PENGUIN  CLASSICS

THE BOOK OF LAMENTATIONS

Rosario Castellanos (1925–1974) was born in Mexico City and grew up on her family's ranch in Comitan, Chiapas, the Mexican state which is the setting for much of her fiction, including a collection of short stories, *Ciudad Real*, and two novels. She was also the author of twelve collections of poetry and five volumes of essays. She held professorships in Latin American literature at universities around the world, and served as Mexico's ambassador to Israel in the years before her death.

Alma Guillermoprieto is the author of *The Heart that Bleeds* and *Samba*. She writes about Latin America for various publications in the United States and England.

Esther Allen has translated a number of books from Spanish and French.

THE BOOK OF
LAMENTATIONS

ROSARIO
CASTELLANOS

TRANSLATED AND WITH
AN AFTERWORD BY ESTHER ALLEN
INTRODUCTION BY ALMA GUILLERMOPRIETO

PENGUIN BOOKS

PENGUIN BOOKS

Published by the Penguin Group

Penguin Group (USA) Inc., 375 Hudson Street, New York, New York 10014, U.S.A.

Penguin Group (Canada), 90 Eglinton Avenue East, Suite 700, Toronto,
Ontario, Canada M4P 2Y3 (a division of Pearson Penguin Canada Inc.)

Penguin Books Ltd, 80 Strand, London WC2R 0RL, England

Penguin Ireland, 25 St Stephen's Green, Dublin 2, Ireland (a division of Penguin Books Ltd)

Penguin Group (Australia), 250 Camberwell Road, Camberwell,
Victoria 3124, Australia (a division of Pearson Australia Group Pty Ltd)

Penguin Books India Pvt Ltd, 11 Community Centre, Panchsheel Park, New Delhi – 110 017, India

Penguin Group (NZ), cnr Airborne and Rosedale Roads,
Albany, Auckland 1310, New Zealand (a division of Pearson New Zealand Ltd)

Penguin Books (South Africa) (Pty) Ltd, 24 Sturdee Avenue,
Rosebank, Johannesburg 2196, South Africa

Penguin Books Ltd, Registered Offices: 80 Strand, London WC2R 0RL, England

The Book of Lamentations translated by Esther Allen first published in the
United States of America by Marsilio Publishers 1996
This edition with an afterword by Esther Allen published in
Penguin Books 1998

LIBRARY OF CONGRESS CATALOGING IN PUBLICATION DATA
Castellanos, Rosario.
[Oficio de tinieblas. English]
The book of lamentations/Rosario Castellanos; translated and
with an afterword by Esther Allen; introduction by Alma
Guillermoprieto.
    p.   cm.—(Penguin twentieth-century classics)
ISBN 0 14 11.8003 X
I. Allen, Esther, 1962–   II. Title.   III. Series.
PQ7297.C25960313   1998
863—dc21   98-11868

Set in Stempel Garamond
Designed by Virginia Norey

146119709

CONTENTS

INTRODUCTION

IN THE 1930's, in Mexico's southernmost state of Chiapas, a little girl travelled to her family's ranch for the holidays. She made the journey as generations of the state's white landowners had done, and as at least one generation to come would still do, sitting on a chair strapped to the back of an Indian. Her mother travelled on the back of another man, her little brother on the back of a third, perched for days on their mounts, up rainforest-covered elevations and down steep ravines, in the suffocating heat of the dry season or through drenching rains. In Chiapas, long after the Mexican Revolution had brought the idea of equality, at least, to the rest of the country's citizens, the owners of the state's most productive land continued to use the destitute indigenous majority as beasts of burden, and considered this the rightful order of things. In the particular case of this little girl, however, several exceptional things occurred: as she grew up she came to understand the twisted nature of the relationship between her family and the people who served them; she remembered what she had seen; and she became a writer. In due course she wrote the novel we now have before us in a fluid and powerful translation whose English title is stunningly apt: *The Book of Lamentations*.

Rosario Castellanos found her calling as so many writers do, out of loneliness. But in her case, the decision to write only served to compound her sense of isolation. There was no precedent for her choice: no woman before her in Chiapas had decided to write, and the idea was as shocking, as against natural law as if, say, an *indio* or a horse had decided to put pen to paper. The act of writing—indeed the very act of observing that precedes writing —was subversive, and banished her from the place that birth and upbringing had reserved for her in the tiny social universe of Chiapas. It is hard to imagine today what it meant not to know one's place in so rigid a society; for Castellanos it meant, of course, that her chances for achieving the expected goals—a comfortable marriage, children, the safe rituals of family and religion —were reduced to zero. But in such suffocating circumstances, not to know one's place could also mean something more terrifying: not knowing who one is, not understanding the face in the mirror, because that face does not resemble any other face one knows.

Her parents defined her condition as an outsider early on. Her founding memory, as it were, was of the day one of her aunts burst into the room, saying she had just had a vision, and that one of Mrs. Castellanos' children would not live to adulthood. "Not the boy!" Rosario's mother exclaimed, rising from her chair in terror. (The boy did indeed die soon after.) Rosario was thus reduced to insignificance, and in the years that followed she was ignored and yet simultaneously overprotected: another childhood memory also involves her mother, this time instructing a servant to swab with alcohol the area on which Rosario was about to perform a school dance routine. The combination of her character, her intelligence and her upbringing left the girl completely unprepared for ordinary social intercourse, and the writer Castellanos remembers the child Rosario, painfully, as neither outgoing nor charming. To be present in the world was in itself a difficulty, and so in her happiest fantasies she reduced herself to nothing more than an eye. "It must be so lovely to be always like a balcony, all empty and carefree, only looking!" she wrote in the opening pages of her first, autobiographical, novel *Balún Canán* [1956, Fondo de Cultura Económica].

That such a childhood would produce such a novel was probably inevitable, although Castellanos did not begin her writing career as a novelist. Strictly speaking, she began writing as a teenager in a dismal "young ladies' school" in Comitán, the coffee-trading Chiapas town where she grew up. Here, she drafted highly successful mash notes for her classmates, and thus bought herself a degree of popularity, although one can imagine that she might have preferred to have the boyfriends. The door to real writing was opened in the late 1930s, as a result of a confrontation with the modern world that the wealthy landowners of Chiapas had long resisted—often by force—and which was finally imposed on them by President Lázaro Cárdenas: he decreed a program of land reform and peasant emancipation that greatly diminished the Castellanos family holdings; embittered, the family left Chiapas for Mexico City when Rosario was sixteen.

In interviews, Castellanos described her encounter with this rude, noisy city as traumatic. Much more so were the deaths, in quick succession, of both her parents, a year later. But in high school she met a gentle and luminously intelligent girl by the name of Dolores Castro, and, with her, fell in with a group of young poets. At last she saw a face in the mirror that suited the person she could be. The Nicaraguan poet/priest Ernesto Cardenal was part of this group, and so were Dolores Castro, the Guatemalan short-story writer Augusto Monterroso, and a fellow Chiapaneco, the great Mexican poet Jaime Sabines.

Castellanos read constantly. She wrote and published her first poems. She spent hours talking in coffee shops with her poet friends. She studied *Filosofía y Letras* at the National University. Her intelligence and sharp wit were no longer a source of shame, and although she would later title a book of essays *Mujer que sabe latín . . .* from the Spanish saying, "A woman who knows Latin will not find a husband or a good end," the fact was that she could now write this truth, rather than simply suffer it.

Castellanos joined the National Indigenous Institute—founded under the aegis of Lázaro Cárdenas, the same president whose active social reforms had so affected her family—and worked there writing and producing scripts for didactic puppet shows that were staged on market day in the most inaccessible villages in Chiapas. Back in Mexico City, she taught at the National University. For several years, she wrote a lengthy weekly column in the newspaper *Excelsior*. She published eleven volumes of poetry. Her numerous essays include the first feminist texts ever published in Mexico. For Mexican women, "[Castellanos] opened wide the door of feminine literature, and began it. In a certain way it is thanks to her that those of us who now attempt to do so are able to write," Elena Ponitowska states. "Before her no other woman except Sor Juana Ines de la Cruz . . . truly committed herself to her vocation."

But Castellanos would never be happy. Indeed, the many friends who loved her felt that she was rarely anything but deeply depressed. Late in life, and unhappily, she married. She had a child. Eventually she was named ambassador to Israel.

Unsparingly, she summarized her life, and the inevitability of her writing career, in an *Excelsior* column:

To recapitulate: first, I was an only daughter, who never attended any school or childhood institution on a regular basis that would allow me to develop friendships. Abandoned to the resources of my imagination during adolescence, it seemed logical to me that I would suddenly be left utterly orphaned. I remained single until the age of thirty-three, during which time I reached an extreme degree of isolation, confined in a tuberculosis asylum, and [then] working in an institute for Indians.

I then entered a marriage that was strictly monogamous on my part and totally polygamous on my husband's. I had three children, of whom two died [through miscarriage]. I received my divorce papers when I was in Tel Aviv.

Add to this that I am shy, and that, as long as I had no obligation to do so, I never went to parties, out of fear that I would lose myself in others, abolish that distance that kept me so safe from any emotional contact.

For company, I virtually never had need of another's physical presence. When I was little I talked to myself because I am a Gemini. Not yet out of childhood I had already begun to write poems. What was the result of my first falling in love? The production of an intimate diary which was first intended as an instrument to bring the object of my love closer but which ended by utterly substituting for and supplanting it.

Given the despairing way in which Castellanos almost always wrote about herself, there is a widespread belief that her death in 1974 in Tel Aviv was an act of suicide. Instead it was the result of one of her many idiosyncrasies—her utter mechanical ineptitude. On August 7, 1974, while trying to plug a lamp into a socket at the embassy residence, she died of electrocution. She was forty-nine years old.

Had *The Book of Lamentations* been published in English at any other time until very recently, it would have been necessary to start this introduction by explaining that Chiapas, a state bordering on Guatemala, is one of Mexico's poorest, that the majority of its three and a half million people are descendants of the Maya, who built fantastic limestone cities in the middle of the jungle more than a thousand years ago, and who today are largely illiterate, impoverished and enraged. But newspaper readers around the world know all this now, thanks to the uprising that started in the former capital of Chiapas—referred to by its old name, Ciudad Real, in this novel—on January 1, 1994. On that day, thousands of Maya campesinos, including descendants of the very same field workers who lived on the Castellanos estate, declared war on the Mexican government. They called themselves the Zapatista National Liberation Army, after General Emiliano Zapata, who led campesino troops into battle eighty years ago and gave the Mexican Revolution its distinctly agrarian cast. The new Zapatistas' rebellion was a throwback both to a long-gone Mexican agricultural past and to a more recent form of struggle—guerrillas for socialism—that had seemed exhausted in this hemisphere. That the uprising should have happened at all, much less endure so stubbornly against all odds, struck millions of people as astonishing. But the rebellion should not have come as a surprise to anyone in Mexico who had read *The Book of Lamentations*.

The Book of Lamentations, first published in Spanish as *Oficio de tinieblas*, in 1962, followed Castellanos' autobiographical *Balún Canán*, and was to be the last novel she published. The plot recreates an Indian rebellion that took place in the vicinity of San Cristóbal de las Casas (the official name of the book's "Ciudad Real") in the mid-nineteenth century. The novel is faithful to the known facts in many respects, including the character who sparks the rebellion when she hears miraculous voices issuing from three "talking rocks"—a woman called Catalina Díaz Puiljá in the book, Agustina Gómez Checheb in real life—and the ritual crucifixion of her foster child, called Domingo in both fact and fiction.

The plot differs from history in one respect: Castellanos decided to set it in the 1930s—the very time when her family was suffering the impact of the Cardenista reforms. She transformed the real-life nineteenth-century mestizo anarchists from central Mexico, who provided the Maya rebels with much of their military training, into a romantically complicated trio: the historical Ignacio Fernández Galindo is the basis for the novel's Fernando Ulloa, the Cardenista school teacher and land reform agitator; Ulloa's assistant in the book, César Santiago, corresponds to Fernández Galindo's real-life aide; while Fernández Galindo's wife, who appears to have been an epically courageous woman, is replaced in the novel by the equivocal, sexually traitorous Julia Acevedo. There is ambiguity in the author's attitude towards the mestizo protagonists of *The Book of Lamentations*. Perhaps it springs from her childhood memories of dispossession. Perhaps, in the case of Julia Acevedo, it is related to the mistrust she appears to have felt for women who were sexually lively and openly seductive.

But the novel's heart is not really with the mestizos (or Ladinos, as they are called in Chiapas). It is with the Maya outcasts of a desolate highland village, who put the white-skinned inhabitants of Ciudad Real to siege because three speaking rocks have told them that justice will someday be theirs. What is astonishing is Castellanos' fluent understanding of the world view of the hopeless rebels; of their sense of how whites behave, of their singular relationship with the Catholic God the Father and his attendant saints, of the ways in which a woman in the Maya community can acquire power and of the ways in which individuals with a tiny measure of power in such deprived communities can come to be distrusted and feared. Castellanos was able to know and imagine all this because in her outcast childhood the people closest to her were the equally hapless Indians who cooked for her, carried her on their backs, sang her to sleep and loved her, as the nanny does the willful, sickly Idolina in *The Book of Lamentations*.

Unlike the modern Zapatistas and their supporters, Rosario Castellanos did not have a romantic, or even optimistic, view of the world. She did not believe that indigenous peoples are perforce purer human beings than mestizos, and she was devastatingly clear-eyed about the distortions of the spirit that ignorance and misery can bring about. *The Book of Lamentations* is a heroic attempt to re-imagine and understand an atrocious event: the rebellion spearheaded by the inhabitants of San Juan Chamula in 1868 which, according to contemporary accounts, culminated in the crucifixion of a child. This book revolves—lovingly, it can be said—around that central horror.

The lack of violence in the current Chiapas rebellion is one of the essential differences with the events related in the pages that follow, but that does not diminish *The Book of Lamentations'* relevance to the present. The desperate urgency with which the

Maya communities dream that they will one day be free of the *caxlanes*—the powerful whites who rule them—continues to this day. The dependence on white revolutionaries who join and give direction to the Maya uprisings in pursuit of their own ideological utopias continues as well. Maya history has been, since the Conquest, a tragedy marked by the Indian communities' enduring faith in the possibility of an avenging, cleansing war. It was an unlikely observer—an awkward girl who wanted to transform herself into an eye because she did not see any room for herself in the world—who understood this better than any other Mexican novelist to date. She turned herself into a mirror in which the Maya people who brought her up could be reflected, and what she saw still has the authority of truth today.

Alma Guillermoprieto,
MEXICO CITY, 1996

THE BOOK OF
LAMENTATIONS

Whereas your glory is no longer great;
Whereas your might exists no more
—and though without much right to veneration—
your blood will still prevail a while . . .

All the children of dawn, the dawn's offspring,
will not belong to your people;
only the chatterboxes will yield themselves to you.

People of Harm, of War, of Misery,
you who did the wrong,
weep for it.

THE BOOK OF THE COUNCIL

CHAPTER I

SAN JUAN, the Guarantor, he who was there when the worlds first appeared, who spoke the yes that started the century on its way and is one of the pillars that keep stable what is stable, stooped down one day to contemplate the land of men.

His eyes travelled from the sea where the fish glides to the mountaintop where the snow sleeps. They passed over the flat-lands where the fluttering wind scuffles, over the beaches' buzzing sands, over the forests, refuge of wary animals. Over the valleys.

The gaze of San Juan Guarantor paused at the valley called Chamula. He was pleased by the gentle slope of the hills that come there from far away to meet, their ravines gently heaving. He was pleased by the sky, hovering near in the early morning mists. There rose up in the soul of San Juan a desire to be worshiped in this place. That was why he turned all the white sheep in the flocks grazing in that valley to stone: so there would be no lack of materials to build his church and so his church would be white.

And there the rocky outcrop remained, silent and unmoving, sign of a divine desire. But the tribes that dwelled in the valley of Chamula, those called Tzotzils, the People of the Bat, did not know how to interpret this marvel. Neither the eldest among the elders nor the men of the Council were able to express a worthy opinion; they produced only confused stammerings, lowered eyelids, arms falling in gestures of fear.

That was why the other men had to come, later. And it was as if they came from another world. They carried the sun in their faces and spoke an arrogant language, a language that wrenches the hearts of those who hear it. A language not like Tzotzil (which is also spoken in dreams), but like an iron instrument of mastery, a weapon of conquest, the striking lash of the law's whip. For how could orders be given or condemnations passed down, if not in Castilla? How could punishments or rewards be meted out, if not in Castilla?

The newcomers did not fully understand the enigma of the

petrified sheep either. They understood only the command that work be done. So they with their heads and the Indians with their hands began to construct a church. By day they dug the foundations, but at night the foundations filled in and became level again. By day they built the walls, and at night the walls fell down. San Juan Guarantor had to come in person, pushing the stones himself, rolling them down the slopes one by one until they were all gathered in the place they would remain. Only then did the men's efforts come to fruition.

The building is white, as San Juan Guarantor wanted. In the air consecrated by its vault resound the prayers and chants of the Caxlán, the pleas and laments of the Indian. Wax burns in perfect self-immolation; incense exhales its fervent soul; a carpet of pine needles clears and perfumes the air. From the altar's most conspicuous niche, the refined profile of the brightly painted wooden image of San Juan looks down, larger than the other images: Santa Margarita, the smallfooted maiden who pours out blessings; San Agustín, tranquil and robust; San Jerónimo, with a tiger in his belly, the secret protector of brujos; the Virgen Dolorosa, with a storm cloud darkening her horizon; the enormous Good Friday cross, expectant of its annual victim, leaning precariously, ready to drop like a catastrophe. There are also hostile powers that had to be tied down to keep their forces from erupting; anonymous virgins, mutilated apostles, inept angels fallen from the altar to the portable platforms and from there to the ground where they were knocked over: inanimate matter, forgotten by piety and disdained by oblivion. Hearing dulled, heart indifferent, hand closed.

These, it is said, are the things that have taken place since the beginning. It is no lie. There are witnesses. All of it can be read in the three arches of the church portal, where the sun takes its leave of the valley.

This is the center. Around it are the three sections of Chamula, the principal town of the municipality: a town with both religious and political roles, a ceremonial city.

The leading men of even the most distant regions of the Chiapas highlands where Tzotzil is spoken come to Chamula. Here they take up the burden of their duties.

The greatest responsibility falls on the president, and after him, the secretary. The two of them are assisted by alcaldes, regidores, elders, gobernadores and síndicos. The mayordomos are there to supervise the worship of the saints, the alféreces to organize the celebration of holy days. The pasiones are assigned their tasks for Carnival.

These duties last twelve months and those who carry them out, transitory inhabitants of Chamula, live in the huts scattered along the hillsides and the valley floor, supporting themselves by working the land, raising animals and guarding flocks of sheep.

When their term is over, these representatives return to the places they came from, enveloped in dignity and prestige. Now they are "former authorities." They have deliberated in the presence of their president and their deliberations were entered into the record by the secretary, inscribed on the paper that talks. They have established boundaries, mediated rivalries, dispensed justice, formalized and dissolved marriages. Most importantly, they were custodians of the divine. They saw to it that no one was remiss in care and reverence. This is why the chosen ones, the elite of the race, are not permitted to enter the day in the spirit of labor: they must enter it in the spirit of prayer. Before commencing any task, before pronouncing any word, the man who serves as an example to others must prostrate himself before his father, the sun.

Morning comes late to Chamula. The cock crows to chase away the darkness. As the men grope toward wakefulness, the women find their way to the ashes where they bend and blow to reveal the embers. The wind circles the hut, and below the roof of palm fronds, between the four walls of mud and twigs, cold is the guest of honor.

Pedro González Winiktón spread apart the hands that had been joined in meditation and let them fall along his body. He was an Indian of good height and solid muscles. Despite his youth (marked by the early severity typical of his people), others looked up to him as an elder brother. The wisdom of his decisions, the energy of his commands and the purity of his habits ranked him among men of respect, and only there did his heart expand. So he was content when, obliged to accept investiture as a judge, he took his oath before the cross in the portal of the church of San Juan

Chamula. His wife, Catalina Díaz Puiljá, wove a serape of thick, black wool that amply covered him down to his ankles, to make those assembled hold him in greater esteem.

Consequently, after December 31st of that year, Pedro González Winiktón and Catalina Díaz Puiljá came to Chamula. They were given a hut to live in, a plot of land to farm. The cornfield was there, already green and promising a good harvest. What more ʙuld Pedro wish for? He had material abundance, prestige among is equals, the devotion of his wife. A smile lasted only an instant n his face, little practiced at expressing happiness. His features ardened. Winiktón saw himself as the hollow stem, the stubble that is burned away after the harvest. He compared himself to ashes. He had no children.

Catalina Díaz Puiljá, barely twenty years old yet already dry and withered, was given to Pedro from childhood by her parents. The early times were happy. The lack of offspring was seen as natural then. But later, when the companions with whom Catalina spun, gathered wood and carried water began to settle their feet more heavily onto the earth (because they walked for themselves and for the child to come), when their eyes filled with peace and their bellies swelled like granaries after the harvest, then Catalina probed her fruitless hips, cursed the lightness of her step and, turning suddenly to look back, saw that her feet left no mark behind her. This, she thought with anguish, was how her name would pass over her people's memory. From that time on she was inconsolable.

She consulted with the elders, yielded her pulse to the diviners' ears. They questioned the cycles of her blood, investigated the facts, intoned invocations. Where did your path swerve, Catalina? Where did your spirit take fright? Catalina sweated, immersing herself in the smoke of miraculous herbs. She did not know how to answer. And her moon did not return white like that of women who have conceived, but stained with red like the moon of spinsters and widows. Like the whore's moon.

Then the pilgrimage began. She approached the wandering peddlers who brought news from far away. She stored the names of the places to be visited in the folds of her mind. There was an old woman in Cancuc who could work harmful magic but was also a healer, depending on what was needed. In Biqu'it Bautisti, a brujo went deep into the night to interpret its designs. An enchanter practiced in Tenejapa. Catalina brought them humble gifts: the first ears of corn, jars of liquor, a young lamb.

In this way the light was gradually hidden from her and she was caught up in a dark world ruled by arbitrary wills. She learned to placate those wills when they were threatening, to excite them when they were auspicious, to transmute their signs. She chanted mind-numbing litanies. She ran through flames, unharmed and delirious. Now she was one of those who dare to gaze on the face of mystery, an ilol, a seer, whose lap is a nest of spells. Those she frowned on trembled and those who saw her smile were reassured. But Catalina's belly was still closed. Sealed like a nut.

As she knelt in front of the metate, grinding a portion of posol, Catalina watched her husband from the corner of her eye. At what moment would he force her to speak the words of repudiation? How much longer would he tolerate the offense of her sterility? Marriages like theirs were not valid. One word from Winiktón would be enough to make Catalina return to her family's hut back in Tzajal-hemel. She would not find her father or her mother there; both of them had been dead for years. There was no one left but Lorenzo, the brother who was called "the innocent" because of his simple nature and the vacuous laugh that split his mouth in two.

Catalina stood up and placed the ball of posol in her husband's bag of provisions. What made him stay with her? Fear? Love? Winiktón's face kept its secret. Without a sign of farewell the man left the hut. The door closed behind him.

An irrevocable decision froze Catalina's features. They would never separate, she would never be left alone, never be humiliated before her people.

Her movements quickened, as if she were about to fight an enemy then and there. She came and went through the hut, guided more by touch than by sight; the only light filtered in through holes in the walls and the room was blackened, impregnated with smoke. Even more than touch, habit steered her, keeping her from stumbling against the objects heaped up randomly in the tiny space. Clay pots, chipped and cracked; the metate, still too new, not yet broken in by the strength and skill of the woman who used it; tree trunks instead of chairs; ancient chests with useless locks. And, leaning against the fragile wall, innumerable crosses. One, made of wood, was so tall it appeared to be holding up the roof; the others, woven from palm fronds, were small and deceptively like butterflies. Hanging from the principal cross were the official insignia of Pedro González Winiktón, judge. And scattered throughout the hut were the professional instruments of Catalina Díaz Puiljá, weaver.

The sound of activity in the other huts, increasingly clear and urgent, made Catalina shake her head as if to chase away the painful dream that was tormenting her. Hurriedly she prepared for the day, carefully placing in a mesh bag the eggs she had gathered the night before, wrapped in leaves to keep them from cracking. When the bag was full, Catalina lifted it to her shoulders. The strap digging into her forehead looked like a deep scar.

Around the hut a group of women had gathered, waiting in silence for Catalina to appear. One by one they filed past her, bowing to show their respect. They did not lift their heads until Catalina had quickly brushed them with her fingers while reciting the courteous, automatic phrase of greeting.

When this ceremony had been completed, they set off. Though all of them knew the way, none dared take a step that was not led by the ilol. Their watchful gestures, rapidly obedient, anxiously solicitous, showed that these women looked to her as a superior. Not because of her husband's position, since they were all the wives of officials and some were married to men whose prestige was greater than Winiktón's, but because of the reputation that transfigured Catalina in the eyes of those whose souls were fearful and unfortunate, those who were avid to ingratiate themselves with the supernatural.

Catalina accepted their respect with the calm assurance of one receiving her due. The other women's submissiveness neither annoyed her nor made her proud. Her conduct was moderate and sensible, in keeping with the tribute she was accorded. Her gift to them was an approving smile, a glance of complicity, a well-timed word of advice, an opportune reminder. And in her left hand she held threats, the possibility of doing harm. Though she kept careful watch on her power. She had seen too many left hands chopped off by vengeful machetes.

Catalina led the procession of Tzotzil women, all uniformly

wrapped in thick, dark serapes. All bent beneath the weight they carried (the goods they brought to sell, the small child sleeping against its mother). All going toward Ciudad Real.

The path, made by years of walking feet, coils around the hills. The earth is yellow and loose, easily blown away by the wind. The vegetation is hostile: weeds, curving thorns. Here and there are young bushes or peach trees in their festive garb, peach trees blushing pink from sweetness, from smiling, blushing pink from happiness.

The distance between San Juan Chamula and Ciudad Real (or Jobel, as it is called in Tzotzil) is long. But these women crossed it, untiring and wordless, their attention fixed on the careful placement of their feet and the work spread between their hands, the coils of pichulej that their busy fingers made longer and longer as they walked.

The mass of mountains flowed into a wide valley. Here and there, as if fallen by chance from the sky, were houses. Shingled shacks, inhabited by Ladinos who looked after fields or miserable flocks, precarious shelter against bad weather. Now and then a stately home rose up in all the insolence of its isolation, solidly built but with the sinister look of a fortress or a jail rather than a place meant to lodge the refined softness of the wealthy.

The outskirts; the banks of the river. From here the domes of the churches could be seen reverberating in the humid light.

Catalina Díaz Puiljá stopped and crossed herself. Her followers imitated her. Then, with whispers and quick, skillful movements, they redistributed the goods they were carrying. Some women were given all the weight they could bear. Others pretended to stagger under an excessive load, and they went to the front of the line.

Silent, as if they neither saw nor heard, as if they were not expecting anything to happen, the Tzotzil women moved forward.

As they came around the first corner it happened, and although it was expected, habitual, it was never any less fearsome or repellent. Five Ladinas of the poorest class, barefoot, dressed in rags, threw themselves onto Catalina and her companions. Without saying a single threatening word, without working themselves up with insults or excusing themselves with reasons, the Ladinas fought for possession of the bags full of eggs, the clay pots, the fabrics that the Indian women defended in brave, mute furor. But in the flurry of their gestures, both parties to the struggle took care not to damage or break the objects they were contending over.

In the confusion of the first moments, several of the Indian women managed to slip away and hurried toward the center of Ciudad Real. Meanwhile, those left behind opened their bleeding hands, leaving the goods to the attackers who snatched up their booty in triumph. Then, to give an appearance of legality to her violence, the enemy threw down a handful of copper coins that the other woman picked from the dust, weeping.

CHAPTER II

MARCELA GÓMEZ OSO was one of those who succeeded in escaping. With furtive, rapid movements, like an animal accustomed to pursuit and danger, Marcela crept through the stone streets of Ciudad Real. She went with her load on her back, walking in the gutter because people of her race were not allowed to use the sidewalks. Confused by the crowd, bewildered by the strange language that pounded at her ears without touching her mind, Marcela moved on, ungainly and amazed. She did not want to go toward the market and turned onto the side streets instead. These were peaceful neighborhoods. The bare feet of the poor hardly disturbed the silence that was scratched by ranchers' gleaming spurs and broken by animals' heavy hoofs.

Marcela leaned into the open passageways and pitched her wares in a high and uncertain voice, carefully pronouncing the only Spanish words she had mastered. From beyond the lush courtyards, from inside invisible bedrooms, came the response, an impatient or halfhearted "No," an impersonal and anonymous rejection. Sometimes the servants took her to their quarters. Then there were cruel jokes, an unbearable dickering that Marcela barely understood but that flustered her and made her tremble like a trapped bird. When the maids tired of the game they let her go.

"What are you selling, merchant girl?"

A woman in her forties, obese, her flashing teeth garishly inlaid with gold, asked the question. She was sitting in a small wooden chair with her skirts spilling out around her, smoking a long cigarette rolled in yellow paper. She had spoken in Tzotzil. Marcela's eyes shone with gratitude.

"Pitchers," she answered.

"And are they well made, your pitchers?"

The Indian girl nodded vehemently as she set down her bundle so the woman could judge their quality for herself.

"They won't crack on me, will they? They're not going to break right away?"

Marcela said no in a tone that was almost anguished. This seemed to satisfy the buyer, who began to examine the clay pitchers one by one.

Marcela remained standing, motionless, desperately trying not to make any noise when she breathed. Sweat ran down her face.

She was in a large room. The door to the street stood wide open, while the back door, leading into the house, was only ajar. A rickety counter and a display case with four shelves were there to give the impression that the room was a shop. But the scantiness of the stock (a few half-empty packages of brown sugar, three bottles of a sedative, some bunches of fragrant herbs) bore witness to the business's lack of prosperity.

"Sit down, merchant girl. It provokes me to see you standing there."

The Ladina's words were veiled in the smoke from her cigarette. Disconcerted by the friendliness of the suggestion, Marcela changed position but remained standing. The woman insisted. "Sit down. Don't worry. You're not tired from walking?"

Marcela gave a vague smile.

"At your age, though, you have strength for that and more. I remember how I was . . . You must be around fourteen now, aren't you?"

"I don't know, patrona. My nana never told me when I was born."

"You still live with your nana? They haven't given you to a man?"

"Not yet, patrona."

The Ladina took a last pull at her cigarette and her chest purred with pleasure. She looked Marcela over attentively. Then, as if to conclude a lengthy reflection, she said, "You're not bad."

Marcela had finally sat down on the ground. Eyes lowered, she was drawing lines on the brick floor. Her ears reddened at the praise.

"You never had a husband?"

"No."

"Why not?"

"My nana doesn't want to send me away."

'That's because you're old enough now to help her with the rk."

"That's why."

"So you're worth something. For you, I'm going to ask for a big bottle of aguardiente."

A harsh laugh, glittering with gold, shook the Ladina's abundant breasts. Marcela felt an indefinable unease, a distant shiver of alarm. The woman changed the subject.

"Well, girl, how much do you want for your pitchers?"

"Twelve reales, patrona."

Marcela ventured the figure without knowing exactly how much it was. She supposed it was a lot of money and that it would be refused. She waited for the buyer's scandalized protests, expecting her price to be whittled down. But the Ladina did not protest. She only commented, "I certainly won't make much on them. All right."

Marcela knew she hadn't asked for the right amount, that she was giving her work away. But it was impossible to take back what she had said. She made one last objection. "Will you take them all, patrona?"

"Don't say patrona. My name is Mercedes. Mercedes Solórzano. You've heard of me?"

"No, patrona."

A distant mumble of "Good, good," then the decision. "Yes, I'll take them all."

With difficulty, Doña Mercedes pushed herself to her feet.

"Wait for me a minute."

She opened the back door and disappeared.

Five, ten, fifteen minutes. Marcela felt a numbness gradually rising through her legs. She changed position and the tingling blood circulated once more.

Doña Mercedes had returned, noiselessly. "It's fine. Leave the pitchers here and come with me. They'll pay you in there."

Doña Mercedes showed the way. She stopped in front of a door and knocked discreetly before opening it. Marcela stood at the threshold.

"This is the one," said Doña Mercedes, gesturing toward her.

A man, ruddy and middle-aged, dressed in work clothes with high boots, was polishing the barrel of a pistol with a scrap of leather. He leaned back indolently in his revolving chair. When the women came in, he raised his head slowly. A keen, rapacious eye evaluated the native girl. There was an imperceptible wink of consent. Doña Mercedes grabbed Marcela. "Come in. They're waiting for you."

When Marcela did not obey quickly enough, the Ladina tugged at her unceremoniously. "I told you to come in."

Marcela swayed and steadied herself on a piece of furniture. Doña Mercedes started to leave.

"Close the door," the man's voice advised.

Fuming, Doña Mercedes walked away. "That Leonardo . . . As if I didn't know what to do!"

Doña Mercedes was a woman of communicative temperament, ill-reconciled to the prolonged solitudes circumstances had forced on her. In the end she had acquired the habit of talking by herself, imagining a vague listener.

"There are things you couldn't believe if you hadn't seen them with your own eyes. Don Leonardo Cifuentes, one of Ciudad Real's highest and mightiest, a gentleman so popular, so well groomed, all he has to do is lift a finger and the vainest beauties come running. This man has a taste for Indian girls. Well, they do say pleasure comes with variety. People who eat pheasant every day are probably craving a plate of beans. But an Indian. . . . It's like rooting around in a pig pen, isn't that so, compadre? I do my best to find girls with a little bit of shine to them, girls that are clean, at least. Anyway, don't think I've gotten so hard-hearted that I do these things without a second thought. In my day, I had high hopes of running around town like some women I know who have more money than they need. But no, there I was, inside my house like a queen, and that's why I had quite a few friends who stood up for me. People could talk all they wanted. It was my good luck that offended them. As far as honor goes, no one has ever been more honorable than me. I'm a mirror for the rich ladies to recognize themselves in.

"Remember how much there was of everything in my house? They always gave me anything I asked for! Nobody who came to see me in those days ever bothered me about anything. After that it was like the cricket in the story. Little by little I was left on my own, with no one to help me out or tell me what to do. But it's sinful to complain. I have a lot to give thanks for, first of all to the Santísima Virgen de la Merced, my patron saint, and then to Leonardo. I remember when I met him. He was tiny, like this!" She measured an inch between her thumb and forefinger.

"Some friends of his, who were already the size of big men, brought him to my house. The poor baby was shaking with fear. Sit down on my bed, I told him. I don't know why I was so familiar with him, as if we were old friends. Come here, I'm not going to eat you. I could feel his heart easing little by little. When I grow up I'll thank you for this, he said. Who would have believed him? A boy's words. But he kept his promise at the right time. And here I am, set up in business next to his house, the Cifuentes house. If it hadn't been for him, where would I have gone? I'd have been one of those poor women without a louse to their names who attack the Indians on their way to market. Or a peddler, or one of the women with stalls in the marketplace. But instead. . . . The wife doesn't look too kindly on me. She says I'm a go-between, here to hide her husband's wickednesses. But I'd like to see her in my place. When it came time to return the favor, we'd see if she'd be such a prude."

From time to time, people in the street walked by the door. Certain of the men greeted Doña Mercedes, furtively raising hand to hat, then looking around and sighing with relief that no one had noticed.

"You used to stay with me a little longer, my friend. Old hypocrite."

Doña Mercedes said this without altering the tone of her voice, without bitterness or resentment, like a woman well acquainted with the fickleness of the world and the pettiness of men. Her two hands, long accustomed to idleness, rested in her lap.

The door in the back of the room opened and Marcela appeared. She came forward, wild-eyed. Her disheveled black hair made a piteous halo around her face. She covered her shoulders with her hands as if she were cold. Doña Mercedes looked at her without interest. "Ah, there you are. Wait. I'm going to pay you."

Doña Mercedes took a packet from inside her blouse. She untied it, removed several coins, and thriftily counted them out. "That's it. Twelve reales."

Marcela clutched the money convulsively. Then with sudden resolution she hurled it at Doña Mercedes. She ran to where the pitchers lay in a heap and threw them against the counter, the shelves, the floor. The fragments flew through the air and scattered across the room in a commotion that drowned out the procuress's cries of outrage. Doña Mercedes screamed down the street after the fleeing girl, "Filthy Indian! You won't get away with your life if I catch you! Look at the damage you've done! Child of Satan! Whore!"

The sounds of the girl's running feet and Doña Mercedes' shouts rebounded off the walls and were multiplied in a babel of innumerable echoes.

Drawn by the noise, a woman pulled back a curtain covering a window. She was Isabel Zebadúa, wife of Leonardo Cifuentes. For an instant her face was visible behind the glass, a face lined by suffering, gnawed by anxiety, stamped with disdain.

She saw the terrified Indian girl, the furious procuress, and understood immediately. It wasn't the first time she had witnessed this scene.

She couldn't keep herself from making a movement of disgust. Quickly she left the window, crossed the room, opened a door. Her pupils dilated as she peered into the darkness. Amorphous objects gradually took shape: a wardrobe, some chairs. At the far end of the room, a narrow bed.

Arms stretched out in front of her, Isabel crossed the room like a sleepwalker. She stopped beside the bed, whispering, "Idolina."

There was no response. She knelt on the rug. Her fingers dug into the sheets.

"Idolina, wake up. Fistful of bitter, bitter myrrh. Little bird legs that don't know how to walk, wake up. When will I see the sun? How much longer until daylight comes back to me? Child of my sorrows, hummingbird, scrawny legs that can't walk, wake up."

The incoherent litany, softened with diminutives, tender, urgent, despairing, shattered into sobs.

Idolina made no move to betray the fact that she was awake. She kept herself rigid, her back turned as if she were fleeing, her eyes obstinately staring at the wall.

CHAPTER III

MARCELA CAME TO a stop, panting. She had run until she felt her heart breaking open inside her. It was impossible to run any more. She took a few steps forward, tottering as if she were about to fall over. She sat down on the edge of the sidewalk, pressed the tips of her fingers against her eyelids and breathed deeply, fearfully.

The whole city with all of its noises was buzzing around her, tormenting her. A door hammered by a gust of wind, the slow mournful ringing of church bells, the resounding crack of a whip against a horse's haunch, a beggar's irritating persistence. And the insults raging out of the gold-inlaid mouth of a prostitute.

Doña Mercedes, the buzzing repeated, Doña Mercedes Solórzano. And Marcela pursued the name, syllable by syllable, letter by letter, as if by grasping it she would enter into possession of all that is prized most highly: night, sleep, death.

Because Marcela retained no more than a confused image of the violence she had suffered. Behind Cifuentes' imperious, voracious movements (which she had resisted as animals do, instinctively, savagely, biting and scratching), Marcela glimpsed something. Not the same thing many women in her place would have seen: the pride of having been chosen by a Caxlán. Nor what others would have seen: the dangerous pleasure of arousing a brutal desire. No, Marcela had divined a paradise: the supreme abolition of her consciousness.

It was only an instant. Letting her hands fall slack, letting go of what she carried in them: misery, anguish. Surrendering it all and being left free. A painful murmur arrived from her body as if from a distant planet. But Marcela was far away, floating in a dense, warm, maternal atmosphere. Why had she been dragged out into the open again? She came back to herself, surrounded by shouting, a pursuer nipping at her heels. And she had run, away or back, she didn't know. But how to go back, oh God, how to go back?

Seated on the sidewalk's hostile edge, her knees together to support her abject forehead, Marcela swayed back and forth very slowly, making a hoarse cooing sound, like a fretful dove.

That's the way. Now the lethargy is weighing your innards down with lead. That's the way. Little by little, the dove is soothed. That's the way.

Midday flew slowly by.

"Hey, look at that one. She's pretty soused."

Two boys, no more than eleven years old, were nudging each other toward Marcela. In their eyes, already tarnished by the spectacle of human degradation, glinted a spark of glee.

Marcela did not hear them. A buzzing was still drilling its way through her, a buzzing that said: Doña Mercedes Solórzano, Doña Mercedes Solórzano. And then the precipice, and then nothing.

"She's acting kind of loony, isn't she?"

"All right, so. . . ."

One of the boys took a slingshot from the pocket of his jeans, which had large patches at the knees. He loaded it with an orange peel that hit its target. Marcela opened a pair of eyes that were wide with shock, bewildered with fear.

"Yessss! Yessss!" the boys shouted, barricading themselves behind the corner, having provoked an anger that could not be vented.

Then the fear and shock were extinguished, as quickly as they had flared up; there was no fuel to feed the sudden blaze. Marcela lowered her eyelids again.

The boys, emboldened at having emerged unscathed from the first sally, were planning another more audacious one. But something held them back. They hid the slingshot and adopted a stance of innocent carelessness and an angelic expression that was contradicted by their tangled hair, dirty hands and disheveled clothes. The act was for the benefit of the two men who were approaching: Don Alfonso Cañaveral, bishop of Chiapas, and a young seminarist, Manuel Mandujano.

"Give alms to this poor woman," the bishop ordered his companion.

Manuel attempted to place a coin in the girl's hand. But the hand was limp and let the coin fall to the ground.

Don Alfonso's eyebrows, already gray, drew together in a frown of incredulous amazement. It was the first time he had seen anyone so indifferent to money. This could only be for a very serious reason.

"Ask what is wrong with her, whether she's ill."

"I do not know how to speak the language, Su Ilustrísima."

"Neither do I. I would have the excuse of not being from here if I hadn't lived in Ciudad Real for more years than you have existed."

Don Alfonso asked to lean on his companion's arm; he liked to exaggerate his weakness. They continued on their way, their voluminous dark capes fluttering around them.

Each at his or her own time, the other townspeople went by with slow, processional steps. The woman who delivered bread from house to house, the pious lady going out to attend vespers, the apprentice leaving his work, the dressmaker who had just locked up her workshop with several turns of the key. Gentlemen with gold-handled canes, out for a stroll between daylight and darkness, whistling to hide their intentions.

Marcela shook herself and stood up mechanically. She looked around in amazement. Who brought her here? How much time had she spent in this place? Why? She did not succeed in understanding; she did not remember. She had one thought in her head: to return to Chamula. She began to walk quickly, often losing her way, until she came to a halt in the market. There, seated on the steps, were the Tzotzil women. Waiting for Marcela. They fell silent as they watched her approach.

Marcela stood in front of them. Silent herself. Her eyes floated in turbulent, unsoundable waters.

From among the assembled women a voice rose, rebuking her.

"Why did you take so long? Soon the sun will set. Because of you we will have to go back in the dark."

It was her right to speak. She was Felipa, Marcela's mother. But Marcela did not respond. Her muteness irritated her mother. In a fragile, absurd screech, she demanded, "Answer!"

What answer could Marcela give? She had entered an unknown house: she had offered her pitchers to an unknown buyer.

"Where is the payment?" Felipa held out her hand to receive it. But Marcela had nothing to give.

"Where is the payment?"

Felipa stood up straight. Her cheeks were purple with rage.

The other women witnessed the scene, astounded. Some of them turned their heads away because it is not good to look upon disobedience.

Felipa came down the stairs, threatening.

"You are going to give me that money, you bitch, you cabrona."

This unexpected word, the only Spanish word in the sentence, resounded like the crack of a whip. An enraged fist rose up and fell on the girl's face. The pain made Marcela break down into sobs.

"What? What are you going to tell me? That you were robbed because you were walking around with your mouth gaping open?"

All the energy that the hours of waiting had built up in Felipa's heart went into the punishment. And the disappointment, too. Not only that day's disappointment. The years of misfortune patiently endured, the years of suffering borne without complaint, all the bitter memory that an Indian silences with drunkenness and prayers added its weight to Felipa's closed fist. And every moan Marcela gave enraged her mother more. She was bathed in sweat, her arm was stiff with cramp, and still she did not want to release her victim. Until an authoritative voice paralyzed her.

"Let her go!"

It was Catalina Díaz Puiljá. From her place on the highest step she spoke. And she had only to be heard to be obeyed.

Helpless, Felipa turned to Catalina. Eyelids submissive, tremulous with exhaustion and anguish, she sought to justify herself.

"I do not deserve to be reproached, madrecita. You yourself witnessed it. I hit Marcela here. But did she have pity on my face? Look at me. I am no more than a poor old woman. My shoulders cannot take the work any more. My feet hurt very much. Before, would God ever leave us without anything to feed our mouths? But now the man has a position to attend to; he neglects the cornfield; debts come to carry away the harvest. And money? Is it there to be swept up with a broom? Is it picked out of the garbage? Ay, madrecita, the things I am telling you. Hunger bites me here, between my ribs, for a long time now."

The ilol made a gesture of indifference to stem this torrent of lamentations.

"Your daughter is a burden to you. Give her to me. I will treat her well."

Felipa was not expecting this proposal. She was taken aback and her forlorn features showed it. She attempted a clumsy excuse.

"I would give her to you, madrecita, if Marcela here were not so neglectful. But you have just seen with your own eyes. She was robbed of the payment for the pitchers. And that's how it is, always. If you send her to fetch wood, she fetches green wood. If you tell her to make tortillas, she lets the tortillas bake on the comal. She loses the sheep from the flock."

Catalina smiled at the childishness of these pretexts.

"If that is so, then it is better she should be with me than with you. You no longer have the vigor to set her straight. I do."

Catalina's tone was conclusive. Felipa assented. To Marcela she said roughly, "Get up. From now on you are estranged from me. You are no longer in my power."

Marcela wiped off her tears with the back of her hand and went to stand behind Catalina. That was how they walked. That was how they arrived in San Juan Chamula.

Catalina pushed aside the bolt that fastened shut the two doors of her hut and entered. Marcela did not cross the threshold, fearful of venturing into a place she had never been before in the dark.

Light quivered out from a thick tallow candle, transfiguring the things in the hut with its spooky, yellowish glow. Catalina took the candle and placed it on a small board that hung from the ceiling.

"You will sleep here."

She unrolled the usual straw petate, frayed around the edges, and spread it out in a corner. Marcela curled up on it. She watched Catalina reviving the fire without daring to offer her help. She asked herself what motive the ilol could have had for placing herself between her, Marcela, and her mother's punishment, and for what purpose Catalina had brought her to live with her. She could not give in to gratitude until her distrust had dissolved.

"Take your dinner."

The girl had gone the whole day without eating. But it was nausea more than hunger that filled her mouth with saliva. She hesitated a moment. Until the tone of Catalina's words—persuasive as someone asking for a favor, inflexible as someone issuing

an order—decided her. She divided a tortilla in half and plunged
it into a sauce of cold beans to soften it. She began to chew with
the thoroughness of someone who can only swallow with great
effort. She was preparing the second mouthful when a gust of air
startled her. The door had opened again, this time for Pedro González Winiktón.

"Where are you, Catalina?" he said, and went to sit down next
to the fire's glowing embers. He seemed not to have noticed the
presence of an outsider. But his wife was quick to inform him.

"This is Marcela Gómez Oso. Daughter of the martoma Rosendo Gómez Oso."

Pedro accepted the news, indifferent. Catalina had to be more
explicit.

"She is going to stay with us."

Now this was something that demanded an explanation.

"Why? Is she an orphan?"

With a slight rustling, Marcela slid down until she was
stretched out full length on the mat. She wanted to leave, to weep,
to lose herself in the darkness, to go far away from this taciturn
man who was examining her with such remote disdain. But she
was subjugated to the ilol's incomprehensible designs. Now the
ilol was saying:

"She is estranged from her mother and belongs to me."

"Why?"

"A Caxlán made ill use of her."

Marcela remained still. She raised to Catalina a pair of eyes in
which admiration and respect fought to be the only emotion
manifested. By what means had this woman ascertained what
Marcela had confessed to no one, what she herself did not know?
She was a very powerful ilol, there could be no doubt. Marcela
rejoiced at being under her authority. In her mind, she repeated
the phrase, savoring it: "A Caxlán made ill use of her." This was
what had happened. Something that could be said, that other people could hear and understand. Not vertigo, not madness. She
sighed, relieved.

But in Winikton's eyes, the phrase gave off a very different
light. As if the years had not gone by and he, still a teenager and
from the powerlessness of his youth, was gazing upon a sickening
sight: his youngest sister, her foot pierced by the nail with which

a Caxlán had secured her to the floor so he could consummate his abuse. Seeing the blood that ran from the wound (slow, thick, black), Pedro let out a wild scream and pounded the earth furiously. At his back, among murmurs of disapproval, a bolt of lightning was unsheathed: the word justice. Who spoke it? None of the impassive mouths had been scorched by its fire. One by one Pedro questioned the men of the council, the oldest among the elders. No one answered. If the ancients possessed this notion, they did not pass it down to their descendants. So Winiktón could not test the term's worth. Nevertheless, each time his race suffered under the Ladinos' highhandedness, the syllables of the word justice resounded inside him like the bell around the eldest ewe's neck. And he walked blindly behind it, along steep and perilous trails, without ever catching up to it.

Later, Winiktón attached himself to Xaw Ramírez Paciencia, the sacristan of the parish church of Chamula, a solitary man who lived in the belltower and furtively sucked the tips of his fingers, impregnated with the taste of charred candle wick, oil and varnish. Xaw insisted on imitating the gesticulations of the priests, which, in his awkwardness, he caricatured. He mumbled prayers in a language called Latin which was even more impenetrable than Spanish, and then suddenly collapsed, struck down by a drunkenness without exaltation or reveries. But he had assisted men of reason, the priests. He had listened to them speaking in former days, and he was a man of long memory. At Winiktón's insistence, he gradually yielded until he finally revealed the only thing he knew: that justice is the task of judges. And then Pedro wanted nothing more than to be an adult, to hold in his hands the scale that weighs the actions of men.

He achieved what he set out to achieve. He was appointed a judge.

The audiences took place in the central chamber of the Cabildo. The judges heard only the conflicts that had not been resolved by deliberations between the families or by the intervention of a brujo. Accused and accuser presented themselves, bearing gifts to excite the benevolence and partiality of the authorities. They took their seats, unsealed the demijohns of aguardiente and offered the drink to those who were there, in order of their rank. Between one swig and another, accusers, accused and judges ranged far and wide around the matter that had brought them together, gratifying themselves in endless reticences. When the liquor had taken its effect and logic was uncertain, the matter at hand was addressed at last. Denunciations were made, punctuated by hiccups; the allegations of the defendants were piteous and absurd. The judges stumbled their way through this thicket of contradictory arguments. Roles were erratically reversed and victim and victimizer exchanged masks by turns. Faced with the impossibility of passing judgment, the judges exhorted the two parties to reconcile their differences. They reminded them of their childhoods spent together, the vicissitudes they had shared, the consideration they owed to relatives and neighbors. The contending parties wept, touched by the judges' evocation, by drunkenness. They took their leave together in perfect agreement. They walked along arm in arm, each one supporting the other's inebriated unsteadiness. They arrived back at their village, allies. But once the drunkenness passed, discord overcame them once more. The judges, in quick exasperation, locked the troublemakers in the calaboose. Jails, however, can be gotten out of. Prison doors are opened by gifts or by time. But the knot: how can it be undone, except by the slash of a weapon? The boundaries between properties were marked out by machete blows; theft and slander were punished by the machete; marital fidelity was nourished with blood.

During his tenure as a judge, Winiktón became familiar not with justice but with its opposite, the wild beast that devours it. After meeting that beast at every crossroads, he was learning about it, trait by trait. He knew its animal cunning, the lair it retreats to, its disguises, the speed with which it flees. Pedro's will to exterminate, his hunter instinct, became sharper and increasingly urgent. He tracked the beast, set out snares for it. And the prey (the prey whose name was garbled when he first heard it) always thwarted him. Now, today, this phrase—"A Caxlán made ill use of her"—coiled itself like a rope around injustice's throat and handed it over to Pedro with the same face it had shown him the first time. There it was, struggling, having just sated itself on the frail flesh of a woman, almost a girl. Pedro González Winiktón recognized it. He trembled with an eagerness to defend; he trembled with a need to destroy. And yet he remained still, immobile, captivated.

Catalina pushed the pot of beans (now steaming) to within her husband's reach. But the Tzotzil dignitary did not notice it. He was absorbed in his thoughts. The beans, untouched, gradually stopped steaming. Then Catalina asked, "You are not going to eat?"

Pedro said no with a gesture. His wife kept her eyes on him, alert and frowning. Winiktón was always reserved, little given to expansions and confidences. So the scarcity of his words could not alarm her. But muteness was usually his way of concentrating more deeply on what surrounded him. And this time Pedro was paying no attention. He was distracted, absent.

Did he dislike it that Catalina had made the decision to bring a guest into the house without asking for his consent? One more mouth, he could be thinking. But in exchange for that, Catalina would have someone to help her with the heaviest work. Catalina. . . . By what right did a barren woman like her try to elude the arduousness of her duties? On the contrary, she should compensate for her shortcoming by outdoing everyone else in her abnegation. Yes, that was what Winiktón was thinking deep inside himself; Catalina had the bitter satisfaction of reading his mind. And rebelliousness welled up like a gush of blood in her chest. Was it her fault she had no children? Was there any measure, however painful, however repulsive, she had not taken in her attempts to cure herself? All of them turned out to be useless. She has a cold womb, the women diagnosed mockingly. She was marked with an evil mark. Anyone could look down on her. Anyone. But not Pedro, not her husband.

Filled with animosity, Catalina turned toward Winiktón, seeking in his expression the evidence that would condemn him. What she found was a countenance flayed by an anguish so dire as to mortify anyone who could look at it. Catalina sought, among all names, one, to throw like a veil over this sight. But what name does suffering have when it is endured by the being we love? Catalina suddenly blew on the candle. The flame went out.

"It is time to sleep."

Quick sounds were heard, small domestic noises. There followed the vast nocturnal silence, the silence that becomes more compact, more real, when the coyotes howl, when the faint-hearted crickets chirp.

Pedro lay down with his back to his wife. His breathing was rhythmical, as if he had gone to sleep. Catalina measured the breathing to measure the depth of his anguish.

"He thinks of nothing now; he thinks of no one."

And this certainty calmed her.

But Winiktón was pretending, doing what some animals do when threatened with great danger: closing the eyes, stiffening the body, mimicking death. Because injustice was there, crouched in one of the corners of the hut.

Pedro's temples pounded against the hard wood. A feeling of imminence was vibrating in the tips of his fingers; it ran through his veins, igniting them, electrifying him. For the first time, his life presented itself to him as a river of continuous events flowing through a channel that brought him to this place, to this precise moment. The influence he had over those of his race, his political position, even the fact that he was the last of his lineage (because it made him more solitary, because it left him freer to accept and fulfill ambitious destinies), everything would take on meaning, find an explanation, reach its culmination, if only Pedro were capable of responding to the challenge thrown down by injustice which, in coming to provoke him, did not stop even at the threshold of his own house.

How was he to fight? Against whom? Pedro's mind burned with sudden, vengeful flames. He saw the Caxlán impaled; he saw fire running through the streets of Jobel; he saw the Ladino throng bent low beneath slavery's whip. Winiktón pounced on these images like a ravenous beast on a slab of meat. Then he pulled away, not sated but in disappointment. No, it was not so easy to deceive him. He already knew, he had seen it too many times: injustice grows greater with vengeance.

"It is impossible to do anything," he said in discouragement.

And his life escaped from him, like water when there is nothing but a net to carry it in.

Carefully, so as not to awaken Catalina, Pedro moved. Now ιt the defeat was complete, he wanted only to flee. He could ɴυt bear the slow nightly vigil of familiar objects, lightless stars, whose center of gravity he was. Silently he reached the door. The midnight wind lashed his cheek.

Catalina did not notice that she was left alone. She was dreaming. Dreaming that she was conversing with water. Dialogue is difficult when the other has a distant face, fugitive eyes, a vagabond attention, hardly hearing a word when the word has already been forgotten, along with the person who spoke it. However, Catalina knew a great deal about patience. She sat down on the bank, to wait. Until the water answered. It solidified into crystals and through the crystals could be seen, first vaguely, then distinctly, a set of human features. The smooth forehead, stony and unresonating, the eyes from which meekness peered, the random laugh: Lorenzo Díaz Puiljá, her brother, the innocent.

CHAPTER IV

CATALINA WENT EARLY to bathe in the stream; she washed her hair with amole root until it was squeaking with cleanliness; she rubbed it with fragrant brilliantine and braided it. Back in her house, she unfolded the woolen rebozo she kept for fiesta days; she held up the necklace of old coins—made of silver with a solid clank to it—that she stored at the bottom of a trunk, and with those two things she adorned herself.

Pedro González Winiktón was waiting for her at the door of the hut. He was wearing a new straw hat bedecked with a torrent of colored ribbons, along with a new chamois sash; in his right hand, he wielded the staff of authority.

They walked among the groups of Chamulas, giving rise to various comments: "There goes the judge with Catalina, both of them turned out in their best. Where are they taking that demijohn of aguardiente?"

"May the morning bring light to your field, Martoma Rosendo Gómez Oso."

In contrast to the light outside—the light goes naked in Chiapas and at noon its nakedness is like a sword's—the hut's shadowy interior was doubly impenetrable. Several minutes went by before the new arrivals were able to give some configuration to the shadows. Rosendo was curled up next to the fire, drowsing. His wife, on her knees, was turning the spindle which grew greater with wool at every rotation. The children—grubby, tattered, fretful—were crawling around on the dirt floor. One of them, the youngest, swollen and deformed by the rags he was wrapped in, was sleeping in a hammock (or was it only a net bag?) suspended from the roof's crosspieces.

Felipa, the martoma's wife, greeted the visitors with suspicion. For more than a month her daughter Marcela had been estranged from her, under the ilol's power, and during that time Felipa had not exchanged a single word with Marcela, not even a glance. Mother and daughter often encountered each other on the path to the spring and passed each other by without a word of greeting, like two strangers. Felipa was afraid, afraid Catalina would harm her if she tried to reclaim what Catalina had singled out as her own. That was how she felt at first. Later, absence showed its good side to Felipa: fewer expenses, more space, fewer obligations. She quickly resigned herself to losing Marcela. She had not foreseen the possibility of getting her back. She must have done some kind of damage, Felipa thought. Careless as she is. And now they are coming to demand compensation. They will probably want compensation as well for the days they fed and lodged her. But we have nothing to pay with. Look around, search the house. All I earn—so little!—is eaten up by my children. Ay, they are like leeches. Nothing is enough for them, nothing leaves them satisfied. And what is left, when anything is left, is squandered by that man there on his position as mayordomo. I keep nothing. Sadness is drying me out.

"Where are you, Felipa Gómez Oso?"

The woman thus summoned bowed her forehead, offering it to the touch of Catalina's fingers. Then, at a distance once more, she watched the ilol's gestures, trying to foresee her intentions.

"You will forgive us for having brought you this gift. Do not accept what it is, but the affection."

Pedro relinquished the demijohn of aguardiente to the martoma. Rosendo received it with a gesture of gratitude. Courtesy required him to invite his guests to partake of its contents. He placed the demijohn in Felipa's hands and commanded her to open it and offer some to everyone.

Felipa obeyed in silence. But the corners of her mouth stretched into a sarcastic grimace. Now she was sure: Catalina and Pedro had come to ask for something. The main thing was to keep her guard up, not to yield.

Rosendo's wife rinsed out a jicara and filled it with liquor. She presented it first to Pedro. He barely wet his lips on the rim before yielding it to the head of the house.

The martoma did not mind drinking. And since the obligations of his post had offered him legitimate occasion to do so with assiduity, his taste for alcohol had grown. So he drank deeply and with evident pleasure. The women would make do with what was left.

All of them remained still, silent. From time to time, the martoma made a show of letting out the sighs required by convention. This was a subtle way of conveying to his visitors that his situation was like that of all mortals: less satisfactory than it should have been. Yes, despite the fact that luck had favored him by exalting him to the high position of mayordomo of Santa Rosa, he was not exempt from the common bondage that afflicts mankind.

"How will the harvest be this year?" Winiktón asked.

Rosendo took advantage of this opportunity to adopt a mournful expression. He did not wish to arouse the envy of those less fortunate than he. The position of judge is an honorable one, certainly. Nevertheless, it is merely the title of a civil official. Whereas a mayordomo holds a religious post. Few men can boast as much, and those few are, without doubt, the best of the best. Ah, what sacrifices are forced on us by modesty. To ensure that he would be able to carry out what was now being demanded of him, Rosendo poured himself a little more aguardiente. He was unable to answer Pedro's question until he had finished drinking it.

"The harvest will be bad this year. The land is no longer young, tatic."

Liar! Felipa thought vehemently. It is not the land that is no longer young: it is you. And if this land does not yield, why did we sell the land we had back in our village of Majomut? It was good land. But you are feeding on your post as mayordomo. Drinking yourself silly the whole day through without leaving the church, you and the other mayordomos and that sacristan who goes along with all of it, Xaw Ramírez Paciencia.

"I do not go to the cornfield often. I must attend to the duties of my office."

Catalina saw how those words flowed across Felipa's expression. That was all she needed. She now knew exactly where to press in order to leave Felipa at her mercy. She said, "We all agree very strongly with the actions of Martoma Rosendo Gómez Oso. They say he will be forced to accept the post of mayordomo for one more year."

Rosendo felt the sweet caress of flattery. No, he could not pretend he was surprised. After all, it was the most natural thing. But he did have to admit that his maneuverings for re-election (his fawning and bribery) were successful because of the skill with which he had plotted them.

Felipa picked up the spindle again to hide her exasperation. One more year in Chamula. Meanwhile, her hut, closed up for so long in the village of Majomut, would collapse. Already, hateful accusations were circulating: greedy neighbors were taking it apart. One more year would be their ruin.

The ilol had calculated the blow well. Now she calmly observed its impact. She waited.

In the pause that followed, a name one of the two women did not dare pronounce was throbbing.

"Marcela is well," Catalina said.

Through the alcoholic mist that enveloped him, softening the crash of outside elements against his reverie, the martoma heard the name. He gave a start as if he had been pricked with the point of a needle. The balloon of his greatness was deflated. Because, tell me this, is it correct that the daughter of the mayordomo of Santa Rosa be estranged from her family, left in the power of strangers like an orphan, like a poor girl whose family cannot feed her? Obviously it is not correct. It is an anomaly only Felipa's weakness of spirit could have allowed to happen. But the anomaly must end this very day. He cleared his throat so the force of his demands would emerge intact. But it was not he who spoke, it was the drunkenness.

"My little girl, my Xmel, since she left blood falls in my heart!"

He hiccuped, moaned. Tears, slow, heavy and ignoble, flooded his cheeks and were lost among the limp strands of his moustache.

Pedro was irritated by the immodesty of this emotion. No one had the right to make such a display of what tormented him. Was he himself not forced to hide it? Drily he interrupted the martoma. "Marcela is the person we came here to speak of."

Catalina choked back an exclamation of disappointment. She was enjoying the state of tense expectation and anxious doubt she had created in Felipa.

"You want to give her back?"

What did the question conceal? An unconfessed hope? An egotistical and self-interested fear?

"No. We have found a husband for her."

A mayordomo cannot allow a common functionary—a civil

functionary at that—to appropriate his fatherly prerogatives and seek a destiny for his daughter. No one but Rosendo may choose Marcela's husband. He wanted to reply, to argue. But his vague, insubstantial gesture fell into the void. By now his muscles were obeying the drunkenness, not his will.

"How much will he pay for her?"

Winiktón was ashamed that a mother would ask the price before anything else. She wants to sell her like an animal, he thought. But after all, Pedro was not invested with any right to criticize the emotions of others. Was he not more cowardly, more despicable than anyone?

"He will pay what is just."

Felipa regretted the question, in which her avarice had betrayed itself. She resorted automatically to the customary formulas.

"That daughter of mine is a very idle girl. You have not yet taken full measure of her."

A mocking smile played on the ilol's lips.

"She does not know how to weave," Felipa insisted. "She does not know how to grind posol; she lets the beans go bad."

Her voice had been rising up the scale until it became shrill. She did not want them to believe what she was saying; she did not want to lower her daughter in their esteem. Catalina remained unfazed.

"The man has agreed."

"Who is the man?"

"My brother. Lorenzo Díaz Puiljá."

Felipa heard the answer, unbelieving. Then she erupted into a spasm of laughter that was painful, aggressive and uncontrollable.

"Why do you laugh?" Catalina asked severely.

The laugh, now inaudible, froze on her face. Covering it with both hands, Felipa, in her weakness, answered, "I do not know."

But she knew. She knew that Lorenzo Díaz Puiljá was an imbecile and that Catalina, to get him off her hands when their parents died, had arranged for him to marry. It did not matter to her that she had to pay an excessive dowry. She had married him off. But a few weeks later the newlywed bride fled to take refuge with her own people and the family had to return the gifts. Catalina would not resign herself to the situation and brought a lawsuit.

The girl had to appear before the judges. She declared that Lorenzo "did not know how to make use of her in the night." The judges agreed to annul the marriage. From that date, Lorenzo had lived alone in the village of Tzajal-hemel.

"My brother is a good man."

Cautiously, trying not to provoke Catalina's wrath, Felipa risked an objection.

"They say . . . they say Lorenzo is a little touched."

"It was unfortunate. A great pukuj carried him off when he was a boy. He was in the cornfield. The great pukuj flew far away with him, to another village. Many people saw him flying. Many of our elders whose mouths cannot contain a lie. Loronzo was found cast down on the mountainside. He never recovered his spirit; he never remembered how to speak."

The efforts of the brujos to cure him were in vain. The boy grew like a tree deformed by a twisted trunk.

"I do not want my daughter to marry badly, Catalina Díaz Puiljá. Therefore I tell you that if she is to be your brother's wife, I will ask for five fat sheep, three demijohns of liquor and a large measure of corn."

"My brother will not give you those things."

"Why?"

"Because your daughter is not worth them."

"How much will he give, then?"

"Nothing."

Felipa turned her eyes toward her husband to force him to intervene in this transaction from which they would extract no gain. A man's voice is always heard with greater respect. But the martoma was slumped against the wall snoring, his mouth wide open.

"Is this a good thing your wife is proposing to me, Pedro González Winiktón?"

The desperate plea for advice was not directed to Pedro González Winiktón, husband of Catalina Díaz Puiljá, but to Pedro González Winiktón, judge, assessor of the actions of men. Nevertheless, now that the first offense against justice was complete (that of the night when Marcela took shelter under his roof and nothing was done to repair the damage inflicted on her by the Caxlán), other offenses were only awaiting their turn.

Without hesitation, without remorse, Pedro answered, "It is good."

"But why am I to hand my daughter over, for nothing, to a man who will not even know how to make her his own?"

Not once since the innocent's first wife confessed in the Cabildo, before all the principal men of Chamula, had anyone dared repeat that Lorenzo Díaz Puiljá was impotent. It was whispered in corners, perhaps; it was a matter for coarse or ambiguous joking. But now Catalina had flushed the cunning animal from its hiding place. She did what armadillo hunters do, asphyxiating their prey with smoke and harassing it with torches. The rumor had shown its face, at last. The punishment would be thrown back in that same face.

"No other man except Lorenzo Díaz Puiljá would accept your daughter."

Felipa was no longer measuring the danger. She took her provocation to its limit.

"Why? Are you going to put a hex on her?"

"In Jobel, a Caxlán made ill use of her."

Felipa could no longer continue to ignore the suspicion that had been jabbing at her since the day Marcela came back without the pitchers, without the money for the pitchers. But an unreasoning fury dictated her final protests.

"It is not true! Not true! My Xmel is not an ear of corn to be stripped of its grains like that, without a second thought. You are slandering her because you want to take her without paying me what she is worth."

Catalina took Felipa by the shoulders and shook her to put her brains back in their proper place.

"Do you want to see your daughter shamed in front of everyone? We will call them. Let them ask her! Let them search her!"

Felipa began sobbing again. The sobs were strangling her, strangling her words. But her head was still moving anxiously, shaking, saying no. Catalina let go of her. She stood up and without looking at Felipa said, "Pedro and I gave it much thought. And we agreed to inform you of Marcela's engagement. Only out of consideration, because when all is said and done you are her mother. Understand it well. And tell Martoma Rosendo Gómez Oso about it when he comes back out of his drunkenness."

Catalina and Winiktón left. Felipa watched them walk away without trying to detain them, without pleading with them until she made them change their decision, without kneeling before them to stave off this new misfortune come to annihilate her.

She sat still for a while, staring fixedly at the spindle that slept between her hands. Then, as if someone were listening to her, she said, "Rosendo, let us go to our village, to our house in Majomut. I swear to you I cannot work any more. I swear this to you. My feet hurt very much."

CHAPTER V

WINIKTÓN WENT TO Tzajal-hemel. On his return, he walked in front and Lorenzo, carrying his household goods, came behind. Catalina helped her brother disencumber himself of his load and took him to her, caressing him slowly and clumsily like someone caressing an animal's furry back. The innocent stared up at her and the limpidity of his pupils clouded over for an instant with recognition. Docile, he let them lead him to the hut where Marcela, gray with alarm and shyness, was waiting. Pointing to her, the ilol said, "This is your wife."

Lorenzo looked her over with an animal's sluggish thoroughness. But neither fright nor happiness nor aversion showed itself on that forehead. Little by little, Marcela became more at ease. Soon she remained calm in the newcomer's presence, as calm as when she was alone.

Winiktón presided over the meal. Catalina had prepared a special dish: venison. They all ate in silence, with the gravity of people who are carrying out a ritual. Lorenzo was the only one who laughed from time to time, for no reason, a slack, deranged laugh. But the ilol reduced him to silence with no more than a light pressure on his arm.

Marcela watched him out of the corner of her eye. Lorenzo's fingers trembled so badly that half of every mouthful he picked up fell, staining his clothes and dirtying his surroundings.

Pedro did not lift his eyes, but he was alert, imagining the gestures his brother-in-law was making. His obsessive preoccupation made his muscles tense, made his jaws grind almost perceptibly. He pretended not to notice the awkwardness of Lorenzo's hands, in a childish effort to ensure that, since he was ignoring it, another person, Marcela, would ignore it, too. He did not want to hear her utter a breath of scorn or mockery. Because who but Pedro did she have the right to scorn? Who but justice would she mock, since both of them—justice and Pedro—had fostered, had permitted this union?

Catalina did not even try to disguise her satisfaction. She had always been responsible for her brother and she had always given him the care he needed. From the time she was a little girl, before they were orphaned, Catalina was Lorenzo's protector, his support. He was not a burden to her. But her position as a childless woman was so precarious that she did not dare aggravate her husband with further demands. Therefore when Pedro was named a judge and it was necessary to go and live in San Juan Chamula, Catalina had not wanted even to suggest the possibility that her brother might accompany them. But she could not leave him without remorse. Lorenzo, far from her, Lorenzo left to his own devices, to the neighbors' good will. The invisible guardians condemn such acts.

If Lorenzo were to marry. . . . The failure of his first marriage annoyed the ilol all the more for the fact that from the beginning she had to consider it inevitable. The bride left her family's house honorably, pushed out by a paternal greed that took nothing into consideration except the value of the dowry. But if the girl initially obeyed her parents' demands, later her insistence upon a separation was inflexible. Neither pleas nor threats had any effect in the face of the reasons she cited. The judges supported her demand and she, seeing herself free, escaped. She went to Jobel first. Later it was learned that she had ended up as far away as Mexico. Lorenzo was alone once more, seeking the company of his sister, who did not want to risk her prestige and Pedro's, too, on another false maneuver. Catalina preferred to wait. But she was only passive in appearance. Ceaselessly she invoked her dark allies, the powers that populate the air, those that rule the night, those that preside over events. She never stopped making them offerings, promising sacrifices so her petition would be attended to. And when Marcela presented herself, defenseless and as if pursued, on the steps of the market of La Merced, when she was so unthinkingly punished by her mother, a dark impulse prompted Catalina to defend her. Afterward, in dreams, she realized that this was the answer to her prayers and that her wait had reached its end. The rest was easy. Marcela's relatives were not an obstacle. The vanity of the martoma's nature was all too well known, his shiftless character, his total servitude to alcohol. As for Felipa, custom did not authorize her to have her own voice. And even if she had, she would never have spoken up effectively on her daughter's behalf, she would never have succeeded in saving her. She liked to moan and lament. She liked to suffer.

So the marriage took place. From now on, Lorenzo would have someone to look out for him. Marcela did not have what it would take to be anything more than what Catalina intended her to be. And if Marcela ever thought about her lot in life, she would understand that she had reason to be content with it. Or would she have preferred to have her family spit on her dishonor? Would she have been able to endure the harsh weather on the mountainside, the shame of beggary in a town of Caxláns? Here she had a place of refuge for her destitution, a name to cover her head, the title of wife to confront others with.

"From Lorenzo no harm can come to her. Though if what Marcela wants is to have the satisfaction of a man . . . she will just have to control herself. She has to pay something for what she lacks."

This reasoning dispelled Catalina's last scruple. She had finished eating her portion of meat and she served herself another.

For weeks Marcela lived in frightened expectation, quivering like a hare. Then, imperceptibly, she began to grow accustomed to Lorenzo's almost vegetable presence.

The pair held each other's hands to go and cut wood, to go and herd the flock, to go to Jobel.

Not love but pity gradually filled Marcela's heart to the brim with a deep and restful water. She drank from it when, with a delicate motion, she drew close to her husband to bring a bite of food to his lips, or when she wrapped him up warmly at bedtime so he would not be cold.

The days went along, one after the other. In mid-afternoon the two women sat under the hut's palm-thatch eaves with the loom stretching out in front of them like a brief horizon. The threads were intertwined with precision, with artistry, and the work gradually began to appear in its perfection: soft to the touch, pleasant to the gaze, useful. At times a word flew between them. Catalina was the one who spoke it. Simply syllables, slight suggestions, the short string that keeps the bird tied down. Marcela would listen distractedly, acquiescing to the sound, only the sound.

Because a great peace—a peace with eyelids of sleep—had spread its balm over the girl's joints in the place where memory was painful, in the place where hope would be painful. What throbs inside her is no longer a bloody entrail but a moment, the marvelous void of this moment.

How beautiful this landscape looked, seen through her transparency. The men returned along the paths of twilight, with the hoe or the staff of office in hand, depending on whether they had been at the cornfield or the Cabildo. Xaw Ramírez Paciencia, the sacristan, tolled the bronze churchbells. Smoke rose from the huts, the timid, hesitant smoke given off by the cooking fires of the poor. Here, there, like the eyes of a fugitive animal, tiny lights flickered. Then night held absolute sway.

But it is essential to be vigilant, not to sleep. Something is always lurking. Catalina was the first to become aware of it. People swear that an ilol needs only to examine a female's footprints in order to tell the number of months of her heaviness. She needs even less when envy sharpens her senses and makes them perceive what is beyond the footprints, beyond what the purple circles under the eyes hold back, what the forehead, cloudy as a mirror, conceals.

Catalina knew but kept silent. She was speechless with what is most painful, most true: hunger. The hunger that makes us twist and moan, that becomes intolerable when we behold the fullness of others.

The ilol spied on Marcela with wide, delirious eyes. How was it possible that this insignificant, stupid girl whom she used as a simple instrument of her designs had succeeded in becoming the repository of the treasure that was denied to Catalina? And what was even more absurd: Marcela was unconscious of her privilege. She continued carrying out her duties, indifferently, routinely; she continued in her daily comings and goings, a little slower now, only a little slower.

Rather than placating Catalina's jealousy, this unconcern only excited it. Ignorance is sometimes too close to mockery, and passivity can be confused with provocation and insult. Exasperated, Catalina shouted (and it was as if someone were lancing an abscess on her body), "You are going to have a child!"

The revelation shook Marcela. Instinctively she raised both hands to her belly as if to stop the thing that was growing within her, implacable, hour by hour, more and more, and that would end by devouring her. She began to feel it: that thing was moving, kicking, suffocating. A spasm of nausea, her last gesture of defense, doubled her over. An uncontrollable longing to tear out the gelatinous mass that was patiently nourishing itself by gnawing at her entrails, a desire to destroy the formless creature that was already crushing her down with a master's heavy foot.

Catalina left Marcela alone during her outbursts. From outside, she watched her struggle against herself in a useless battle whose only possible outcome was defeat. But when the girl, her hair flattened down with sweat and her eyelids reddened by her efforts, surrendered to exhaustion and huddled up in a corner, Catalina came to her with the potion she had prepared to help her recover. Marcela tried to push it away in vain. In the end, she always opened her mouth to swallow what was offered. Afterward she wept at great length, with jagged sobs and sighs that were quickly extinguished because her torn muscles ached. And the thing, that thing, stayed in there, swelling out her belly grotesquely, weighing her down.

How difficult it was to walk up the sheep paths; how problematic to stand up or sit down on the tree trunk used as a seat. Pedro would sometimes help Marcela. Lorenzo laughed when he saw the awkwardness of his wife's movements, the delay in her reactions.

One day when Marcela went to herd the flock without anyone accompanying her, she did not want to return. She abandoned the animals and walked without following a trail, stumbling, unable to dodge the thorns that scratched her clothing and skin, made her bleed. She went along aimlessly, aghast at her decision and at the warm and obscene burden she carried within her, stopping from time to time to vomit, until she fell down next to an anonymous rock.

Woodcutters who were passing by found her there and sent word to the judge's family. Between all of them they carried Marcela back to the hut where she convalesced slowly under Lorenzo's opaque gaze, Winiktón's guilty aloofness and Catalina's efficient ministrations. Thanks to the latter (to her power, the ilol preferred to say), the danger of a miscarriage was averted. Now, every time a momentary discomfort made Marcela shift her position too rapidly, Catalina ran to restrain her, warning her, "You are going to have this child. I do not care if you want it or not. After all, are you the one it will belong to?"

Marcela, whose fiber had been sapped by adversity, no longer protested. She nodded humbly. She watched the preparations for the birth without interest or even curiosity, as if the event had nothing to do with her.

The men of the household busied themselves building the pus, the steam bath, next to the house. They bound reeds together and filled in the cracks between them with mud, leaving only a narrow crawl space for an entrance. Catalina arranged for the most famous pulsetakers in the region to come and pray before the hut's central cross to banish evil influences and the grim desires of enemies.

The others were keeping close track of time, but not Marcela. She was there, laid out flat like the land where the flocks graze. Defenseless, parched under the August sun.

And when the day came it was not like other days; it revealed itself to be overshadowed with omens. The sun and the moon were doing battle in the sky. The tribe of the Tzotzils witnessed this battle in terror, striving with screams, a deafening beating of drums, a frantic clanging of bells, to ensure the triumph of the strongest.

When Catalina heard the news of the eclipse she ran to Marcela's side. She had made a mask out of tree bark to protect Marcela from the eyes of the great pukuj who was now roaming free.

The mask fell over the ravaged face of the woman in labor. Her body had suddenly entered a zone where the force of youth was quickening its every cell, stripping her naked for pain, making her infinitely sensitive for the moment when she would be torn apart. And the rebellion within her, which had seemed drained of all life, surged up anew, pitching about in fury like a colt refusing to cross a river that is too turbulent.

Outside people were running, ululating, while the panic-stricken animals howled, gobbled and whinnied, breaking their bonds, leaping fences, abandoning their familiar surroundings. Because they had scented the disaster.

The pulsetakers did not want to come, so Pedro lit the candles at the foot of the cross, knelt down and covered his ears with his hands in order to hear neither the panic nor the agony, only the other voice.

"Look at her, Pedro González Winiktón. Injustice is breeding in front of you and you have tolerated it. What is the name for what you have done? Pedro González Winiktón, you are a judge. Judge yourself."

Catalina dragged Marcela to the most solid pillar of the house and tied her to it so she could wrestle with herself there, so she could struggle. Lorenzo watched this kneeling female figure, its face extravagantly covered by a mask, without knowing what to do. Custom ordained that the man should tighten a band around his wife's waist so that the child would follow the natural path "and not go upward." But what could an innocent understand about such things? Catalina took him away from there. She alone would receive the newborn, cut the umbilical cord (over an ear of corn, to propitiate the fecundity of the planted fields), swaddle him.

Marcela was released from the pillar, gasping. Pedro ran to hold her up. Awkwardly, fearful of causing pain, Winiktón bathed her neck which was lustrous with sweat. On the hot embers, the chili water that would restore the new mother's forces was bubbling.

Outside, the clamor of the eclipse had ceased. Now Marcela's mask could be removed without danger. The face appeared: serene, sweet, asleep.

The next day, the new mother entered the steam bath with the baby. In the wet heat that the stones exhaled, Marcela became acquainted with her son. The skin was a sturdy color and he had the tenacious almond-shaped eyes of her race. But the hair was curly, like a Caxlán's. Marcela was repulsed; she rejected him.

The child would be brought up in Catalina's lap. She was his godmother and chose his name: Domingo Díaz Puiljá, after her and Lorenzo's father. She believed this would perpetuate their father's memory. But everyone called the child something else: "the one born at the eclipse."

CHAPTER VI

WHEN PEDRO GONZÁLEZ WINIKTÓN ceased to serve as a judge in the capital of Chamula, he returned with his family to the village of Tzajal-hemel.

Everything spoke of abandonment, in the hut, the animal pens, the cornfield. The roof's palm thatching had worn away in large rents through which wind whistled and rain dripped. The doors no longer fit their frames and in the corners cobwebs dangled, thick, dirty and torn.

A fallow period had not made Winiktón's plot of land more fertile. On the contrary, the cornfield's furrows were overrun with weeds; rainstorms had opened up innumerable deep channels and the field's borders had been demolished by animals that grazed there, placid and unpunished.

Pedro, helped as much as possible by his brother-in-law (the women were busy with the household tasks and herding the flock), worked eagerly. He planted the field on the auspicious day, watched over the growth of the corn, freeing it of cizakas and entrusting it to the timely arrival of the rains.

The season progressed, serene and without disturbances; for many it was a fruitful one. But Winiktón's harvest did not correspond to his efforts or his needs. The slopes where his corn was planted were too steep; the small, irregular and stony patch of ground no longer yielded much. The future would only make the scarcity they were now enduring grow worse.

Nevertheless, the rent had to be paid on time, in work and in cash, to the owner of the land, a Ladino who lived in Ciudad Real.

Mealtimes in Winiktón's family were quiet. Pedro polished off his food quickly without daring to lift his eyelids so as not to see the faces of those around him. In every gesture, every expression, he read a recrimination, a useless cry for help. And the child, hanging in a net bag in the center of the shack, cried desperately from hunger.

That crying followed the former judge wherever he went; in

vain he went further and further up the mountain, chasing the fleeing tracks of a stag; in vain he dizzied himself in the tumult of the plaza; in vain he participated in the ceremonies. The baby's cry went with him, rang out here and there, in the caves on the hill, at the corners of the market, near the church and the Cabildo. The baby's cry only expanded in the great darkness of night when Pedro looked for a refuge and a truce in drunkenness.

The elders gave him advice.

"Do as we do, tatic; one cannot be like the animals, without a shelter or a corral. Seek the shadow of a patrón; he will help you when you are in need; he will stand beside you in hard times."

This was what the old men said, but they did not talk about the humiliation, the exhaustion of the peon who lived permanently on the patrón's estate, or of the temporary laborer whose own land was left uncultivated. And Pedro, who had been a man of authority in his tribe, whose most intimate acts and most secret thoughts were bound to his judge's investiture, could not lower himself to become a Ladino's footman, a ranch hand, a servant boy in a stately house.

Propped up with loans, grown accustomed to austerities, Pedro held out for one year more. But the harvest cheated him again. The child was crawling through the hut by now, thin and dirty. He no longer cried; he no longer had the energy to cry. He moaned softly and fell asleep next to the stones around the hearth where the embers glowed.

Pedro González Winiktón agreed to leave. When the enganchador arrived in San Juan to enlist a crew of indentured workers for the patrón of a lowland finca, the former judge requested that his application be noted down in the book.

When he was asked his name, he said Pedro González. He did not speak the name of his chulel; he safeguarded his soul from the strangers' power; he left the deepest and truest part of his being out of the agreement.

The crew, made up of men from all parts of Chamula, went down to Ciudad Real first.

From the moment they walked away from their villages, a strange transformation came over them. They ceased to be Antonio Pérez Bolom, a harpist residing in Milpoleta, or Domingo Juárez Bequet, a hunter of mountain cats and a famous pulsetaker, or Manuel Domínguez Acubal, well-versed in questions of enchantment and witchcraft. They were only a fingerprint at the bottom of a contract. In their homes they left memory, reputation, personhood. What walked along the trails was an anonymous, solitary man who had rented himself out to another's will, who had become estranged from other interests.

Pedro deeply resented this change. From the moment he became part of the group of enganchados, the others' gazes rested on him with an indifference that stripped him of his prestige, his attributes, and reduced him to a thing, a thing that could be put to some use, perhaps, but that had no value in itself.

The enganchados' entrance into Ciudad Real was a grotesque parade. People came to a standstill, whispering and laughing, when they saw the Indians walking in a single file down the center of the street as if they were afraid of going astray or making any movement, any action not dictated by their guide.

The Indians interrupted the flow of traffic, stumbled into each other, hurting themselves with their heavy leather sandals; they endured the Ladinos' scrutiny with a discomfiture that exacerbated the townspeoples' mockery instead of placating it.

Finally they arrived at the enganchador's office. Waiting their turn, they sat down on the edge of the sidewalk where some of them began patiently examining themselves for lice and rapidly eating the lice they captured.

Each Indian was subjected to an inspection. Their dates were noted down, a photograph was taken of them and their cards were filed away. In that way, the enganchador assured them, he had taken possession of each one's chulel. And what good would it do them to run away from the fincas, to go off without finishing their job or settling their debts? How far could they go without a soul to sustain them? On the other hand, if they knew how to merit it, the enganchador would give back, at the end of the time for which they were bound, the card that for now remained deposited with him as a guarantee of their good conduct.

Debts, the enganchador had spoken of debts. Winiktón had not expected to hear the word. But Don Remigio Flores repeated it many times: "Listen closely, Chamula; we're going to tally up our accounts. The minimum salary is seventy-five centavos per day: six reales. That makes twenty-two pesos with one fifty-centavo piece per month. From that I deduct my commission, the advance we give you for travel expenses, the rent on your lodgings at the finca, the price of the machete and the other little things you ask for in the patrón's store. . . . Add it all up, and the first month you come out behind. Later, if you behave and don't squander anything on liquor, if you don't feel like getting new breeches and new sandals, if you don't need medicine for malaria, then you might catch up a little."

Don Remigio spoke with convincing volubility and though he knew the Tzotzil language well enough, in these explanations involving numbers and calculations he preferred to use Spanish. So Pedro, although he made an enormous effort to follow his reasoning, had to resign himself to assenting blindly. Later, when all of them were sleeping in a heap in the doorway of the enganchador's house, Pedro turned Don Remigio's words over and over in his head.

"How is that?" he said to himself. "I leave my house, my family, my village; I walk for miles and miles down the mountain. I suffer from heat, my body aches with sickness; I do not idle the time away, lying all day in the hammock—I put in the full day. And when the hour arrives to return home, the result is that I return emptyhanded. To my way of seeing, this is not good. It is not just."

Worried by this discovery, Winiktón yearned to share it with those lying nearby. They were sleeping deeply, snoring, and when Pedro tried to wake them they grumbled threateningly and, bundling themselves tighter in their blankets, fell back into their lethargy.

It was not yet dawn when the enganchados got underway. They went quickly and in silence; the rest periods were so short there was no time to do more than devour a mouthful or drink down a gulp of posol.

Nevertheless, Pedro spoke. Addressing those who could hear him, he said, "The agreement with Don Remigio is not just."

"So? What did you expect? It was your fate to be born an Indian," one of them answered, with a worried look at the capataz. The others nodded and hid their faces.

Indian. The word had often been thrown in his face, an insult. But now, spoken by someone of the same race, it served to establish a distance, to divide those who were united at the root. This was Winiktón's first experience of solitude and he could not endure it without remorse.

"I am the guilty one," he reflected. "I separate myself from the others, I ponder things that are not legitimate."

He promised himself he would erase the ideas that were obsessing his mind, but in the most unexpected moments, triggered by the most trivial details, they resurged. His efforts were also useless in another respect: the flow of confidence that had once united him with his companions was not re-established. There remained an unchanging mistrust, a reserve that the days made irrevocable.

The mountain range had gradually left behind its steep volumes, where even the eyes could not find rest, to settle into soft hills and, finally, expansive flatlands, swollen with a warm air of almost carnal density.

Pedro contemplated this new landscape with a disturbance he did not know how to define. Some inner rigidity whose tension was sustained by the mountain yielded here. He was walking in the same rhythm as the others and was prompt to obey the commands of the capataz. But during the march and amidst his obedience, a greedy eye was gathering in the color of a fleeting bird, sensitive pores were assessing the fertile earth underfoot, the rough tree trunk with a slash through it that served as a signal.

At night, instead of giving in to exhaustion as the others did, Pedro stayed awake. Never had the sky been so close, the clusters of stars within such easy reach of the hand. The constellations slipped by, silent as a great river. It was the smaller beings that signalled their presence with noises: the crackling of the dry leaves on the ground, the bleating of an abandoned suckling lamb, the jabbering of the monkeys, the seething voice of the jaguar.

After so many days of travel, Tapachula could seem to those who arrived on foot (and even more to these Chamulas, accustomed to the misery of their villages or the shameful poverty of Ciudad Real) like a splendid place. Nature had not stinted on any of her luxuries here: beneficent plants, abundant fruit, ornamental parasites. The buildings, which would have been modest somewhere else, seemed trivial here. From what severity of climate did their inhabitants need to protect themselves, from what fierce elements did they need to take shelter? A bit of shade was all that was necessary, and to achieve that, a few gigantic leaves supported with a thin framework of flimsy vines and twisted, unpolished logs were all that was needed.

But in the center of the city the view changed; cement and mortar replaced wood and palm leaves, and walls surrounded an interior that the archways without doors insisted on revealing: courtyards from which vegetation was banished because it was uncontrollable, hot concrete, cracked everywhere by invisible seeds on the verge of germinating, sprouting, growing.

In the galleries, large hammocks were slung: pale women with shadowy eyes sleeping the sleep of pregnancy or distractedly abandoning a flaccid and already sterile breast to a suckling child. Barefoot children, large-bellied and colorless; domestic animals, sleepy and panting; an ancient woman fanning herself with a mechanical motion that she no longer put any hope or conviction into.

The Indians were sweating. They had torn off their woolen serapes, which were intolerable in this climate, and they would have liked to relinquish the solid mass of their bodies, as well, where the heat ensconces itself and torments.

"It will be difficult to work here," Pedro thought. "We are not accustomed to these ways."

The finca to which the Chamulas were bound (La Constancia, property of a German, Don Adolfo Homel) was five leagues from Tapachula. In the big house, spacious and well-ventilated, fans hissed, there was a small machine that made ice, and wire screens protected all openings from invasion by insects. Thanks to these comforts, life could be pleasant there. But Don Adolfo's family could bear no more than brief stays and day-long excursions. They lived in the city, where the Homel girls—white-skinned and blue-eyed, with merry dispositions—were one of the most sought-after and enthusiastic elements in clubs, charitable societies and other such organizations.

Their mother, Doña Ifigenia, kept back in a discreet shadow. She had had the good sense not to pass on the color of her skin (the dark skin of a Zoque Indian), the rawness of her intellect or the crudeness of her manners to her descendents. She had also had the prudence not to make herself visible as Don Adolfo's wife when wealth came to crown his efforts and aristocracy rewarded his virtues. Doña Ifigenia moved from the kitchen to the ironing room, happy with the large gold earrings that dangled from her ears and her filigreed necklaces, waiting to become a grandmother in order to be useful once more.

Don Adolfo, for his part, never regretted having made such an unequal marriage. He had needed a docile, submissive woman who would live in awe of her husband's superiority. Who could better satisfy those criteria than Doña Ifigenia? She never tried to compare herself to him and the language barrier had placed a tangible limit on their intimacy from the beginning. This distance was soothing to Don Adolfo because direct personal relations made him uncomfortable. He was incapable of establishing them even with his daughters, for whom he was content to fulfil the role of provider.

Scrupulous in the management of his affairs, exacting, active and well-informed about the branch of business he was in, Don Adolfo was a difficult patrón. Administrators often resigned from his employ, disappointed at being unable to rob with impunity and command without supervision. Despite these difficulties, Don Adolfo refused to do without an intermediary in dealing with his peons. It enabled him to be unscrupulous in his demands for more work and to enjoy his earnings without remorse.

For Don Adolfo had a sensitive heart. Although on his finca recourse was had, when it was deemed necessary, to the stocks, the calaboose, the whip, it was only because he appreciated discipline. And if, in the finca's store, aguardiente was sold on credit at higher prices than in the market, if the workdays lasted from sunup to sundown, it was only because he respected tradition.

However, as a tribute to hygiene, he installed a latrine in the shed where the Indians lived. He opened a school and paid a teacher for other reasons; the government's new legislation had, of course, profoundly touched his Germanic instinct for obedience. Furthermore, he did not agree with the arguments by which his neighbors justified their failure to comply with the legislation.

"Your Indian who gets above himself is a lost Indian," they said. "When those so-and-sos know how to read and write Ca-tilla the devil himself won't be able to handle them."

"On the contrary," Homel replied. "The Indians serve ı

grudgingly and since they aren't very skilled they can't be very useful to us. But with education everything will improve."

Don Adolfo liked to pronounce words like that one: education. It awoke within him a nostalgia for a homeland whose memory was increasingly vague and capricious. A homeland where (since his reasons for emigrating were no longer at the forefront of his mind) all was prosperity and abundance, owing, naturally, to the primary and secondary schools and universities where education was dispensed. In America, however. . . . Climate and race were the determining factors in its backwardness, that much was clear —but only because both elements weakened mankind in its fight against ignorance.

"Educated men," Don Adolfo would repeat, "make prosperous nations."

And he imagined a world without misery, without conflicts, once all men had reached the same level of knowledge. The patróns of the neighboring fincas listened to Don Adolfo talk, their misgivings mingled with admiration. As a foreigner, it was his right to speak these grand words which in another man's mouth would have seemed pedantic and out of place. But did he really know much about his adoptive country and this area of Chiapas if he thought measures that were effective in Europe wouldn't be counterproductive here?

"When the Indians know what we know they'll seize what is ours."

Don Adolfo shrugged. He was old, and the thought that what he had put by would find its way into the hands of greedy sons-in-law did not move him to defend it.

So the school began to operate at La Constancia. The owners of the neighboring fincas stopped worrying about it when they saw that it had very scant success.

Classes were held at night, after the Indians had completed their day of hard labor and when echoes of the marimbas and exploding firecrackers with which the peons of other fincas were enjoying their leisure came from all directions.

The Indians did not openly oppose Don Adolfo's order that they attend classes. They lowered their eyebrows submissively and murmured phrases of gratitude, though deep in their hearts they felt themselves to be the victims of a new abuse. That was why, as soon as the capataz looked away, they disappeared from his sight. They were discovered hours later under a tree somewhere, sleeping the heavy sleep of drunkenness.

Don Adolfo did not understand such ingratitude. He was astonished, because he had believed that the Indians would rush to take advantage of the opportunity he was offering them to better their living conditions. But he was not a man to lose sight of his goals and so he told the capataz to punish with severity those who disobeyed his orders. After that, the classes were attended by distracted students, unable to remain still in front of a sheet of paper, clumsily clutching the pencil, rebelling against the teacher's instructions, wary of the punishment that could suddenly befall them.

There were those among them who made an effort to comply with this new duty. Pedro González Winiktón did so with the seriousness he had once brought to his position as judge. Quickly, to complement this habit, a real interest in the teacher's lessons sprang up inside him, an interest that did not dim when the class was over.

Pedro stayed awake, his eyes fixed on his San Miguel primer, pondering the signs that were slowly penetrating his understanding. What pride he took in presenting himself before the others the next day with the lesson learned! What a feeling it was to discover the names of objects and speak them and write them and thus take possession of the world! What amazement when he heard "the paper that talks" for the first time!

Don Adolfo, kept abreast of this process by the teacher's reports, retired Winiktón from the heaviest work to keep him at his side as a footman. Pedro accompanied the patrón on his rides across the finca and his trips to Tapachula. He became familiar with the city and entered doors that otherwise would have remained permanently closed to an Indian. From the entryways, from the kitchens, from the courtyards where he waited for his master, he came to know the houses of the rich; he learned the uneven paving stones of the municipal buildings and glimpsed the great rooms of the clubhouses. He would have liked to go nearer and listen to the gentlemen chatting, now that he understood their language.

But even if Winiktón had been standing closer to the regular get-together of Don Adolfo and his friends, it would have been difficult for him to follow the thread of their conversation, so rapidly and tumultuously were they all commenting on the great event: the arrival of the president of the Republic in Tapachula.

"We'll have to throw the house out the window for his reception."

"They say he's no lover of luxuries."

"What about our position? We can't do less than everybody else. In Huixtla they set up triumphal arches from the train station to the Palacio."

"And what do you hear about the highlands?"

"There it's done out of fear. They have the agrarian reform on their backs and the ranches are being redistributed on the president's orders. . . ."

"Won't it be our turn soon?"

"No risk of that. Coffee can only be profitable when it's grown on large expanses of land. What's more, who disputes our ownership of the land? We didn't take it away from the Indians."

"Fortunately the Indians only pass through here."

"Even when they decide to stay."

"They can't take the heat."

"Order, please, gentlemen! We're getting away from the matter at hand."

"The girls will have to wear regional costumes."

"Don Adolfo, your daughters will lead the way, as usual."

"We'll have to hold a banquet at the Coffee Planters' Club."

"And why not an outing to the sea?"

"Too rigorous. . . ."

"It's all part of the fun. Anyway, they say the president is a very simple man, very approachable."

But not in the way the landowners would have wanted him to be. The president had very little time and didn't want to waste it in homages but used it to meet with people; at an early hour, his hotel room was open to the avalanche of citizens who wanted to speak to him: campesino groups, workers' committees, widows wanting scholarships for their children, people requesting jobs, aspiring political appointees. The president listened to all of them with the same respect, the same attention. His green eyes, so surprising in that tanned face, interrogated, discovered, assessed.

The landowners organized a hasty conclave.

"The president has said he wants to visit one of our fincas."

Every one of them would have wanted to offer his own. But prudence held them back. How to outfit an unpresentable house in such a short time? Where to hide the querida and the bastard children? How to make the peons' barracks look like dwellings fit for human habitation?

"We'll have to take him to La Constancia, Don Adolfo."

The man they were speaking to smiled affirmatively. Here is where my abstemious ways, my habits of order and cleanliness, my faith in progress, my foreigner's virtues find their public recompense at last, he seemed to say.

The president visited La Constancia. Proudly its owner displayed the machinery that processed the coffee beans and the groves that were in season. The committee visited the enormous embankments where the beans were drying and the warehouses where the coffee was stored. Don Adolfo was on the lookout for his visitors' approval and when it came he reddened with pleasure.

During the meal, conversation turned toward the new laws enacted by the government. This was the moment Don Adolfo was waiting for. Though it was not on the program, he suggested that, to help their digestion, they take a stroll through the parts of the finca reserved for its employees.

The president and his entourage saw the sheds that served as dormitories, the bustling kitchen and the school.

"We strive to carry out your mandates, Señor Presidente," said Don Adolfo, "insofar as our means will permit."

Uncomfortable in their Sunday clothes, the Chamulas were offered up to the visitors' curiosity. The president turned a face lit up by an affable smile toward them. For several minutes he spoke slowly, choosing the most easily understandable phrases, about the effort men like them had to make to be equal to other Mexicans and lead a worthy and respected life. But this effort, he added, would no longer be hampered and punished, as before, by those in power who wished to continue to exploit them. Now the Indians could count on the support of the authorities; justice would be done to them, the lands of which they were the original and legitimate owners would be restored to them.

The patróns nodded their assent, though inside themselves they continued to feel a trace of anxiety. Their confidence that a politician's promises are carried away by the wind calmed them down; moreover, this particular audience, with its deficient understanding of Spanish and its habit of hearing without listening, wouldn't pay much attention to those promises. They may have been right about the rest of the Indians. But not about Pedro González Winiktón.

Many of the ideas escaped Pedro and others he grasped imperfectly. But he was strongly impressed to hear on the president's lips a word that resonated so deeply within him: justice. Unable to represent it to himself in the abstract, Pedro linked it inextricably from that time on to a fact with which he had intimate and immediate experience: the possession of land. This was what the ajwalil had come to announce to them. And in the handshake by which the president took his leave of each one of those present, Pedro saw the seal of an agreement.

It was a memorable day for all. The patróns commented on its incidents for weeks, calculating the advantages and disadvantages the president's policies could bring them and the ways of making the most of some while avoiding others as much as possible.

The talk with the president left a mark on Pedro that was not erased even when he went with his companions to the brothels of Tapachula for the first time.

The Indians arrived in a group, emboldened by their collective number and by alcohol, laughing and pushing each other.

It was a miserable neighborhood with streets in which the air formed brief, furious dust devils. Above the roofs, palm trees nodded with a continuous murmur.

In the doorways, the windows, crudely painted women smiled tired smiles, muttering a few inviting words.

Pedro watched them as he passed with furtive interest, with the mistrust of an animal observing members of another species. He expected the same response as the Ladinas of Ciudad Real gave: brusque disdain, a jeering burst of laughter. But none of that happened. For a few coins, any of these women gave her body over to the quick and brutal embrace of the Chamulas.

Pedro rested his head on a female lap, at peace. How different from his wife's tense and always disappointed body was this docile flesh, humble in receiving pleasure, generous and skilled in giving it! The encounter took place without words, without the oaths by which Catalina called upon eternity.

After that night, Pedro could read, under the proud appearance of white women (all of them, even those in Ciudad Real), the secret avidity, the contraction of the supreme moment in which all masks melt away, the lawless repose that follows. They were no longer mythical beings made of a substance different from his own. They were females, yes, females: clay that the male hand shapes to fit its whims.

Such discoveries gave Winiktón a different perspective on things. He no longer felt inferior to anyone, and to proclaim his equality he abandoned his coarse cotton clothing to wear long pants and multicolored sweaters; he replaced his sandals with cheap shoes and, with a gift of money from Don Adolfo, he was able to buy himself a watch.

It was the custom of the enganchados to return to their villages displaying their acquisitions. From afar they announced their presence by playing a sad, monotonous melody on a new accordion, occasionally bursting into cries of joy and exultation.

The families, attracted by all the clamor, left huts and work to see the new arrivals. The children clapped with delight at the festive feeling that pulsated in the atmosphere. But the men turned their heads away with false indifference and the women's mouths twisted in frank disapproval.

A few weeks later the tribe had reabsorbed the enganchados. One day they put the shoes away in the trunk because Chamula's mud puddles and the rough terrain of its hills demanded more durable footwear. Another day, they pulled out the coarse cotton breeches and the wool serape because they were uncomfortable in garments that set them apart from the others. The accordion and the watch were sold in order to buy things that were more useful and more urgently needed. From their tongues, from their memories, the Spanish words were erased little by little until they disappeared.

Pedro, who upon returning had reassumed his rank as a former authority, rapidly yielded to the pressure of his group and by no external sign could a rebellion against traditions, an independent criterion for judging facts, an assimilation to Ladino ways, be detected in him. But in secret—in the same way Catalina exercised her powers as an ilol—Pedro went over his notebooks, repeating the lessons of his primers and remembering, with painstaking application, what he had learned in Tapachula.

In conversations with the principal men, Pedro spoke of the president and his promises of justice. His listeners heard him with impatience and unease. The life of the Chamulas was laborious, but they were well acquainted with the routine of sufferings they inherited and passed on to their children. And suddenly here was this man speaking a new word which meant great upheavals. To say justice in Chamula was to kill the patrón, to raze the hacienda, to lie in ambush for the police, to resist the merchants' abuses, denounce the enganchador's manipulations, avenge the mistreatment of children, the rape of women. To say justice in Chamula was to keep a vigil, day and night, sustained only by the promise of a faraway man whose good faith no one had yet put to the test. It was preferable to remain silent.

"But I have seen him," Winiktón repeated desperately. "I am the witness and the guarantor that what the great ajwalil says is valid."

Xaw Ramírez Paciencia cleared his throat before answering.

"It is good, my son, that you keep the news of these things for more suitable times, for their proper season."

The rest of them gravely agreed. The old men took their leave, crippled by a nameless anger they had no way of releasing. What had this upstart, this Pedro, said? That the generations to come would be exempt from or indemnified for the labors they had endured. Was their condition a chance circumstance then, which could be remedied? No: it was fate, the mandate of dark powers, the will of cruel gods. What a mockery of their beliefs, what a sneer at their life, their humble virtues, their submission, all now stripped of their merits if Pedro had spoken the truth!

Only the young men, whose spirits had not yet been wholly bridled, retained from these discussions a certain restiveness, a seed that would have to break through the hard crust of inertia and conformity in order to sprout.

CHAPTER VII

DOÑA MERCEDES SOLÓRZANO had been keeping her store closed lately. The real reason Leonardo Cifuentes had set up a business for her in one of the outer rooms of his own house—not to line his pockets but as a front behind which she could arrange fleeting sexual adventures for him with the humbler servants and even the Indian women—was no longer important. Not that Leonardo had mended his ways or given up his pastime. But now all his interest, all his attention was focused on one woman, the woman who had been dubbed "La Alazana"—the Roan.

The situation of Cifuentes' go-between had become even more secure as a result; she had made herself indispensable in bringing his machinations to their desired conclusion. What better person to turn to than Doña Mercedes, with all of her experience? This was an intrigue among fine, upstanding people, however, so it was necessary to proceed with a certain degree of dissembling. First, the facts had to be concealed from the ever-suspicious Isabel, who had patiently endured her husband's passing adventures with her inferiors but could not be expected to react the same way to a rivalry with a woman who was her social equal. Care had to be taken as well to avoid arousing the jealousy of Fernando Ulloa, La Alazana's husband. Perhaps those precautions were exaggerated. Men from other parts who have seen a bit of the world are often not as punctilious as the gentlemen of Ciudad Real when it comes to matters of honor.

La Alazana herself, who had bestowed her friendship upon Doña Mercedes (thereby demonstrating the commonness of her spirit), complained of Fernando's indifference. She was not too reticent to confess that just two years before they had run away together, so in love that they dared to defy their families' opposition and society's prejudices. We legalized our life together afterward, La Alazana hurried to add. But Doña Mercedes Solórzano, who was well versed in the world's ways, would not have put her hand in the fire to attest to the truth of this statement. She was careful not to let her conjectures rise to the surface.

She smiled with a gleam of her gold-capped teeth and skillfully asked more questions, inciting further confidences, in order later to give a full account of every detail of the conversation, as Cifuentes demanded.

"We've been through a lot of hard times together, Fernando and I. But that doesn't bother me. It was all right because we loved each other. But now an ambition, I don't know what for, has taken hold of him. Every day his indifference is more obvious. He doesn't notice me any more."

"Why don't you leave him, niña?" the go-between asked slyly. "For a woman of your class, all this going from place to place like a stray puppy is no good. It's not for nothing they say the rolling stone gathers no moss."

"I don't know. I haven't thought about it. And what would become of me if I left my husband? I can't go back to my parents' house."

"You'd have more than enough protection, niña. Look at you, so pretty. . . ."

La Alazana's expression of distaste (not very energetic, not like someone trying to defend her honor; more like someone who feels her modesty has been wounded) prevented Doña Mercedes from completing the compliment.

"Well, then, be that way," the go-between mused silently. "I know what you're figuring out for yourself. If only Leonardo were to put you on solid ground with a bit of capital so that when your boyfriend wants to set sail you won't have to go off with him. And you have a good eye for the cold, hard cash. Because that's what Cifuentes has coming out of his ears. All that's left is for him to feel like giving it to you. Yes, I know, right now he's offering it because he's at the stage of trying to keep you all wrapped up for himself. It's easy to see you haven't given in to him yet. But there's a long way to go from that to creating an obligation. Anyway, lady, fight your fight—what do you have to lose?"

And La Alazana fought her fight with a very good chance of winning. Because Leonardo was just itching for her, as they say. Since he couldn't do anything else for the moment, he limited himself to making sure that the very best of everything from his fincas, the aguardiente aged in his stills, was sent to her house rather than his own.

Those were the only presents La Alazana accepted. She always refused, with a joking comment to minimize the hard impact of the negation, the jewelry and fine fabrics of which Doña Mercedes was the bearer. But the go-between turned out to be difficult to discourage, especially since a soul that was greedy and not very firm in resisting temptation could be glimpsed behind La Alazana's affected modesty.

Doña Mercedes' insistence won out for the first time when she offered a wrap from Guatemala made of fine silk embroidered with vivid designs. La Alazana accepted it, but not without adding, "Please tell Señor Cifuentes that I don't wish to slight him, especially in consideration of the friendship he has shown for my husband. I'll wear this shawl at tonight's dance."

That dance! Even before it took place it had already been the cause of much fuss and murmuring in Ciudad Real. For it was the first time the Cifuentes family was opening up its house for a party. Up to that point, their reclusive attitude had been traceable to two causes. Idolina, Isabel's only child, had been confined to her bed for years, immobilized by a paralysis the doctors were unable to diagnose or to heal. As for the other cause, the fact that the Cifuentes family was making such a public display of gaiety was, in some way, a provocation. For it could not have escaped their notice that although they were acknowledged and admitted within the circle of a few families—the good families—in Ciudad Real, this was due only to their increasingly vast wealth. Dazzled by the glitter of gold, many no longer saw the murkiness of Leonardo's origins. They also managed to forget the scandal of his marriage, which was Isabel Zebadúa's second. But those on whom such favors were bestowed should always remain conscious that the benevolence they were enjoying, a benevolence that was all the more extraordinary in a society that boasted of its strict standards, was out of proportion to their merits.

Many times, Doña Mercedes had advised Leonardo, "You must be prudent, don't flaunt your money or make a show of your good fortune. Because envy has a mouth and speaks. And when, as in this case, there are dirty stories to tell. . . ."

But Leonardo had suddenly lost his keen sense of propriety. Encouraged by his successive strokes of luck, eager to cover himself with yet another kind of prestige in La Alazana's eyes, the prestige of the sumptuous host, he took pains to see to it that this dance would far exceed what people were used to. He hired the best marimba group in Ciudad Real, but he also had a brass band brought in from Acala. Flowers from the local nurseries weren't enough for him; he had tanales shipped in from Comitán and dazzling red flamboyanes from Tuxtla. The banquet was to be prepared by a famous cook, brought in from Soconusco just for that purpose.

It would have been natural for Isabel to see to all the details, from making sure that the hired hands neatened up the garden to ordering the maids to shine the doorknockers. But Doña Mercedes had to take charge of everything because Isabel came and went, completely aloof from the preparations for an event she had opposed from the beginning. When she had to admit to herself that Leonardo had crossed wills with her, Isabel, too proud to lower herself to reproaching him, retreated into total silence. She shut herself up in her sewing room, bent over her embroidery frame. Not even curiosity could make her lift her eyes each time a parlor maid hurried through the room to carry out another of Doña Mercedes' instructions.

But maintaining this stance demanded an effort that Isabel lacked the energy for. With every breath she choked back a sob of impotent rage, a howl of trampled dignity. To escape the questions of outsiders, Isabel isolated herself, avoiding even her daughter. Alone, she gave free rein to her wrath in fevered, sterile rantings that led her only to extreme resolutions that were impossibly violent. Because Isabel, despite the momentary rebelliousness her fury aroused in her, was by temperament and conviction a submissive spirit whose habit was resignation, whose vice was forgiveness.

Leonardo, however, was a man whose enterprising nature had been marked only slightly by the prejudices of a class he had acceded to by adoption. His status as a parvenu gave him a critical perspective. Every time his desires conflicted with the norms that society proclaimed untouchable, Leonardo ignored society and satisfied his desires. Thanks to this, Cifuentes considered himself, at the age of forty-three, a fortunate man. And crafty, too, he would add, with a roguish wink. Because craftiness gives me what luck denies me.

At times his cunning maneuvers had gone so far, according to people of ill will, as to constitute actual crimes. But—his good luck again—no one dared accuse him of anything. And the suspicions gave him an ambiguous aura of rakishness that kept the men he frequented in check and made the women he pursued give in to him.

Little by little, this conjunction of circumstances strengthened Leonardo's certainty that his power was incontestable and his whims legitimate, a certainty he accepted unquestioningly and imposed on others without a second thought. No religious dread, no moral idea, no intellectual reflection argued against his impulses once they had started on their blind, headlong plunge. Yet Cifuentes was capable of supposing, in the crude naiveté of his egotism, that those he trampled underfoot wouldn't turn against him in hostility, but gaze at him with gratitude.

Surprise, therefore, was his first reaction to the lack of interest with which his wife witnessed the accomplishment of a project into which Leonardo had put so much enthusiasm. When he approached Isabel on the morning of the dance, his mood was not conciliatory but sarcastic.

Isabel was embroidering when her husband entered the sewing room. He gesticulated to make his presence felt, but Isabel pretended not to notice him. She couldn't go on pretending when his voice, deliberately obsequious, unbearably hypocritical, issued an invitation: "I hope you will honor us with your presence tonight."

Isabel's fingers tightened around the embroidery frame. Leonardo went on, "Because I suppose you must be aware by now that I am giving a party in my house this evening."

Well might Isabel have replied to that "my house," so possessive, so inaccurate. But a spasm of anger made her throat contract.

"By the way, I've been wanting to thank you for all the trouble you've taken. I have no doubt that thanks to you the dance will be a great success."

Isabel had let her chance to demand an apology escape. Now she would have to defend herself, prove she hadn't been shirking her duties as the lady of the house. Heatedly, she attempted an excuse, "You didn't need me. Doña Mercedes is here."

She pronounced that hated name with the childish resentment of a woman who sees her place usurped by another.

"It doesn't matter to you whether I have someone to take over for you or not. It's your obligation as the lady of this house. . . ."

"As the lady of this house I am not obliged to throw parties for your querida!"

It was the first time that word—querida—had defiled Isabel's lips. All of Leonardo's other diversions were so fleeting that they didn't deserve the title. And now that Isabel gave it to La Alazana, she did so with a tremor, knowing she was transforming a hazy and ambiguous intuition into an established fact.

"You, Isabel? Jealous!"

Cifuentes registered it with incredulity, not because the irreproachability of his conduct made it absurd but because his wife's age made it ridiculous. But Isabel didn't grasp that nuance in his tone; she was listening only to the meaning of his words. And, overly anxious to allow herself to be convinced to the contrary, she hazarded, "As if you hadn't given me reason enough to keep a sharp eye on you. . . ."

"Yes, I've given you reasons. That's why I find it strange that now that you have no reason. . . ."

"Are you going to deny what I've seen with my own eyes? You've got your head in the clouds and you're drinking the wind over the famous Alazana."

The trace of spite in the nickname sent Leonardo beside himself with rage. He grabbed away the embroidery frame Isabel was shielding herself with.

"La Alazana, as servant girls and common people in the streets call her, has a name: Doña Julia Acevedo. And she is the wife of a respectable man, a friend of mine, whom I would be incapable of insulting."

The speed with which Leonardo leaped to defend the foreign woman enraged Isabel to such a degree that she rose to her feet, her features pale with rage, and delivered a frenetic accusation: "It would be the first time I had seen you so scrupulous. You weren't like that with me."

Startled by the abrupt attack, Cifuentes could do nothing but make threats: "Don't say another word. That was a different story."

"Yes, that was different, because Isidoro, my husband—listen to me say it: my husband—not what you were to me afterward —was more than your friend; he was your brother. Who was it who took you under his wing and forced his parents to take you into their home because you were only an orphan and the nuns treated you badly and let you go hungry . . . ?"

But Cifuentes had already recovered his aplomb and the insult left him unscathed. With an ironic inflection he answered, "You should be proud of yourself, Isabel. In order to win you, I didn't hesitate to overlook the duties imposed on me by gratitude, friendship, decency itself. I made the wife of Isidoro Cifuentes fall in love with me while Isidoro Cifuentes was still alive. And I married his widow before his period of mourning was over."

A final hope was dying in Isabel's next question: "Why did you do it, Leonardo?"

Cifuentes shrugged, to strip the query of any importance, to keep from giving an answer.

"You don't know! Well I do. Greed was what tempted you. Isidoro was rich."

Like someone mustering up the patience to explain to a child or an imbecile a fact that is evident to the eyes of any normal person, Leonardo said, "You've always been extremely good at misunderstanding my motives. You misinterpreted me from the beginning. You thought the best way of keeping me tied to your apron strings was to keep the fortune you inherited away from me. That was a big mistake. I'm rich, too, Isabel. And I got rich without needing to touch a centavo of your inheritance."

Bitterly Isabel had to admit this was true. "You're a wealthy man. And you didn't need any of what I could give you in order to become wealthy."

Leonardo assumed an almost genuine expression of astonishment. "You knew that, Isabel? You'll have to forgive me. I did whatever I could to hide it, but. . . ."

Isabel cut off the joke. "So you killed Isidoro Cifuentes for nothing."

Leonardo hesitated an instant, only an instant, before answering. Not a muscle in his face had twitched. But in that instant of silence Isabel saw the patent sign of his guilt.

"The town gossips say I did. And you say so, too. But if it were true I wouldn't be here; I'd be taking some hard knocks in a prison cell. Isidoro's death was an unfortunate accident. No one can prove otherwise."

"And who was the witness?" Isabel shouted, stung. "You were. The pistol was yours, you were showing it to him. Who would have thought it was loaded? A new pistol you hadn't used even once. You aimed here, at the heart, in play. And the shot went off. An accident. I say it was a crime."

With studied calm, Leonardo moved one of the sewing room's chairs. He sat down on it, crossed his legs, took, from the case he kept in the pocket of his jacket, a cigarette, lit it and blew out great mouthfuls of smoke. Not until then did he say, like a man who has reached the conclusion of a very round-about argument, "And you find out about it how many years later, Isabel? No, don't count them, it would make you too sad. But all that time you've lived with a murderer, your husband's murderer. The authorities wouldn't believe in your innocence. They wouldn't hesitate to charge you as an accomplice."

"And what does that matter to me? Don't you think I would prefer anything to this hell?"

Poor Isabel! Such exaggeration, always. What was hellish about this life? Leonardo found it acceptable enough.

"And while you're pursuing your own inclinations it doesn't matter to you if you neglect your daughter's health—"

Leonardo interrupted with a gesture of irritation.

"Please, Isabel. Idolina is the daughter of your first marriage. Don't confuse the dates and try to put her off onto me."

Isabel shot an accusatory stare at her husband.

"You hate her. You'd like to see her dead, just like Isidoro."

Leonardo made a grimace he didn't succeed in congealing into a smile.

"Why would I hate her?"

"For what she knows."

"She doesn't know anything. She believes what you have drilled into her."

"She can talk; she can tell the truth about you. . . ."

"To whom? She's been glued to her bed for years. She has no friends; no one visits her."

And then, more slowly, as if the possibility had once been of some concern to him, "Even if she did talk, no one would listen to a poor little creature who's been unhinged by illness and isolation."

Leonardo's cigarette had burned away. He threw it onto the carpet and stepped on it. Then he stood up.

"Now, Isabel, I will beg you once more to honor us with your presence at the dance this evening. None of Ciudad Real's finest families will be absent. It doesn't suit me to present either the spectacle of a home torn apart by bickering or of a woman who does not fulfill her duties."

And, not because he wanted to share the plan that for months now, since the moment of La Alazana's arrival in Ciudad Real, had been preoccupying him, but just to show off a new plumage to impress her with, he added, "It doesn't suit my political ambitions."

After Leonardo walked out, Isabel remained still for a moment. Then, with automatic servility, she bent down to the carpet to rub away the stain left by the cigarette ash. What would Don Alfonso Cañaveral say if he came in here during the dance! He was always so exacting when it came to cleanliness.

With this simple gesture, Isabel was already tacitly preparing to obey her husband and attend to the guests. Her change of attitude was foreseeable. The scene that had just ended had left her exhausted. Despite her efforts to ignore it, a certain uneasy feeling was stealing over her: remorse. It seemed more difficult now to carry out a decision she had made in a different frame of mind. And of all Leonardo had said, her memory was feeding on a single phrase, the last one. When he spoke of his political ambitions, wasn't he giving in, in a veiled way, to Isabel's jealous demand? She preferred to interpret it that way. Although politics was no longer an occupation in which gentlemen put their leisure time to noble use and squandered their assets. Ever since the state government had moved from Ciudad Real to the lowlands, any upstart from the coast, any obliging fellow from Comitán, could flaunt his appointment to one position or another. Leonardo had other motives. But Isabel didn't expect fidelity from him, only discretion. She herself would collaborate in concealing his true motives by pretending to believe in the false ones.

Isabel reproached herself for having recklessly judged La Alazana. What was so reprehensible about her behavior? Her way of walking freely through the streets by herself could well be perfectly innocent. She walked alone with her hair loose like . . . yes, like a roan mare, an alazana. There was a reason they gave her that nickname.

At the prospect of meeting a foreigner, a woman of ambiguous habits, a "temptress," Isabel felt a flicker of anticipation.

A temptress . . . I must have read that in some novel, thought Isabel. His Excellency the bishop is right to forbid them. And if Leonardo visits the woman it isn't to see her, it's to see the husband. They have some business dealings, I think. And even if they don't. Men aren't used to being cooped up indoors, glued to their wife's apron strings. Especially when there are no babies in the house with funny faces to laugh at and new achievements to celebrate.

God had manifested his displeasure with this marriage by not granting it any offspring. There was only Idolina, the stepdaughter, whom Isabel coddled in secret so Leonardo wouldn't say she was still demonstrating her love for Isidoro.

Isabel tiptoed around as cautiously as a new bride. Because no matter how many years they had spent together (she always got tangled up whenever she tried to count), Leonardo remained an enigma to her. Never, not even when passion bound them together in its blind knot, did they belong to each other deeply. And the great thirst he aroused in her was never sated.

The demon abandons those he seduces, His Excellency Don Alfonso would declare, trying, as her confessor, to dissuade Isabel from making an unsuitable alliance. She confessed to the bishop the first movements of her soul toward the temptation to commit adultery that Leonardo represented. She spoke vaguely, without being very exact—how could she be more exact?—about the vertiginous intensity with which evil thoughts were overwhelming her. (She appeased her scruples by telling herself that priests know they are obliged to fill in with their malice what we leave out with ours.)

The evil thoughts—if only I were free!—were so obsessive that at times Isabel found herself looking around as if the clamor of the words had made itself heard outside of her brain and was giving her away. Then, when they brought Isidoro's corpse. . . .

It was the first time Isabel had stood in the presence of death. But it wasn't as horrible or as solemn as she had feared. Isidoro's face had an expression of tranquility, repose, saintliness. The bullet hadn't disfigured him. An almost imperceptible hole in the middle of the chest; a small round stain of his blood. And another, the same size and shape, on the palm of his right hand. From the gesture he made when he felt the wound.

Perhaps people began suspecting it was a crime from that moment. Isabel didn't know. No one around her was close enough to her to dare repeat such rumors to her. But in the confessional, His Excellency Don Alfonso was prying: "You're sure you didn't lead Leonardo on with sinful promises?"

"No, Monseñor. No, Monseñor." Isabel could deny it wholeheartedly because the two of them had never once exchanged a word that needed to be concealed. Between them was silence, a palpitating, magnetic, portentous silence, a terrible inevitability. Anguish. An anguish Isabel would not have exchanged for the most absolute happiness.

That Lent the bishop's sermons all dwelled on finalities: death, judgment, hell. He described them with images so vivid, features so appalling, that the worshippers, wringing their hands in fear, cried out the error of their ways for all the world to hear and demanded absolution, weeping. Only Isabel, sunk down on her prie-dieu, ran through her rosary beads with distracted fingers.

It was whispered that Leonardo was courting her. She denied it with a movement of the head but her denial looked more like that of a hopeful bride than of an inconsolable widow. And why should she have to be an inconsolable widow? She was still young, she was healthy. Isidoro was rotting away underground; he was erased from her memory as quickly as a dream.

Isidoro never enjoyed the resounding, almost insulting existence of other beings (Leonardo, for example). Neurasthenic, taciturn, tormented, anxious. Perhaps he didn't die in an accident; perhaps he committed suicide in one of the fits of melancholy that tortured him and were growing longer and more intense.

Isabel was the last person who wanted to voice this suspicion. But was it not her moral duty to do so if Leonardo's good name was falling victim to evil tongues? In consultation with her confessor, she was categorically forbidden to allude to it. The reputation of the dead cannot be touched, said His Excellency. The living can defend themselves. Don't worry yourself about Leonardo Cifuentes. He can take care of himself and then some.

Everyone persisted in accusing him. And deep down, very secretly, Isabel, too, was uncertain of his innocence. But she didn't want to feel that she was linked to the crime and even less to admit that she had been its motive. Her spirit did not have the strength to carry the weight of guilt or the gravity of remorse. She searched the past to find another reason underlying Leonardo's act. She came up with envy. Isn't it natural that two boys who have grown up together would turn against each other if one of them enjoys all the privileges while the other always takes second place? Even Cain, in the Bible, did the same thing to his brother Abel because of the inequality of the treatment they were given.

The whole town admired the magnanimity of Isidoro's parents when they took Leonardo into their home as a small boy. But afterward, no one witnessed the small pettinesses, the constant comparisons between the legitimate and the adopted son, in which the latter always had to come out behind. A child whose sharp intelligence and vehement feelings were noticed by everyone cannot be treated that way without consequences. Who knows what blood runs through an orphan's veins? It might be more noble and more proud than the blood of his benefactors. And what had they given him, apart from their name? The crude education of a cowherd. While Isidoro was given a full, liberal education. He couldn't complete it; his intelligence was not very solid. He came back from Paris without any diploma to show for his years there.

He did bring back a tuxedo that had diamond buttons and a shirtfront gathered in little tucks. He was wearing it the night he declared himself to Isabel. She accepted him, looking at those tiny stones.

After that everything was so strange. . . . Two weeks after the wedding, when they had settled down on one of his father's fincas, Isidoro locked himself in his room and refused to speak to his newlywed bride. Her eyes overcast with weeping, Isabel, leaning on the balustrade in the gallery, watched Leonardo galloping through the paddocks. And she wished she could run to him out there and beg him to save her from so unhappy a fate.

Isabel still recalled the period of her pregnancy with nostalgia. Months during which her body, which had now reached its plenitude, swelled with an elemental sensuality that existed not in acts but in an enormous repose. The slow swaying of the rocking chair, the siestas on the sun porch, her hair falling loosely through the hands of the Indian woman who combed and combed it with a tortoiseshell comb.

Idolina was born there, on the ranch. Around the time she was due, Isidoro claimed an urgent and unpostponable need to make a trip to Ciudad Real. Business, he said. But Isabel, who had deciphered his character by then, knew it was a pretext. What Isidoro wanted was to run away from the pain his wife would have to endure. With the same repulsion, he withdrew from the corrals every time a calf was about to be branded or a steer was being treated for worms with creosote. Isabel watched him leave with a smile of contempt. Even the considerate gestures Isidoro sometimes bestowed on her couldn't be credited to the meticulousness of his courtesy or the depth of his affection. He was a weak man; that explained everything. And women like Isabel do not forgive weakness. They value as a sign of manliness the whip the male uses to force the female to yield; they store the memory of their humiliations among the relics of love.

"Leonardo, now, he wouldn't have to do any soul-searching before he dragged by the hair a female who resisted him or acted headstrong or surly or capricious."

Leonardo, in Isabel's dreams, in the interminable wanderings of her mind during the interminable forty days that followed he labor. Rain blanketed the windowpanes. And there, next to th mother, tiny, wrinkled, red and shivering with cold, was th daughter.

Idolina, her grandparents predicted, will be just like Isidor She quickly gave everyone reason to believe the prophecy wou come true. When she celebrated her first birthday she was shov ered with toys, gifts, parties. They thought they were making h happy. But the excitement of seeing so many unfamiliar fac around her, of receiving so many new things, was so great that she came down with a very high fever and spent all night in a delirium. Afterward, that peculiar, morbid way of folding in on herself each time a situation seemed not even hostile but simply out of the ordinary, became a habit. Timid, insecure, the little girl never let go of Isidoro's hand. And when Isidoro had to be away from the house, Idolina would curl up anywhere that a piece of clothing, an open book, a half-written sheet of paper would speak to her of her absent father. She would curl up and weep like an abandoned puppy.

She won't be able to bear the pain, Isabel said to herself when they laid out Isidoro's body in the parlor. She tried to hide the sight from Idolina. But the child's curiosity outwitted all of the adults' precautions and Idolina witnessed every detail of the funeral. Without a tear. With the same frown of resolute attention she had on her face when she practiced a difficult scale on the piano.

To the others, to Isabel especially, this attitude seemed very strange. It's because she doesn't understand what has happened, they decided. They forgot that Idolina had a very precocious understanding of absence. And now that the absence was definitive, she was never heard to ask why or to mourn it. She didn't protest when all the dead man's personal effects were given to the poor. For months she checked carefully on the mourning crepe that overshadowed her father's portrait.

Idolina turned to Isabel with a raw, demanding attachment that couldn't have been satisfied, even by absorbing the totality of Isabel's life. From that moment on, Isabel could not take a single step without her daughter following in her shadow. She lost all patience with this relentless tenacity; with scornful gestures, with mockery, she succeeded in pushing her daughter away.

Isabel's new marriage changed Idolina profoundly. For weeks she refused to eat anything. She grew skeletally thin. Each time she looked at herself in her wardrobe mirror, her eyes were glazed over with a malevolent happiness. Isabel had to give in, lower herself to pleading, serving each mouthful with her own hands. Idolina refused them all, stubborn in her will to let herself waste away.

Leonardo, who had little use for hysterical women, derided the two of them. It was the first crack in his union with Isabel. What was more, when he wasn't excessively absorbed in his work, he used the free time for uncouth diversions, with the lowest kind of people in Ciudad Real.

Isabel hid her husband's misconduct as best she could. The only place she risked complaining about it was the confessional, and there she received no advice but only the reprimand of someone who had strongly warned her about the error she was going to commit: "The demon abandons those he seduces. . . ."

Isabel's heart was poisoned by this compulsory discretion. The venom began to filter into her talks with Idolina, first in complicated allusions, later in shameless confidences that pulsated with a hidden urge to expose the depth of her unhappiness so that her betrayal would be forgiven.

How the young girl—for she was already a young girl—savored the tale of Isabel's every new disillusionment. An image was engraving itself in her avid mind: the image of the unscrupulous man to whose brutality and voracious cynicism Isidoro had succumbed and Isabel was sacrificed.

Idolina's only comment was a soft monosyllable, just enough to keep from turning the complainer away by her indifference. But she gave no other sign of sharing the outrage. She saw Leonardo as the instrument of a punishment. And she needed so badly for Isabel to be punished!

One winter night the mother and daughter were in the parlor. Isabel had lit a brazier to take the chill out of the air and was passing the time poking it with a pair of heavy iron tongs. Idolina was irritated by the brief but repeated and almost rhythmic sound of the metal. She breathed the air tainted by the warmth with increasing repulsion. After a painful and lengthy hesitation, she raised the lid of the piano and stiffly and stubbornly began practicing an exercise.

"Bravo! Bravo!"

It was Leonardo applauding, standing at the threshold with a lumbering, drunken defiance. The mocking look that accompanied his exclamation was still on his face. Idolina clenched both fists and let them fall heavily on the keyboard. Hatred was strangling her. She wanted to hurl herself onto Leonardo, knock him down, destroy him. She turned violently to face him, stood up, took a few steps. And suddenly collapsed, writhing, frothing at the mouth, unconscious. When she came back to herself she could no longer move without help.

And then the days, the years, all alike. Until today.

Outside, in the galleries, in the courtyards and rear yards, the whole house was bubbling over with preparations for the dance. Whispering, hurrying, the light shuffle of feet.

A sudden burst of light from a lamp that had been lit chased the shadows away from the sewing room.

The cathedral bells rang vespers.

CHAPTER VIII

"AND WALKING THROUGH the night the ijc'al appeared to them."

Ever since she was small, Idolina had loved to hear horror stories; she demanded them when the late afternoon shadows were transforming familiar objects into phantasmagorical beings and when every sound was a mysterious warning. She witnessed with a shiver of terrified pleasure the metamorphoses of the yalambaqu'et, which drops its bones along the path as it goes; the evil mischief of the xuch ni' which sticks out its nose during the commemorations of San Andrés. And the wiles of the most terrible of them all, the ijc'al, a tiny black man who spirits away those he finds alone in the dark. If they are men he decapitates them and uses their heads as pillars in his house; if they are women he forces himself on them and after the months of their pregnancy they give birth to monsters.

But this time, despite the storyteller's best efforts, Idolina was not captured by the tale. At several points she gave signs of distraction, and finally turned her face violently toward the wall, a gesture of impatience those who took care of her knew very well. Her profile, sharpened by sickness, was distorted when reflected on the wall by the ghostly light of the candles.

The storyteller, an Indian woman with a submissive demeanor, dressed in the fashion of the women of Chamula (the coarse wool fabric that still smells of sheep), seemed not to understand the disgust and irritation Idolina's movement expressed. In a monotone, she repeated the last phrase: "And walking through the night the ijc'al appeared to them."

Idolina covered her ears. Her forehead was furrowed. Tears she didn't try to hold back brimmed in her eyes.

"Be quiet, nana. I don't want any more stories."

"Niña," the woman began a timid reproach. But her tone only exasperated the sick girl.

"I don't want any more! You're torturing me!"

The nana withdrew from the bedside and went to huddle in a corner of the room. Idolina didn't take her eyes off of her, and when she was certain that the nana had decided to remain there and in that stance she said querulously, "Why did you leave me by myself?"

The Indian woman was about to stand up and return to her place next to her mistress. But she stopped when she had risen to her knees. "Everything bores you. You're very chinaj."

The sick girl sat up, supporting herself with her right elbow on the pillows; she passed the back of her free hand over her forehead as if to erase her look of ill humor. Her lips barely curved in a conciliatory simper.

"Come here."

The Indian woman shook her head.

"You won't come, nana?"

There was more incredulity (the incredulity of someone who was obeyed even in the most insignificant of her whims) than admonishment in the question. Idolina saw the uncertainty that had come over her servant's mind. The nana's breathing was laboured. But she did not obey.

"Look how your heart leaps under the blouse. Blood is falling from it."

"Niña," the woman answered at last, "you have behaved very badly to me. I will not go to you."

"All right," Idolina acknowledged unconcernedly. "Then I'll go myself."

The statement was enough to make the Indian woman run, tangling herself up in the folds of her tzec, to restrain her patrona. But she didn't manage to keep Idolina from throwing back the sheets that covered her and sitting up at the edge of the bed. Her naked legs, excessively white and thin, hung down without touching the floor.

"Niña, you're going to freeze to death, por Dios."

But the girl laughed at the Indian woman's fears and with a quick movement pushed aside the blankets meant to protect her from a chill that was not banished even by the brazier burning peacefully in a corner.

The nana let her arms fall along her body in the inertia of powerlessness. In front of her the bedclothes were piled up in shapeless heaps that took on grotesque proportions in the dancing shadows.

Hanging on to one of the bedposts, Idolina stood up, sinking her feet into the carpet. She was waiting for a look of forgiveness on the Indian woman's face. To hurry it, she took the tip of her braid and pretended to kiss it.

The nana did not try to evade this caress. She said, in affectionate mockery, "Try that on someone who does not know you like I do."

"And who made me this way?" the girl shot back. "You brought me up, so you're the one who brought me up badly."

There was between the two of them the kind of dialogue that can only be established between a mistress and a servant as the result of a lengthy dependency on the one hand and a tender loyalty on the other. Their relationship was a constant play of reciprocal concessions and impositions whose mechanism had been perfected by an exclusive intimacy.

"Good. We're calming down."

The nana had gathered together the bedclothes and put them back in place. After fluffing up the pillows, she said, "Now you can lie down."

But Idolina wasn't listening to her. Still leaning against the bedpost, she was trying to catch the bustling sounds from outside.

"The marimba band has just come in."

The woman took advantage of Idolina's distraction to push her until she was sitting down on the edge of the bed.

"I've never seen a party," the girl reflected gravely.

"When you are good and healthy, mi niña. Then."

Idolina added somberly, "When my stepfather and she are dead. When this house has gone up in flames. When you and I have gone off to travel other lands."

The Indian woman was frightened to hear, on such resentful lips, the words she herself had once pronounced. As if to hold them back she put her hand over Idolina's mouth. But Idolina pushed it away.

"That's what the ashes said."

There was so much hope for freedom in Idolina's acceptance of the promise that the Indian woman turned her face away with a guilty blush.

"It was a game, niña."

"It wasn't a game!" Idolina contradicted vehemently. "You swore to me. . . ."

And then, as if suddenly crushed by doubt, she added, "But you also swore you'd let me see the party."

"It's for your good, little dove. Lie down. If someone comes they shouldn't see you like this.

"Who on earth would come?" the girl asked in a bitter voice. "She . . ." (she wouldn't refer to her mother any other way). "She only comes when she has nothing else to do. Because she has to. 'How are you? Very well, it's plain to see; I'm very glad,' " said Idolina, mimicking Isabel's voice and gestures. Then, abruptly, as if the image she had summoned up had led her to an unbearable certainty, she cried out passionately, "I can't wait any more. The ashes said. . . . But nothing ever happens. And I'm rotting away between these walls. Until when?"

"Santísima Virgen de la Caridad, please protect us!"

The nana crossed herself to conjure away the demon that had taken possession of the girl. Idolina was pounding at her temples with clenched fists. Her fit of frenzy left her gasping and drained.

"Give me my shawl," she ordered.

The tone admitted of no reply. As the Indian woman obeyed she went on warning the reckless girl.

"It's our secret, niña. If they see you, if they find out you can walk, the wrath of God will descend upon our heads. On mine first, for having covered up the deception."

But Idolina wasn't listening. Devoured by restlessness she urged the nana, "Softer, softer; now the guests are here."

In a final attempt to dissuade her, the woman said, "The tiles in the gallery are very cold."

Idolina turned to look at her with a flash of anger. "They put pine needles down."

When she went past the lamp, Idolina blew it out. They would have been in total darkness if not for the brazier's reddish halo. Stealthily, Idolina pushed the door ajar.

She was ending a confinement that had lasted many years. Because from the date of her first attack Idolina had not left her room, not even to consult a doctor. The doctors came here, and not only from the farthest reaches of Ciudad Real, but also from

Guatemala and even from Mexico, that remote place called Mexico.

The doctors stationed themselves at a prudent distance from the invalid's bed and it never occurred to them, not even as an evil thought, to ask if they could be permitted to go to her side and examine her. They did ask a lot of questions, pronouncing the technical words in a pretentious tone. Since Idolina didn't know any of those terms and was ashamed to acknowledge her ignorance to a stranger, her answers were vague and often contradictory. To distract their attention from this defect, Idolina exaggerated her pains with moans and complaints. The doctors looked at one another in perplexity, wiping the lenses of their eyeglasses with silk handkerchiefs.

Afterward they solemnly withdrew from the room to meet in the adjoining one for a buzzing exchange of remarks whose conclusions they never considered it appropriate to communicate to the members of the invalid's family. With intricate script and a magnanimous flourish they signed the bottom of the sheets from their prescription books and ordered the nearest pharmacy to stock up immediately on the prescribed medication which, in general, was no more than some innocuous substance.

This system of treatment ended by having a definitive influence on the girl's spirit. Unconsciously, she yielded bit by bit to the conviction that her case was so exceptional that no one would be able to diagnose it. And the more confidence those around her had in a new treatment, the greater the intensity with which Idolina's symptoms flared up and her pains grew worse: she had made it a point of honor not to allow herself to be cured.

Which did not prevent the eminent foreigners (this was what Mexicans were usually called) and compatriots from charging very large fees for their consultations.

Leonardo's protests and Isabel's voice promising to take care of all the expenses reached Idolina's bed. "Because"—the statement made the sick girl's face twitch into a sarcastic smile—"a child's health is something that has no price." Cifuentes' irritation grew to the extreme of proclaiming that if his wife was determined to ruin herself by giving in to the whims of an inconsiderate child, she could do so very much on her own and very much with her own money. He, Leonardo Cifuentes, swore by his own name that he would never contribute even one centavo to prolonging this stupid farce.

Perhaps it was her stepfather's words that first aroused Idolina's doubts about the authenticity of her sufferings. To dispel them, she forced herself to feel worse and to show it. She couldn't rest until all those around her (marks of worry and sleeplessness mercilessly imprinted on their faces) were vying with each other to please and serve her.

In the beginning, the girl had wanted to avenge the betrayal, as she called her mother's second marriage. Her spite drove her to make terrible resolutions—flight, suicide—and despair would have given her the incentive to carry them out. But her father's death taught her a great deal about the speed and ease with which the living, the absent, forget, console themselves, change, substitute. She understood that her complaints were a better way of prolonging the torture she was inflicting on Isabel. Her first attack had had spectacular results: the couple's union was ruptured. Of course they were still living under the same roof. But they were no longer bound by their former complicity.

After that, Idolina's attacks no longer succeeded in giving rise to such paroxysms of anguish. Repetition lessened their effect until they descended to the level of everyday events. Bit by bit, the mother allowed others to take charge of caring for the sick girl. She satisfied her scruples by offering higher salaries than any other patrona in Ciudad Real. But, unaccustomed to receiving such handsome remuneration, servants were suspicious of the job and quick to resign from it on the pretext that it was too much work (when in fact they were afraid of a possible contagion).

Isabel then remembered an Indian woman, Teresa Entzín López, who had suckled Idolina from the first week after her birth. She had her sent from the ranch.

· From whom could she expect greater abnegation? And Teresa went beyond what was expected of her. She stayed awake all night and didn't allow herself an instant's rest during the day. When the crises ended and Idolina's condition stabilized, Teresa was her inseparable companion.

She surprised everyone by the tenacity with which she began learning Spanish. And she, who was so awkward at making herself understood even in Tzotzil, her own language, mastered the foreign one with a certain fluency. She entertained the sick girl with recollections of the events of her youth, the traditions, superstitions and legends of her race. But she never told her why she abandoned that race to live among Caxláns. Nor was Idolina interested in knowing why. She wanted only to be distracted.

But too many idle hours remained. The two of them, mistress and servant, invented futile pastimes that did not succeed in absorbing them. Weaving was cast aside because it was too monotonous, embroidery was too fatiguing and the rest was useless. Tedium. Tedium. Tedium. Even the nana's stories were losing their savor.

Idolina had no friends among the girls her own age. On one occasion, Don José María Velasco's daughter, a very devout young lady dedicated to the practice of charitable works, wanted to pay a visit to the invalid. Isabel and Leonardo received her in the parlor with a courtesy that did not quite conceal their coldness, and drew out a conversation that was difficult, languid with silences and frequently extinguished. Estela Velasco waited in vain to be invited to go to Idolina's room. She even courted the invitation by alluding several times to the girl's health and the contribution that the affection of someone the same age and of the same class could make to her recovery. A friend, she explained; because solitude isn't good for anyone. But the Cifuentes couple let the allusion drop with their most hermetic smiles.

Estela left the house and went directly to the home of His Excellency, Don Alfonso Cañaveral, to recount the failure of her initiative.

But at heart Isabel was not indifferent to Estela's reflections, which moved her to visit her daughter's bedside three or four times. She left it feeling unhappy with conversations in which every word had a wounding edge of reproach. Isabel thought it would be best for both of them to suspend their interviews. Now she only sent things to the invalid's room, things she thought might distract her. Among those things was a deck of cards.

Idolina and Teresa didn't know the rules of any card game and every match was the occasion for disputes. Idolina finally took over the deck and excluded her wet-nurse altogether to embark on games of solitaire in which the cards were identified with flesh-

and-blood people. The king of swords, for example, corresponded to her stepfather because both suggested cruelty, power and harm. The wench of doubloons was her mother and the horse of clubs was the current attending physician. Idolina grouped them in strange conversations and gave them voices so they could carry on dialogues in which she gave vent to an imagination fired by bitterness and isolation.

The Indian woman witnessed these ravings with a jealous unease. Pretending to pay no attention, she withdrew to a corner of the room where a brazier was always burning. As she watched the embers, Teresa had the idea of talking to herself in an unintelligible and continuous drone.

It didn't take much to arouse the sick girl's curiosity and even less to make her feel cheated of the devotion that was her due. Taking her eyes off the cards she cast them on the still form of the Indian woman, deep in whispering contemplation.

Idolina began to wonder, with more anticipation than fear, whether this woman who looked so insignificant, so humble, might not be a canán, possessor of a fire nahual, endowed with the power to transform herself into fire and dictate her commands to the flames. All at once she asked, "What do the ashes say?"

Teresa turned, startled. Whether it was because Idolina's words had taken her by surprise and she didn't know what to answer or because the nature of the revelation being demanded was so serious it had to be built up to gradually, the fact is that the nana delayed her answer.

Idolina's interest grew more pressing. From then on she did nothing but implore the Indian woman, whose silence had strengthened Idolina's suspicions as to Teresa's true nature and made her suppose, as well, that while stirring the ashes Teresa could see into the future. She had seen something, that much was certain. But what?

After several weeks of skirmishes, and not until the intimacy between them had been reestablished, no longer weakened by the sick girl's distractions or the maid's evasions, Teresa finally reached the point of sharing her discovery. "The ashes say you'll get well."

Idolina gave her a look of scandalized reproach. The prophecy did not agree with her intentions and Teresa should have known that very well. She was going to contradict it, negate it, but the nana anticipated her, intercepting her anger: "The ashes say this house will burn. They say the husband and wife will die."

Idolina turned anxiously toward the mouth that had spoken. She didn't want to find out when or how it would happen; it was enough to be sure it would happen.

"Is that a promise?"

The Indian woman answered unhesitatingly, "Yes."

Idolina and her nana did not speak of this again, though neither one of them stopped thinking about it. Idolina was silent out of fear that the certainty of the predictions would melt away at the slightest indiscretion. And Teresa kept quiet as if she were awe-stricken by the greatness of what had manifested itself through her. Though they corresponded to her desires, those omens were beyond her. In that disjunction took root her belief that such ideas could not have sprung up inside her of their own accord, but must have been received by supernatural means.

On one of her rare visits to the sick girl Isabel saw that something in her had changed. An undefinable force was enlivening her, a happiness that, without wasting itself in ostentatious gestures or mincing effusions, was there, present and certain. Isabel disliked this atmosphere, in which a tension was threatening to erupt, in which an impending event could be felt. Her inquiries brought no clear explanation, so she decided to attribute it to an improvement in the state of her daughter's health.

As if to confirm this supposition, the invalid became less obstinate in her resistance to following the doctors' prescriptions and began viewing the beneficial effects of the medicines with a skepticism that almost had to be forced.

Idolina made use of the time she spent alone with Teresa to try out, with her help, some movements. The paralyzed limbs were gradually giving up their rigidity. At first the movements were awkward; they began slowly and almost always required the nana's help to be completed.

When Idolina saw herself standing up for the first time, reflected in the wardrobe mirror, she was frightened. Her body looked very different from the way she experienced it from within. Her height was exaggerated by the long, loose shape of the nightgown. In her face, gnawed by the years of enclosure and suffering, a pair of enormous pale blue eyes, perpetually incandescent with fever, were the only sign of beauty, a tormented and singular beauty.

The day Idolina took her first steps through the bedroom was not the day her will to be healthy finally won out. It was the day she found the formula which reconciled that will with her desire to use her own body to punish her mother's conduct. The formula consisted in nothing more than keeping the fact that she could walk a secret.

It wasn't necessary to tell the nana to be discreet. She understood that the sick girl's recovery was news that must not get beyond the walls of the room. She had no qualms about keeping quiet because her allegiance was to no one but Idolina. And because she thought that the ashes' promises needed silence in order to be fulfilled.

The murmur of the preparations for the dance reached this silence. Idolina refused to believe that the doors of her house, kept shut for so many years by mourning and shame, were now about to open for entertainment. Isabel had to confirm the truth of the rumors. No phrase of excuse, no sign of vexation and even less of disapproval. As if the party were something completely natural, possible and habitual. Everything seemed to indicate, moreover, that it was taking place on Isabel's initiative.

To eyes not as blinded by abhorrence as Idolina's, the despair Isabel was hiding so as not to give her daughter a reason to jeer would have been clearly visible. But Idolina preferred not to express an opinion on the coming event. The crease of haughtiness that always marred her face barely contracted.

The next day, however, a yellow color had flooded across the sick girl's body, tinging even the sheets that covered her. She couldn't keep down any food and she refused to allow the doctors' advice to be followed. With her eyes closed, she heard the pleas of her mother and the weeping of the Indian woman, without responding.

Isabel, who, though she would never have avowed it, felt herself to be the cause of this latest setback in her daughter's health, took leave of her as if she had been offended. From the doorway she declared that she was not going to worry about such an ungrateful person, who so abused the patience of those who had the unfortunate obligation of attending to her. Idolina answered, sitting up in bed with her eyes flaming, that she would only be grateful if they let her die in peace. Isabel hesitated a moment without giving voice to the answer that was swelling her throat with rage. In the end she turned her back and left the room with a slam of the door.

This scene achieved what the doctors had strived for in vain: the girl reacted. She was galvanized by a new plan: she wanted to attend the party, erupt with her tragic face amidst the happiness of others. She would not say a word, but who could fail to interpret her presence as an accusation flung by the dead at the living. Who would not see the girl as a victim?

Teresa was horrified. It was a reckless act. Idolina's condition would worsen, punishment would rain down upon the two of them. None of these reasons made a dent in the invalid's resolve. Only when the Indian woman expressed the fear that the promises of the ashes would not be fulfilled did Idolina's determination weaken.

But not to the point of giving up the plan entirely. Her isolation had been bearable until then because her bedroom was a refuge against people like her stepfather whom she found hateful. But from the depths of her seclusion, Idolina had always longed for company, tenderness, intimacy, friendship. In every echo of the footsteps that rang out on the sidewalk, she waited for the sound of the person who would come to free her. She had learned to distinguish, with a solitary person's terrible sharpness of perception, the hurry of those who were young, joyful, going out in search of happiness, and the hurry of the anguished, those who are rushing to postpone their destiny. In the authoritarian harshness with which their canes struck the paving stones she recognized the gentlemen's rank and she could gauge a man's self-assurance by the scrape of his spurs. And in the most furtive, the most imperceptible shuffling, she read the barefoot humility of a servant or an Indian.

Though Teresa would run to lean over the balcony and describe what she saw, those figures continued to move across the recluse's dreams, nameless and faceless.

Now, for the first time, a reality that had always been inaccessible to her was close by. And Idolina could not retreat, however fearful she was of advancing to meet it. To satisfy both demands, she gave in halfway. She wouldn't attend the dance publicly, but would be an invisible witness to it from a concealed place.

That place was a sort of attic which looked out on the house's courtyard and galleries from a height slightly above the rest. It had been constructed on the whim of one of the owners, separated from the other rooms, and only a few yards from Idolina's. At first it was used as a library. But the volumes gradually disappeared, sold, devoured by rats, or eaten away by the damp. Nowadays, trunks, useless furniture and old dresses were heaped up in it beside the remains of the books.

Stealthily, Idolina opened the door a crack. After making sure no one was there, she stepped out. Slowly, despite the fear of being seen that was goading her on. Slowly her foot sought the place where the sharp pine needles would hurt it least, where the resin was least sticky. Meanwhile the nana went ahead to unlock the door, then returned to the girl's side in time to help her go up the few steps that gave access to the attic.

Together Idolina and Teresa went in. The room was dark, illuminated only by the lights that came through the window from the courtyard below. The girl rested her forehead, burning with emotion and fatigue, on the window's glass. Beyond it was life, the world.

Idolina looked down, defenseless, eager to allow herself to be fascinated. Her first impression was confused, lacerating: disordered noises that hammered at her brain, sudden flashes of light that tore at her retinas. Not until she had calmed down a little (and the artery in her neck was no longer throbbing as if it were about to burst), not until her senses, dulled by the long confinement, had grown accustomed to the spectacle that presented itself to them, did Idolina begin to contemplate, to understand, to assess.

Her first emotion was disappointment. How paltry what she saw now was compared with what she remembered or had imagined! The courtyard was large, true. But not as large as the one she ran across when she was a child. Then, the only thing big enough to cover it was the open sky. Now a canvas awning was sufficient, patched with large stitches and vibrating in the furious March gales that were beating against it.

The Paniagua brothers' marimba, the most famous in Ciudad Real, had been set up in one corner of the courtyard. In the opposite corner, the band from Acala was tuning up its instruments: the trombone, solemn and ridiculous; the clarinet, sharp and defiant; the cymbals, gleaming and clattering; the potbellied drum.

In the space left between them the musicians had set up the dance floor, whose waxed, polished tiles would make the dancing fast and weightless.

On the gallery's pillars were lighted torches of ocote pine that burned with an ample flame, crackling and fragrant with resin. Around the slenderness of other pillars were twined palm fronds and ivy runners.

Seats were lined up along the sides—long wooden benches and folding chairs, so the dancing couples could rest. Inside, along the walls of the receiving rooms, were the places reserved for the older people, the placid, respectable people who couldn't be exposed to the weather's fickleness. Old men with little lashless eyes and a worried, malicious gaze. Married women blooming with motherhood, their small, plump hands, constellated with rings, crossed in their laps. Standing near the doors were the gentlemen. All wore black suits, though some had opted for a pair of eye-catching yellow shoes as the final touch on their outfits, rather than the traditional patent leather slippers. These were the newly rich, coarse people suddenly come up in the world due to a favorable fluctuation in the price of coffee, cattle dealers who sold their herds in Guatemala, bootleggers. Ciudad Real's proudest families tolerated them at their gatherings but made them pay a high price in gibes and loans for admission.

The priests, wrapped in the severity of their dark cassocks, were at the center of other groups: spinsters, beyond all hope by now, who spoke to them in a manner at once protective and submissive; unmarried women who had seen the best years of their youth go by without yet resigning themselves to defeat but without daring to compete at a disadvantage, and who pretended to disdain such amusements by demonstrating their affinity for serious, moral discussions; married women who made a show of the sway they held over their husbands by forcing them to pay tithes to the church and who expected special consideration from members of the clergy for that reason. And finally, timid men who were uncomfortable with the crude expressions and manners of the other men and incapable of approaching the eligible women and so came to breathe this asexual and insipid atmosphere.

The servants came and went offering glasses of various liquors—from the harsh comiteco which more than a few ladies accepted without putting up a fuss, to the cloying fruited mistelle made with peach, apple or jocote. There were slices of cold meats, crunchy cracklings, and cream cheese to nibble on.

The buzz of voices, faint laughter, bursts of merriment, grew and expanded, filling the whole house. The master of the house, Leonardo Cifuentes, could not complain. No one had turned down his invitation. The party was a success.

At the announced time, the music began to play. The marimba's low, opaque tones scattered out into the air and were multiplied, making everything throb with a deep, sweet nostalgia, a vague presentiment of plenitude and good fortune, a remote, chaste sensuality.

The emotions summoned up and made present by the music rose like a wave out of Idolina's heart and disturbed it. Agitated, she watched the couples sliding gracefully across the waxed dance floor. Idolina would have wanted to be one of the girls who were dancing. That one, waiting for her companion's words with such modest expectation. This one, who settled her hand on the sleeve of an evening jacket with an assured gesture of possession and control. The one over there, who shook her head with the same rebellious gesture as a colt rejecting the bridle. No one was excluded from Idolina's eagerness to be. Not even the one who was waiting, anxiously trembling on the edge of her seat, for someone to ask her to dance. Or the one who responded to the courteous request of an obese married man with a disillusioned smile, or the one who, abandoned by her more fortunate companions and wishing to conceal her disappointment, pretended to entertain herself by counting the floor tiles. Or the one who, constrained by her allegiance to the rules of a certain religious society or by her fiancé's absence or prevented by her parents or by the tradition that deprives all married women of the right to participate in any youthful diversion, remained at the margins and watched the others dancing, eyes big with envy.

Idolina's soul, ordinarily so uninhabited, was now overflowing with the reality these other women conferred on it. A gesture, a set of features, gave her enough material to invent a personality, to imagine a situation in which she was the center.

The squeaking of the door's rusty hinges brought Idolina out of her trance. Startled, she turned toward the noise. There, outlined against the light from outside, was the silhouette of a woman in an evening gown. Teresa choked back a moan of terror.

"Who is there?" an imperious voice demanded.

With the audacity of one who, having lost everything already, no longer has anything to risk, Idolina tried to slip by the woman and out the door. But in the darkness she ran into another body. A pair of hands around her waist stopped her. She tried to free herself; there was a quick struggle, but her opponent's dexterity and strength won out and Idolina fell to the floor.

Motionless, Teresa observed this episode from a corner. She was about to take a step toward the girl when she saw that the intruder was leaning over her.

The blaze of light from the courtyard exploded against a head of hair that was unbraided and as red as the flame from the ocote pine torches. Idolina saw this and along with it a face that was flushed and disconcerted by the violence that had just taken place.

The intruder stood up. When she saw that the other woman did not, she asked in perplexity, "Why don't you get up?"

"She is sick," the Indian woman interjected.

The intruder appeared to ponder this answer. She let out a brief laugh.

"So you're Leonardo Cifuentes' famous daughter."

Idolina was struggling to stand up, aided by the nana. She replied, "Leonardo Cifuentes is not my father."

The intruder stood next to the other two women now. She pulled Idolina over to the window in order to scrutinize her, following the outline of her face with the tip of one of her fingers.

"You don't look like him."

Idolina pulled sharply away from the touch.

"And yet," the intruder added, "he worries a lot about you, about your health."

Teresa whispered in the girl's ear, pleading with her to let them leave. But Idolina did not listen, studying the beauty and aplomb of this woman. In some part of herself she was still struggling against the overpowering influence she was giving in to. The marimba rang out in the distance.

"When he finds out you are well, Leonardo will be very glad."

The nana tried to catch Idolina's eye. But Idolina was saying to the intruder, "I am in your hands."

The effort it cost her to acknowledge this truth made the blood flood into her face. Then Idolina suddenly frowned severely.

"Why did you come in here?" she asked.

The intruder made a vague gesture as if to say the answer was obvious.

"I was going to the powder room; I don't know this house and I got lost."

Something in that voice always left a glimmer of doubt. Something that sounded of too much deliberation, too great a coincidence. A voice that was incapable of complete deception but was even less capable of being completely sincere. And the self-control in the words the intruder spoke when she came in, when she sensed another presence in the darkness, was feigned; she hadn't completely contained the quivering that comes over a person who suddenly feels she has fallen into a trap. Idolina understood this. But now that lucidity was intolerable to her. She didn't want to draw a conclusion from the evidence, only to stick to the literal meaning of the sentences.

"Who are you?"

"My name is Julia Acevedo."

She had forgotten to add her married name. She lowered her eyes and said with an almost imperceptible trace of disgust, "Why are you barefoot?"

Idolina tried to hide her feet under the hem of her nightgown.

"They don't buy shoes for me because they think I can't walk."

Teresa was studying the intruder's face but could find nothing there to orient herself by. Idolina added quickly, "My father's portraits are in here."

"You loved him very much?"

"No."

The negation came out of Idolina with such spontaneity that she was unable to conceal it with evasions or lessen its brutality with explanations. What had uprooted Isidoro from his daughter's heart? Bitterness; a sudden bitterness, an explosive disappointment. Idolina had experienced her father's death as an affront, an unfulfilled pact, a broken oath. It was the first betrayal she endured.

She had never before been conscious of such feelings. But judging herself for them was not important to her; any act that would have struck her as reprehensible in another person became good if she were the one who carried it out, without any need to seek motives to justify it. This time, though, she had spoken out loud, exposed her naked intimacy to a stranger. She trembled as she awaited the verdict.

Julia stripped the moment of its gravity.

"I didn't love my father either. He was a drunk."

It wasn't the vulgarity of what she confided but the casual and unconcerned way she did so that offended Idolina. She straightened herself and moved away from this unknown woman at whose mercy she had so unthinkingly placed herself.

The suspicion that she was walking on uncertain ground could not escape Julia's quick intuition.

"You'll have to get used to my ways," she said. "We Mexicans are very frank. I have nothing to hide."

It was a threat. But Julia immediately counterbalanced it.

"I only hide my friends' secrets. And you're my friend," she repeated as she brushed the girl's forehead lightly with her lips. "No one will hear from me that we have met. You keep quiet, too."

And after lifting her index finger to her mouth as if to impose silence, she left. Her perfume, a female perfume, dense, real, took longer to fade away.

Teresa pleaded in anguish, "Let's go, niña, let's go before they come."

Idolina looked impatiently at the nana.

"Julia Acevedo is my friend."

Without heeding the other woman's wailings, she went back to look down from the window. Not like the first time, when her attention was pure, wandering and dispersed. Now she was looking for something. She saw Julia, wrapped in a silk shawl, standing in the middle of the courtyard. She seemed to be waiting for someone. At her back, Leonardo's footsteps declared his approach. Julia turned to him, her face lit up with a cynical and inviting smile.

Idolina couldn't look any more. Her eyes were clouded over with tears.

CHAPTER IX

MANUEL MANDUJANO PACED through the galleries of the Palacio Episcopal. His footsteps rang out sharply against the tiles and faded away, mingling with the house's other sounds: the daily chores in the kitchen, barns and stables, the banging of the pail hitting the sides of the well, the strident cry of the guët, a wading bird that, according to a popular superstition, announced the arrival of a visitor. All the racket of an awakening morning.

With one hand the young priest nervously buttoned and unbuttoned his cassock, with the other he held his breviary open in front of him though he rarely focused his gaze on it. Manuel's mind was wandering, no matter how he tried to concentrate on prayer. He hadn't slept the previous night, and this morning his head ached and there was a bad taste in his mouth. What was more, the sudden summons from His Excellency at so untimely an hour heralded some news. He was worried. And the bishop was making him wait.

Not for long. The great front door creaked as it opened. Don Alfonso Cañaveral came in, still wearing the vestments he had donned to say mass.

Manuel closed the book and went to open the latch on the screen door that separated the entrance hall from the courtyard. The bishop thanked him for his solicitude with a tired smile.

"Good day, hijo."

"Did you have a good night, Monseñor?"

"Tolerable. We old men don't sleep much. Getting up so early must still be a mortification for you, though."

"Teachers such as yourself taught me to mortify myself."

The bishop responded to this flattery with a slight shrug.

"Tell them to set out breakfast. I'll change clothes."

Without waiting for the young man's assent (he knew him to be at his disposition, like all of his subordinates), Don Alfonso went to his rooms. He had been fond of Manuel for many years now. There is always something moving about adolescents; they are still intact and it is possible—why not?—that something could be realized in them which their elders did not achieve. The bishop was well acquainted with the boy's aspirations and with the ambition that had sustained him during his years as a seminarist. Now that he was about to put a brake on his momentum and cause the direction of his life to take a sudden swerve, he wondered if he wasn't doing so with an obscure complacence.

"As if I were envious. . . . He has what I lack: character. I've always been too serene, I've never caused any disturbances. I always believed this to be my principal virtue. So why, now, am I having these doubts? No one can do anything about it at this point. And what am I accusing myself of, ultimately? Of not having done what I could do? No one does. No one knows what he is capable of doing."

A quick knock on the door and the voice of Doña Cristina, the housekeeper, announcing that the table had been prepared, interrupted Don Alfonso's reflections. Quickly he finished dressing and went to the dining room.

What does his way of fixing his gaze on a neutral point mean? the bishop wondered. This young man is looking out at me from his austerity, from his innocence which hasn't had time to be corrupted. He does not admire me; on the contrary, he condemns me; he protests again the luxury of this house. I know the serving dishes could be more modest, the furniture more common, the decorations less lavish. And he says I taught him to mortify himself! He mocks me. He cannot understand that nothing here is superfluous. Solitude, idleness, fear of old age made me as persistent as a bird that gathers bits of straw wherever it can to make its nest with. None of this belongs to me. It will pass into the hands of my successors, others will enjoy it, strangers who won't even know how to appreciate it.

Such thoughts made all Don Alfonso's efforts to haul to this remote town the crystal jug, the ivory carved by Guatemalan craftsmen, the exquisite specimen of the weaver's art, suddenly strike him as monstrous and vain.

"Let us make our thanksgiving," said the bishop before taking his seat.

The two priests began their muttered prayer as Doña Cristina was about to cross the threshold. She stopped, her hands hidden beneath her apron, until the blessing had been spoken. Then she approached them to serve the meal.

"Regarding what we were saying before," Don Alfonso went on—Manuel's questioning gaze forced him to be more precise—"about mortification. I have had occasion to observe you during meals. You always reject the most appetizing dishes. Doña Cristina"—here he made a gesture that was answered with a smile of gratitude by the woman he alluded to—"is worried that her culinary abilities have declined. She doesn't know that youth is an age that mistrusts pleasure."

His Excellency was going to continue developing this paradox but was discouraged by the incomprehension of his audience. Doña Cristina (though naturally he had not spoken for her benefit) was looking at him with stupid veneration and seemed about to fall to her knees. And Manuel couldn't hide his distraction. After a few seconds of silence he answered with visible reluctance, "When youth has not forgotten the hunger of childhood it is unlikely to know how to appreciate the refinements of the palate."

"And other refinements as well, Manuel."

His Excellency dismissed the housekeeper with a wave. When they were alone, he prepared to speak. Clearing his throat to rid his voice of any nuance of condescension which could appear insulting, he said, "Last night, at the Cifuentes' party, your behavior was not quite so correct as one would have wished."

Manuel's ears reddened.

"Etiquette is not my strong point, Monseñor. My teachers taught me to be polite to God, not to men."

"You went there with your mind set against the owner of the house. Stories are told about Leonardo Cifuentes, tales of exploits that are not very edifying. But what are we to do? It is not for us to judge, but to pardon."

"Very convenient . . . as long as we are not the offended parties."

"And when we are, we know what we must do: turn the other cheek."

"Is that a warning, Don Alfonso? Very well: choose the cheek you prefer and start delivering the lesson. Last night I made a mistake."

"Don't exaggerate; it was no more than a lapse in tact."

"With everyone in general or with one person in particular?"

"Very particularly with Ulloa's wife."

Manuel frowned; he did not recognize the name. Don Alfonso had to add, "Julia Acevedo—the woman they call La Alazana. You were very harsh in your criticism of her."

Like a bolt of lightening the image evoked by that name flashed through Manuel's mind: the insolent neckline, the flaming hair, the frank laugh.

"And with good reason. Her immodesty. . . ."

"You must learn to make the distinction, my son. Immodesty, yes, if this were just any woman. But in a lady it is elegance."

"And what proof do we have that La Alazana is a lady? Not her appearance or her manners, certainly."

The bishop closed his mouth, disconcerted. For him Julia Acevedo's social standing was so obvious that he was unable to substantiate it. After a few seconds of searching, he replied, "The best families in Ciudad Real receive her."

Manuel smiled sarcastically.

"They do not receive her. And if they did they would be as gullible as you are, Monseñor. Who is this ambitious upstart? No one knows her."

"She's the wife of a gentleman."

"Is he a gentleman or a swindler trying to pass himself off as a gentleman?"

"What makes you think that?"

The young man shrugged, "A simple hunch."

"A rash judgment, Manuel."

"Can I help it if things that are strange look strange to me? And that pair is strange."

"Fernando de Ulloa's position is clear: he is a civil servant who occupies a post of some importance in the administration."

"Which isn't enough to make the people of Ciudad Real receive him like the prodigal son, kill the fatted calf and, to top it all off, believe every story he tells them."

"Coletos are not a hospitable people."

"Nevertheless, their reserve breaks down once in a while. Not out of hospitality: out of boredom. Whatever disrupts the routine or provides a distraction is welcome. And La Alazana knows how to ingratiate herself—she bedazzles the men."

Don Alfonso reddened and lowered his eyes. With the tip of his knife, he drew uneven lines on the tablecloth.

"The women, at their husbands' insistence, will open their doors to her. They won't regret it. Julia knows how to repay hospitality: she introduces the lax ways of other towns. Ah, how they envy her, these women who are always shut up in their houses, how they would like to behave with her shamelessness. And we, the shepherds, are letting the wolf into the sheepfold to decimate the ewes when our duty is to chase it off with clubs."

"To the parable you cite I can oppose another: that of the wheat and the tares. Do you know how far the roots of the evil extend? Do you know if in your attempt to root it out you will not also destroy what you want to protect? For many years I have led my congregation without upheavals, to the satisfaction of all and with the blessings of my superiors."

This final phrase brought the skirmish to an end and re-established the principle of authority. Manuel bowed his head, mumbling an apology.

"I have never at any moment sought to criticize your attitude, Monseñor. Only. . . ."

In any case, the zeal Manuel so imprudently exhibited was not sincere. What did that foreign woman matter to him? But he had waited for his conversation with Don Alfonso so anxiously that wasting it in idle gossip was irritating him to the point of making him forget the courtesy he owed his bishop. Bitterly he asked himself for the thousandth time a question that had always been the thorn in his side: What good is it to have drive, to feel you are capable of any and everything, when you are poor, when you are no one? Just Manuel Mandujano, the orphan, brother of his only sister, Benita, who, because of the difference in their ages and other circumstances, was more like a mother to him.

So many sacrifices, she said with a sigh (but also with a sense of pride), so many sacrifices for the boy's education. Because from the moment he discovered how to decipher the words in his primer, everyone, teachers and schoolmates alike, was amazed by the accuracy of Manuel's memory and the quickness of his mind. He learned to read, write and solve elementary math problems more rapidly than the other students. That should have been enough for him, as it was enough and more than enough for others. But it was a pity to waste such a talent in an ordinary civil post.

What to do? Benita, a member of the Ladies of the Sacred Heart and other religious societies, listened to her confessor's advice and took great pains from then on to inculcate a vocation for the priesthood in her brother.

To a boy raised among clouds of incense, the skirts of pious women and the hustle and bustle of the sacristy, the possibility of the priesthood was not repellent or shocking. And the sentimental outbursts, the effusions of enthusiasm so common in adolescence could be interpreted as the call of Divine Grace. In other boys, such effervescence naturally led to a bed in a brothel, a fistfight or a drinking binge. In this one, without money or friends and tied to the apron strings of a much older sister, no other outcome was available but enrollment in the Seminary. The fact that his board and tuition would be free was an added temptation. For the moment, at least, the Mandujano legacy (a shack and a plot planted with fruit trees in the Tlaxcaltecas district) would remain intact.

Within the bramble-covered walls of the Seminary, Manuel found a happiness he had not known outside them. In his sister's company, he was inhibited. After all was said and done, she was a woman, and one cannot talk to women. Now Manuel felt strengthened and ripened by his interaction with men. He discovered himself through them; he affirmed himself; he was constantly modifying himself. He found schoolmates to share his small secrets and his immense revelations; teachers who would place in his hands the formulas for triumphing over life, vanquishing the world, saving himself.

Triumph, vanquish. Manuel's choice of vocabulary was not Catholic or even Christian. It betrayed pride, ambition, audacity. But since that always remained implicit and Manuel's limbs were well oiled with humility, it wasn't easy to deduce the motives that underlay his conduct. One man, Don Alfonso, who was his spiritual advisor and therefore the person closest to his intimate thoughts, suspected something. But other, more apparent facts always more than counterbalanced the suspicion. The brilliance he displayed in his studies, for example. Manuel's intelligence, which was not particularly adventuresome or innovative, poured itself, docile, into the mold of the ecclesiastic disciplines.

Where his moral conduct was concerned, he was irreproachable. His sensuality, like that of all those born in the highlands, was shrouded. Neither his ascetic features nor his habitually reserved expression allowed anyone to glimpse the jolts of his flesh. He found a discreet outlet for them and hypocrisy did not mark him with even the smallest stigma of guilt.

It had never been Manuel's ambition to become a saint. He dreamed of ruling over a diocese, guiding the multitudes from the pulpit, plotting vast intrigues. He always occupied the center of the stage; his kingdom was always of this world.

And why not? He had more of what it took to win than the others; he had ideas, character. When he was given the parish of San Diego, his first parish, his first stop on the road to his destiny, he believed the moment had arrived to take action.

"Please do not think I called you here so we could exchange comments on last night's dance."

Don Alfonso's words seemed to awaken Manuel.

"Is it a serious matter, Monseñor?"

"No, not serious. A bit troublesome to your vanity, perhaps. And very awkward for the affection I bear you."

This introduction augured yet another reprimand. Manuel mustered up all his calm in order to listen to it.

"Once again it has to do with your character, my son. Such vehemence, such outbursts. . . . Personally, I admire them. But the civil authorities have no grasp of subtleties and find your activities to be seditious."

Manuel's activities? The parish of San Diego was not centrally located. The parishioners were primarily families of antique lineage, left little by little at the outskirts of the town by the expansion of more recent powers-that-be. Without any inheritance other than their names, without any skill by which to rebuild their fortunes, without a craft by which to earn a decorous living, these families shut themselves up in houses that were half in ruins, turning their backs on a city that had ostracized them.

The demands of his ministry had allowed Padre Mandujano to step across the thresholds of those dwellings and see the gardens

engulfed by weeds, the interior courtyards where the womens'
hands were eaten by lye, the dark rooms where useless objects
accumulated.

He entered the rooms of the dying. What a rank smell of mold,
unaired sheets, abolished future!

When he first arrived in San Diego parish, Padre Mandujano
wanted to break through these peoples' isolation, incorporate
them into the community, make them participate in the interests
and satisfactions of others. He failed. As the afternoons began to
darken, the men of those houses still went to the closest cantina,
well muffled up in their cloaks, to drown the humiliation of their
lives in cheap liquor. The women still slipped out surreptitiously
to offer to sell their former friends a book from their grandfather's
library, the last silver spoon, the lace that had once adorned a
legendary ballgown.

These rich people who had come down in the world and the
craftsmen they lived among were like oil and water. Neighbors,
pedestrians in the same streets, parishioners of the same church,
they neither spoke to one another nor acknowledged one another's existence.

The craftsmen's doors were always wide open. From inside
their houses came the sound of work, of the machine's rhythmic
movements and the worker singing as he labored. The courtyards
thronged with dirty children, domestic animals, clients. And on
Sundays the family went to church, elbowing their way through
to the best pews (on which they had had their names ostentatiously painted) and maintaining, during the service, a composure
all the more meritorious for the effort it cost them. They cast
sidelong glances at the aristocrats, with a solid satisfaction where
the present was concerned, but with a secret envy of the past.

This was the public Padre Manuel addressed. His eloquence
vibrated between the church's baroque walls, rang down from the
gilded altars, glanced off the somber altarpieces. His listeners
cleared their throats in covert impatience, shifted in their seats,
hissed to silence the noises each one of them caused. And in their
vacant eyes and distracted expressions, Padre Manuel had ample
and grievous evidence that he was not being heard.

Late at night, in the solitude of his bedroom, Padre Manuel

meditated. The relationship between the priest and his parishioners is a curious one. The nature of the priest's role inhibits the secular man; he changes the subject when the priest approaches; he does not dare include him. He wants to establish a distance. But the priestly character is like the tip of a scalpel. It pierces. Under cover of the confessional, and with an almost defiant shamelessness, souls lay themselves bare and stories are told.

The stories told by Coletos, Padre Manuel mused, were like plants. An excess or a defect of temperament, a hereditary flaw, a careless upbringing can be the seed. Then comes the gray seedling of the years and the unvarying customs. The thick bark of reputation, social standing. And suddenly the red flower blooms: scandal, violence, crime. Nothing produces the illusion of randomness like a slow, patient logic.

But the seed, the root, does not grow by itself. It feeds on beliefs, practices and aspirations that are legitimate, on rigid prohibitions: on morality, in other words.

And Coleto morality is very peculiar. In their dealings with each other, the people of Ciudad Real are exaggeratedly scrupulous, the most prudish sticklers. They want to keep up their good names as honest merchants, professionals in every sense of the word. But this same honest merchant, this consummate professional doesn't hesitate for an instant at the chance to rob an Indian. Even more: he's proud of having done it. He tells the story as a funny anecdote that never fails to gladden the hearts of his listeners. When they sell "used" cloth to a man from Oxchuc; when by some underhanded legal chicanery they dispossess a family from Chenalhó; when they kidnap a young girl in the street to enslave her in their domestic service, they can boast of the feat without anyone finding it in the least reprehensible. It would only be censurable if in some indirect way it damaged the interests of another Ladino. But apart from that, who would condemn someone for shaking a tree that belongs to no one in order to enjoy its fruits? Who could possibly take seriously the aberrant belief that trees are people and should therefore be respected as such?

The most cherished virtues of the women of Ciudad Real are chastity and modesty. Inconvenient virtues, these, requiring a constant vigilance over oneself, a renunciation of the pleasures of vanity and the flesh, a sacrifice of the primary impulses. Perhaps some women are capable of incarnating them. But many are very adept at feigning them.

And what stiff necks they all had, men and women alike! Pride in their ancestors, in their prosperity, in their race. A pride that had remained intact for centuries and was beginning to crack only now.

Because Ciudad Real was no longer a closed city. The government had opened up roads and the roads brought it closer to other cities. Travelling ceased to be the remote plan passed down from generation to generation without ever being carried out, and became an immediate possibility, an accessible and easy experience. Coletos travelled; they crossed the mountain which for centuries was their obstacle and their defense, their bulwark and their challenge. They saw, they touched, they compared. And they preferred not to communicate their observations. Anyone hearing them talk could believe nothing had happened. Nothing. An insect is nothing and it eats away at the foundations of a house.

Foreigners now come to Ciudad Real, as well. Curious people who are astonished by all they see, who are alarmed, who judge. Blabbermouths who comment on everything and kick up a fuss. Rigid, disdainful people, like Fernando Ulloa.

As a defense against this disturbing intrusion, Coletos needed to rekindle their old prejudices. Padre Manuel interpreted that need, which he himself felt, and from the pulpit he fulminated against these emissaries of Babylon, these bearers of dangerous ideas which would inevitably give rise to abominable habits. For the first time they listened to him with real attention.

Padre Manuel abandoned the rhetoric he had learned at the Seminary, the senile formulas of an oratory whose time had passed, to adopt a direct, vigorous language in which the weakness of the argument was concealed by the impetuousness of the delivery.

Attendance at Padre Manuel's sermons grew larger with each passing Sunday. Worshippers from other parishes came from afar to watch the lightning bolt of wrath that was unsheathed before their eyes and flashed for a short while, dazzling them, helping them endure a week of gray routine and colorless inertia.

Padre Mandujano fell into his own trap. He had discovered his own force and wanted to increase it, make use of it. Did he forget to be prudent? Who, when drunk, doesn't forget to be prudent?

"I did nothing out of the ordinary. A talk on Sunday. . . ."

"In which you incited the people to rebel against those who govern them."

"Those who govern are unjust. Their injustice exempts us from obeying them."

"But the crisis the Church is going through right now can transform any incident into a provocation. You know they are persecuting us in Tabasco, humiliating the priests, burning the churches and desecrating the images. The same thing can happen here."

"And we are to confront this threat with our hands folded in our laps?"

"The Church needs no martyrs. A martyr requires an executioner. And it is a sin without remission to try to make our adversaries into executioners. What is needed is common sense and discretion."

Manuel stared at Don Alfonso. The bishop had the reputation of having been energetic and combative in his youth. And this empty husk was what Ciudad Real had left after grinding him down for years with its all-too benign climate, its too easily accessible countryside, its too tranquil way of life. Manuel felt a jab of alarm. No, a thousand times no! He would seek out the wilderness, the inhospitable sands, the blank horizon. He wanted to live, to pant with exhaustion, to walk, to move, to fight.

"I am neither sensible nor discreet."

"Don't be proud of that. You're forcing me to send you to a place where your defects can do no harm."

Manuel stood up. A look of incredulity convulsed his face.

"Do you mean you have yielded to our enemies' demands and are ordering me to leave my parish?"

"It is for your own good, my son. Even though you don't believe it and right now it seems as if I'm being sarcastic, I have always been concerned about your future. And what future can you have if you stay in Ciudad Real? You are being watched, and they will have you on a very short leash. Are you going to resign yourself as I have? A quick mass, a cup of chocolate at the same hour every day, the regular gathering of your circle of friends, a nice fire in winter, a nice lamp at night. And prevaricating, and absolving mediocre sins, eunuchs' sins."

"Never!"

"You see? And if you were to attempt something, to organize assemblies, for example, the government would call it political. And come down on you fast and hard."

"So then?"

"You have to get away from here. In this town of shyster lawyers, we priests are superfluous."

"Yet we still have influence. I've seen the haughtiest gentlemen bow down to kiss your ring, Ilustrísima."

"Yes, they do bend their knees but they no longer pay tithes. Never make any kind of alliance with the rich, Manuel. They always demand more than they give. The poor, on the other hand. . . . How consoling the Gospel's promise is: 'For ye have the poor always with you'! I had never fully understood it until today."

Don Alfonso could not help observing the incongruence between his exclamation and his furniture. He hastened to add: "You'll say it's easy to sing the praises of poverty from a comfortable chair after a delicious breakfast. But we bishops are obliged to keep up the protocol our position imposes on us."

Padre Mandujano nodded. He was having a hard time following this lecture, whose direction he was unable to predict. The old man repeated, "You will have to leave."

"To go where? On the coast they're not exactly models of religiosity."

"No, no. To the interior."

"There's nothing in the interior but Indians."

"Whom our Holy Mother has abandoned to their fate for a very long time now."

As if that mattered! Manuel was on the verge of answering. But he restrained himself in time.

"You are a Coleto before you are a priest, and therefore you're accustomed to despising the Indians," Don Alfonso continued. "In a Christian, this is a lack of charity. And in a politician— because you are one whether or not we want to acknowledge it —it is a miscalculation."

Manuel's lips parted in a smile.

"In our reckonings, the Indians are a quantity that does not count, Monseñor."

"It hasn't always been that way. Remember the missionaries in the early days of the Conquest."

"And what was the result of all that? Failure. They were generous men, but mistaken. . . ."

"However, the Jesuits. . . ."

"They are indeed the true sons of light, as the Gospels define them: they have the wisdom of the serpent."

"I'm glad our opinions coincide. Well then, the Jesuits undertook a very interesting experiment with the Indians in Paraguay. Do you remember it?"

"Vaguely. I think they tried to found a kind of utopia, which didn't produce any results either."

"It produced results."

"Even if it did," Manuel interrupted impatiently. "These are different times."

"Yes. Our Holy Mother forgot the Jesuits' lesson. But secular people took it up. They're the ones who have begun to think about the Indians again. Do you know why Fernando Ulloa is here? To redistribute land. Later, teachers will come to teach them to speak Castilla, to read, to write. Do you realize what this means? Thousands of souls which by divine right belong to us will be snatched away by the unjust government you are fighting. And why will all this happen? Because we did not want to remedy our blameworthy negligence in time."

"You're very quick to take alarm, Monseñor. Let the teachers and engineers come; let the Government strive for all it's worth. They won't be able to do anything. All their good intentions will be smashed against the Indians' indifference and stupidity."

"And what if it doesn't turn out that way?"

Manuel shrugged. "What can we do? We're very poor . . . and there are so few of us!"

"That kind of rationalization is for cowards. If everyone thought as you do Christianity would never have been disseminated. Remember the situation and the tiny number of the Apostles. . . ."

"But the Holy Spirit dwelled in them and spoke through their mouths and. . . ."

"Commanded them to go forth and preach and they went forth and preached. The only supernatural thing about it was their obedience, so inflamed with faith that it moved mountains. And don't tell me that was an exceptional episode. The story of the Apostles is repeated in every priest."

Manuel gave in with a bitter smile.

"And now my time has come, Monseñor?"

"The Spirit moves where it wishes. I will do no more than put you in a suitable place."

Manuel began to grow alarmed. The grandiloquence of Don Alfonso's language could only be forewarning a very grave decision.

"I want you to take charge of the parish of San Juan Chamula."

The name gave birth in the young priest to a thousand confusing images: unruly Indians, barbaric bouts of drunkenness, Ladino merchants fleeing in the middle of the night to save their lives, though not their properties, from looting and fire.

"For months the Chamulas have been restless. They learned about the Agrarian Reform and they are demanding that it be carried out, that the ejidos be redistributed. Their agitation has increased with Ulloa's arrival."

Manuel made a gesture of powerlessness.

"You don't know what a parish priest is to an Indian!" Don Alfonso enthused. "A representative of God. Who knows? Perhaps even an incarnation of God. And this after so many years of abandonment, of neglect by us! It is an admirable thing."

"Have you thought about the fact that I do not know the language, Monseñor?"

"You won't have any difficulties. There is a sacristan in the parish who speaks Castilla well. He can serve you as an interpreter and help you learn Tzotzil."

Manuel understood that to any objection he might make Don Alfonso would have a response that would strip it of all validity and weight. For powerful reasons (and which was the most powerful: the pressure of the civil authorities? the convenience of keeping an eye on an area where the Government wanted to make some changes? or simply envy of a more daring and brilliant rival?) Don Alfonso had decided to appoint Manuel parish priest of San Juan Chamula and no argument would dissuade him.

He could have used his authority as bishop, the young man thought, he could have given me an order. But he is afraid of my rebelliousness, and so he piles up a stack of sophistries to convince me of the necessity of my appointment there. An apostolate among the Indians. How absurd! He himself doesn't believe what he's saying; he's nothing but a poor old coward and meddler. Perhaps in his own way he thinks highly of me and defends me. I should still be grateful to him for taking the trouble to lie.

"I will leave when you tell me to, Monseñor."

But deep inside himself, Manuel still had not accepted it and was planning to appeal the appointment as soon as a decorous period of time had elapsed and experience had provided him with reasons. No, his stay in Chamula would by no means have to be permanent.

"I'm glad to see you so willing, Manuel. I expected no less from you. Before you go I'll give you my instructions in writing. Now you must make preparations for the journey as quickly as possible. We will take care of outfitting you: you must make sure you are well equipped with clothing and provisions; all expenses will be charged to me, of course. It will also be indispensable to have someone along to help you. I would let you have Doña Cristina, my housekeeper. She is a magnificent woman, very serious, very conscientious, and, at her age, safe from any wicked thoughts or rumors. But she is so much at home with me that it pains my conscience to send her away from the Bishopric."

"Don't trouble yourself, Monseñor. My sister Benita will undoubtedly agree to go with me."

"If that's the case then everything is settled. May God go with you, mi hijo."

Don Alfonso gave the young priest his ring to kiss. As he was paying his reverences, a great relief swept over the bishop's mind. The step, which had appeared so difficult, was taken. Certainly the boy had put up some resistance, but less than his fiery temperament had made the bishop fear. Nor had he seemed very suspicious. He had yielded, accepting his superior's explanations.

Manuel walked away from the Palacio Episcopal with a confused and disappointed heart. Among all his illusions of triumph there remained only the somber prospect of confinement to an insignificant town to carry out a nonsensical mission. Meanwhile his schoolmates and teachers would forget him and he himself would forget his aspirations and allow himself to be worn down by inhuman customs. Manuel breathed with difficulty. He was suffocating, like an insect squashed under a rock.

Benita was frightened when she saw him come in.

"You're very pale. Has something upset you or caused you pain? I'll go to the kitchen and fix you some aguardiente with water and nutmeg."

"Make some for yourself, too," her brother suggested roughly. His tone was enough to hold her back.

"Manuel, what is happening?"

"What is happening is that I took a vow of obedience and today I had to fulfill it. The bishop has appointed me to another parish."

"You aren't going to stay in San Diego?"

"No: complaints have been made against me."

"But, who? Who?"

"The Freemasons are becoming alarmed because according to them I'm doing subversive work."

Benita did not understand what her brother was being accused of. She asked humbly, "It's all slander, isn't it Manuel?"

"You convince them of that, if you can. And convince Don Alfonso that for his own convenience he should support me and not let himself be intimidated by those devils. But the bishop is a prudent man; he doesn't want to have any problems in his diocese and he is ridding himself of me by sending me to San Juan Chamula."

"What is that?"

"An Indian town."

"To an Indian town? You?"

"And you, too, if the sacrifice doesn't seem too great."

"But these bishops are insane, may God forgive and protect me! To send you away, you of all people. You were the best student at the seminary; you have all the most prominent people in Ciudad Real enthralled by your sermons . . ."

Benita wiped away a nonexistent tear with the corner of her apron. Manuel couldn't resist the temptation to exacerbate her ingenuous and defenseless pain.

"Nevertheless they'll complain that they didn't get their money's worth out of me. So much wasted on educating me, just so I can end up serving them in a church that could very easily be overseen by a priest who was completely ignorant."

Suddenly Benita ended the discussion. "Patience, hermano. What date is your departure set for?"

"As soon as possible."

"We must begin making preparations."

"Will you go with me?"

Benita nodded silently. She was moved and, though ashamed to admit it, she had to acknowledge that she was happy. The years of Manuel's education had been years of solitude for her. One day each month she rejoiced in his visit; one day each month her tidy spinster's house was turned upside down by her brother's presence. And when his day of leave came to an end, Benita kept, like a sacred relic, the ashes the absent boy had carelessly let fall on the bedspread; she lingered over the task of scrubbing the traces of mud left on the doormat.

During that time, Benita had lived in fear that when Manuel completed his studies he would leave for some distant place or would become so important a personage that his humble origins would embarrass him. But, thanks be to God, her fears had been in vain. The Virgen de la Caridad was answering her prayers. Benita and Manuel would never be separated now; Manuel would depend on her totally once more; he would demand care, attention and pampering from her as if he were a child again.

From the doorway (who could go near this forbidding man?) Benita turned to look at her brother, tremulous with expectation and gratitude.

CHAPTER X

AFTER DINNER (some boiled beans and a cup of coffee, served in pewter dishes), Padre Manuel Mandujano shut himself up in his bedroom. A task he had been putting off for a week awaited him: writing to Don Alfonso. Manuel knew he had a lot of news to tell, and he knew it was important news, as well. Nevertheless, half an hour later, under the warm and silent glow of the lamp, he had done no more than trace some meaningless arabesques on the paper, trying out flourishes for his signature.

Before now, perplexity had never restrained him in the confrontation with a blank sheet of paper. He had quickly filled in the space with the monotonous, clear and impersonal handwriting taught at the Seminary. Today, he remained suspended. He had dates, figures, facts at his disposal. Everything was scrupulously exact, but he refused to consider it true. Still, when they are written out, incidents adjoin one another so closely that their proximity looks like coherence.

For what seemed like the thousandth time, Padre Mandujano put down his pen. His thoughts dwelled obstinately on one image: that of his predecessor, the last priest of San Juan, a reprobate, drunk, lecher and blasphemer. He had been transformed into that by something worse than isolation: a life shared with those strange, hermetic beings, the Indians.

Padre Manuel's countenance darkened. Would his fate be as dismal as that man's?

These apprehensions had been uppermost in the priest's soul from the day he accepted the mission to Chamula. He was oppressed by the certainty of failure, the anguish of knowing that a bottomless chasm was opening at his feet, an abyss that would devour him in the end. And his downfall would have neither the merit of a sacrifice freely consented to and carried out nor the fecundity of a martyrdom. It would be like a rock falling down a well. A mournful echo, then nothing more.

At the very beginning of his stay in San Juan, Padre Manuel drove off these bitter prospects by throwing himself into an exhausting bout of physical activity that left him wanting nothing more than rest.

He had put off travelling to the outlying parts of his parish for the moment. Even so, he had more than enough work simply trying to make the large, broken-down parish house inhabitable. Rain trickled through the roof's broken tiles and ran down the walls, staining them and impregnating them with a dampness that soon became green with mold. Rats, bats and opossums had found a convenient shelter in the rooms. And the freezing wind of Chamula battered at the rickety doors, the empty, unglazed windows.

Benita did what she could to help her brother. But what could a woman do under such circumstances? Manuel had a man's work to do, a strong man's work.

The residents of San Juan spontaneously presented themselves to place themselves at the parish priest's disposition. He accepted the offers of some, those who seemed most experienced. And with the help of the sacristan, Xaw Ramírez Paciencia, who translated his orders from Spanish to Tzotzil, he was able to clear away a little of the rubble heaped up in the kitchen, to patch up the gutters and chase away the animals who were living in the house and causing so much damage.

Because provisions were scarce, Benita prepared frugal meals, hardly any better than what Xaw was used to eating. Xaw scrutinized her with an almost imperceptible expression of disappointment. Why did the new arrival scorn the "tidbits" by which his parishioners tried to show him their affection? Was he unaware that many of them had resigned themselves to going hungry so that their parish priest would have a well-furbished larder? But Padre Manuel rejected the gifts he was offered. The other priests had behaved differently. Was it because this one thought he was worth more and therefore had greater pride?

Manuel did not notice that his attitude toward his parishioners' gifts (which stemmed from his disgust at anything that came out of their filthy huts and from his slowness to feel gratitude) was giving rise to resentment. He continued devoting himself to his labors, oblivious to the distance that was growing up around him.

Among the many rooms of the parish house, Padre Manuel chose those where the ravages of abandonment were least visible and made them his sister's bedroom and his own.

His bedroom furniture wasn't luxurious or austere, just inappropriate. It consisted of an enormous walnut bed, what they call a matrimonial bed, which was donated by a rich, devout widow who hadn't resolved to divest herself of the mattress as well. Padre Manuel didn't want to alleviate the lack of a mattress even with the heap of hay suggested by Xaw, and preferred to lie on the hard wooden boards.

"You Indians sleep on the ground"—he offered the example with forced joviality. "What am I made of, that I can't take anything but softness?"

"You are a Ladino, padrecito."

Ladino! In Ciudad Real, Padre Manuel could be proud of a status he shared with the rich and powerful. But in San Juan it was an ambiguous privilege which provoked mistrust, fear and aggression in those beneath him.

"We are all equal in the eyes of Our Lord," Padre Manuel affirmed resentfully.

Xaw nodded with a silent smile. Neither respect nor his shaky command of Spanish would allow him to continue the discussion. But an uncontainable wave of repulsion was growing inside him. Was this man not an imposter?

The rest of his furniture consisted of a table of ocote pine, good enough for writing but heavily scarred by use, two leather armchairs so low to the ground that no one but a dwarf could have been comfortable in them, and some other chairs, also made of ocote pine, which were flimsy and unstable. Presiding over this laughable decor was a crucifix. An ivory crucifix. A gift from Don Alfonso when Manuel finished his first year of study at the seminary.

Padre Manuel always kept the crucifix with him. He did so out of habit and a kind of superstitious attachment. Now the two of them had wound up in the parish house of San Juan Chamula. But did this chunk of matter make the priest's solitude any more tolerable, his helplessness any less piercing? Manuel shifted his eyes away from it almost with reproach.

There were few reasons indeed for contentment. His first visit to the church left him dumbfounded. Was it possible that only a short distance away from Ciudad Real, the seat of the diocese, Christianity had failed to penetrate? Was it possible that no one had noticed or denounced the fact that the natives were practicing a warped religion? Thanks to Don Alfonso's warning, Manuel had anticipated a certain level of idolatry, the level a converted people always introduces into Catholicism, and which Catholicism tolerates and absorbs. But what he found in San Juan went far beyond anything he could have imagined and revealed a state of absolute paganism.

Statues lay on the ground where they had fallen, unrevered. Face down, nothing to protect them, exposed to a destruction the impatient Indians accelerated with abuse. Some were already missing their heads, others had broken hands, noses that had been chipped away, eyes that had fallen out. And the colors! They weren't the colors of aging, of the natural deterioration of the wood, but greenish tones, a simulation of rot.

Padre Manuel's first thought was that mere carelessness had left those images looking so preposterous. But he quickly became convinced that the Indians' attitude toward them arose from an active desire to deface, humiliate and punish. Because other images had been treated differently, though Manuel would not have gone so far as to affirm that their fate was any better.

There were hated figures and favored figures. The Indians manifested their favor by swathing the sacred statue in rolls and rolls of fabric, producing an obesity that was increasingly out of proportion with the size of the body parts that remained uncovered. The disproportion could grow to a point where the figure lost its human form. The saints looked like enormous tortoises standing upright, with a tiny, timid human head emerging from the massive shell.

And what to say about the adornments? Palm-leaf hats, tiny mirrors that scintillated among the profusion of fabric, small jicaras, diminutive clay vessels.

When Padre Manuel wanted to find out why a certain painting of the sacrifice on Calvary had been draped over with a cloth, the sacristan's solicitude in explaining things to him seemed to vanish, to be replaced by a reticent ambiguity. And when Padre Manuel tried to move aside the cloth to see what it hid, Xaw placed himself between the priest and the image, offering various incoherent reasons for his behavior. The priest didn't think it was the right time to pursue the matter. He wasn't going to bring the enmity of this people down on himself right now, when he had no weapon in his hand to fight with.

Benita, who was more intrusive, uncovered a painting of the Virgen Dolorosa on the pretext of cleaning the dust off of it. When Xaw came running, it was too late. The two women had already seen each other. And now, the sacristan lamented, danger was lurking in the motionless painted eyes.

Xaw himself was certainly disconcerting, too. As evidence of his own merit, he told Padre Manuel that during the period the parish had been unsupervised he, in his capacity as sacristan, had taken over the functions of the missing priest. For that reason, all the children born during that time had been baptized, no one had died without benefit of the last rites, and as far as cohabiting couples were concerned, they were a disgrace that other places could be ashamed of, but not San Juan. Xaw's greatest pride was in having legalized all unions by a church wedding.

Very gently, so as not to keep him from confiding anything more, Padre Manuel asked Xaw if he hadn't also confessed and given Holy Communion to the parishioners. The sacristan said no. By way of an excuse, he said that the brujos were in charge of inquiring about sins and establishing the conditions for their forgiveness. And the brujos would, very justifiably, have become angry if anyone who wasn't one of them had tried to compete :h them.

"And Holy Communion?" Padre Manuel persisted.

Xaw had not administered it. He had of course seen on innu-....rable occasions how the priests made the host, but he had never hit on the recipe that would enable him to make it himself.

Padre Manuel paused for an instant at such simplicity. Inside, he was boiling over with anger. Anger at the ignorance of this man whose proximity to the altar and familiarity with the holy services had taught him nothing. And anger, too, at the laziness or stupidity of those who had not managed to catechize even the one person who was in the best position to receive their lessons.

As the days passed, he undertook to change Xaw's opinions. With the relentless zeal of a man who has little outlet for his need for activity, Padre Manuel endeavored to instruct Xaw on the most elementary notions of doctrine. For that purpose, after saying mass (a mass that reverberated in an empty church because it was the hour when all the town's inhabitants were at their chores), Padre Manuel invited Xaw to share his breakfast. It was difficult to convince the Indian that he could, that he had to sit at the table with the priest and not on the floor as was his custom. Xaw obeyed but without ever quite being able to conceal the unease the situation caused him. He barely managed to eat. He prepared each mouthful with exaggerated meticulousness, then swallowed it quickly without taking the time to savor it, and as soon as Padre Manuel was distracted for an instant, he seized the opportunity to take a ball of posol surreptitiously from his knapsack, then eagerly awaited the priest's briefest absence to prepare it and drink it. Padre Manuel became aware of this one day when he returned earlier than Xaw had anticipated and Xaw didn't have time to hide the jicara of posol, which was still full.

It would perhaps have been more charitable to allow the Indian to eat by himself and as he liked. But that would deprive Padre Manuel of his only opportunity to speak slowly and at length with Xaw, which was at mealtime. Over the table, casually, the priest reviewed the catechism. He was shocked, first of all by the extraordinary limitations of his pupil's vocabulary. The simplest and most ordinary Spanish words had to be repeated four or five times and explained with abundant examples. And when the explanation had ended, no one remembered what the initial word was any more.

Manuel made an effort to pick up the thread, trying in vain to find in his student a trace, however slight, of comprehending attention, of interest. Xaw's face remained impassive at the most vehement proofs of the existence of God and his incarnation in the person of Christ, or of the Church's faithfulness to the revealed truths. The only commentary he allowed himself was an occasional coarse interjection, an uncontainable belch, a brazen yawn, a resolute spit. These reactions made Padre Manuel rigid with fury; when at last he decided to forbid them, the sacristan received the order grudgingly, bitterly. The new arrival had not understood that in the Tzotzil's unpolished mind, the interjection, the belch, the yawn and the spit were the most courteous demonstrations of deference he could offer to the speaker.

Padre Manuel had to modify—and how often!—his methods of teaching the catechism. Not because Xaw's individual case mattered to him any more, or because what produced good results with him could later be applied to the others, but out of a blind obstinacy that had forgotten its objective.

First, the priest had to give up his intensity. Facial expressions, changes in the register of his voice, any superfluity whatsoever distracted Xaw, taking his mind off the matter at hand and making him stare at the speaker as if he were an actor. No vehemence, then. Simplicity. But simplicity, after a while, becomes monotony. And how simple can you be with someone who doesn't speak your language?

Padre Manuel noted how sympathy, benevolence and tolerance were diminishing within him until they were entirely used up. Every clumsy move Xaw made irritated him as if it had been done deliberately. Brute of an Indian, he repeated to himself, Indian beast, miserable Indian. And to think that there's someone who wants to consider you a person! He should end up here so he can beat his head against the wall like me!

Putting his scruples aside, Padre Manuel reprimanded his student with excessive harshness; he was not adverse to the idea of corporal punishment, which kept suggesting itself.

At times, in an instant of abrupt lucidity, he wondered how it was possible that in such a short time he had already arrived at that point. He was lacking not only in gentleness, as a priest, and in charity, as a simple Christian, but even in the most basic dictates of humanitarianism. Was the demon that corrupted his predecessor *already* at work within him? And Padre Manuel would repeat that *already* as if violence were the inevitable and foreordained end of a process of evolution, as if the only horrible thing about his own case were the speed with which he had reached that end.

But this brief, superficial remorse melted away, exacerbating an anxious need for justification. After all, who was this sacristan? Who could guarantee his good intentions? When he functioned as an interpreter he undoubtedly distorted the words, misinterpreted the sentences. And not in good faith, no, but with the insidious purpose of hindering the priest's plans. As if it weren't enough that those plans were absurd!

And how slowly everything moved! The parishioners were prepared to pay the tithes and other offerings that the Church exacted from them annually; they were prepared to give the necessary alms and to tender money in exchange for the sacraments. Their generosity was all the more laudable in light of their poverty.

But their practice of religion ended there. They remained at the margin of true Catholicism. The priest could not instruct the people of Chamula on their spiritual duties or excite them to confession and penitence because the language barrier interposed itself between him and his flock. Given that barrier, how was he going to persuade them to eliminate some of the rites with which they tainted the church? The Indians would protest in outrage, as they did when Padre Manuel tried to prevent the mayordomo of Santa Margarita from getting drunk every time he had to change the statue's garments in a ceremony that required inebriation.

"The hand of God has forsaken us."

This certainty was affirmed in Padre Manuel after the first Sunday he spent in San Juan.

During the week, the enormous plaza surrounding the church was kept relatively clean because there was not much traffic of men and flocks through it. But on Sunday, everyone, even those from the most remote parts of the region, gathered there very early, doubled over beneath the weight of the goods they wanted to sell or exchange. Without caring about the mud or the incessant rain, they spread the merchandise out on the ground and huddled next to it, abandoning the children to their play. As the hours passed, this multitude could be seen shifting itself like a great animal made ungainly by its own size and weight. The men came and went, aimlessly by now, swaying from the alcohol gulped down at the conclusion of an agreement, leaning on their wives who were just as drunk or on small children who fell, dragged down by the strength of their elders. Mud was everywhere. They thrashed around in it in fist-fights, in lewd acts, splashing blood and filth all about them. Asking the guardians of order for help would only add another element to the general unrest, for the guardian came to deliver blows right and left with his staff of authority. And then he demanded a brimming measure of aguardiente in payment, or else he would haul one of them (anyone, whoever happened to be closest at hand) off to jail.

The project of attracting the Indians to religion and transforming them into conscientious and active members of the Church seemed more unfeasible than ever to Padre Manuel. But although this conviction had ascended by now from the mute depths of his being to his brain, where it took shape in words, those words were not set down in the letter the priest wrote to Don Alfonso. An incomprehensible coyness, a sharp jab of pride rejected them and replaced them with others that were vague and routine.

And there was the letter, already folded, more concrete, more real than the events it did not mention; with a weight and a truth to it that the doubts and misgivings of the person who had written it would never be able to achieve. There it was, ready to be sent. The piece of paper would go off, light and easy, while Padre Manuel was condemned to remain in San Juan, wildly striking out around him with a stick, as in the parties of his childhood when, blindfolded, he tried to break the piñata.

"I never hit it," he thought in sad self-mockery. "It was probably just as well. I'm one of those people who don't know how to duck away from catastrophes in time. If the piñata had broken, it would have fallen on top of me."

With a quick puff, the priest blew out the lamp. He knelt in the dark for his nightly prayers. The persistent murmuring of the brook had become so habitual that he would have noticed it only if it had stopped for a moment.

And suddenly a deafening noise, a torrent of music inundated and shook the atmosphere. A barbaric music, a childish tune repeated to the point of exasperation, weirdly swollen by the organ's enormous, hollow sonority.

After an instant of stupefaction, Padre Manuel stood up. He groped for something to make a light with and when he found nothing he opened the window impatiently. The wind and rain hurled themselves in at him like an ambush of wild beasts. With difficulty, he could see the church in the distance, dimly lit up. He headed there at a run.

The portal yielded to his push. Inside the nave the Indians had congregated. Not simply on their knees, but flat out on the ground, they protected the dying flames of votive candles with the hollow of their hands and moaned, writhing. Others were upright, lurching, already cockeyed from drinking, facing the altars in boorish complaint over wrongs done to them. The crest of

the great wave of music, the childish tune, was continually breaking after sustaining its nothingness for an instant in space. And
then it began again.

Padre Manuel did not even try to scream out a demand that all
of this cease immediately. His voice would be lost in the more
powerful current of sound. With rapid footsteps he went up the
stairs to the choir loft. There, surrounded by religious and civil
officials, was Xaw Ramírez Paciencia, also drunk, playing a Chamula tune on the organ.

"You!" Padre Manuel exclaimed.

In that one syllable were compressed his surprise, his discouragement at the failure of his lessons, his disappointment at seeing
himself uncomprehended and betrayed by the only man he had
any reason to trust, and his indignation at the sacrilege that was
being committed.

"Tell them all to leave this place! The House of the Lord de-
serves to be respected."

Xaw stared at Padre Manuel stupidly. Perhaps he did not understand what he was being ordered to do. His fingers continued
to press down on the same keys again and again and again, without a pause, with a mechanical inevitability.

Padre Manuel's moment of defiance resounded against the
walls of the church and gradually died out. Those who were still
lucid enough to realize that something out of the ordinary was
happening peered up with alert faces. The officials who surrounded Xaw gripped their staffs of leadership threateningly.

The priest did not see that threat when he flung himself at the
sacristan. He lashed out, blind with rage at himself or at Xaw, he
didn't know. With a shout the officials advanced on him.

"Be still!"

The voice brought them to a halt. Padre Manuel heard it from
the ground where he was lying. Now the voice spoke to him.

"Get up, priest."

It was not a request. It was a scornful command.

Painfully, Padre Manuel rose to his feet. He tried to stand erect,
with a serene bearing and gaze. But his face was still convulsed
with anger.

"Who are you?" he finally managed to ask the man who had

spoken. At the same time he made an effort to fix the features in his memory, features chiseled as if by fire or by the blows of an ax in a simple, tough material.

"I am Pedro González Winiktón, the former judge."

The voice corresponded to the face. Firm, decided, manly. And he had spoken in correct and fluent Spanish, without the flute-like intonation, the "sing-song" Ladinos loved to make fun of.

Padre Manuel and Winiktón remained face to face for a moment, examining each other as if each wanted to decipher in the other's expression whether they would be allies or enemies. Two equal forces were recognizing each other.

All at once Father Manuel broke the spell. He turned on his heel and left.

CHAPTER XI

WHEN A SMALL TOWN (and Ciudad Real was a small town, despite its name, its pretensions and its history) sees a stranger arriving, a shiver of misgiving, curiosity and expectation runs through its inhabitants.

But who comes to Ciudad Real, a place so remote, so far off of all beaten tracks? Travelling salesmen come, more out of habit than for the amount of business they can do here. They arrive with their bulging briefcases, their air of efficiency, their needless haste, their false assurances. The visit makes a little stir in the ooze of commerce. When the day is over, the travelling salesman raises a racket in the cantinas, provokes disputes with the men, flusters the girls. When he departs, he leaves behind him an unsettled debt, an insult left hanging, a precarious virginity. Or he carries off, clinging to him like a bramble, a desperate spinster for whom the adventure comes to its end in the next town.

Government employees also come to set up house in the town for a while. Their prestige is ambiguous, their rank difficult to determine with any precision. The honorableness of their origins is doubted; their situation as salaried employees is looked down on. But still their habits are imitated, their ideas are feared, their peculiarities are admired.

Fernando Ulloa was a government employee. His mission was to map out the region of Chamula and distribute plots of communally owned land called ejidos to the indigenous communities; in other words, he was to establish on the large landed estates the regime of small properties that was required by the law.

Fernando Ulloa's arrival in Ciudad Real alarmed the owners of the vast fincas, who dusted off documents, consulted their cunning lawyers and held long, mysterious meetings.

How to make Ulloa forget his duty? How to transform him into an ally, a servant of the landowners' interests? Opinion was unanimous: by bribery. Fernando Ulloa had no asset but his profession, no income but his salary. His shameful poverty, concealed by a thousand ingenious tricks, suddenly showed through in the threadbare elbow of a shirt, the indiscreet shine at the knees of his trousers. To round out his budget, hadn't he agreed to teach a course in mathematics at Ciudad Real's Instituto Superior?

It was true that Fernando Ulloa had no children. But his wife did not appear to be one of those self-abnegating, long-suffering women. She had to be an expensive wife.

She had to be because Julia Acevedo was beautiful, though not in the same way as Coleta ladies, who were very vain about the whiteness of their skin, sign of a noble ancestry, and the abundance of their flesh, evidence of a financial well-being that enabled them to lead a life in which gluttony and idleness remained the supreme luxuries.

No, Julia Acevedo was different. Tall, slender, agile. A female silhouette walking alone through the streets; a voice, a laugh, a sonorous presence rising above the whispers; an insolently red mane of hair, often left unbound in the wind. Nothing more was necessary to make the devout women, pale from years of enclosure, cross themselves behind their windows; to make the men dream and chomp at the bit of their respectability; to make the old people offer words of advice and predict catastrophes.

Oblivious to this image of herself, which she would not have recognized, Julia was bored. Housework had never interested her and the satisfactions of her life with Fernando were so precarious that Julia sought distractions beyond herself and her home, a clamor that would make her giddy and keep her from thinking about her problems and disappointments.

After being abandoned by her husband (a neglectful and uncouth Spaniard, or Gachupín as Mexicans call them), Julia Acevedo's mother had attempted to replace the paternal authority with her own hardheadedness and lack of tenderness. She was obsessed by the idea of preserving her daughters (there were three of them, to top off her misfortunes) from the failure she had endured; she wanted to make them into women who could earn a living by working, who could dispense with a husband's support. That only became possible, in her opinion, by learning a lucrative profession.

Without considering the girls' individual aptitudes, Julia's mother enrolled them in the Instituto Politécnico, since the scarcity of their means barred them from the private schools or universities. Julia's sisters, more docile or perhaps more clear-sighted, satisfactorily completed their pharmaceutical studies and both now held positions that were modest but had good prospects for the future.

Julia, however. . . . Her intelligence was as quick as it was fragile, her enthusiasm as indefatigable as it was voluble. At first she had attended classes, hoping that the teacher would say something that would provide a solution to her inner conflicts, illuminate the confusions she struggled with or confer meaning upon her acts. She quickly grew disenchanted and absences began to accumulate next to her name in the class lists.

Despite her mother's scolding, Julia took up with a group of young people slightly older than her whose main preoccupation was politics. For long hours they discussed theoretical and tactical matters with an avid and boisterous passion that squeezed every subject dry and then tossed it aside like a useless piece of rind.

Julia listened, attentive, without any notion of the time that was passing and without caring about her obligations. She became familiar with many terms—social justice, equal distribution of wealth, penetration of foreign capital, agrarian reform—without having any clear understanding of their meaning. She was one of those women for whom the world, her own destiny and even her personality do not reveal themselves or take on a definite shape except through amorous contact with a man.

The brief and fruitless adventures in which Julia hazarded her adolescence lost all importance when she met Fernando Ulloa.

What had first attracted her? His manly attitude, his prestige as the leader of the group? Or the sharp clarity with which she could see herself reflected in another person's consciousness, the lucid response to all of her perplexities?

Julia's mother was opposed to a love affair that could easily have been transient, but her opposition only succeeded in precipitating events. One night Julia packed her bags and ensconced herself in Fernando's room because she "couldn't take it anymore."

Fernando, in a burst of romanticism, decided to stand his ground against all objections to the situation. Among the young people in the group (all of them from good families), the pair of lovers enjoyed an ascendancy no one dared dispute for the daring way they had taken control of their own lives.

Julia's mother swallowed her pride and pleaded with her to legalize her position by getting married. Julia refused. A married woman, a respectable bourgeois lady. . . . where would that leave her aura of the convention-defying heroine? Moreover, she was beginning to notice signs of bitterness in Fernando, unavowed, unconscious, which she did not want to aggravate.

After a few chaotic and carefree weeks, Fernando realized that they had nothing left to pawn and no other means of borrowing money. It was time to face up to his responsibilities. He gave up his student ways and found a job in Tepic.

The pettiness of provincial life wounded Julia deeply. It wasn't just the poverty and the lack of intellectual stimulus and suitable friends: the adventure had lost its novelistic quality and become routine, and the criteria of the people here were very different from those of the group of students at the Instituto Polytécnico. In Tepic, society frowned on the lovers, mocked them, left an empty space around them.

This reaction, which Julia hadn't expected, disconcerted her. Gradually she began to grow colder and her impulsiveness diminished as she yielded to her adversaries' perspective. She became petulant, was always on the lookout for grievances, and no explanation, no apology would appease her for very long.

What did she want? Fernando would ask in exasperation, to get married? to leave? Julia didn't answer. How could she talk about the urgent, implacable need that had suddenly awoken within her to wield respectability, wealth and power? It was so sordid, and nevertheless for Julia it was the only thing that was true.

Fernando fell silent as well, offended by her tenacious silence, vaguely suspecting what was now expected of him and ill-disposed ever to concede it. Why sacrifice himself once more? This tension between the two of them, these occasional outbursts of anger and tears, this tacit reproachfulness were the only compensation for his past generosity.

Julia, who was becoming irritated at the certainty of having disappointed Fernando, understood she could no longer rely on him. To achieve her ambitions she had no other tool but her own shrewdness. In Tepic, she had lost the match; she had been marked, once and for all, by the unfavorable judgment of society. But she had gained experience. Somewhere else she could use her wits to reach a position in which she could not be humiliated, in which others would revere and even fear her. She dreamed of the day Fernando would be transferred.

She had to wait two years. But Julia didn't waste the time. From the distance fixed by the disdain of those around her, she observed the habits and fashions of those she had exalted as models: the aristocrats of Tepic.

Julia polished her manners and applied herself conscientiously to the task of erasing the style her middle-class neighborhood had imprinted on her. She retained just the dose of insolence necessary to assess the defects and vices of those she was imitating, thus keeping herself from falling into an annihilating vertigo of admiration. In a final stroke of inspiration she used her father to invent a genealogy of noble Spanish ancestors whose accent she practiced when she was alone.

When the couple arrived in Ciudad Real, Julia could have a reasonable amount of confidence in her eventual triumph. Her look and her bearing were, she believed, those of a lady.

Nevertheless, the Coletos, with the wiliness of provincials who are always afraid their good faith will be abused and who would rather make a mistake because they're too clever than be right out of ingenuousness, demonstrated a certain reserve. Their greetings were extremely friendly, their conversation interlaced with a great deal of flattery, but they never left open a chink through which intimacy could filter.

Leonardo Cifuentes seemed to be the only one who was accessible. Julia was not unaware of his motives and was inclined to take advantage of them. But she feared the drawbacks of an indiscreet passion and the rumors it would give rise to. She sought to create more solid, more acceptable links.

The only family to whom Julia Acevedo had been presented up to now was Leonardo's. She had, therefore, a pretext for frequenting them, and it suited her to do so in order to silence idle talk.

Slowly, cautiously, Julia penetrated the domestic orbit of the

Cifuentes family. First came the parlor, with its demand for distance and ceremony; then, when the weather permitted, the galleries. The ferns nodded, the palm trees spread out their fronds, the climbing vines hung down. At her feet, the tiles were seeping with dampness and the roof's crosspieces were suspended above her.

But though Leonardo was always very attentive, Julia found Isabel, for all her courtesy, inaccessible. Isabel's curiosity—her only motive for making a momentary overture to the stranger—was satisfied by two or three not very explicit (and of course not very accurate) allusions to Julia's past and an unremarkable commentary on her current situation.

In the end, Isabel's predominant trait was her pride as a lady of Ciudad Real who disdains all interaction except with her equals and who recognizes no superiors. At every step of the conversation, she found ways to mark the differences that set her apart from the other woman. And Isabel's unfamiliarity with the world kept her from being aware of the deficiencies in her own polish, the limitations of her experience and the almost nonexistent development of her faculties. She was a Zebadúa, and that fact alone placed her in a category no criticism could reach; she was one whose exaltation required no further effort, whose level of perfection required no further discipline. Zebadúa. The name was a talisman, and anyone born in possession of it was no longer in need of any further quality to add to his or her person.

"Zebadúa?" La Alazana once commented. "What a strange name! I had never heard it before coming to Ciudad Real."

Isabel shot her a pitying glance. Naturally she hadn't, since that code was not part of the common knowledge of the coarse and vulgar public. An acquaintance with it was reserved for the select few. But in Ciudad Real, no one who had any claim to being anyone was unaware of the significance of the name Zebadúa.

Because of this simple and irretrievable lapse, Isabel placed Julia on a plane of absolute inferiority. Therefore she could permit herself to reject the friendship that this parvenu of ambiguous aspect and reputation was offering her.

With her eyes half-closed—aloof, bored—Isabel listened to the other woman's picturesque anecdotes, the little witticisms Julia tried to distract her with. But she was too old, she had suffered too much to be seduced by the chimes of laughter that rang out around her. How greatly she preferred solitude, a monologue with her familiar shadows, reviewing the minutia of her misfortunes.

Jealousy was the electric shock that provoked the corpse's last spasm. After all, the wife reasoned, what can this woman take from me? I've had no part of Leonardo for many years. If someone's going to get some use out of him, what do I care who she is? Wasn't my husband chasing around after Indian girls like a colt on the loose? Now he'll calm down, he'll have a regular querida. Let him have his fill of her. Is he making me look ridiculous in the eyes of Ciudad Real? Someone else looks even more ridiculous, and he's not complaining. Go ahead, Leonardo, be as shameless as you want, squander your money on this little whim of yours. You know very well that at the end of the day when you're flat broke you'll have no right to expect anything from me.

But while these arguments did their part to appease the rebellions and fears of Isabel's self-love, they left a distaste, a bitter memory that was certainly not conducive to a sympathetic understanding between the two women.

"There's nothing to be done with that woman," Julia had to accept in discouragement. But other ways of breaching the barrier remained to be examined. For example, Doña Mercedes Solórzano. From the beginning she had exhibited a loyalty to Julia that was perhaps too conspicuous to be sincere. But even if it were sincere, her status as a servant, the lowliness of the functions she performed made Julia's interaction with her a double-edged sword. Julia tried to conceal that interaction while maintaining a hidden complicity with the procuress because she was afraid—and rightly so—of making an enemy of her.

The news of an inhabitual presence in the house reached Idolina's bedroom. A visitor in the Cifuentes house? How is such a thing possible? How did she get past Leonardo's mistrust and Isabel's standoffish nature?

"She came to inform on me," thought Idolina, who was unable even to imagine that other people established relationships with each other or had interests of which she was not the crux.

Fear of being given away obsessed her. She saw herself unmasked, overwhelmed by her mother's reproaches and her stepfather's insults; she saw herself made a laughingstock and felt incapable of enduring so many humiliations. She decided to die.

But when Julia was standing in front of her, smiling without malice, seeming as unaware of their first meeting as if it had never happened, Idolina's fears were calmed, though in secret she felt disappointed. It wasn't until later, in their daily conversations, that she began to tense into a state of alert. She noticed that every time she complained about some ailment, every time she tried to take refuge from unpleasant obligations in her illness, Julia would stare at her with such an ironic look on her face that a cold sweat would run down Idolina's back. Julia opened her lips. Was she going to give away her secret? No, she was pleading. Her entreaty didn't quite veil the threat that was implicit in the authoritarian tone of her voice, a threat meant to force the girl to give up her invalid's privileges and concern herself a little with other people's convenience.

"What do you mean you don't want to eat?" Julia remonstrated. "No, it isn't that you feel worse. It's because you spend the whole long day in bed. No one would be hungry after that. But if you would just get a little exercise. . . ."

"Exercise?" Isabel said in amazement, gesturing toward the bed where her daughter lay.

"Idolina, you know perfectly well that what I'm asking isn't impossible. I only want you to show your will power, put a little of yourself into it."

The girl nodded, pale with fear.

"Look, you could start by sitting up. No, not in your bed against that pile of pillows. In a chair: sit up straight, like this."

"She's going to get very tired, Julia."

"As soon as she gets tired she'll rest. We aren't here to torture her, are we? Let's see: Idolina, lean against me to get up. No, leave the others alone: this is between us. Hang on to my arm. Come on, a little tighter. And your feet, solid on the ground."

"I can't," the girl moaned.

"I've seen you more determined on other occasions."

The allusion to the scene in the attic was enough to make Idolina submit to Julia's orders. She tried to walk—the chair was two steps away—feeling the fictional support La Alazana was offering her vanish.

"You see?" Julia exclaimed, triumphant. "It's just a matter of deciding you want to. Now, rest a while. Tomorrow we'll move the chair a little further away."

Isabel witnessed these sessions with a surprise that was somewhat disturbing. She had always wanted, or had always believed she wanted, for her daughter to be cured. And now that the cure was becoming a reality, it was turning out to be difficult for her to adapt to the new situation. Idolina, healthy: the two words that had appeared contradictory for so many years were now joining together to form a certainty that Isabel did not want to name.

"What's wrong?" Leonardo asked her. "You don't look very glad about it to me."

Isabel blushed, as if she had been caught in a guilty moment. Her mouth filled up with a tumult of rationales. It's just that Idolina's improvement is so sudden, she would say, the effort Julia demands from her is so inconsiderate . . . all this apparent progress could suddenly end in a shattering relapse.

"Relapse into what?" Cifuentes replied. "It's all pure sham. What's happening is that this time my crafty stepdaughter has met her match."

So it appeared. When Julia was there, Idolina didn't dare allow herself an explosion of temper, a fit of weeping, a paroxysm of restiveness. She humbly sought out the foreign woman's eyes, and as long as her visits lasted she was docile in following Julia's suggestions and even tried to anticipate them.

Idolina's soul, beleaguered by anguish and helplessness, gave in—with no more than a confused and ineffectual resistance—to La Alazana's influence. And how effusively friendship welled up in that arid breast! No demonstration of affection seemed sufficient, any demand was easy to fulfill and there was no declaration of loyalty that the girl was not quick to swear. But in the same way, how painful it was to discover that her new friend had other affections, other interests, other obligations, even! Wide-eyed, Idolina followed the play of Julia's features as she was talking about herself, her past, her plans. With bitterness, she confirmed the insignificant role she played in the other woman's life. At those moments she feigned indifference but was desperately anxious to arouse Julia's compassion and be consoled.

"Don't play games with me," she once pleaded with Julia.

No, La Alazana wasn't playing games. She knew she could use the teenager's submission as a weapon against the older members of the family. Stirring up the girl's animosity toward her family at some moments, her thirst for affection at others, Julia was securing a control over her that neither Isabel nor the nana dared dispute.

In their interminable conversations, Julia encouraged Idolina to confide in her. At first she was reluctant; it was painful for the girl to recall her years of isolation. But to satisfy Julia's curiosity, she spoke. Little by little her recollections, disjointed ramblings in which everything came out in a jumble, became bolder and more abundant. Childhood anecdotes, tiny details of her long enclosure, the fantasies of a silly girl. But when she mentioned her father's death, Idolina's voice took on an adult gravity.

"They killed him, she and my stepfather."

"Dios mío! How horrible!"

Encouraged by Julia's apparent credulity, Idolina's imaginings took on the shape and consistency of truths. The girl succeeded in convincing herself that she had witnessed the crime and, what was more, that she had heard the criminals planning their exploit and congratulating each other on its success. La Alazana listened carefully, with well-timed gasps. And Idolina's satisfaction at appearing before Julia as the protagonist of an extraordinary episode was great. That fact alone established a certain equality between the two of them which enabled the younger woman to give herself over wholeheartedly to the manifestations of a feeling that grew ever stronger and more absorbing.

"You won't regret having trusted me," Julia said once. "I'm not looking for anything but your happiness."

"What is my happiness?" Idolina asked.

"You're no different from anyone else, little one. Why do you keep pretending to be sick? The only thing you'll achieve by that is for your mother and stepfather to get bored with the farce and put an end to it."

Idolina smiled with a trace of bitterness.

"I've known that for a while now; they want to get rid of me, kill me, the same way they killed my father."

"Don't be an idiot, little one. As if it were so easy!"

"You don't know them. They're capable of anything."

"But you don't have your hands tied behind your back, and what's more you're not alone. We'll defend ourselves."

"How will we defend ourselves? My father couldn't and he was a man."

"They betrayed him. But you know what to expect from them, you're already on guard."

"I'm afraid, Julia," Idolina whispered.

"Of who? Leonardo? He's nothing but a big oaf."

"And her?"

"In her own way she's weak too. She says she loves you. Fool her, make her think you love her back; that way she'll stay calm."

"I'm afraid," Idolina repeated, trembling. "I want to go away from here."

"Me, too. We're rotting away in Ciudad Real."

Yes, they would leave. Now, for the first time, Idolina was certain that freedom, her freedom, was possible. She had to win it and the only way would be to follow Julia's orders to the letter. Did Julia want Idolina to eat her food? Very well, Idolina wouldn't leave a single crumb on the plate, though it still repelled her to eat so much and, even more than that, to admit to others, to her mother, that she was hungry. Julia forbade her to lie down during the day. From the chair's rigidity, the girl gazed nostalgically at the fluffy pillows, the sheets invitingly folded back. But she refused to give in. When the fatigue of her position grew unbearable, she stood up and, rejecting the nana's support, tried out a few steps across the room. Alone—at last she was able to walk alone! She did it in front of Isabel, her eyes brilliant with defiance.

"You see?" she exclaimed, shaken with rage. "My will is more powerful than yours. I've turned out to be the stronger one."

Isabel left the room, wounded by the tone of the words, though she didn't understand their scope or their significance.

Absorbed in their confabulations, Idolina and Julia forgot what was going on around them. But Isabel was attentive to the rumors in the street, the gossip the city was bubbling over with.

Idolina's recovery had been so swift and in some way so inexplicable that it could not have failed to elicit comment. Most of the reactions were malicious, and Isabel waited almost impatiently for the opportunity to convey them to Julia.

The opportunity didn't take long to present itself. Julia came and went in the Cifuentes house as if she were its owner. But her favorite place was the sewing room. It was so nice there, the atmosphere was so warm and protected. The furniture was inviting; it wasn't severe like the furnishings in the parlor. And the carpet, worn from long use, had lost its colors so aristocratically. Isabel rightly preferred the room as well. She spent hours there bent over her embroidery frame, making tiny stitches until the sun's light dimmed. The servants had been instructed not to enter the room unless they were expressly called for. But those orders didn't matter to Julia, who did as she pleased.

Isabel knew how to avenge the intrusion. In her sly Coleta way, very smooth, very sweet, very calm, she delivered one pinprick after another to the vanity, the pride, every bit of the vulnerable, sensitive surface the other woman exposed.

"The people of Ciudad Real are incomparable," Isabel exclaimed exaggeratedly. "There's no one like them for coming up with nicknames."

"In small towns there's no other form of entertainment," Julia yawned.

"But here they're really something special; they don't spare anyone, not the morning star itself. Why don't you try to guess the nickname they've given you?"

"Who?"

"You."

"I don't have the slightest idea."

"Promise me you won't be upset; it's just that they're so terrible. . . ."

"All right, go ahead. I can see you're burning up to tell me. . . ."

With a little laugh, Isabel agreed to pronounce the syllables, very slowly.

"They call you La Alazana, the roan."

"Alazana? Why?"

"It must be the color of your hair. It's what they call the mares that are that color."

The taunting insinuation made every plebeian element in Julia's soul churn. But with an effort to smile, she pretended the joke had amused her and Isabel pretended to believe her. The conversation went on like that.

"The doctors don't understand how my daughter has recovered."

"They don't understand how she got sick, either. They aren't very quick off the mark, those doctors. Their brains must be full of cobwebs."

"And they're the ones with the advanced degrees. Imagine what other people think, common people, the vulgar, as they're called."

"What do they think?"

"That what happened with Idolina was something to do with witchcraft. That you have a pact with the devil."

"Of course, a roan mare is capable of committing any atrocity."

"You're not going to believe me, Julia, you're going to laugh because it's really the limit. A group of ladies—and the most prominent ladies in Ciudad Real—went to talk to His Excellency Don Alfonso Cañaveral, in order to find out what the truth of the matter is."

"It's odd that the bishop didn't ask me to make a statement."

"He came to talk to me."

"And what did you tell him?"

Isabel raised her eyes from her work and looked squarely at her interlocutor.

"I don't care what means you used to cure Idolina. For me, it's enough to see her good and healthy."

But Isabel was very careful not to say she believed Julia was innocent of the supernatural machinations she was accused of. Her reticence enraged the foreign woman.

"Well, when they ask you you can tell them that what the girl suffered from was fear."

"Fear?"

"This house is so big, so dark! At night the shadows of the trees in the garden look like souls in Purgatory. And then there are the stories the servants tell next to the fire, stories about terror, apparitions . . . murders."

Isabel was uncertain where Julia was headed. But the last word put her on her guard.

"There was no murder here. Idolina's father died in an accident."

"Yes," Julia conceded, "an accident. Did the authorities investigate?"

"Why? It never occurred to anyone that there was any irregularity."

Isabel tried to hide her unease. But her breathing had quickened.

"We're getting off the subject, Julia."

"Let's get back to it: fear of this house, of its stories, of the dead and the living, paralyzed Idolina, nailed her to her bed for years."

"But how absurd to torment herself like that over something she imagined, a hallucination!"

"A suspicion, Isabel."

"She couldn't speak? She couldn't tell me, her mother, what was frightening her? How could she think I wouldn't help her?"

"Perhaps Idolina didn't have enough trust in you."

"Yet in you, someone she hardly knows. . . ."

"Does it bother you that it was me?"

"I'm going to seem ungrateful, but I want to be sincere. It pains me to see my daughter, so surly, so rebellious with me, melting like wax in someone else's hands. What secret potion did you give her in order to take possession of her will?"

"It's a secret," La Alazana said maliciously. "A secret she and I share."

"I'll never succeed in deciphering my daughter's character. I thought it was enough to love her, pamper her."

"Idolina complains that she didn't receive the tenderness from you that she had the right to expect."

"She doesn't understand that we women weren't born to live alone or ignored. We're worth very little without a man's respect."

"Is that why you married again?"

Isabel lowered her face, confused.

"I don't know. . . . It was so many years ago. . . ."

"Children have a tremendous memory. Idolina says she remembers everything."

"And what is everything? The inventions of her jealous mind!"

"Blood will tell, Isabel. You're jealous, too."

"Me? Of you, perhaps?"

"Of me. Because of Idolina."

Isabel suddenly stiffened.

"You haven't had any children, have you?"

Julia hadn't wanted them. In order to give herself fully to Fernando. In order not to tie him down with yet another knot. And also because she feared her own enslavement. No, it wasn't fear of the pain or the danger. Wasn't an abortion worse than a birth? Nevertheless, she aborted. Deliberately. And with so little remorse that the need to share her secret, even with Fernando, had never troubled her.

"But imagine what a mother's love is."

Julia shrugged in a gesture of obliviousness, indifference.

"For a child, one is capable of the greatest sacrifices."

"But why generalize? We would do better to speak of a specific case. Of your case, Isabel."

"I'm not an example. I was never indispensable or even necessary for Idolina to go on living. A nobody, an Indian, took over my place from the beginning. Now it's you."

Isabel made a desperate effort to appear in control of herself. But her emotions were overwhelming her. She looked at Julia with insecure, vanquished eyes, shipwrecked. Out of the contradictory waves of greed and disappointment, lustfulness and remorse, Isabel had rescued no more than the salt of her white hair, the net of wrinkles across her forehead, her cheeks, her lips. Julia took pity on this mask of defeat and made a movement as if to erase it. Isabel dodged the caress as if it had wounded her.

"Don't sing your victory song so quickly, Julia. Just so you don't get too proud of yourself, I'll tell you that the woman you pushed out of Idolina's heart was not her mother. It was the nana, the Indian, Teresa."

"Yes, I've seen how she takes care of her."

Isabel made a gesture to show Julia that she hadn't fully understood her words.

"It isn't a recent thing. The roots are very old. When Idolina was born, I had no milk. They wrung my breasts, they made me drink gunpowder dissolved in liquor—

"How revolting!"

"—and it was all useless. The baby was already hoarse from crying so much. She was hungry and I couldn't give her anything to eat."

Isabel passed both hands through her hair, as if to smooth it down.

"We were living on my first husband's finca. The middle of nowhere. The rainy season had trapped us there and my time came. It was my first child, and without anyone to give me advice, I had to work things out as best I could. A doctor? Not even to be dreamed of! Among the Indians there are some experienced midwives and one of them took care of me. I got through labor without much difficulty. The problems began afterwards. Idolina was crying from hunger."

There was a pause Julia didn't want to break with any comment or question.

"I knew that not far from there was another woman who had just had a baby: Teresa Entzín López. I had her brought to me. I offered her the Virgin's pearls to act as a wet nurse to Idolina. She didn't want to. She was skinny, weak. She claimed her milk wouldn't be enough for two mouths. She even fled from the finca. But I ordered the vaqueros to find her. They scoured the mountain as if it were hunting season and found Teresa holed up in a cave with her baby in her arms. The only way to get her back to the big house was to drag her."

Isabel stopped, suffocated by the intensity of the memory. The she added.

"And I was on my own through all of this. My husband had looked for any pretext to leave, to get away from the cry of hunger that was tearing apart my soul."

"And Teresa agreed to stay?"

"Agreement had nothing to do with it! 'You've made me angry,' I told her. 'Now we'll have to come to an understanding by force.' In the sheepfold next to the big house there was a set of stocks. I had her put there, day and night. And she fooled all of us. To persuade us to free her, she pretended to be willing to do as she was told. Later I discovered that she was giving Idolina less milk in order to give some to her own daughter. I had to separate them."

The story seemed to end there. Nevertheless, Julia wanted to know.

"And the other baby?"

"She died."

An expression of such surprise and disapproval appeared on Julia's face that Isabel was forced to justify herself fiercely.

"And why shouldn't she die? What was so important about her? Teresa's no more than an Indian. Her daughter was an Indian, too."

"And you condemn her for her race?"

"I didn't say that," Isabel snapped. "You foreigners come from another world and don't understand what goes on in Ciudad Real. I've heard what Don Fernando preaches: that we Coletos are savages, that we treat the Indians worse than animals. But it isn't true, por Dios! We baptize everyone with the same water, and there is no money or color or language that will set us apart from each other in the eyes of the One who will measure our worth in the end. No, it isn't that we disdain them; they're the ones who debase themselves. You don't know their ways. I've lived for years among Indians. And I swear I have seen this with my own eyes: when a ewe is lost and the lamb is left helpless without a mother, the women take care of it. They nurse it, even if they have to take the breast away from their own babies, even if hunger finishes them off. And my child, a Ladina, was going to be worth less than an animal is worth to them?"

La Alazana hesitated before answering and Isabel wanted to finish her argument.

"So, from a distance and in cold blood, someone like you can be outraged, can gasp. But trapped in that situation, listening to Idolina cry, hour after hour, inconsolable, you don't hesitate. I did what was within my power to do. And in my conscience I did the right thing."

Isabel had worked herself up. Her pale skin was inflamed with purplish blotches.

"And there you have the proof that I didn't do anything wrong: Teresa herself, who hasn't left us since then."

"Did she have anywhere else to go?"

"All right, it wasn't out of gratitude but out of convenience, as always. Teresa wanted to go back to her husband and he met her with a club. According to him, Teresa was guilty of killing his daughter. He wanted to punish her. She was afraid she'd be killed and took refuge in the big house. When we came back to Ciudad Real, Teresa came with us. She went from being a wet nurse to being a porter. The idea was not to separate her from Idolina, whom she had grown very fond of."

"She showed it when Idolina was sick."

"That was later. I've never been in favor of having children grow up tied to an Indian woman's tzec. They teach them all kinds of nonsense. Idolina, I'm ashamed to say, learned to speak their language before speaking Spanish. And as long as we kept Teresa nearby, trying to straighten her out was like trying to carry water in a basket. So we thought it best to send Teresa to work for another family. But when Idolina became so ill and there was no other servant who could keep up the pace, we brought her back."

After Isabel had confided in her, Julia began paying attention to the Indian woman. She searched the impassive face in vain for the traces of an episode so cruel, a generosity so immoderate, an abjection so profound. She saw nothing more than an almost mineral oblivion, an inhuman resignation. In the end, she lost interest in Teresa. Occasionally, she happened to see her carrying out her tasks in silence. Since her presence was no longer indispensable, she almost never appeared at Idolina's side. Who was there to notice this or, having noticed it, to be concerned about it? She must be drudging away in some corner, since there was never any lack of work for her to do. And since Teresa had a very special aptitude for passing unperceived, several days went by before anyone noticed that the nana had deserted the Cifuentes house.

CHAPTER XII

AT NIGHTFALL (and in San José Chiuptik, nightfall is foretold by the thick fog that covers the valleys) the flocks return from the countryside and the men from their toils. Here and there a small flame flickers, and when there is no rain a bonfire of ocote pine crackles in front of the chapel, diffusing its reddish glow into the atmosphere.

Groups of Indians, numb with cold, huddle around the fire. Their huts do not provide enough protection against the weather so they seek this brief, fleeting heat, company and conversation. Someone takes out a cane flute, clumsily carved. The music a shepherd uses to make his long solitudes bearable, the stammer of a race that has lost its memory. The others listen for a while. At a distance, the woman who is grinding corn suspends her work, lost in a reverie that frees her for an instant from fatigue and mind-numbing routine.

But at the first gusts of wind heralding the storm, the flute falls silent, the groups disperse, the fire goes out. Only the bell, left to the wind's caprices, continues to ring meaninglessly.

Quick steps in wide hallways, hands that hurry to close doors, fasten windows shut. A few minutes later the storm howls without witnesses around this massive construction in stone, mortar and iron, the hacienda's big house.

The horsemen who are making their way through darkness and flashes of lightning enter the space between the group of huts without having their presence given away by the barking of a dog or the vigilance of a guard.

"We were lucky to get to a place where Christian people can receive us, patrón. We can spend the night here."

Fernando Ulloa made an affirmative gesture. A small gush of water ran off of the brim of his rubberized hat.

"What place is this?"

"San José Chiuptik, Don Leonardo Cifuentes' finca."

The speaker, Rubén Martínez, the engineer's young assistant, spurred his horse on. He knew where to find the lock on the main

135

gate and how to open it. After that, he yielded the lead to his boss.

"Ave María! May we lodge here for the night?"

An Indian leaned out from the kitchen with a pine torch in his hand. He was too far away to hear the question. The horses moved forward, slipping on the flagstones and accompanied by a furious, belated barking.

"It's best if you get down here, patrón. I'll take the horses to the stable."

Fernando Ulloa felt too tired to argue. He obeyed. His waterproof poncho hampered his movements.

The Indian with the light in his hand had reached them. He helped the engineer up the steps of the gallery. They went to the widest door and knocked. When it opened, a familiar silhouette stood out against the lighted doorway.

"But it's my friend, Don Fernando Ulloa!" Leonardo Cifuentes exclaimed, cordial and surprised. "This way, ingeniero, careful, we don't want you to trip. Please do me the honor of taking possession of our house."

Fernando stammered out excuses for the untimeliness of his arrival. But the other man was guiding him into a room that seemed enormous because of the height of the roof, the thickness of the walls and the scantiness of the furniture; in the middle of all that space, a brazier was burning.

"This is a very fortunate coincidence, ingeniero. I knew you were passing through here and I meant to invite you to spend a few days with us."

"Thank you very much, Don Leonardo; I wouldn't have wanted to trouble you, but night fell and we got lost; instead of going to San Juan Chamula, where we were headed, we ended up here, I'm not sure how."

"A fortunate coincidence that gives me the opportunity to take care of you and serve you. Leave your poncho over there, anywhere. Please make yourself comfortable. In the meantime, if you'll excuse me, I'll go and give orders for your room and your dinner to be prepared."

Leonardo went directly to the kitchen. The assistant was there, having a cup of coffee by the fire.

"What kind of time is this to arrive, Rubén? I'd almost given up on you."

"We had to go around and around in circles. Our blessed engineer is mistrustful and finds his way with some device he takes out of his pocket. But in the darkness and the rain, he got confused."

Leonardo seemed to accept this and handed the young man some coins. Then, turning toward the servants whose faces could hardly be seen among the smoke and shadows, he said a few phrases in Tzotzil that made them spring into action. When he left, he was followed by a mestiza girl of uncertain age, one of those women who are worn down not by time but by hard work and deprivation.

"The bedroom is ready now," she whispered.

She had done her very best: flowers on the table, fresh pine needles on the floor, filtered water in a glass jug.

"Good," Leonardo said curtly. "Now make sure they don't see you. It would be best for you to sleep at the home of the administrator or one of the vaqueros."

The woman bowed with the docility of a whipped dog that doesn't understand the mechanism of its punishments and fears them. Nevertheless, she hadn't stopped smiling. Her smile, in which numerous and unnecessary gold teeth gleamed, had an involuntary, sinister quality. She covered her head with a faded shawl and ran into the darkness.

The dinner was abundant: chicken broth and baked chicken, beans, plantains, eggs. Fernando had to refuse some of the dishes, against Leonardo's insistence. He was done in. He told his host he would be grateful if dinner could be brief and he could be taken to his room quickly.

He slept without feeling the hardness of the bed or the thinness of the blankets. He was awakened very early by the jabbering of the chickens and the bellowing of animals in the corral. Distant, insistent and obsessive, the sound of the rain could also be heard.

"You can't be thinking of leaving today," Leonardo told him when he saw him dressed for the road.

"I have appointments in Ciudad Real," Fernando responded.

"I wish it were possible to go in all this mud! But you're running the risk of getting stuck. What do you think, Rubén, my friend?"

The assistant exaggerated the dangers of the journey. But Fernando wasn't listening. Why had Cifuentes used the familiar "tú" when he addressed Rubén? How had such an intimacy sprung up between them, given the inequality in their age and social standing?

"The bad weather doesn't look as if it will last. By tomorrow morning it will have cleared up."

Leonardo and Rubén were obviously right. How ridiculous to suspect that there was some agreement between them to keep Fernando in San José Chiuptik!

At breakfast, leftovers from the night before were served. On a ranch, luxury consists in abundance, not delicacy or variety.

"Please forgive me for not taking very good care of you, ingeniero. Where there are no women, a man has to adjust to a certain amount of discomfort."

Leonardo had touched on a topic that made him eloquent and voluble in his resentment. The women of Ciudad Real, he complained, don't think they are sullying themselves by marrying a rancher. On the contrary: the ranchers have more solid capital and a more noble ancestry than the merchants. But when it comes to going with the husband and living on the ranch, then the thing becomes more difficult. The family raises its voice to the skies. What humiliation! What scandal! The parents didn't spend all that money educating their daughters (piano, embroidery and fine pastry-making) only to see them holed up on the mountain. And for their part, the daughters weep and make sure they're always pregnant or nursing so no one will dare ask them to do anything that goes against their whims.

"And a man can't sacrifice his interests to be tied to his wife's skirts. She wants her comforts, too, and you can't just shovel money out of the ground. So we come to the ranch alone."

"There must be some men who are unwilling to resign themselves to that."

Leonardo smiled as if to himself.

"If you don't want to resign yourself, you make your own arrangements."

Fernando did not encourage further confidences. The rancher had to keep speaking in general terms.

"A wife always has her place and no one will take it away from her. But with a querida there's no need to beat around the bush; she takes what she's given and thanks you for it. It's easier to live like that, isn't it, ingeniero?"

Leonardo's feint could have one of two consequences: either he would find out whether he was right about Julia's being Fernando's mistress and not his wife, or he would provoke a violent reaction. He wasn't afraid of that: violence was his element. But neither outcome occurred. Fernando nodded distractedly. Was he the kind of cynic who controls his own passions in order to profit from the passions of others? Leonardo imagined a thousand traps around him, a thousand possibilities for extortion that his provincial astuteness was unable to envision. He would try, then, to gain some ground, to bring Fernando over to his side, to involve him in his own plans to such a degree that it would no longer suit him to go against them.

They rose from the table and went into the main room.

"It's a pity we can't go out to the fields. I'd like you to see the ranch. I don't want to boast, but. . . ."

Leonardo hesitated, torn between his desire to show off and his wariness as a landowner. Fernando took advantage of the pause.

"In any case, I'll have to go over it at some point. You know I am making a map of the region."

Leonardo bit his lip; that was precisely what was bothering him.

"Why make useless work for yourself, ingeniero? We already have maps; every owner of a finca has his own. And there's no one who won't put them at your disposition."

Fernando sat down in the leather armchair and stretched out his legs.

"It's odd," he observed casually, pointing to the brazier. "The Spaniards who settled here never thought of building fireplaces. I've never seen a single one in the houses in Ciudad Real, and now I see that the ranches don't have them either. In Europe there are fireplaces in climates less harsh than this one. . . ."

"Have you been to Europe, ingeniero?"

"For a few months."

"The deceased"—this was how Leonardo always alluded to Isabel's first husband—"was in Europe, too, and for a few years, not a few months. And I assure you, he wasn't any the wiser for it when he came back. Perhaps the same might be true of you."

It was the Coleto's time-honored tactic: provoke the other man (the other man is always an adversary), make him lose his temper, show his face. But this time the tactic yielded no results. Ulloa kept smoking, calm and indifferent.

"That remains to be seen."

The answer bewildered Leonardo, who thought of himself as a man who knew men and could manipulate them at will. But the engineer belonged to a new species, a species Leonardo hadn't yet succeeded in classifying.

For the present, Ulloa was serving the government, a government looked upon with mistrust by the landowners, the men who were on the side of order. He was a civil servant, and thus corruptible by nature, since the civil service is the last refuge of indigence. In Ulloa's case, this certainty was encouraging, because his mission—to enforce the new agrarian legislation that was to provide the native communities with lands and modify the boundaries of the haciendas—would cause upheavals of a magnitude no one could foresee. Why then would this man, whose price had been set in consultation with the other landowners, not come to a prudent arrangement with them? Why did he let opportunities to bring up the subject pass and, instead, ask questions that were irrelevant?

"Do the peons here in San José Chiuptik have a contract for their work? Are they paid the minimum wage? How many hours a day do they work? Who sees to their education and their health?"

Leonardo began by answering unconcernedly, with factual information and disdainful comments. But he saw such a mixture of surprise and reproach in the other man's eyes that he felt like a fool. He wanted to argue, justify himself. But the long exercise of arbitrary power, the smooth orbit without resistance or objection in which his conduct had always moved had never made it necessary for him (or for any of the other ranchers of Ciudad Real) to provide himself with any justification.

Ulloa's interrogation caught him off guard, helpless, naked, and exposed him to the cruel light of a mind which judged by criteria that were very different and even opposite to those he had, until then, considered to be the only valid ones.

Leonardo Cifuentes had no illusions about it: Ulloa condemned him and for that reason alone had suddenly acquired an intolerable superiority, as intolerable as the silence that rose up between the two men.

"What are you thinking about, ingeniero?"

"I would not have wanted to have to rely on your hospitality."

"Do you have any complaint to make?"

"What worries me is that I'm unable to demonstrate my gratitude."

Leonardo pretended not to understand what the other man meant.

"On the ranches, we always have a room available for visitors. We know what it is to need one. And, gracias a Dios, we can meet the need. But if you have to turn to an Indian, he'll close his hut to you and refuse to sell you something to eat at any price."

Fernando accepted this sadly.

"They live in dire misery."

"They're like animals. What are we going to do about that, ingeniero?"

Ulloa was irritated by the bad faith of Cifuentes' complicity. He said, in a tone so smooth it could have seemed insulting: "What we are going to do is give them back what belongs to them. . . ."

Leonardo waited for the end of the sentence, almost without breathing.

". . . the land."

Then he smiled, relieved.

"So they've come to you, too, with their tale about how these lands are theirs and I don't know who took them away from them! It seems you believed them."

"They showed me their property titles."

"Signed by who? The King of Spain, or some other gentlemen who may have had some authority way back when but nobody remembers now."

"Antiquity doesn't lessen the validity of a concession of land."

"But common sense does. When we came to this region, there was nothing but uncultivated land, forests that had been cut down and burned-off clearings. The Indians couldn't do anything else with the land during all the centuries they were its owners. We were the ones, with our sweat, our effort, who made this place into fertile and productive property. Tell me, in all fairness, who has property rights here, us or them? And it's not just a question of justice, but of the best use of the land; thanks to us even the Indians have work and earn money. But look at the Indian on the loose who doesn't live on a finca or acknowledge a patrón's protection: he eats his own fleas because he hasn't got anything else to eat. There's not another loafer to compare with him."

Cifuentes had stood up and was pacing the room with long steps. From time to time, he stopped to underscore a passage of his peroration with a gesture or an exclamation of "Carajo!"

"No one is much interested in working for someone else's profit. But when the Indian is his own patrón the sense of responsibility he cannot have now will be strengthened."

"And according to you, all it takes is a tiny patch of land to be a patrón."

How mistaken Fernando Ulloa was! Being a patrón implied a race, a language, a history that the Coletos had and the Indians were incapable of improvising or acquiring. Patrón: a man who maintains a house in Ciudad Real with his wife and his legitimate children, many children; who has one querida in town and another on the ranch (apart from occasional adventures with little Indian girls and little mestiza maids; apart, too, from excursions to the less reputable side of town). Patrón: a man who makes bets during evening parties at the Gentlemen's Club, who, during a wild spree, lights a cigar with a large bill out of pure ostentation; a man who risks his fortune on a political adventure, a military coup. A man who provides his sons with a liberal education and his daughters with a good husband. A man who travels, once or twice, to Guatemala, to Mexico and, in extraordinary cases, to

Europe. A man who has seen to it that after his final departure he will leave a handsome legacy to ensure the well-being of his dependents.

"The ejido is indispensable, of course, but the Indians will also need a small amount of capital that a bank will supply."

The hacienda, whose boundaries extend as far as the strength and greed of the neighboring landowners allows, will be broken up into a thousand pieces. The peon will no longer come to plead for a bushel of corn, a yard of coarse cloth, a new machete, a gram of quinine. He will no longer run up debts in order to buy a demijohn of posh for a fiesta, a family ceremony, his day off, or to satisfy a vice. He will no longer die and leave a pledge of loyalty to the patrón as his children's only legacy.

The Indian, made equal, raised up by a government order, will no longer walk the way he does now, always sticking close to the wall as if seeking protection there; he will not slip past like a furtive animal, fearful of the reprimand, the command he never succeeds in interpreting, the question for which he has nothing but insufficient and stammering answers. He will no longer stand before his master without daring to lift his eyes.

When this Indian speaks he will not do so in a little mouse voice, incredibly faint, "so as not to show any disrespect." He will speak in a normal tone, and if he has learned Spanish, prudence will not keep him from speaking it in front of Caxláns. It will no longer be a crime to address the patrón as he would any other man.

"Until now, the Indians have lived under a tutelage that lent itself to many abuses. But they will reach the age of reason once they know how to read, write and cultivate their land scientifically."

"What? You're dreaming, ingeniero! An Indian can't be taught anything. We tried it ourselves, it's like trying to get blood from a stone."

Fernando listened, his expression unchanged.

"Perhaps you didn't know how to teach."

Leonardo paused. He had never considered that possibility. He shot back hastily: "And while we're all busy learning, who's going to work and what are we going to live on?"

"There will be some lean years, but that's not important. Af-

terward, everyone will be better off than they are now, I promise you."

Leonardo watched his opponent for an instant. Did he really
believe what he was saying? Or was he simply trying to increase
the bribe?

"You're more educated than we are, ingeniero; you've travelled, you've seen a bit of the world. But we know the color of
our cattle very well and it won't be easy to change our opinion:
an Indian, here or wherever else you like, is always poor and
ignorant. Nothing can be done about it."

"We're going to do something."

"I hope the cure doesn't turn out to be worse than the disease.
You, with what are undoubtedly very good intentions, are riling
up the Indians by preaching that we're all equal and have the same
rights. I'm not going to ask you to understand and approve of
customs you aren't familiar with; nor will I ask that you take my
word for the fact that it's best not to shake that particular hornets'
nest because if it gets stirred up there's no one who can calm it
down. What I will prove to you is that the government is biting
off a whole lot more than it can chew. And not for the first time."

Leonardo had recovered his calm and sat down, moving his
chair closer to the engineer's.

"I'm going to tell you what I have been told. We have always
been on the side of order, and we are very sedate in our little
corner here as long as we are left to arrange our affairs in our
own way. But suddenly revolutions come and everything gets
blown to bits."

Leonardo had lit a cigarette and was puffing on it with delectation.

"They say that when the French invaded, some military types,
the kind that are always trying to make a deep bow with someone
else's hat, promised they would send volunteers from Chiapas.
Volunteers! Who would want to go? Who cared if foreign troops
were disembarking in Veracruz and taking over Mexico City? The
French were never going to come to Chiapas. There weren't any
roads."

"If they had gotten here, what would the Coletos have done?"

"Received them with open arms, because they were orderly
people, decent people like us. But the liberals in Tuxtla and Co-

mitán (very recently converted liberals, the ones who got rich buying the Church's property for a song) were determined to send troops from Chiapas. Naturally the patróns weren't going to fight, and neither were their sons. In order to keep from embarrassing themselves, they sent the Indians from the haciendas. They were the lucky volunteers, and they had to be caught the way you catch a steer: with a lasso. Yes, ingeniero, I'm not exaggerating: it's recorded in the documents. In the list of the troop's expenses is the sum spent on ropes to tie them up.

Leonardo laughed out loud, but his laughter died when he noticed the other man's seriousness.

"Our peons took part in the battle of the 5th of May and they didn't make us look bad either. But when they came back here: disaster! They were raring to go because they'd been told that in the North and in Yucatán there was a caste war between Indians and Ladinos. It didn't take much for them to start getting impudent, and remember, they had learned to use firearms. . . . To make a long story short, the bad example was contagious and there was an uprising, and Ciudad Real was about to disappear from the map."

"But you Ladinos won in the end."

"It certainly wasn't because of any support from the government, which has always tried to harm us. President Juárez—I'm sure you must worship him—didn't send a single soldier or rifle to help us defend ourselves. But Guatemala offered us its army. Out of loyalty, a loyalty Mexico never thanked us for, we didn't accept any help from the Guatemalans and we fought alone. The losses were great, and what was our sacrifice for? A few years of peace, and now the threat of instability again."

"The two situations are very different. How can you compare them?"

"No, you don't notice the resemblance because you aren't from around here. But you can almost touch the agitation, the anxiety. They're agitated, too. For no reason at all they're fleeing from the haciendas and going to join up with the communities of unindentured Indians. They're getting bolder because there are more of them and now they've seen that they can count on the support of certain authorities who, whether they know it or not, are provoking another uprising."

"Times change, Don Leonardo. Nowadays there is no reason blood has to be shed. The battle will be strictly a legal one. What more do you want? That's where you Coletos are most at home; those of you who aren't lawyers hold forth even longer than the ones who are."

"You flatter us, ingeniero. But it's our opinion that a bad settlement is worth more than a good lawsuit."

"You can try. I'm sure there is no lack of corruptible civil servants, either."

Cifuentes sat back, uncomfortable.

"That is a strong word. We don't need to rely on a man without honor; we want a man who sees the light of reason and helps us maintain order."

"And will his assistance be offered for free?"

"Every form of work must have its compensation. We're very generous when we want to be."

"And do you have a viable candidate?"

"You."

Fernando didn't appear to be shocked or offended. He limited himself to asking, with a certain remote curiosity, "What made you think I would accept your proposition?"

"It is to your advantage, ingeniero."

"Would it also be to the advantage of. . . . of those who trusted me?"

"If you mean the government, you'll be doing it a large favor by keeping it out of a mess."

"I was referring more to the Indians."

This answer was so unexpected it left Leonardo without a response. But he recovered instantly.

"You want to help them, don't you? On that we agree. Why can't we also agree on how to help them?"

"The only way is the way set out by the law."

"Who made the law, ingeniero? As far as I can tell, it was made by someone who doesn't have the faintest idea of the problem. The law demands that a minimum wage be paid to the peons, which turns out to mean that the patrón will lose money, and that a school be established on every finca and, naturally, be maintained by the owner. And then there aren't any teachers, or if there are they don't speak the language. And since the Indians don't understand Castilla they just sit there in a daze."

"Those issues don't fall under my jurisdiction, Don Leonardo. I came here for the redistribution of the land."

"You come here and you spend a few days here and you arrange this and that and then you leave and never give another thought to what happened. We and the Chamulas are the ones who stay behind. You leave them all stirred up and us angry. Who's going to see to it that what you ordered is carried out?"

"An inspector, undoubtedly."

"All right, let's say that an inspector comes. He'll have an area many miles wide to cover. The roads. . . . you already know what they're like, ingeniero. And as far as lodging goes, the owners of the fincas aren't going to want to open their doors to those who are coming to damage their interests. You can figure that your lucky inspector will be able to take the grind for a month or two. After that, he'd rather let things take their own course. And that is supposing, mark my words, that he is very honorable and no one starts waving money around under his nose."

"Don Leonardo, I'm only responsible for what I'm supposed to do."

"That's nice work! Light the fuse and let everyone else take the heat. Because the way you're leaving things, there's going to be a fight. And the Indians will be on the losing side; we patróns are still stronger."

None of these warnings had the slightest impact on Fernando; he felt he was backed by a legal code, a political orientation, the steadfastness of the government.

"We ranchers here in Chiapas aren't going to be the only ones to protest this. Throughout the Republic, landowners are growing alarmed and joining together to fight. We're going to be forced to dig out the problem at its roots."

To straighten out the legal code, change the political structure, replace the government. Fernando Ulloa knew that in Mexico these were not remote possibilities and that even the most insignificant privilege of the wealthy had never been attacked without unleashing a disproportionate, bloody and ultimately triumphant reaction.

At that point, the ranchers were prepared—in order to keep the peace, they said—to concede some improvements in the treatment of the peons. But what they would never tolerate was for the Indians to believe they had won a right to anything. The patrón must always be the divinity who dispenses favors, freely given benefactions and well-deserved punishments. The circumference of his existence was not going to be violated by a trial, by a summons from his inferiors.

For their part, the inferiors carried the feeling that inferiority was their authentic condition so deeply in the marrow of their bones that they were offended by those who tried to foist a new burden on them: dignity.

Dignity was something the Indians had relinquished long ago and thought they had lost forever. But now, suddenly, they were finding it intact, with all its weight, its conflicts and its lacerations, and a man in a position of authority was inciting them to recover it. Such urgency could only produce uneasiness in the old people, rejection in the cowards, and uncontrollable rage in those who were discontented—the young. All of them went to an extreme —in some, it was an extreme of servility, in others, an extreme of rebelliousness. The air was dense with uneasiness, restlessness. What events would the law give birth to?

Fernando Ulloa didn't know; like his opponents, he was groping fearfully toward what was to come. Common sense inclined him to fall in with Leonardo's arguments and acknowledge the judiciousness of his advice. But it wasn't only his intelligence, his ideal of justice or his ambition to make Mexico a prosperous country, it was the deepest part of himself that swung around to reject such a transaction, to label an alliance with the ranchers impossible and monstrous.

Because Fernando Ulloa wasn't merely a middle-aged employee with a salary that didn't stretch to meet his needs and who had achieved less than he set out to. He was also the orphaned child of the campesino who defied his masters and followed Emiliano Zapata across the southern mountains that were ringing with shouts of freedom. He was the son of the helpless widow who was driven to the city by hunger. He was the boy who, during the years when other boys play, worked at menial, degrading tasks to earn a few centavos. He was the applicant for meagre scholarships. He was the boarding-school student who never had enough to eat, who never had any books except those his schoolmates loaned him. He was the hard-working student who earned the highest marks, one of the group chosen by the professors for a brief trip to Europe to give them further training and polish. Later, he was also the man who, without quite knowing how, became entangled with Julia, and in order to support her, abandoned his education and never received the degree for which he and his mother had made so many sacrifices.

If this postponement (he never resigned himself to calling it a definitive renunciation) had caused Fernando any pain, perhaps he had compensations of another order. But for his mother, eaten away by illness, the disappointment, the sudden loss of her reason for being, was annihilating. She died.

And it was she who rose up in all her despair as an unreconciled soul to say "no" to Leonardo, and it was the blood of his father, the obscure revolutionary who never saw the face of victory, and it was the years of hard work and postponed hopes, and, closer and more painful, the failure of his union with Julia. All of it shouted "no" to Leonardo, "no" to prudence, "no," "no," "no," to a shadowy compromise, to bending the law, to a paid compliance. A deeply scarred loyalty held sway over Fernando; it kept him beyond the reach of the other man's hints.

"What have you decided, ingeniero?"

Ulloa stood up and slowly walked over to the window. It was still raining.

"There is nothing to decide. My course is set."

"Is that your final word?"

"Yes."

This Fernando Ulloa was turning out to be a hard nut to crack. But Cifuentes wasn't discouraged; there was still insistence, intrigue. There was still time, a period of time the ranchers would know how to prolong.

Suddenly Fernando felt a stinging in his feet, a sense of asphyxiation, an oppression, an anxious need to leave, to break out of this prison of rain, mud and hills.

"I'll be going right away."

And, in answer to a question the other man hadn't asked, he added, "I have classes to teach tomorrow at the Instituto."

It didn't occur to Leonardo to try to detain him. There would be other occasions for continuing the dialogue. He stepped politely to one side to allow his guest to depart.

CHAPTER XIII

THE BUILDING THAT HOUSED the Instituto Superior was originally constructed as a convent. With the triumph of the liberal troops and the expropriation of goods from the clergy, it became government property. What use could be made of it? It was very large and very dark for an office building, but not sturdy enough for a barracks. The decision was made to convert it into a school.

The result was an irritating general inconvenience, an air of improvisation contradicted by the antiquity of the furniture and the smudged decrepitude of the maps and engravings. The dark, narrow, damp cells—instruments for the mortification of the flesh—fulfilled their mission on teachers and students who justified their miserable accommodations by attributing to them their inability to teach, or their lack of interest in learning.

Despite all this, the inhabitants of Ciudad Real were proud of their Instituto, the only and therefore the best one in the state. Every year, its prestige attracted young men from all over Chiapas and even from towns on the borders of Tabasco and Guatemala. Languid natives of the lowlands, wily men from the heart of the country, and happy-go-lucky fellows from the coast brought income to the town's boarding houses, liveliness to its avenues and sentimental unrest to its young girls.

The Instituto did not depend on specialists for its faculty. From the first, it relied on the good will of men who had acquired one degree or another to safeguard their careers or else had engaged in such a lengthy practice of their chosen professions that it was the equivalent of a diploma. Each one taught what he could. There was an abundance of lawyers, because the School of Law had been founded during the colonial era and had operated without interruption ever since. And since, by a tradition based on laziness, it was believed that a lawyer was capable of imparting any subject within the humanities, the Instituto could consider itself well supplied in that respect. But there was a real scarcity of technical expertise, a lack of doctors, chemists, engineers. That was why Fernando was asked for his assistance, but not without being warned, between obeisances, that the salary was merely symbolic and in no way a sufficient recognition of his merit or a compensation for his labors.

Fernando accepted the position without worrying about its drawbacks. He had never hoped to resolve his financial problems by giving a course in mathematics. And he had a very keen interest in renewing his contact with students, a contact he had lost since his departure from the capital.

So he began to prepare his classes carefully and to be present for them punctually. He didn't let the students get away with doing nothing; he required a great deal of homework from them and made them participate actively in the subjects he was covering.

The boys were not accustomed to demands like these and were upset by them. Fernando was mistaken in supposing he would find in them what he and his classmates had possessed during their adolescence: a curiosity that motivated discovery, an urgent need to get their bearings and form a vision of the world, a generous interest in things.

His students were all the sons of ranchers and rich men, and even before they inherited their family properties they had inherited the prejudices that would eventually enable them to enjoy those properties without remorse, as well as the rationalizations by which they would unscrupulously defend them. The idea of their own importance was like a thick carapace around them; proud of the role they would one day play in society, they learned the little vices of their class very early. They believed that abusing tobacco, having a strong head for alcohol, and giving immoderate reign to their sexuality would confer the patents of adulthood upon them. The fact that someone like Fernando, who lacked any prestige in their eyes, should come to put their convictions into question and try to replace them with others that went against their feelings, habits and interests left them completely unfazed. It only made them laugh. They heard Ulloa's explanations with mocking patience; they asked him trick questions; they put the little stone of a scornful observation in his path for his enthusiasm to stumble against. In a dim and formless way, Fernando was aware of his failure. But that wasn't enough to change his objectives, alter his conduct or diminish his fervor.

Fernando Ulloa's presence was a living reproach to the other teachers who were fossilized in the routine of a profession exercised without vocation or any particular aptitude. Like any reproach, it disturbed the somnolence of their ruminations. They woke up just enough to keep a watch on the new arrival with a gaze that eagerly sought any pretext for mistrust. Fernando's every word or gesture was pondered and commented upon by his colleagues. Without knowing it, Fernando Ulloa had become the defendant before a group of judges who would look more harshly upon his virtues than upon his defects.

The hostility Fernando aroused in those around him was exacerbated by his ignorance of the customs of Ciudad Real, the careless way in which he wounded many sensibilities, his imprudence in expressing his opinions. His various lapses in tact were meticulously recorded in the dossier that was being assembled against him. After a few weeks he was known only by the nickname, "the Communist," that a gleeful teacher of first year civics had come up with.

For most of them, the term Communist had no meaning. But it rang in their ears like a forewarning of something sinister and threatening that was embodied in this man whose story nobody knew.

The rumor—Communist—had a few isolated repercussions among the civil and ecclesiastical authorities. There was some suspicious questioning of the establishment's director, and knowing smiles were exchanged by the professors. But the real cry of alarm went up from the parents.

A student, Roberto Zepeda, unhappy with the grade by which Fernando had rated his idleness, thought it was a good idea to mention to his mother that the teacher—in a mathematics course which obviously did not lend itself to such high-flown pronunciations—maintained that all men were equal, that Indians were men, and that therefore they deserved to enjoy the same privileges and advantages as Ladinos.

Señora Zepeda listened to this nonsense in horror and immediately communicated her dismay to Señor Zepeda. But he preferred to take the whole thing as a joke, declaring that neither the harangues of a sanctimonious old woman nor the affectations of a spoiled boy who was still clinging to his mother's petticoats were worth paying any attention to.

Allied by this condemnatory ruling, mother and son turned to someone who could make their complaints resonate: a priest.

Padre Balcázar, bored with the moral insignificance of his parishioners, paid inordinate attention to the whisperings of Señora and young master Zepeda. He initiated inquiries among the other students and found them to be in agreement with Roberto. He decided that Fernando's reputation and sobriquet were well-founded, and, once in possession of those elements, he dusted off his books, compared the opinions of various authorities, and applied himself to such a degree that he managed to transform a vague nebula of irrelevant or very sketchy facts into a full-fledged accusation: if Fernando was a Communist—of which there was not the slightest doubt—he was also a sworn enemy of the Church, a threat to the established order and a corruptor of youth.

These arguments in hand, Padre Balcázar paid a visit to the director of the Instituto, Dr. Palacios, a man whose respect for the clergy was well known.

In heart-rending phrases, the priest pointed out to the doctor that both he and the school he was in charge of were throwing themselves into an abyss. His imprudence, for Padre Balcázar exempted him from any guilty premeditation, would be justly punished by the heavens if, having been warned, he did not cast the diseased sheep from the fold.

Palacios defended himself with a few weak allegations. He resisted the idea of giving in without a fight to the consequences of this chat, which were obvious: after hearing Padre Balcázar's admonitions, he would have no other option but to request Fernando Ulloa's resignation.

The priest did not understand how his will could possibly encounter the least resistance in Palacios. They were from the same town, of the same race, their backgrounds were identical. He did not realize that Palacios was a young man and that the air of Mexico (where he had received his medical education) had blown away many of his former prejudices.

Palacios was, moreover, an ambitious man. He wanted to get into politics but, unable to enter that world directly, he took the academic post he was offered as a springboard to leap off when the time seemed right. But before that, it was to his advantage to try to distinguish himself in some way, to set himself apart from his predecessors, a grey cortege of civil servants who limited themselves to keeping the school from closing down, but without worrying about making any improvements in it.

Dr. Palacios had already accumulated some enemies and provoked a lot of misgivings with his zeal for innovation. His first one was to review the textbooks used by the school and judge them anachronistic; he ordered them replaced with more current works which were accepted in the Republic's other educational establishments.

This change, and the attendant effort it required for the teachers to understand their subjects from different points of view and explain them with formulas other than the ones they had used for decades, naturally gave rise to some discontent. The director let the professors fume and grumble until their scant energy was absorbed by the new pedagogical methods and they abandoned their protests as useless.

The initial commotion caused by the new textbooks hadn't yet died down when Palacios, a former student of the Instituto who was well versed in the habits of each of the men under him, took further measures. The absentee professor now found himself forced to give irrefutable proof of his attendance; the one who trafficked in passing grades had a committee assigned to review and justify his evaluations; and the one who wasted time in lengthy anecdotes that had nothing to do with the syllabus had to begin sticking to it because he knew he was being watched.

There was nothing for the teachers to do but applaud Dr. Palacios' attitude, since that way they appeared not to deserve it. But when an upstart arrived in their feudal domain (because that was what they considered the Instituto after so many years of being its only and irreplaceable usurpers), they trembled. Ulloa represented an element they had never expected to have to deal with: the competent competitor.

Palacios had enough talent and objectivity to appreciate Fernando's intellectual capacities, and he was satisfied with the way the engineer played his role as a spur to puncture the other teachers' laziness. He would have wanted to lead an entire faculty made up of people as fit for their tasks as Ulloa was, since the Instituto's prestige would then grow and its director would be viewed in a positive light by the government inspectors. But now, through an unforeseeable combination of circumstances, far from having his desire fulfilled, Palacios was being pressured to get rid of Fernando Ulloa. For his attempts to mollify Padre Balcázar were in vain; even more, his promise to call the matter to the engineer's attention and warn him to abstain from troubling his students with subversive exhortations was heard with considerable skepticism. No, the priest wanted Fernando Ulloa to be taught a lesson and would accept nothing less. As Dr. Palacios invoked the higher interests that he, too, had to take into consideration, Padre Balcázar withdrew from the office muttering anathemas against the cowardliness of worldly men and citing the passage of the Gospel which advises that a millstone be hung around the neck of whosoever shall offend the little ones.

From that moment on, Dr. Palacios knew Fernando Ulloa was a lost cause. His apprehensions were confirmed as the incidents multiplied. Several students stopped attending the Instituto in order to keep from contaminating the purity of their Catholicism; anonymous letters rained from the sky, heaping up a most singular assortment of accusations against Ulloa; serious, discerning people affirmed that His Excellency was pondering the appropriateness of laying an interdiction against the establishment.

Dr. Palacios didn't want this matter, which had already gone too far, to compromise his own position any further. He understood that he had to provide a public redress, so one morning when Fernando arrived to teach his class, the proctor refused to give him the key to the classroom because, "according to instructions from my superiors, you have been deemed unworthy to remain a member of the faculty."

This news was communicated to Fernando in front of numerous witnesses and with the secret pleasure a servant takes in humiliating someone who, by virtue of his higher position, is always humiliating him.

To everyone's disappointment, Ulloa was more surprised than angry. He wanted to find out who had given such a ridiculous order and badgered the proctor with questions. But the proctor shrugged insolently, refusing to give any explanation. For their part, the witnesses showed the circumspect faces of those who are fully informed but prefer not to get mixed up in the matter.

Fernando tried to meet with Dr. Palacios but that was impossible because he "was out of town." So he had to retreat back home, shaken by contradictory feelings.

Shut up in his study after having given a slam of the door in response to Julia's curiosity, he paced back and forth, seized by a blind fury he didn't know how to vent.

Who was so interested in hurting me? he wondered. Undoubtedly he had been the victim of an intrigue, the object of slander, caught in a trap. He examined his own conduct and found nothing reprehensible. On the contrary, during the months he served as a professor, he never strayed from the most scrupulous ethics. And now look how they repaid him! With a humiliation that was all the more offensive for being anonymous and collective.

He reviewed his memories. Among all the people he had frequented recently he couldn't find a single friendly face, a single kindred spirit, a single cordial gesture. In light of what had just happened, he finally read the hostility of the stances, the hypocrisy of the words. Guided by his bitterness, he groped his way, exhuming almost forgotten phrases, nameless faces and unfinished episodes that now, at last, reached their outcome.

After that, Fernando withdrew from a society that had declared war on him to dedicate himself to the duties of his position, duties that were becoming increasingly intricate and daunting. He maintained no contact with anyone except for a few formal exchanges with Don Leonardo Cifuentes, who visited his house, and the obligatory communication with his assistant, Rubén Martínez.

Ulloa began to observe Rubén as if he—a Coleto—were a compendium of the characteristics of all Coletos. In Rubén, he stalked the mechanisms of the conduct of a town that had rejected him, and he found a mean slyness that offended him. How could this naive young man think to deceive him with his excessive adulations, his docility which was no more than a means of getting his own way? Because even events as apparently random as having ended up in San José Chiuptik one stormy night obeyed a preconceived plan of which Rubén was the agent.

The ranchers, Fernando said to himself, have placed someone near me to spy on my movements and intentions.

Despite this discovery, Fernando did not watch his back. He continued to depend on Rubén to organize his journeys through the interior, and Rubén continued to be the intermediary who set up his meetings with the owners of the fincas. Moreover, in the conversations their isolation brought them to, Fernando gave free rein to his words without stopping to think that the other was undoubtedly going to twist and misinterpret them, and, of course, pass them along.

Fernando would begin to hold forth at the slightest provocation. So Rubén, on occasion, would timidly allude to his poverty, the humbleness of his origins. He didn't want sermons and wasn't even asking for advice. He simply liked to complain about a situation that, ultimately, suited him.

But Fernando wanted to incite him to an active discontent. At least, he told himself, he should know whom he owes his misfortunes to. By doing that, and by not evincing any distrust despite having abundant reason to do so, Fernando believed he was attracting Rubén over to his side.

"Do you know why the Revolution took place, Rubén? So that the differences between you and the rich people who exploit you would no longer exist, to give you a dignity that others would respect."

Rubén acquiesced with exclamations of wonder: "Oh really!" "How about that!" But at heart he was uneasy and hurried to ask Don Leonardo Cifuentes' advice about quitting this job.

The advice must have been affirmative because, without further ado, Rubén disappeared one day. He went off, saying to anyone who wanted to listen that the engineer was "in league with the devil" and leaving Ulloa with an amount of work that was too much for him to handle alone.

CHAPTER XIV

IN HIS URGENT NEED to find a substitute for Rubén Martínez, Ulloa placed notices in the town's only newspaper (a weekly called ¡Plus Ultra!) and in the movie theatre which filled its intermissions with advertisements.

These measures were not effective, despite the fact that an adequate salary was offered and opportunities for work were neither frequent nor abundant in Ciudad Real. But those who would have applied for the position had been given careful instructions by their spiritual advisors and did not approach Fernando even out of curiosity.

As the days passed and this situation continued unchanged the engineer was beginning to think about going to Tuxtla to find the assistant he needed. Then he received a visit from César Santiago.

"Come in," Fernando said, recognizing one of his former students. "To what do I owe this miracle?"

For an instant he thought César had come as an emissary from his schoolmates to ask that he return to his teaching post. His dismissal had been so shameful, so unjustified! But the young man was already unfolding a copy of ¡Plus Ultra!

"I just saw your advertisement. . . . I was away for a few days. . . . I hope I haven't come too late."

"You're the first," Fernando answered, suspicious that this was some kind of a joke. "On whose behalf are you applying for the job?"

"On my own behalf."

Fernando had taken a seat after inviting his guest to do the same. He still felt distrustful.

"I don't think you could fit it in with your studies. You'd have to spend most of your time outside the city."

"That doesn't matter. I've decided to leave school."

Now César's image was becoming more precise in Fernando's memory. He was a mediocre student and Fernando had had to scold him on occasion for his negligence. But, after all, he was no different from the others. Many of them who had the same defects managed to complete their education.

"And what led you to make this decision?"

César stammered; it was difficult for him to say.

"The Instituto isn't the same since you left."

Ulloa smiled bitterly.

"I didn't leave of my own volition."

"Anyway, it isn't the same any more."

César was silent; he couldn't clarify what he meant.

"All right. Let's say you discover you don't have a vocation to become a professional, so you give up your studies. What does your family think?"

"Before they find out, I want to make myself independent, earn a salary."

"The salary I'm offering won't be enough for you. You're used to certain comforts, certain luxuries."

"Others start out with less."

Fernando shrugged.

"I assume you know what you're doing, but I can't understand what would make you leave a secure position and throw yourself into a difficult life in the company of a social outcast. Have you thought about the consequences joining me will have for you?"

César gave a cautious smile.

"I know what these towns are like, ingeniero. Once they have it in for someone they don't stop until they've finished him off. Why do you think I had to leave Comitán?"

It was a story of pettiness and humiliation that César told in its entirety, without hiding any details.

The Santiago family lived in Comitán and in not very remote times had owned a flourishing butcher shop in the neighborhood known as La Pila, a lusty district filled with carefree people who saw many possibilities in life. The fiestas in honor of San Cara-lampio, the neighborhood's patron saint, were the most famous in the area. There was an extravagance of fireworks and gambling booths, and the whole town and even neighboring towns came for the parades of flowers to the church. But a Pileño must never seek to leave La Pila or become part of the town's high society because he would be ignominiously rejected. Pileño you were born, Pileño you stayed.

This was the mistake of Don Timoteo Santiago, father of César (whose true name wasn't César, but Caralampio, after La Pila's patron saint). Don Timoteo was a man with some drive who wanted to go up in the world, by what means he didn't much care. When the persecution of the Church began and he saw an opportunity, he didn't let it go to waste.

The priest of San Caralampio, Padre Cancino, had unlimited confidence in Don Timoteo. Seeing that the authorities were taking increasingly severe measures against the clergy, he put all his properties in his friend's name. Those properties were not insignificant, for the parish paid well: a cattle ranch in the tropical lowlands, various orchards on the outskirts of the town, and two good houses in the best neighborhood.

Then it so happened that the strain of the persecution against the Church hastened Padre Cancino's demise and he died suddenly without time to make a will. There were two legitimate heirs, two destitute spinster sisters. But Don Timoteo did not see fit to recognize their rights. Thus, in one fell swoop, he came into possession of one of the most considerable fortunes in Comitán.

Poor Don Timoteo! He hadn't derived much enjoyment from his booty. If anyone—anyone from the right circle, of course— ever addressed a word to him, it was only to make him the butt of jokes or deluge him with innuendos.

Was this out of moral rectitude? No. Don Timoteo wasn't the only one to enjoy an ill-gotten wealth. What was more (and though this might seem to detract from his inventiveness), it should be clarified that the idea of fishing in the turbid river of circumstance would never have occurred to him, and even less would he have dared put it into practice, if he hadn't been encouraged by the example of others. But those others' backgrounds were not as unsatisfactory as his. Many were from good families and their excesses were concealed by their family names. What was unforgivable in Don Timoteo's case was that, despite his position, he still had the unmistakable air of a butcher, and rather than concealing it, he heightened it with the absurdity of his manners and the insolence of his accessories.

The privileged members of Comitán high society made him feel their reprobation by every available means. They gave him a nickname, "The Golden Calf," which alluded both to his former trade and to his current circumstances. They knew exactly how to jab at this parvenu's vanity: by excluding him from every gathering, thus denying him the opportunity to strut in front of others.

Because when it came to showing off, Don Timoteo had come up with more than enough ways to do so. Hadn't he bought the house of Don Sebastián Revelo, a gentleman with titles of nobility proving his illustrious descent from some Andalucian family or other? Before he was hung for his gambling debts, Don Sebastián had to sell off all that was left of his inheritance, which passed into the hands of the former resident of La Pila.

The satisfaction with which Don Timoteo moved his ordinary feet across the antique carpets! The voluptuous complacency with which he stroked the plush of the furniture, the velvet of the curtains, the silk of the tapestries with the hot palm of his hand! Who would ever have thought it. . . . He, Don Timoteo, the owner of a set of china inscribed with an anagram and sheets embroidered with initials. All right, the initials weren't his. But the sheets belonged to him; he was the one who used them. What a pity he never had visitors he could dazzle with his opulence!

To top off his problems, Don Timoteo's wife, Doña Serafina, who had fought tooth and nail to get ahead during the family's impoverished years, had acquired, now that she had sufficient leisure to enjoy life's pleasures, a tendency to grieve over the salvation of her soul. She became very devout and spent the whole day nosing out places where a mass was going to be celebrated or a ceremony performed. She found a confessor in whom to confide her cares, and Padre Damián displayed admirable skill in depicting the horror of the sin her husband had committed by raising himself up with the inheritance of the Cancino sisters. He harped so insistently and so energetically on this subject that the poor lady was crucified on the horns of a terrible dilemma: restore the fortune to its rightful heirs or be forever damned. As the decision to restore it was not hers to make (and her pleas did no more than exacerbate her husband's hatred of the church), Doña Serafina had no way out but to become a thief herself. She robbed on a small scale, of course, in order to give alms to the clergy and put out even just one of the flames of hellfire that were going to torment her family throughout eternity.

The Santiagos' two sons grew up in the vortex of these conflicts. Caralampio (who, with his father's money, had bought the right to use the more elegant name César), was attached to Don Timoteo and refused to judge the conduct to which he owed his own well-being. But despite his effort to understand his father he never reached the point of admiring him. He couldn't keep from seeing that the ex-butcher would never deserve to play a leading role in the social life of Comitán, and that people of good breeding were right to make fun of his ignorance and lack of manners. As the song says, the tree that grows twisted never straightens its branch. Even less so in old age. The scions of that tree, César felt certain, would be polished, would learn how to conduct themselves, would no longer allow their rustic origins to show. He himself, for example, had an alert mind and a normal capacity for acquiring knowledge. It wouldn't be impossible for him to learn, educate himself, and frequent the best people, untainted. As for his younger brother, Límbano. . . .

He was a sickly boy, and during his childhood he monopolized the small amount of coddling that a mother overly absorbed in procuring a means of subsistence and assuring a future for the family could give. But that coddling was the source of such satisfaction that Límbano fed from the breast for a number of years that had never before been equalled in all the annals of Comitán. At an age when one is beginning to retain one's memories for life, Límbano was forced to abandon this oh-so-pleasant habit by Don Timoteo's brutal punishments and César's relentless sneers. However, this separation from the mother was only exterior. The umbilical cord that attached him to Doña Serafina remained intact and through it he continued to feed on his mother's words, feelings and convictions.

The moral conflict which, for Doña Serafina, had an outcome that was unorthodox but eminently practical (when her conscience reproached her for embezzling from the conjugal heritage she soothed it by recalling the adage, "Thief that robs from thief gets a hundred years' relief"), was for Límbano a dead-end street. Adolescence doesn't understand or make allowance for the rationalizations of adulthood, the subtle delusions, the specious reasonings by which virtue is feigned. As soon as he caught sight of a duty, the young man threw himself into fulfilling it, and no amount of reasoning could turn him away from his goal. He wept, he pleaded that the ill-gotten fortune be returned to its rightful owners. When neither his tears nor his pleas were successful he began making threats. The idea of a righteous poverty repelled him far less than that of an affluence with such sordid origins. His histrionics didn't even succeed in infuriating Don Timoteo, who heard him with the tolerant composure of a Great Dane listening to the yipping of a Chihuahua.

Desperate at being no more than a boy in the eyes of the adults when he had already taken upon himself the responsibilities of a man, nostalgic for his lost childhood and the warm darkness of the maternal breast, Límbano assumed the fetal position of a corpse; he curled up in the grave's lap. He killed himself with a shot in the head before he reached his sixteenth birthday.

The tragedy, everyone said, repeating the term with which the local newspaper had referred to the event, plunged the Santiago home into mourning. Their dead son's grave became an abyss the couple could not cross. Don Timoteo found refuge only in his absorption in money, and he hoarded and tallied up his holdings in solitude. Doña Serafina persisted in her devotions, her prayers for souls in Purgatory, in the hope that Límbano was among their number. Because according to the priest he could have had, at the moment of his passing, the perfect repentance that would save him.

Pair of doddering old fools, César, now the sole heir, grumbled to himself. If I, their son, their flesh and blood, see them in a bad light, how much worse will they look to people who aren't even related to them and don't know how to share their neighbor's pain.

Sympathy, what might be called sympathy for the Santiago family's misfortune, was demonstrated by very few people in Comitán. And when the first rush of horror had passed, when the noise of the shot had died down, the onlookers began to ponder the event, now in full possession of their faculties. Their reflection led them to this verdict: the Santiagos had received the punishment they deserved. And under the shelter of this extenuating certainty, the event and its consequences could be spoken of lightly, with disdain or even mockery.

And how the Comitecos delight in mockery! A town of sharp, ingenious people, quick to retort, with a deadly skill at coining nicknames. "Putting them in their place" was their favorite entertainment.

How could the Comitecos fail to laugh at the misfortunes of Don Timoteo and Doña Serafina! Naturally, their chuckles didn't reach the ears of the interested parties. As the saying goes, there's none more deaf than he who will not hear. Furthermore, the Santiagos almost never went out and weren't on friendly terms with anyone. He was entirely absorbed in his business dealings and she spent all her time scampering from church to church. The only one still within reach of the evil tongues was César. But he wasn't an easy prey either. His friendlessness forced him to become proud and reserved, and anyone who approached him did so at the risk of scurrying back with his tail between his legs. Because —oh, the impudence of it!—the boy boasted about his money. Who could tolerate that kind of showing off? No matter how fine you think you are there's always someone finer, and a Comiteco doesn't let anyone lord it over him. César's enemies quickly learned how to get back at him by provoking him so as to have the pleasure of laughing in his face, bringing his dirty laundry out into the open. César defended himself but he was outnumbered and in the end he had to give in and hide away in a corner to nurse his indignation.

Without saying goodbye to anyone (who would a Johnny-come-lately like him say goodbye to?), the boy left for his father's finca, the finca that had put a curse on Don Timoteo and all his descendants. But the blot on the family honor was a lovely one. Even its name was lovely: Las Delicias. With a big river to win it some respect and a lot of small, useful brooks. Good land, fruitful land, plenty of people. Indian men in white breeches and palm hats; Indian women enveloped in their blue tzecs; people with pride enough to do their utmost to preserve their rank as the best peons in the region. Some of them seemed as if they already wanted to become Ladinos. Not in their customs or clothing, but more generally: they had light-colored eyes, curly hair and a pallid tint to their skin. They were the "priest's children," so to speak, the region's finest fighting cocks.

And like good fighting cocks, they were temperamental. César had his altercations with them. The boy wasn't used to commanding, and severity was a two-edged machete that cut him when he gripped it. For that and other reasons, César had become melancholy after a few months on the finca. He spent the whole day locked in his room, not speaking to anyone. Meals? He picked from one dish or another without giving strength or substance to his body. The hashes he was served on the ranch disgusted him. And he was afraid someone would try to poison him or slip him a potion of some kind. He guarded against betrayal in the big house as he did against ambushes in the fields. The Indians are so cowardly, so contemptible. . . .

César went back to Comitán.

But it was impossible to live there either. Let's say he fell in love with a girl, one of the girls from the classy part of town called La Rovelada, for instance. When is one of those girls going to deign to glance at a Pileño? Their lineage is illustrious; they have white skin and an elegant demeanor; they give themselves airs. And they think anyone who goes near them is a fortune-hunter. Why would César be hunting a fortune? The Santiago family is as rich or richer than theirs. But it's their family name that makes them so proud. And, on the other hand, César doesn't want to lower himself by dragging his wing around after a more common girl. So there is nowhere to look.

But without a girlfriend, who will he serenade? The marimba rings out late at night in the lonely streets. . . . When the marimberos are carrying it, it reverberates like a barrel of water on a burro's back. Then you take up your position in front of a given window and say: here it is. The numbers follow each other like beads on a string: waltzes and danzas, decent music, honest songs. Without any commotion, so the girl's parents won't hear and speak ill of the suitor, the bottle passes from hand to hand. Clink, clink, have a swig. It burns in your gullet and invigorates you against the early morning chill. And when your friends start shouting *Viva!* their voices are stronger and more in earnest.

The next day, of course, you wake up hung over. Then comes the chicken broth with roasted chilis. The steam dampens your face as you drink it. Between sips, you savor your memories of the night's revelries. The commotion at the Lochas' place, which got to the point where shots were fired—only one shot, though, and no one heard it. The oaths of friendship and more than friendship—I'm your brother, your brother!—with your companions. And the hope that the girl I told you about, the one who was sleeping last night, so far away from any sound, while the men set up the marimba outside her balcony, will someday sleep at your side, warm and delicious, you with her, and she with you.

But none of this is for César Santiago. Maybe he can go along on another man's serenade a few times, if he decides to put up with the ribbing. He has no friends but his enemies and no woman but the "seagulls," the girls who live in the houses of ill repute and paint their faces like clowns at a town fair. Is César supposed to marry a common, run-of-the-mill girl? That would be just great for his pride and Don Timoteo's pretensions.

Then what should he do? There's no way out but to leave Comitán. To travel. Not very far, if the stone is to gather any moss. It's never good to go too far from home, from your people. Just a little way. To Ciudad Real.

With his parents' permission, César left. He took with him many illusions, a good enough sum of money, and some luggage that he would augment when he arrived at his destination.

He moved into a boarding house for students. Galleries with blooming flowerpots, a gilded metal bed and spinster landladies. After spending his first few days getting used to his new environment, he went to enroll in the Instituto Superior de Chiapas.

What reason did he have to feel out of sorts here? His classmates were polite and refined. He didn't miss the Comitico expansiveness, which often comes to seem like vulgarity. The Coletos are very formal; they may well be hypocrites, but their discretion protects others from unpleasant barbs and malicious jokes. Friends? Santiago had no expectation of making any so soon. No late-night revels, because in this climate you have to be careful to stave off pneumonia. No frugal domino matches behind closed doors, under clouds of exhaled smoke. No chasing servant girls down the alleyways of the less frequented neighborhoods; no assaults on Indian women at the outskirts of town, no circling around the local Venuses. Perhaps a walk under the arcade that borders the town square, between one light rain and the next, to stretch the legs; a hot, spiked punch drunk down hurriedly at the counter; and the rest of the day spent studying.

Like so many other ambitious men, César wanted to erase his lowly origins with an excellent education. His case was already difficult in itself because it cost his mind (unschooled in scholarly discipline) too great an effort to grasp what he sought to imbue it with, and what he did take in he took in uncritically. And there was another obstacle: César had enrolled at the Instituto to solve a personal problem. But he found nothing in the classrooms but hollow words, abstract formulas that were in no way related to the experiences and urgent needs of his life.

The only one who was able to speak to César's needs was Fernando. And then only in passing, since the subject he taught could not have been drier or more remote.

But the students were preoccupied by an enigma that had nothing to do with numbers: the engineer's mission. For what purpose had he come to Ciudad Real? Were the rumors true, the ones that said he was going to strip the rich of their lands in order to redistribute them among the poor and the Indians?

There was a malevolence hidden in questions like that, a wounded susceptibility, a set of threatened prejudices Ulloa was unable to perceive. His answers gave an overall vision, a general theory in which the particular cases that were before him lost all importance, at least in his eyes.

According to Ulloa, Mexican history could be represented by the gradual expansion of a circle: that of the owners of wealth. From the conquistadors to the monks to the Spanish colonists to the criollos, those of Spanish blood born in America. . . . There was still a long way to go before that wealth would reach the humble masses of the population. Considerable interests were opposed to the unfolding of this process; thus, every new expansion of the circle had been achieved at the cost of drowning the country in rivers of blood, making it an easy prey to foreign plunderers, and throwing it into the most brutal chaos, which was fertile ground for false redeemers and corrupt caudillos.

Why not do as other countries did? In them, the historical process, which is delayed but does not stop, flowed through the channel of a legal standard. At a certain moment, Mexico replaced the improvised proclamations of soldiers with the painstaking work of experts.

The first attempts failed because the legislator worked in the solitude of his chambers. The legal structure, sprung like Minerva from the head of Jupiter without passing through the heat and muck of any maternal entrails, turned out to be inapplicable to our peculiar circumstances, though it had been calculated on the most perfect models in Europe and North America.

Mexico had made the law an idol to be revered and not a functional instrument to be put to use. How can a law be functional if the legislator who drafts it does not take the concrete facts of the reality he seeks to govern into account?

And what was Mexico for the Mexican people but an enigma, a vague specter, a nameless monster? It had to be reduced to clear notions, exact figures. As full an awareness as possible had to be gained of the natural resources available, the quantity of persons among whom they had to be distributed, and the way in which they had to be exploited in order to give the greatest possible yield.

Once the lies of propaganda and the exaggerations of optimism were put aside, the countenance of the fatherland was found to be an immense and desolate horizon. Misery, ignorance, moral rot. A soil that is either exhaustingly sterile or exuberant to the point of annihilation; a population pulverized into innumerable isolated villages. A man whose work does not keep him from the slow agony of hunger. Another man who knows no voice but the whip's.

And the truth becomes apparent. Where does Mexico's wealth lie? The mines are stripped of their riches, the prosperity of the cities declines. Nothing is certain but the land.

What a pity, what a waste, what a crime that vast expanses of land lie fallow! What a scandalous price their owners demand to rent those lands out, since they do not want to sell them! A just government (and in politics, justice takes the form of skill) has the obligation to wrest the land from the "dead hands" that are now in possession of it and place it in the empty hands of the campesino, the Indian, those who sow and will share their harvest with all.

But those dead hands, which were once the sacred hands of the priest, the monk, are now the powerful hands of rich men, which have become claws that will not release their prey. What, then, is to be done? Struggle, combat. Not only against the landowners, those who are opposed to the redistribution of the latifundios, but also against the great crowd of those who have been turned into fanatics and refuse to accept an improvement in their lot because they have been made to believe it is a sacrilege.

"The Government has enough strength and will use it, if necessary, but it is also on the side of right and prefers to convince both the egotists who don't want to give up a single one of their privileges and the faint-hearted who don't dare claim any of their rights that a country is not great if it is not just, that a society is not prosperous if it is not equitable, that goods are not goods if they are not enjoyed by all citizens."

Ulloa's students listened to him with distaste and unease. To all the teacher's arguments they opposed a terse rejection, an insistent, "And what about us? Why do they have to spoil things for us? Let the people who don't have anything work it out for themselves as best they can. It's no concern of ours, and the Government doesn't have any business meddling in it either."

All of this was grist for César's mill. So: those who had set themselves up as his judges, his father's judges, were the very landowners who, in order to amass and hang on to their fortunes, had unscrupulously and unstintingly resorted to the violence of conquest and legal chicanery. The power that had made them so haughty was now foundering. Because now, Fernando had announced, justice would be done at last. Everyone, old and new money alike, would be measured by the same yardstick. Everyone would merge in the great act of restitution to the disinherited that the Government was preparing to make. And those who were carrying out this restitution would know how to make the most of it.

In his disciple's eyes, Ulloa had the prestige of an expert, the appeal of a politician. A groundswell of admiration grew up in the scrawny chest of the boy from Comitán. To listen reverently to his oracle, to defend him from the biting criticism of others—these were the ceremonies of the new cult César had given himself over to. So why not leave the Instituto entirely, if Fernando had no place there, and abandon everything to share in the engineer's task and his eventual triumph?

Fernando had listened attentively to César's words and though the boy's motives still struck him as confused, he accepted him as his assistant. At least César wasn't an accomplice of the men who were trying to block his mission.

CHAPTER XV

WHEN WORD GOT OUT in Ciudad Real that César Santiago had become Fernando Ulloa's assistant there was a murmur of disapproval. How dare that boy disobey a tacit command everyone else had respected? People began paying attention to him, watching him closely in order to discern the traits of a personality that had seemed insignificant until then but was now beginning to be dangerous.

Everything about Santiago fed their suspicions: his accent and his words, his clothing and his manners, his gestures and his habits. The owner of the boarding house would remark to her neighbors that César had refused a certain dish today at lunch and the neighbors received the tidings as obvious proof of his guilt. An aging bachelor, member of a religious brotherhood, pointed out that César had passed in front of a church, the Iglesia de Caridad, without uncovering his head.

"It's true that no image of Our Lord is displayed there . . . but in any case, it's a sign of respect."

The owner of a store selling "clothing and novelties," communicated the total price for the purchase of a rubber poncho, riding pants, field boots and other implements that César would undoubtedly use to accompany Fernando on his circuits through the interior.

Accustomed to the brutal rejection of the people of Comitán, César didn't notice the secret hostility that surrounded him here. On the surface nothing had changed: the same greetings, the same handshakes, the same polite questions about his own health and his family's. The situation would have gone on like that indefinitely if the owner of the boarding house, tormented by her exacting conscience, hadn't taken the drastic step of telling César, in the most honeyed words, that she was going to need his room "because an orphaned cousin was coming to live by her side."

César was somewhat displeased by this request. Being a boarder in Señorita Morales's house was to his liking; his room was spacious and airy, with furniture that was old but solid and handsome; the food was abundant and a good plate of stew or refried beans, his favorite, was never lacking. The care and laundering of his clothing left nothing to be desired. But César was confident that these advantages could also be enjoyed elsewhere, and Señorita Morales's reason for asking him to leave seemed so valid that it never would have occurred to him to doubt it for a second. But when he had paraded from one boarding house to another without finding accommodations, he realized that his former landlady's orphaned cousin was just as false a pretext as all the others by which he had been denied lodgings.

César told Fernando Ulloa about the predicament he was in, and Fernando, not wishing to allow his assistant to continue undergoing the humiliation of rejection, offered him a place in his own house.

He made the offer without consulting Julia. He didn't consider it essential to do so, given that the house was too large for the childless couple and many of its rooms were closed up for lack of use. And servants were inexpensive and easy to find. Why would Julia become furious, as she did, when she learned that a stranger was going to live under her roof? Fernando didn't want to plumb her underlying reasons; in the years of living with her, he had grown used to sudden explosions of rebelliousness or temper, fits of weeping, outbursts that quickly evaporated without a trace. He attributed them, out of good-natured laziness, to the instability of the female soul, the unpredictable physiological ups and downs, the oppression of the horizonless routine in which women are submerged.

But this time, at least, Julia's motives were different. She had grown used to wandering alone through the vast house, arranging its every corner to suit herself. She was irritated by the presence of a witness. Not because she was doing anything wrong. What was wrong with receiving visits from Leonardo Cifuentes or having conversations with Doña Mercedes Solórzano? Why, then, was she being spied on like this?

For in Julia's eyes César Santiago was a spy. She found him suddenly behind her, silent, cunning, as if waiting to surprise her at something. She was sure he took advantage of her absences to snoop around the rooms and that he listened behind doors whenever he could. But he was skilled at slipping away, and Julia could never accuse him of anything in front of Fernando. So she took revenge in her own way. She forgot to order the maids to change her guest's sheets or mend his socks; his breakfast coffee was almost always cold, and sometimes César had to sleep on the sofa in the parlor because the key to his room couldn't be found anywhere.

César didn't put up any protest but pretended to sympathize with Julia over these irregularities. If she didn't immediately hit upon a plausible excuse (stammering, as she offered it, so it would be less convincing), César invented one to safeguard her prestige and his own dignity. But he smelled the intrigue that was being carried on against him and attributed it to motives that were more base than those which in fact existed.

For César, the truth of the rumors going around Ciudad Real about La Alazana's conduct was so patent that the only proof he lacked was precise knowledge of the occasions she took advantage of to commit adultery with Leonardo and the means she employed to keep the affair hidden.

His avowed admiration for Ulloa increased his disdain for Julia. How is it possible, he said to himself, that a man of such quality married a woman who is so common and so ill-natured? But that being the case, at the very least it would have been logical for the woman to live in a state of perpetual adoration and gratitude for the man who had lowered himself to her level. Yet nothing like that happened. Julia was thoroughly incapable of appreciating Fernando's good qualities and treated him with an absolute lack of respect. As if incited by bitterness, she didn't miss an opportunity to wound him with cruel sarcasm or ironic observations. César, who had lived in a world in which women are submissive or, at the very least, hypocritical, found her attitude scandalously unjustifiable.

Occasionally he tried to say something about it to Fernando, whose husbandly passivity seemed to César to stem entirely from obliviousness. But Fernando only smiled, robbing the matter of any importance. Basically, if he tolerated Julia's fractiousness, it was out of a kind of pity for a weaker being, a small, wild thing in captivity that lashed out harmlessly at those around it. Furthermore, Fernando still saw in Julia the enthusiastic girl who fell in love with him and followed him, renouncing her own future.

Other elements besides those Santiago could observe added their weight to his estimation of her: the instants of abandonment and tenderness, the helplessness and dependency on Fernando which Julia had from the beginning of their relationship and which he considered to be still intact, certain childish traits of her character.

For the rest, the transformation Julia had undergone over the course of those years was so gradual that Ulloa, without failing to notice it, did not give it the importance it really had. Julia's inner hardness was taken by her lover to be a superficial dissatisfaction; her cynicism was nothing but flippancy and her greed for wealth and prestige was only the natural frivolity of her sex.

This allowed Fernando to exempt his mate from the feeling that, in him, always remained strongest: responsibility. His passions had chilled, his tenderness had dried up, but no one would ever relieve him of the obligation to protect Julia and take care of her, to help her in her helplessness and her blunders.

But this attitude, which was held in reserve for moments of great crisis, did not come into play in their daily life together, which was increasingly routine and passionless. And if Julia had hoped that Leonardo's presence would bring a new tension, a new interest, to her conjugal relations, she must have felt cheated. Ulloa's lack of jealousy offended her as a sign of his disregard; she did not see it as a flattering proof of his confidence.

Fernando's attitude was disconcerting to César, and he didn't stop making veiled allusions to it until one day Ulloa condescended to explain his point of view: Julia had no friends and it wasn't because she hadn't tried to make them.

"I would be in the same situation if it weren't for you. And I have the stimulus of my work, too. I get absorbed in the problems it presents, I see new people, new places. But my wife is shut up in the house all day long."

"But that's natural."

"Who knows. A child would distract her, but she doesn't have one. There isn't much work around the house, and anyway the maids take care of that. I can't take her out because I'm always away and there isn't much to do in Ciudad Real anyway. You can't go to the movies more than twice a week, when the program changes. And even then you have to resign yourself to watching a movie that dates from the year one and doesn't interest you in the least and you can't even tell what it's about because the film keeps breaking and the sound doesn't work very well. And the people in the balcony take their discomfort out on the rest by spitting on the orchestra seats and shouting crass comments."

"Of course, the señora is used to a different milieu."

"In her student days, Julia liked to read novels and things like that. But where can you find a novel here? The only bookstore in town sells nothing but textbooks and school supplies."

"Well, yes, there's nothing left but boredom."

"Leonardo entertains Julia, I confess I don't know why, because to me personally he seems like a numbskull. I won't forbid her to talk to him."

"But people could start whispering. . . ."

"People are never happy with anything. What do they say about me? That I eat children raw. And about you? That you sold your soul to the devil."

"We are men; we know how to defend ourselves. But in a woman, honor is a very delicate matter."

"Honor, César?"

"In these towns, friendships between men and women are unusual. Don Leonardo himself could misinterpret the freedom you are allowing him."

"Let's suppose Leonardo does fall in love with Julia, it's natural. She's young and attractive, different from all the other women a rancher might have dealings with around here. But Julia will know how to keep him at bay; she's not some inexperienced young thing who'll fall into a seducer's hands. She knows her duty and, in addition to that, what could attract her to Leonardo? There is a gulf between them, in their educations, in their manners, even in their ages."

This type of thinking was a sign of Fernando's profound egotism, because the slightest doubt about Julia's virtue would have required him to devote some attention to it, and all his attention was focused on his work.

A tour through the municipality of Chamula was now being planned, no longer to determine the boundaries of the haciendas, but to recognize the heritage of the communities and villages, reinstating their property titles, which until now had been ignored and violated by the ranchers.

In order to carry out this task, Fernando Ulloa and his assistant needed the whole town's collaboration. On the first day of their arrival in San Juan, the engineer summoned the town's principal men to an assembly in the central hall, the Cuarto del Juramento, of the Cabildo Municipal.

At three in the afternoon, the room (cold and enormous, strewn with pine needles in honor of the visitors and without any furniture other than a rectangular wooden table in the center) was full of Chamulas. Most of them were elderly but a few young people had shown up as well and they formed a group apart, the most restless and troublesome one.

When Fernando and César entered the room, everyone stood up to greet them. A light brush with the tips of the fingers, a few muttered, unintelligible words and they were back in their places.

The air was unbreathable; the crush of men, the mingled odors of resin, the very cheapest cigarettes, sweat, and damp wool had all condensed in the atmosphere. The doors were opened wide and a gust of fresh air relieved the queasiness.

Fernando asked for an interpreter because he had a lot to say and it would need explaining. None of the old men volunteered (though there were those among them who spoke Castilla). They had come because they were used to obeying the orders of Ladinos, but they mistrusted them and inside themselves were prepared to resist.

Among the young men there was a brief discussion; a few of them spat to clear their throats, in a sign of assent, and finally Pedro González Winiktón separated from the group and went to Fernando's side.

Fernando spoke slowly, as if he were addressing a child, choosing the easiest words and repeating them as if repetition would make them comprehensible. He said that he was a friend to the Indians and that he had come from very far with a request from the president of the Republic that they be given back the ownership of their lands. When each man is the owner of his own plot of land it will be necessary for all men to work, to bring in good harvests, and to take them to sell in the markets. With the money they receive, he said, they can clothe themselves better, they can buy medicine, they can send their children to school.

The old men listened and out of the whole speech they grasped only that they were being directed to place in the hands of a stranger the papers they had treasured up and handed down from generation to generation, which represented all that was most precious in their eyes.

Winiktón had transformed the engineer's words into the expression of his own dream. He said that the hour of justice had arrived; that the president of the Republic had promised to come, strip the patróns of their privileges and give the Indians satisfaction for all the offenses they had endured, all the humiliations, all the outrages.

The old men heard him in stupefaction and the young men with enthusiasm. If there had been any alcohol, how easy it would have been to sweep them off their feet, put a rifle or a torch in every hand.

Xaw Ramírez Paciencia had sat at the very back and was making an almost inhuman effort to pay attention, to listen. He looked around him to register the reactions of the listeners. Why were they taking leave of their senses like this? Had not Xaw himself warned them what the priest, Padre Manuel Mandujano, had preached? That they should pay no attention to this deceitful advice, that these foreigners were pukujes, devils come to bring perdition and damnation upon them.

The assembly concluded and each one took a ceremonious leave of Fernando, and made a brief bow, as was appropriate, towards César. All of them promised to look through their trunks and among their belongings to see if they found a document like the ones the Caxlán was requesting; if they were lucky and found something they would bring it to hand over to the engineer. Meanwhile, he and his assistant could spend the night here, since it was the place the Chamula authorities had designated for the town's guests.

"Here? In the Cabildo?" Fernando asked incredulously.

Yes. The one of greater respect—Ulloa—could sleep on the table which was large and solid and would bear his weight well; the other could make himself comfortable on the pine needles.

That was what they did, and since there was no light and the stub of a candle they were provided with burned away very quickly they went to bed early. Their cigarettes glimmered in the darkness.

"What do you think of the reception they gave us?" the engineer asked.

"We can't expect anything better; we have to accept some discomforts."

"I'm not talking about that. I got the impression they didn't understand what we told them. Otherwise I can't explain why they reacted that way."

"Some of them seemed very glad."

"But the others looked at us with such mistrust. . . ."

"Indians are very ungrateful."

"Don't say 'Indians' as if you were talking about people from another planet; try to understand their attitude; think about how you would behave if you were in a similar situation."

Santiago smiled with a hint of mockery.

"They're suspicious; that's natural. After all, they don't know us; we're Ladinos and they don't have a very high opinion of Ladinos. It's up to us to convince them that our intention is not to harm them but to see to it that the law that protects them is carried out."

"The old men are very reluctant. We can't count on them."

But César wasn't too sure about the young men either. Who knows what they're thinking, who knows how they interpret what we say to them? The brightest of them was undoubtedly Pedro González Winiktón, who had offered to serve as their interpreter and guide.

The long excursions began right away; the Caxláns, Fernando and César, went on horseback, and Winiktón went on foot along with a little boy he treated as his son, Domingo Díaz Puiljá.

Familiar with the trail and light on their feet, the Indians would go ahead. Pedro would stop in front of a boundary stone, and Fernando would note down a few figures and take measurements with some strange devices that were carried by a pack mule. From time to time he would shake his head in impatience or doubt.

The engineer had learned to drink posol. At the edge of a stream or a spring, he would dismount to beat the corn paste up with water. He would chat with his assistant or ask Pedro who owned the sheep grazing nearby, who had planted that cornfield, what Don Olinto Serrano—who rented out that land as if it belonged to him—was like.

Pedro, precise and eager to help, answered as fully as he could. And he, in his turn, would ask, "Has Fernando Ulloa seen the law? Where is it? Is it true that it says every campesino must be the owner of the plot of land he works? Will the ranchers no longer be able to call themselves the owners of great expanses of land and evict towns that were established there centuries before?"

Pedro recalled the exoduses of his childhood. His parents had their hut, their cornfield, in a village that no longer exists. Suddenly the troops came and threw them out with blows from the butts of their rifles; the soldiers went off with the sheep and chickens and left them in the middle of a road with the few belongings they had been able to save and no shelter to sleep in. They looked for a place to settle on the highest and most barren hill, until they were thrown out of there in turn.

"And my parents had titles, papers. It did them no good at all."

At times a sudden storm made Fernando and his companions run to take shelter beneath a tree, in a sheepfold or in an Indian family's hut.

There they would sit around the fire with the smoke smarting in their eyes, amid a smell of boiling food and human bodies at close quarters, the animal scent that persists in newborn babies, especially. Outside, the water ran down between the roughly joined planks and the half-rotten straw of the roof. The little children watched from a corner, quiet, ragged, big-bellied. Creeping along, trying not to make any noise or attract the attention of the strangers, they went over to their mother who was laboriously grinding the nixtamal, her eyes lowered, embarrassed and mute.

The master of the house would open the door to them at Pedro's request, because Pedro was a former authority and was known as an honorable man. If he was accompanying these Ladinos there was no reason to fear any harm from them. Hospitably, the owner would uncork a demijohn of aguardiente and invite the visitors to partake. All of them drank straight from the bottle, even the boy Domingo. All except César, who was repelled by the custom.

But while Santiago remained on the margin, a current of fellow feeling and friendship would be established among the other men.

Little by little, the owner of the house would yield to persuasion and begin to speak.

And in that way, today here and tomorrow somewhere else, each man finally says what he has kept inside himself for years. They come with their complaints as they would go to the altar of a saint. And it is the same monotonous chant, the same litany of abuses endured, poverty, sickness, ignorance. These men's misfortune has something impersonal and inhuman about it, so uniformly is it repeated again and again.

Yes, some of them complain, and that is fine; complaining is the custom of a vanquished race, an abject generation. But not all of them are in the same mood. There are those who raise their voices in protest, who make demands. And there are those who propose ways of remedying the situation.

Ulloa answers them. He knows they will not accept any evasions. And he promises. He, a man of reason, will speak with the Ladino authorities. No, they must not rush into anything or go beyond the law, because the law foresees everything, protects against everything. The machine of justice, paralyzed until now by pettifoggers and shysters, has only to be set in motion. Fernando has experience; he knows how to handle deceitful men. Yes, he comes from somewhere else, "from the farthest reaches of Mexico." And it is true that he knows the president and can bear out Pedro González Winiktón's testimony that the president exists. And that the president has the power to order that the Indians be given back what is theirs.

"Fernando, take out the paper that talks; note down what you hear so you can keep all of it in your mind. Here is Crisanto Pérez Condiós and the story of when they indentured him by force to work on the fincas. Here is Raquel Domínguez Ardilla, with whip marks that have not yet scarred over on her back. And you must know about the sister of Domingo Gómez Tuluc, kidnapped in the streets of Jobel to work as a servant in a rich man's house. Put down, with those letters, that the soldiers entered the village of Majomut and razed everything in their path. The accusation that the Indians had set up a still to make liquor was a lie. But now, who will give back the stolen chickens, the wrecked loom, the life of the children whose bellies were ripped open by bayonets? No one will give an unfrightened gaze back to the women or a soul without bitterness to the men. It must be told. Note it down, Fernando; write it, Caxlán."

This man, César meditated, as he watched the engineer bent over his papers, is getting in way over his head with his promise to use the law to help these wretches. What law? In Ciudad Real, in the highlands of Chiapas, there is no law but force. And force is what the ranchers have. The Indians would have it if sheer numbers were all that mattered. There are many of them here, and these aren't the only ones. There are still more higher up in the mountains, waiting for a signal, a voice, to bring them together. But Fernando doesn't have what it takes to be their leader. He's full of good intentions and fails to anticipate other people's malevolence.

"If they left it to me, they'd see how I'd play the game."

CHAPTER XVI

CATALINA DÍAZ PUILJÁ turned the spindle while her sheep grazed. From time to time she cast a resentful glance around her. No one.

She was alone; day and night she was alone. Ever since the pair of Ladinos had been making the rounds of the villages with their words and their numbers, Pedro González Winiktón had not been the same.

But when had it been any other way? Catalina made an effort to remember, to revive the husband she had had during the early times, the man who was clear water, cool water she drank from when she was thirsty. Not this enemy who had since taken his place, always sunk deep inside himself, sad and remote, thinking —about what?

It had been some time since Catalina had stopped blaming herself for Pedro's indifference. It was true that she was barren and he was well within his rights if he wanted to repudiate her. But he never did. Why was she losing him now that they had a son? Because Domingo was hers; he did not belong to Marcela Gómez Oso or Lorenzo Díaz Puiljá. What did they know, poor things, about the gift that had been entrusted to them? Between the girl's inexperience and the man's imbecility they would have ended up letting Domingo die. Catalina was the one who saved the baby, snatching it from Marcela's lap.

Marcela, a bad mother, did not even have milk to nurse him with. The ewes that had just given birth, the she-goats, had to be milked in order to feed the little one.

Catalina knew secrets for preparing herbal infusions and potions, and that lore alone had freed the little boy, time after time, from the clutches of disease and fever.

Domingo grew up in the folds of Catalina's skirts; he learned to walk holding Catalina's hand. Marcela only watched from afar, indifferent. And Lorenzo, from farther still, laughed without understanding anything; he laughed by himself, stupidly, when there was no reason to.

Pedro loved the little boy and sheltered him in the shade of his years. When the boy was old enough, Pedro took him along to the mountain, to the cornfield. He explained the names of things to him, the habits of the animals, the properties and behavior of plants. The father spoke, glad to pass on what he had been storing up over time. The son listened attentively, respectfully. And when the day and the work were over, the two of them went back to the hut even closer, even better friends.

In front of women, composure must be maintained. They are not meant to hear manly things. In their mouths, everything turns to chatter and babbling. They must be taught by example to be serious.

Catalina knew this and approved of it. The boy (he was still a boy, barely ten years old) was already demanding the treatment a man is accorded. Containing herself, the ilol approached Domingo to serve rather than coddle him. Her hands abandoned their caresses, her lips their tender names. But Catalina's renunciations, this distance, was the soil in which the boy's manhood was germinating. He was going to be a man like Pedro, cautious, severe, held in high esteem by others. That was what he was being prepared for, and it was good. But when Pedro began to frequent the Caxláns, who were always there now, and when he was imprudent enough to converse with Fernando and César in front of Domingo, Catalina felt a painful jolt, as when a female tapir sniffs a danger to her babies in the wind.

It was useless to try to separate them. Anyway, Catalina was not accustomed to manifesting her disapproval of Pedro's conduct directly. This time she put her reputation as an ilol to use and announced that her second sight had revealed to her that the two Caxláns' stay in Chamula had no other end or purpose than to bring harm to the people of the tribe, by denouncing the clandestine distillers of aguardiente or by selling the information they were able to gather from their observation of the town to the ranchers and enganchadors of Jobel.

The rumor reached Pedro's ears after having passed through so many mouths that its origin was no longer identifiable. In Catalina's presence, Winiktón spoke harshly of the faint-heartedness and bad faith of those who were spreading such gossip. Catalina argued that those who looked upon the Ladinos with distrust were not to blame. When had an Indian received anything good from a Ladino? Except for the monks and the priests. But those men share only the speech of the Ladinos and are different in every other respect; they are of the race of angels, so great is their power to mete out—and how incomprehensibly, at times!—rewards and punishments.

"Oh really? Certainly you are not going to tell me that the priest of San Juan, that man Manuel Mandujano, has any strength. It is not true! I have seen him fall to the ground, knocked down by rage and by fear. I have seen him tremble at the sound of my voice!"

Catalina enfolded herself back into silence. But like a spider in its web, she was tirelessly spinning ways to separate Pedro from the newcomers whom he spoke to in Spanish about matters she did not understand and which left him pensive, irritable and uneasy.

As if to alleviate the weight of his preoccupations, Winiktón went out looking for someone to share them with. He took great care in choosing the men he spoke to. Never respectable old men, men of council. Not even Xaw Ramírez Paciencia, whom he no longer visited so as to avoid going to the parish house.

No, Pedro's new friends were young men who were disrespectful like he was. They were the ones who had returned from working on the coastal fincas, made insolent by their travels, or the ones who had gone further, down to the isthmus, up to Mexico, those who no longer found it good to continue living as they had lived until then. Poverty enraged them like an injustice. A man (they pronounced the word with all the pride of a valuable discovery), a man does not have to endure it.

"If the Ladinos do not recognize our rights, we must reclaim them. By force, if necessary. By war."

They have seen weapons at close hand, they know how to use them, they know how an army is organized and some have been soldiers. The smell of gunpowder excites them. And in their dreams they hurl themselves against an enemy who has no face yet, no name.

At the hour of killing they will shout: Patrón! Ladino! Caxlán! Because Caxláns die too. Have they not seen them fall at the crossroads, cut down by blows of the machete? Or burned to ⌊cin⌋ders by the flames of a raging fire?

Who wielded the machetes? Who set the fire? Indians. Indians
know how to kill from behind. Now they must learn to fight
head on, with their faces bared. Indians are numerous. There are
many more of them than their enemies. Why should they be
afraid?

Ah, how easy it is to talk, Catalina thinks. The man who talks
gallops like a horseman across the plain. And suddenly he stumbles on a rock: the question, "Where are the weapons? And the
money? And the leaders? Before we have raised our machetes the
Ladinos will have finished us off with their bullets."

The horseman reels, then recovers his balance.

"We must get what we need."

Now comes the deep crevasse which went unnoticed in the
vertigo of the mad dash: "How?"

And here is Pedro, assured and enigmatic, who says quickly:
"I know how."

He knows how. The others fall silent, won over by the authority of the one who affirms. And they wait.

The conversation continues outside the hut, in the village, in
the fields. Catalina follows them from afar, worried, rejected.
What are they saying now? Men's words, oaths. And Winiktón
does not keep Domingo out of these strong winds. Why? Domingo, Domingo. To pronounce the name is to chew a bitter root.

"They snatched him from my lap as if he were already grown
up and ripened. They left me alone again. Bruja, evil woman, ilol!
They punish the harm I did, the harm I want to do. San Juan
Guarantor, have pity on me!

"When I bend down to blow on the fire, steam from the pots
envelops my face and drenches it with moisture. Hot drops run
down my throat, my shoulders. And still I am cold; my teeth
chatter, my joints ache. Ay, my eyelids close by themselves because I do not want to see the sun. How dark it is in here. I have
to feel my way, as if I were at the bottom of a cave. A cave! An
echo resounds against the hollow rock. Lizards crawl, hunting
moisture. My feet slip on the cold slabs of stone. And this wet
darkness penetrates to my bones. It is as if I had died and were
buried, wrapped in an old petate. And I do not have the dog with
me, the dog who must help me cross the rivers. The dog, the tiger
of San Roque, protector of brujos. No one, no one. It is impos-

sible to go forward. I am going to rot away here, in the grave, in the cave.

"But sometimes I find little stones to play with. Little stones and big ones. Moss. No, no moss, I do not want to sleep. Stones. Like the ones I once found.

"They were my secret. Lorenzo knew about it. But Lorenzo was carried off by the great pukuj and has forgotten everything. His head is like an empty bell. Only I know where the cave is, where the stones are. There are three of them. They have faces like a person's face. They speak. I have heard them speak. But I ran away because I was afraid. I was a little girl and shadows frightened me. Today . . . today I am not frightened even to live with a man who is not mine and not to know who he belongs to. I lost him, they wrenched him away from me. Like the trees along the roadway, I had all my wealth spread out around me. Anyone who passes by covets it. And I, blind, unmoving, I stand here being torn apart, being stripped of everything. I don't know how to defend myself. I cannot. Now I am going to open this fist which cannot keep hold of anything. I am going to untie the knot of my love that held nothing more than air. I am alone. This must be understood completely. Alone."

When thoughts are painful, the pain peers out from the face. Everywhere, in the pasture, at the river, in the hut, at church, Catalina bore the mark of her suffering. The women drew back from her in fear and kept a watch on her intentions from a distance. They could not be good intentions. To do harm! What does the wounded beast want except to bite those around it, to rip them to pieces. The circle of isolation around Catalina was closed. And she remained at its center, with the cold fever that racked her temples, the delirium that filled her eyes with absurd images, the hunger that made her dig up memories long buried.

To go back in time, to erase this day of the absent husband, the abducted son. If she could go back to the beginning! When work was as joyful as play, and play. . . .

Running through the mountains, clambering among the boulders and suddenly the astonishment of that discovery. The cave hidden by the underbrush. Catalina fell, hurting herself on the sharp gravel, the thorns. She looked at the small opening without daring to go in. She left, frightened. But she would go back. She went back with Lorenzo. A man is a protection. Together, sister and brother pushed aside the brush. He went in first. She peered in from the edge, fearful. She wanted to scream, run away. But she followed him. Her heart was beating with such force that the whole cave resonated like a temple's lugubrious drums. Then, how cool and dark it was! Bats flapped their wings. Finding them here was a good sign. The bat is an auspicious spirit, a nahual. But there is something else here besides the scurrying of small animals that have been startled. When the intruders' eyes had grown accustomed to the darkness they could make out other shapes. Grotesque petrified ferns. And stones. Yes, stones. There is something about them that seems strange: their form is not fortuitous like that of other stones. All at once the two children break into a terrified run. Outside, at a great distance from the place of danger, they tell each other about their impressions. "What did you see?" "The face of a brujo, a demon. And you?" "I cannot say." Lorenzo stammers; he is slow to express himself. And even more when he is startled. He cannot speak. He is mute. The words that remain to him are few, incoherent. After that he will be silent forever.

The experience of the cave remains a secret. Catalina does not talk. Night after night, for months, the memory stalks her. Time and again, curiosity will drive her towards the mysterious site. But fear does not allow her to go in. She stays there, in front of the cavern's mouth. She knows obscurely that the day she crosses that threshold she will die.

Catalina left her childhood behind her as she would leave a battered hut that offered no protection from the elements: without nostalgia. She entered into her life as a woman sustained by Pedro's love. And then came the years of tunneling into rock without being rewarded by a single drop of water. Everything everywhere was desert and thirst. Suffering instructed her in a dark knowledge. Others feared her. She herself, at times, was afraid to be the instrument of supernatural powers. The bolt of lightning could strike the beings Catalina loved. Pedro, always the first; then Lorenzo. And then Domingo, little Domingo. Marcela was not the one who carried him inside her. The jealousy of brujos gave things a deceptive appearance. Catalina was the mother. The father was not a nameless Ladino from Jobel. The father was

Catalina's husband. The boy had been born of the love between the two of them and grew up under their joint care.

"Lies! Do you not see that you have lied, for years and years, Catalina? If what you say were true, if you were the boy's mother, would you be treated as you are treated? The man's indifference, his aloofness, are the punishment for your sterility. And now Domingo is being taken from you, carried away from you, taught to forget you. Where is your power? That was a lie, too. Your frown is a cloud without lightning, your left hand is a catastrophe that has been successfully warded off. What good are your invocations? The ears of the gods are deaf, their promises were in vain. They abandoned you, too, without hope; ay, you worshiped them. Punishment, everything is punishment. Did you ever reveal what you knew about them? No, you let them rot away in the damp, dark oblivion of their cave. Green with moss they must be now, cracked by time. No one takes them offerings or candles. You cheated them of the adoration that is their due by not telling anyone what you found or demanding that their images be revered."

She had to go back to the cave, display the idols to the community. Catalina's absences, her searches, went unnoticed by her family. Pedro was too absorbed in his conversations with the Caxláns. And Domingo always went where Pedro went. The others . . . the others did not count: Lorenzo the idiot and Marcela, who lived in a fog.

Catalina remembered the direction but not the precise place. She climbed rocks, heedless of the flock; she got entangled in brambles. Unafraid of hurting herself, she brushed aside the undergrowth to find the cave's hidden mouth. And the more lost she became, the more fruitless her efforts were, the more the fever would grip the ilol. She had to find that place! She had to. She attributed all her misfortunes to this single cause, and all her hopes were fixed on this single point: the cave, the cave, the cave.

Desperate, Catalina turned to Lorenzo, as if he could answer her questions. She clawed at his arm, twisted it to wring a revelation from the tortured flesh. Marcela watched this scene, open-mouthed, without daring to intervene; all her sister-in-law's actions were always incomprehensible to her, though she never failed to consider them mysteriously correct.

Catalina let her brother go and went to sit next to the fire. She was cold, yet sweat drenched her back and the palms of her hands. Shivering, she held a cup of coffee and drank it anxiously. The flames' glow danced across her gaunt face, tracing grotesque shadows. A great fatigue left her limp. Tears rolled down her sallow cheeks.

No presence came now in response to her prayers, her invocations. Catalina started like a skittish mare at a sound, a murmur. But the sounds and murmurs of the world brought no message, no word destined for the ilol.

As if they could tell what was happening, people avoided contact with her. No one sought out Catalina any longer to ask for advice or request some form of vengeance. Her left hand hung down lifelessly. Her right hand was empty.

Catalina began to speak. Her words were a confused mingling of threats and promises:

"The time is growing ripe; the great days are approaching, our days. The woodcutter's ax is chopping the tree which must fall in order to destroy many people. I am telling you and you. Do not let what is coming catch you off guard. Get ready. Be prepared. Because a great peril is coming soon."

Those who happened to be walking by and heard her continued on their way with a vague unease. She had powers, the gods had not left the ilol helpless. The enormity of her revelations gnaws at their insides; look at her, with her scorched lips and her delirious gaze, her hair in a snarl. Look at her on the mountain, moving like a sleepwalker. It is because she is listening. The voice is multiplied in echoes: north and south, east and west. Here, here, no, further ahead. She advances, falls back. She trips, her clothing rips, the thistles bite. Where are you walking, Catalina Díaz Puiljá? On the surface of the earth or deep inside your soul? You arrived, at last. Where memory, rising up from your feet, coming in through your eyes, awaking in your touch, begins to recognize and says: it is here. Do not falter; go nearer. Go down this pathless slope; duck under that branch, peer down into the entrance. The smell—remember?—a gulp of damp, unhealthy air. Cross the threshold, go in. You see nothing yet. Wait to get used to the darkness. Now go on. You were already here once. Your heart resounds, as it did then, in the hollow space around you. The stones are there, in that corner. But there is nothing! They have disappeared! You dreamed of something that did not exist; your treasure has been robbed. Wait. You were not dreaming. There are the stones: three of them, as before. Three. The world is yours, Catalina Díaz Puiljá, destiny belongs to you now. Go out, shout it to the four winds. Let them come! Let them bow down before you, all of them! Pedro! Domingo! Everyone!

Catalina's cries were lost in the vacant immensity of the countryside. She wanted to run but she did not want to leave her discovery; she embraced it, mortifying her skin against the mineral harshness. She could not move it.

They will come soon, the woman said to herself; they have to look for me. But the hours went by, night and day, all the same inside the cave.

They will come. They came. They found Catalina next to her stones, fainting from joy and hunger.

CHAPTER XVII

AT WHAT MOMENT does infidelity begin? Julia Acevedo couldn't say exactly when she started listening to Cifuentes' propositions as if they were acceptable. Her own conjugal disappointments did more to undermine her resistance than her seducer.

Fernando made Leonardo's bed for him, she concluded malevolently. And perhaps her decision to yield herself to the rancher was no more than the despairing gesture of a gambler who bets the last she has on a single card.

So Julia faced Leonardo. This is a fight, not a trap, she recited to herself in the early days of their affair, to give herself courage. She was confident in the attractions she knew how to play up, the pleasure she knew how to give. She was sure she could handle herself well enough to keep from losing control of the situation. But she wasn't counting on Leonardo's callousness, the masculine complacence accustomed to receiving tributes, not gifts. And her greatest social asset, the fact that she was a foreigner, was eclipsed by a brutal new designation: mistress. She was Leonardo's mistress, and that fact automatically put her at his mercy.

The lovers' meetings were not easy. La Alazana prepared for them with great care, in the firm belief that discretion alone would close gossiping mouths. There were no witnesses, but there was plenty of testimony. And since scandals are repeated, not invented, those who took it upon themselves to inform the public needed only to repeat the old story, warmed over once more. The story Leonardo and Julia, who were living it, thought they had originated.

Julia Acevedo was waiting. Her throat was dry, her tongue stuck to the roof of her mouth—and this wasn't even the first time. She strained to hear the faintest sound from the street. She had given the servants the evening off on whatever pretext she could think of (the neighborhood fiesta, because there's always a fiesta in some neighborhood somewhere), and she was alone in the vast house. Alone and almost in darkness. One candle flickered in a corner of the main room.

Julia clasped her hands together on her chest as if in prayer. Her heart was pounding rapidly. Thank God the sound of its beating was drowned out by the racket in the street: firecrackers, a sudden galloping of hoofs, some drunkards' stumbling footsteps, tuneless songs. Thank God! But in all that commotion how would she be able to hear the sound she was waiting for, the grating of the key in the lock, the short squeak of the opening door.

Nervous, La Alazana peered into the passageway. The moon's light projected freakish shadows on the brick pavement. A cold, remote moon. But then, what time was it? Julia had lost all notion of time. This night is eternal. It began centuries ago and will never end.

"What will he think if he sees me like this? I must be calm, control myself. This is a fight, not a trap."

La Alazana went to the kitchen and revived the fire to warm up a cup of tea. To help strengthen her will, she lit the lamps. When she examined herself in the mirror she was satisfied with what she saw. Her expression was undaunted; an artificial layer of pink concealed the whiteness of her face.

Julia returned to the main room, picked up a book and settled down on the sofa. When Cifuentes came in, she could raise her head in genuine surprise, as if interrupted by chance.

Leonardo paid no attention to these details. He was after his own pleasure and he demanded it straightforwardly. Boastful of his prowess, he was glad to be spared any feeling of gratitude.

In their conversations afterwards, Leonardo showed off: carefully adjusted memories of former adventures, explanations of his current plans, business, politics. For added bite he would throw in a few insulting references to her husband, Fernando. "Do you know what he's up to now? He's preaching to the Chamulas. That they're equal to the Ladinos, that they'll own the land they work on. As if Indians could understand what he's telling them."

Julia was silent. The tone of his voice, his coarse words always made her tense. Occasionally she attempted a smile but only succeeded in producing an ill-timed grimace. To free herself from subjugation to this man, Julia could only try to ignore his presence, erase him from her imagination and her mind. She closed her eyes, lost herself in absurd thoughts, hypnotic repetitions:

"Pablito nailed a nail, a nail did Pablito nail; one, two, three, four, one hundred; Jesus Christ my Saviour and the one true God . . . when there are oranges, oranges, when there are lemons, lemons."

Julia was growing drowsy. But she started back to consciousness when she heard Fernando's name. What was it about? Of course, the Indians. "Don't even mention them to me! The Indians! I hate them all. Foul, miserable brutes. You can't walk in the streets of Ciudad Real without tripping over a drunken Indian, being bashed over the head by the load some Indian is carrying around like a blind man, or else slipping on the pieces of rind they leave everywhere."

Leonardo laughed, pleased by the spirited description. Now that he thought about it, he had felt the same disgust for the same reasons. But never in a thousand years would he have been able to say it the way La Alazana had said it. She was funny. And to possess this sense of humor that he didn't understand, that disturbed him, Leonardo rolled onto Julia, imposing the roundness of his flesh on her, filling that mouth with the only language the two of them shared: the language of pleasure.

Julia resisted until her opponent's desire was at its utmost. Then she yielded, unleashing her instincts little by little until she gave herself over entirely.

It calmed her down, at least! And when she was alone again she gazed at her surroundings as if everything were new and she were beholding it in amazement. Events still succeeded each other with the monotony of their ordinary rhythm, the foundations of the world were intact, the catastrophe had not happened.

"I am an adulteress," Julia repeated, to convince herself of a fact whose reality did not change her essential being. She was different only in the eyes of others: she had become the object of their contempt, their rejection.

Isabel listened to the gossip about her rival with secret delight. Finally she could leave to others the arduous task of suspecting deceptions, the sad necessity of discovering them and the unwelcome privilege of punishing. Her unruffled behavior filled the murmuring voices of Ciudad Real with admiration. Just look at her—a true Santa Rita de Casia! A fine example for all the quick-tempered young wives who martyrize their husbands over nothing. The bishop himself paid a special visit to Isabel to recommend patience, the only quality among all Christian virtues that is comparable to charity.

The bishop's exhortations made Isabel laugh inwardly. But long years of hypocrisy enabled her to improvise a more appropriate reaction. "It's not my own situation that pains me. All this is very little compared to what I deserve for my sins. What worries me is my daughter."

"What does Idolina have to do with this?"

"She has become very attached to . . . to that woman."

"How can this be? La Alazana is an improper, I would say even a dangerous companion."

"I know, Monseñor, but I can't forbid Idolina to see her. She's so lonely!"

"You must keep a close watch on them, at least. Are you present when they see each other?"

"No."

"Why not?"

"It's more than I can bear, Monseñor!"

"Yes. I understand. But someone will have to intervene."

"Tell her yourself, Don Alfonso. Idolina pays no attention to anything I say. If I ask her for something, she'll do anything she can to give me the opposite."

Idolina listened to His Excellency's sermon, her jaws stubbornly clenched shut. This old man was a nobody, even if he was covered with silks and amethysts. Ranks, titles. . . . Idolina knew what appearances hid: dirt and lies. Let the adults who created them and worshiped them believe in these distinctions. Adults! Primly sticking out their little fingers to pick up a cup of chocolate, wiping the corners of their mouths with the edge of a napkin, gathering up their skirts to keep them from dragging in puddles. But when they are alone they flaunt their vices. Idolina did not know what those vices were, where they were practiced or how. But she sensed the atmosphere of carnality emanating from women and men alike, she caught their winks of complicity, their hungering look-out for what they called "the chance." Idolina was intensely conscious of their disdain for her because she was a girl, because she would never grow up, because she would never decipher their secrets, because she would always look on from outside, from the opposing side, at the assembly of satisfied, surfeited adults. With all her wounded purity, corrupt innocence and aimless passion, she hated them.

What is the old man talking about? Clearly he enjoys listening to himself. He savors the easy glide of his words. He is pleased. But you can't listen to him. He is treacherous. Among his circumlocutions Idolina grasps his intention: he is trying to separate her from Julia. Why? He says Julia is not a fit companion. No? Then who is? Idolina doesn't know the girls of Ciudad Real. And she fears them. From behind her window she has watched them go by. They walk with their eyes lowered. They whisper. At dusk, they go into the street with their faces concealed behind a shawl. Where are they going? What are they looking for? The next day they remember and smile at each other. There is no place among them for Idolina; she belongs to another species.

The bishop doesn't dare state the definitive accusation against Julia in so many words. But between one reticence and another an image emerges: adultery. And the outline of the protagonists is sketched in: La Alazana and Leonardo.

Idolina's first impulse is to shout that people are telling lies about them. But an instant's consideration silences her. Her stepfather is certainly capable of such a thing. And the thought of how her mother must be suffering anesthetizes Idolina, keeps her from thinking of her own pain.

Until afterward when she feels the wound in solitude. She has been betrayed again, in the same way, with the same man. Idolina hates Cifuentes with a loathing in which secret admiration and an obscure envy are mingled.

There she sits in a corner, powerless, while the blood pounds inside her and she gasps for air.

The guilty parties are beyond her reach. How can she punish them? She makes up incantations, chants them. If only Teresa were here, her nana! When she realizes that her words have no meaning, no effect, she falls silent and returns to the point from which she started: the crime, a crime whose enormity is making her head explode. She stands up. It is midnight and the fire in the brazier has gone out. Stumbling, she goes to the candle and lights it. But the idea that brought her to her feet disappears in the pale light of the oscillating flame. What did she want? Yes, to complain, to protest. But not tomorrow. Centuries would go by before sunrise. She searches anxiously for paper and a pencil. Then she, Idolina, who can barely write, is filling one page after another with the large, shaky letters of someone unaccustomed to doing things with her hands. It is a tumultuous narrative, an infantile confession, a last cry before drowning. When she finishes, she is shaking as if after a great physical exertion. She folds the sheets of paper and puts them in an envelope. Only then does she realize there is no one to send them to. Before blowing out the candle, she sets fire to a corner of the manuscript. In the sudden brightness, she returns to her bed.

Now she shivers with cold. The momentary relief granted by writing has disappeared. Yes, she could die. But not at some vague future moment. Right now. It doesn't matter how, and she's unable to imagine the details. She's terrified of the pain, the supreme moment in which the body perishes. No, she wants to die without complications, without horrible delays, as easily as if it were happening in a dream. Idolina dead. A pale serenity endowing her face with a certain beauty . . . but her jaw drops open and has to be tied shut with a handkerchief. It doesn't matter, go on. Around the bier the candles flicker, languishing in their funereal jaundice. And the guilty parties, what do they do? Laugh? Shrug their shoulders, indifferent? No, that's impossible, that's not fair. "I killed her!" her mother would moan, wringing her hands. "I killed her!" she would scream at the people who came to express their condolences and when they heard her they would turn their backs on her, horrified.

And Julia? Julia would have to leave Ciudad Real, tormented by remorse.

Idolina's cheeks were wet with tears. She wept with self-pity; she wept as she imagined the bitter, vengeful memory of her that would stay with her torturers forever.

To confound her plans and even her wishes, her health gave no sign of faltering. As much as she scrutinized herself, constantly on the lookout for any hint of an ailment, she couldn't find the slightest symptom to worry over. She went back to her old tricks and pretended she was sick. But Julia wasn't deceived.

"Get up, lazybones. You're just going to lie there and waste a day as beautiful as this one? Look at the sky. Not a cloud. It's practically a miracle in a town like this where there's never anything but rain and more rain. Come on, get up and come with me. At least the outskirts of Ciudad Real are pretty. The Peje de Oro, the fields, the orchards. And the peaches are ripe now. Juicy and sweet. Don't you like peaches? No, I don't want any excuses. You're feeling weak and exhausted? Come on, your face is turning pink—you can't get away with telling lies."

Julia made Idolina get dressed. Together they walked through the streets of Ciudad Real.

"Why don't people say hello to us?" the girl observed suspiciously.

"Because they don't know us," her companion answered with apparent frankness. "You've always been shut up indoors and I'm not from here."

Idolina wasn't satisfied with this explanation and continued to reflect on her suspicions.

They don't say hello because they despise us. She's immoral and I tolerate her. What they're saying about Julia and my stepfather is true.

In her effort to get at the truth, Idolina remembered certain details, certain odd allusions; to this evidence, she added Isabel's jealousy. But all her suspicions collapsed when confronted with Julia, her words, her gestures. Her face was so clear, her laugh so spontaneous. No, it isn't true, it can't be true!

It was true. By then, relations between Julia and Leonardo had entered a more secure phase. The lovers had settled into a routine after weeks of stimulating their thirst for each other with fear— a fear Fernando's behavior did nothing to provoke. His absences gave them a wide margin of error and his returns were always foreseen far in advance. Guilt was too weak a feeling, in both Julia and Leonardo, to sustain an atmosphere of agitation, regret and fear for very long. The passion of the affair's early days was drifting toward a tranquil, conjugal affection.

But this was not what the rancher wanted in a lover, and certainly not what he expected from a lover like Julia. He confided his disappointment to Doña Mercedes Solórzano.

"What are you telling me, child! I suppose it's like the old saying, 'Faces we know, hearts we don't.' But listen, take my advice: keep quiet. Don't tell anyone about this and don't let them suspect it, because all you'll do is make people laugh at you. If you knew how jealous your friends are! They're saying La Alazana is a choice morsel while they have to make do with whatever moth-eaten thing they can find because nowadays it's not like it was back when there were so many good-looking women around. Let them keep on saying it. Why should you give them the satisfaction of knowing it's not true? And if you want to have a little fun with someone else, no one's going to give you any problems. I know you, you sly dog. You're hankering for a maid's starched apron or even an Indian girl's faded tzec. Leave it to me, I'll take care of everything. I was beginning to miss having something to do for you. Don't you think I know that in jail and in bed is where friends meet?"

Cifuentes did not accept her offer. For the moment, he did no more than think it over. Because when he added it all up, in the final analysis, Isabel, his wife, had succeeded in keeping him in a state of tension and expectation far longer than this new woman.

Julia's glowing good health immunized her against hysterical outbursts, her perfect confidence in herself and her attractions freed her from jealousy, and a certain moral insensitivity easily calmed her scruples. For her, even the most complicated adulterous liaison would quickly become a normal situation.

Leonardo observed other symptoms as well. Julia was taking on a satisfied, matronly look that infuriated him. He began to annoy her just to see how she would react: last-minute excuses for not coming to her house, strange perfumes suddenly releasing their scent from between the folds of a handkerchief, inexplicable moments of distraction. Doña Mercedes, ever the faithful servant, delicately pointed out to Julia the danger that Cifuentes might, one day soon, get fed up with her.

Julia took heed. All she needed was for this rancher, this peasant to whom she had condescended, to whom she had lowered herself, to give himself the luxury of humiliating her. The insult went beyond Julia personally: the provinces were scoffing at the elegance, the good taste and, ultimately, the superiority of the capital.

How have I been careless? Julia asked herself, squeezing an indiscreet blackhead in front of the mirror. Her instincts told her how to make up the lost ground. It was simple: her caresses were painstakingly counterbalanced by moments of coldness, feigned absences, deliberate forgetfulness. But Leonardo, an old hand with a great deal of experience in these matters, sensed the deception from afar and watched it coming with a sarcastic smile.

In these skirmishes, they were playing against each other to establish their position, the dominance each one wanted to have over the vanquished adversary. The man's experience was winning; the woman's vulnerable nature was losing. But a chance event neither of them had foreseen determined the final outcome of the match.

"What about the shawl I gave you?" Leonardo asked. "Why don't you ever wear it? Don't you like it?"

"There's never a place to wear it. I never go out. And when I'm here I need something warmer. I'd catch cold if I wore your shawl."

The pretext was valid. But to Cifuentes it smelled of something false, something thought up on the spot. A few days later he asked again. "And the shawl? Don't tell me it's too cold today. The heat in the courtyard is enough to suffocate anyone."

"You're right," Julia answered vaguely. "It's a beautiful day. In Tepic they must be roasting right now."

She began to evoke her house in Tepic, the events of her stay there, the people she had known. The nostalgia in her voice irritated Leonardo. So she wasn't happy here? What more could a woman like Julia ask for? Suddenly he interrupted her. "Slow down a little, Julia. We were talking about the shawl."

"What about the shawl! What do you want me to do with it, frame it and hang it on the wall?"

"I want you to wear it, to make me happy."

"Listen, I'm not going to play the fool for anybody. If what you want is a woman who'll be your puppet then you can look for her somewhere else because as far as I'm concerned you're in the wrong place."

She looked beautiful like that, her face flushed with anger. A fierce scowl erased the hint of fleshiness that so badly suited her type of woman. Cifuentes was excited enough to plunge into the fray. "Careful what you say to me! Don't make me angry . . ."

"And if I do make you angry, what then? Are you going to tell me you'll find another querida? Go ahead, hurry up. You're only standing in my way here."

"I know what you're looking for, you cunning sow: you're trying to find any reason to show your disrespect for me."

"I don't owe you any respect."

"Who do you respect then? Poor Fernando?"

In an instant, the veneer of good manners Julia had acquired with such difficulty, maintained so carefully, was stripped off. Hands on her hips, she retorted, "Look who's talking! If Fernando is 'poor Fernando' then it's because of you!"

"Just like Isabel when I mention Isidoro. . . ."

"What does Isabel have to do with this? We're talking about me here, and only me."

"You're the one who brought her into this, with your flattering compliments. They seem well rehearsed. How many other men have you used them on?"

"Leonardo, you're going too far. . . ."

He answered, and everything was resolved in a bout of tears. Kisses, made all the sweeter by the icy insults that still lingered on their lips, passionate caresses that had to struggle against hostility, and finally complete inebriation, oblivion, annihilation. Two swimmers who had left their clothing of prejudice, irritation and mistrust on the shore. But after the brief immersion they had to return, put their clothes back on, and continue their dialogue.

"And the shawl?"

"The shawl again! How can I put it on now? It's too luxurious; it's meant for special occasions."

"When there is a special occasion you waste it. Why don't you wear it to matins at the cathedral of San Cristóbal?"

"I never thought of that."

"How odd!"

"Nombre de Dios, leave me alone."

"It's not because some other man will start complaining if you wear it?"

"I have enough headaches with you to keep me from wanting to get myself into some other mess, too."

"Then. . . ."

There was no explanation. Julia hated arguments and it couldn't have been easier to placate Cifuentes. Except that when she went to look for the shawl, she found the place where she had put it away in her dresser empty.

"How strange!" she said, quickly rifling through the other drawers. "I'm sure I left it here."

But the evidence mounted: the shawl wasn't there and it wasn't anywhere else. Julia searched even the most unlikely places in the house: the attic, the kitchen, the storage room. Nothing. As if the shawl had never existed.

Naturally she suspected the maid. At the first chance, she went into her room to continue the search. She forced open a chest, lifted the rug, moved the bed. Before leaving, she put everything back in place, but not carefully enough to keep the servant from seeing that someone had been in her room and raising a tremendous outcry: "I'm poor, but honest. I can hold my head high because no one is any better than I am. Not like certain ladies I know who hide their wicked doings behind their money."

The maid had to be appeased, begged for forgiveness, given a raise. And still the shawl had not turned up.

Leonardo became ever more insistent and ridiculous. Finally he cornered La Alazana, who, now that she felt guilty, was unable to steer the conversation away from the subject or turn it into an argument. She ended up confessing everything.

Leonardo was enraged. Was this the treatment he deserved? Carelessness might seem natural in some women, but not in Julia who keeps her house like a mirror, like a silver cup. If you ask her where the last bit of birdseed for the canary is, she knows. But she doesn't know what happens to gifts from the man she loves. Well, she must not love him very much if she appreciates his attentions so little! Of course, that's if she didn't lose the shawl on purpose.

La Alazana enveloped herself in a disdainful silence. To be criticized like this, to have the money Leonardo spent on gifts for her thrown in her face, it was too much! Because it wasn't jealousy. No, it was pure, flouted avarice that was causing all this commotion. The rancher's actions demonstrated very clearly what kind of family he came from, what kind of manners he had. Julia decided to put him in his place. Until he asked for her forgiveness, until he forgot about the accursed shawl, she wouldn't see him again.

Their quarrel lasted a few days. During that time Leonardo began to feel an anguished restlessness. He would find himself walking toward Julia's house out of habit, ready to take out his key and go in. And he had to control himself, endure it.

"You miss your sweetheart," Doña Mercedes observed. "And she's probably missing you, too, poor little thing."

"Hah! She's probably dancing around her house with joy at having gotten rid of me."

He said it to be contradicted, so that Doña Mercedes's comforting words would make his painful suspicions disappear. But her reasons seemed weak, her arguments easy to refute. The situation had to end.

Doña Mercedes was the emissary of peace. It required a great deal of effort to convince Julia. She was presented with a new shawl, richer and more beautiful than the one that had been lost. Adorned with this prize, Julia celebrated the triumph of her domination of Cifuentes' will.

CHAPTER XVIII

THE VILLAGE OF Tzajal-hemel had been transformed into a shrine, the destination of pilgrims from throughout the region of Chamula.

To the farthest reaches where Tzotzil is spoken the news traveled: the ancient gods have come back to life!

This, then, was the moment everyone had waited for. The elderly, their eyes clouded by age, were grateful to have lived long enough to see their waiting come to an end; the men in the prime of life welcomed the marvelous news with joy and reverence; the women, astonished, understood nothing except that their burden of suffering was to be lightened; the children moved easily in the atmosphere of miracle.

"The place where the gods of the ancestors chose to reveal themselves lies beyond a long distance. But that does not matter. Scout, you go ahead. We will follow you along the narrow footpath. Stop here to catch your breath, because the slope is steep and does not end soon. Protect yourself from the storm under those leafy trees, in that low pen where the sheep take shelter. Careful! Do not slip in the mud or stumble on the rock. Adjust your load so the offering will arrive undamaged: pom, the wild incense, the smoke that dissolves in praises; slow-burning wax candles; jars of aguardiente that inspire a fluency of prayer in those who drink them. Do you not know that each time God looks with malevolence upon the world and wants to destroy it (because our sins irritate him, because he is ashamed of our misery), men placate him with these gifts? God grants his alliance among sacred libations, among flickering lights and pleasant chants; this is known by those who transact with him, those who listen to his commands and serve the people as guides.

"It is said by Catalina Díaz Puiljá, and repeated by those who go after her. If you once knew the grotto where the gods appeared, you will no longer succeed in recognizing it. Look: where there was no more than mountain and brush, there are paths, paths that are frequently traversed. And the interior, once dark and damp, is now clean, sprinkled and fragrant with pine needles. In the center, what is that shape rising up? It is a wooden box, a kind of altar where the idol reposes. The box is unpolished, it was not planed well and you must handle it carefully or you will get splinters in your fingers. That is because the hands of Indians made it here.

"There are better workers in Jobel, no doubt. But it is not good to profane our ceremonies, to allow Caxláns to mix with them. No alien hand must touch even a board. The candles, the liquor, we made them ourselves, too. And the thing that is wrapped around the saint, what is it? It is a shawl. It came from far away, from Guatemala; it was woven there, by the hands of Indians as well. It has the additional virtue of having been the property of a woman who has fire on her head; flames spring from her and spill down her back and do not burn her. Do not fear any evil from her; she is not a Coleta, she is not from Ciudad Real. She is a foreigner and the wife of our protector and father Fernando Ulloa. Her name is Julia Acevedo.

"How strikingly the stony blackness stands out against the extravagant colors of the shawl. Look at its motionless face, its sealed mouth, its eyes fixed on a day that does not exist. It has been reborn here, in our midst, and nevertheless the distance between its hearing and our lament is like that between the stars!

"From Huistán and Yalcuc, from Jolnautic and Yaltem, from Zacampot and Milpoleta, from all directions we have arrived. The thread of tears that salts one person's cheek joins another thread of tears and another and another to flow here, to inundate the plain, to cover the hillside.

"And the god, is he at all moved? Does he ever say: enough! He has been born again, it is true; it is true that he reclines before us. But he has forgotten our tongue and no longer succeeds in speaking to us. And you be silent, too, pilgrim. You cry out uselessly; and therefore your harvest of corn will not be sufficient to your children's hunger; the patrón will grow fat on your debts and the malign powers will feed, as always, on your flocks. And you, woman, what are you whispering in a corner? It would be better for you to close your lips. The Ladina attacker at the outskirts of Jobel wrestled away the cloth you wove? Patience: wait for the sheep to be covered with wool again; shear it again, and weave. But do not go down to the city, be careful not to go near Jobel because the idol's arm does not reach to defend you there.

"Look at it there, sleeping, mute. Ay, how much better it would have been to stay in our village, in our house, and not to walk all this way so our eyes could look upon this sad, sad spectacle.

"In vain, in vain you tear your hair, oh multitude! Uselessly you beat your chest, you break down in howls and pleas! God, the god you came to worship, sleeps. He sleeps like a newborn. Or like a corpse."

Catalina never left the idols. Her hut could crumble away, abandoned; her family no longer received any form of care or attention from her. She was here, day and night, waiting. Waiting for what, she did not know.

When Catalina came back to herself after her discovery, she was surrounded by people of the tribe. She could not speak. Only her eyes remained fixed on the stone figures. The others looked at them as well, and understood. And when they left that place they spread out in all directions to announce the news.

With the offerings brought by the pilgrims the cave was decorated and by their labors it was kept clean despite the flow of visitors and the daily tumult. Drunk with the collective devotion, Catalina breathed an air of enthusiasm those first days, in the expectation of a supernatural immanence.

Who could defend Catalina against the intrusion of the sacred? No intimate companion, no stable affection. Only disembodied shadows, insubstantial words, mirages. Pedro, impassive, silent, frowning; Pedro, devoured by an unknown passion, a flame whose burning kept all external annoyances at a distance. Domingo, eager for novelties, forgetful of the gratitude he owed to the person who raised him. And the others: an idiot and a woman with whom it is impossible to speak because one cannot speak with objects. More real, more truly present were these unknown guests come from who knows where. Submissive and demanding, like all worshippers, the pilgrims came, filled with hope. Was it possible to let them leave without having fulfilled their hopes? Naturally, all eyes converged on Catalina. "What the idol's silence does not say, you must speak."

(You! You! The syllable echoes in a hollow brain; it oppresses and deepens an anguished breathing; it throbs in an uncertain pulse. You! If only you were able to hear. . . . Close your eyes, Catalina, do not be distracted by the sputtering of the candles, the murmur of the prayers, the sounds of life from outside. Focus. This call is weaker than a newborn's wail. Track it down among the confused and pointless noises. There is nothing but a voice. Its voice.)

Those who stood near Catalina could see her pallor. A heavy sweat run down her temples, drenching her neck and blouse; her rigid limbs convulsed. Suddenly she let out a cry and fell to the ground, writhing.

The whole assembly saw her fall and no one made the least movement to assist her, as if in some tacit way they had all agreed that the nature of the event taking place before their eyes outlawed any human intervention.

At the supplicants' feet, Catalina moaned; a thick, copious froth came from between her clenched teeth. The ilol twisted like a reptile being hacked apart with a machete. Frozen in terror the others watched her, trembling at the imminency of a revelation.

And Catalina spoke. Incoherent, meaningless words. Images, memories crowded together on her tongue. Her memory overran its limits to encompass experiences, lives that were not her own insignificant and impoverished one. In her voice the dreams of the tribe vibrated, the hope snatched away from those who died, the remembrance of an abolished past.

The sheaf of powers bound fighting around Catalina's name came undone and through the shreds of her personality the collective yearning overflowed, driven by delirium.

None of those who surrounded the ilol could understand either her evocation of past events or her prophecy. But all were infected with a wild jubilation that begged their hands to turn it into action. At last! At last! The period of silence, inertia, submission has ended. We are going to be reborn, like our gods! We are going to spring into motion so as to feel alive! We are going to speak to each other, you and I, to confirm our reality, our presence! Yes, it is true what we have seen, what we have heard. And it is not over. Here is the instrument the divinity used to make itself manifest. Here it is. Now that the sacred has withdrawn from her she resembles a dead body, the rind of a devoured fruit. Who will dare approach Catalina? Who will dare assist her now that her true nature is known? Only the priests, the brujos, may touch her without dying.

And only the priests, the brujos, were able to interpret Catalina's words. Their speech was obscure, too; they were feeling their way among ancient symbols, forgotten for a hundred years and more. But to themselves and the others they made the gift of a promise: the promise that the time of adversity had reached its end.

Catalina heard them in astonishment. She felt cheated. The great force that had possessed her should not be dammed like that, trickling out, as if in little drops, in the timid language of those men. Catalina had been, for a moment, the channel of a torrent, the precipice over which a cascade thundered. And now, withered, she fell silent.

Between all of them they took her back to her house. It was nighttime and some of them hoisted torches of burning wood. The wind fought with the flames. And all at once a chant welled up from the multitude. They proceeded slowly, adapting their footsteps to the religious rhythm of their voices. And the whole mountain vibrated and threw back magnificent, sonorous echoes.

The woman who returned to the hut of Pedro González Winiktón that night was no longer his wife. She was a stranger. She sat down next to the fire, staring into space as if she were interrogating it. She did not want to move, she did not want to speak. When the judge wanted to find out from her what had taken place Catalina could do no more than cover her face with her hands and sob. Other women gave an account of the day's events. Pedro's first reaction was anger.

He understood perfectly. One of his possessions, a piece of his property had been seized: Catalina. And he had no means of recovering it but violence. To hit his wife until the pain (ah, the rictus that was the familiar companion of her face!) erased the strange look of distraction and absence. Yes: to punish her for her abandonment, her betrayal. Pedro felt naked, flayed alive, now that Catalina's love, now that her need for him had been eclipsed.

The presence of strangers in his house, in his village, held him in check. And seeing them so attentive to the ilol's desires, so obedient to her instructions, Pedro allowed himself to be overcome little by little by a superstitious respect, an obscure terror.

What irritated Pedro at first—the constant intrusion of unfamiliar women in the hut—later became indispensable to him. He was afraid of remaining alone with Catalina, he was afraid she would turn her eyes charged with forebodings to rest on him, or settle them on Domingo.

Fear of the fixed gaze of a madman, the gaze that does not discern, that does not rescue what it sees from anonymity.

Her gaze was the same for those who came to serve her, to worship her. Did she even know they were there? In any case, Catalina gave herself over with total passivity to the solicitude and submission of others.

Catalina had become something worse than an invalid; though perfectly able to carry out any action, any movement, she refused to do so. She lost the habit of attending to her own humble daily needs. She lay in wait for a distant ecstasy: she pursued it with the net of incantation, the trap of prayer.

Catalina's place was in the cave. There she prayed aloud, accompanied by the chorus of the pilgrims. She invented a ritual in which the memory of old ceremonies once witnessed rose to the surface along with certain gestures that always express the need to propitiate the mysterious powers that surround us.

Catalina and her followers were creating a complex, delirious liturgy in which the ilol herself was the venerated center. Curses and praises came to pour out upon her, and from her emanated the light and the promise. Catalina did not make the slightest gesture without the certainty of being a flame by whose light the others glimpsed a divine reality.

Pedro did not even try to stop the avalanche of events that crashed down around him. Like the others of his race and in his circumstances, he believed in the truth of what was manifesting itself. Hopes a thousand times dashed by misfortune sprang up anew, vigorous. In the convulsive rapture which he, too, shared, he felt the pulsation that foretold events which would direct all their lives into a new channel. "Humiliation will no longer strangle you with its iron noose. Amends will be made for injustice. The gods live again in order to tell us that you and you and you, you will be free, you will be blessed."

Pedro observed something more, something that was still invisible to the others. If the suffering we have endured were not enough (he said to himself) to make us worthy of redemption, we have other merits: that of having had the wisdom to gather around a man who has stooped down to hear our complaints, who knows the extent of our misery and who has plumbed our anguish: Fernando Ulloa. He is taking the measure of what we are owed and once he has finished he will go and seek out the government, as far as the city of Tuxtla, where the ajwalils will sign the papers of restitution. We will be, from that moment, Indians with land, Indians equal to the Ladinos. And that will be the first of God's words to be fulfilled.

What Pedro knows is a truth. But a truth that is only just germinating, that still cannot survive the harsh climate or the light. Pedro makes a silence to protect it.

Does anything weigh more than a secret? The judge has no one to speak to. He often remembers Xaw Ramírez Paciencia.

Xaw was content among his people. They needed only to see him coming and all of them, even the principal men, would incline their heads to request the brush of his fingers on their foreheads. And they listened to his words with attention, hoping to find in them the thread that would guide their actions.

Xaw had performed the functions of the absent priest in San Juan for years. Unlike the brujos, he did not have an ambiguous reputation. He was respected for being the one closest to the altar, for being the only one who knew the name of each of the saints.

Xaw carried out his appointed duties in good faith. He believed in all honesty that the hallucinations induced by alcohol, the absurd fancies of a mind befuddled by senility, were inspired wisdom, warnings from the beneficent divinities. He communicated them to his listeners as such and on them fell the remainder of the task: to obey.

Xaw never thought of profiting from his ascendency over the others. The sacristan had passed the age of passion; he was alone, his wife long dead, and for his needs what he had was more than enough; he had no ambition for anything else. But with what delectation he enjoyed his prestige and the tribe's deference!

For that reason, when he learned of Padre Manuel's arrival in Chamula he felt a slight stab of jealousy. Was a Ladino going to dispute the rank that for so long he had usurped? His attitude

toward the newcomer was devious and defensive. The incidents
of the first days appeared to confirm the old man's sad conjectures. Manuel was very vain about his authority, conscious of his
hierarchical status and the importance of his mission.

But very quickly Xaw was able to convince himself that the
presence of a priest should not be cause for alarm or concern. On
the contrary. In the eyes of the Indians, Manuel Mandujano was
the materialization of the Caxlán god. Incapable of representing
him to themselves in abstractions, the Indians preferred to have
that god before them, visible, in flesh and bone. Like all divinities,
this one was incomprehensible. He thundered from the pulpit in
a strange language, he handed down absurd mandates, he was
moved for unknown reasons. He could be feared, yes, and worshipped. But love him, give themselves over to him, trust him?
Never.

Thus the services of an intermediary were indispensable. And
that was precisely what Xaw was there for. He translated the
priest's words to the others in his own very clumsy way; he explained entreaties and excuses to each side, mixing everything up
and complicating it even further. And the result was that Padre
Mandujano stopped being a rival and became a useful ally. Ah, if
Xaw had not had such proximity to his person, if he were not so
closely acquainted with the hollowness Padre Manuel covered
over with his anger, if he did not witness every day the lethargies
of Padre Manuel's will, the weaknesses of his body, Xaw, too,
would have believed in Padre Mandujano as in a god.

A healthy skepticism modified the sacristan's attitude toward
the priest. Of course Padre Manuel Mandujano could be judged,
and judging him had become Xaw's favorite pastime. Of course,
too, Padre Manuel Mandujano could be deceived, and in cases of
conflict with his parishioners, he could always be swayed towards
the other side.

But though the Tzotziles had more than ample evidence of
their sacristan's loyalty, they showed themselves to be ungrateful.
Was it not true that they no longer came in the same numbers
and with the same frequency as before to ask for Xaw's advice or
instructions? Was it not true that they neglected to celebrate the
religious fiestas and let whole weeks go by without visiting the
church once? Something was happening, and Xaw's keen sense of

smell immediately put him on guard. Something was gestating somewhere. Xaw knew the symptoms well. He feared them.

For example: the others became reserved when Xaw was present. They were silent or referred only to matters of no importance, as if in the ardor of their conversation a secret might be betrayed. For there was a secret, that was one thing that could not be doubted. A secret all of them shared, except Xaw. All of them went about in a state of agitation, as if in expectation of some event. Would the harvests be poor because there is no rain? Would hunger come and take our children, our brothers and sisters from us? No matter. All of them have their eyes turned somewhere else, as if waiting for a sign. And something all of them perceive in the atmosphere, something that is imperceptible only to Xaw, is making them go. They do not conceal it. They join together in large groups and leave. Where? They all know except Xaw. They return in a state of exaltation, a light of confidence and defiance in their eyes. Among themselves they hold animated discussions of the journey's incidents. They fall silent when they see Xaw approaching.

He does not know how to take revenge. His complaints are extinguished without finding an echo; the blade of his ironies is blunted against his listeners' indifference. And Xaw does not dare confront the situation resolutely and ask: "What is happening here? Why have I suddenly become a pariah dog?"

By carefully stalking it, Xaw is able to waylay a name. The syllables make their way through the mists of deception and stupidity into the sacristan's brain. And there they sparkle. Alone, apart, Xaw cannot explain the reasons for his certainty. But he knows: it has been revealed to him. In this name lies the solution to the enigma that is tormenting him. What has toppled him from his high position and taken away his badges of preeminence is a word: Tzajal-hemel.

It was there they were all going, full of hope; from there they returned, panting with an excitement Xaw was unable to describe. The sacristan approached some of them, eager to partake of this new foodstuff. And what he learned about it made him decide to undertake the journey himself.

To the priest he gave the pretext of a visit to a sick relative, and he left unaccompanied. He doubted that those who refused to share their discovery with him would accept him. But as he drew closer to Tzajal-hemel he found increasingly numerous groups of pilgrims all going in the same direction. They were singing ancient, monotonous songs; they were playing an obsessively repeated rhythm on the accordion, the guitar, or their rudimentary violins. Their staggering gait, clouded eyes, and uncertain voices gave away their drunkenness.

They were on their way to a solemn occasion, then. Xaw soon had the opportunity to verify that.

Tzajal-hemel, which used to be a sad hillside on which a few miserable shacks were scattered, had an animated and boisterous air today. People from all parts of the region were congregated here. Those from Tenejapa, with their long, vertically striped shirts, those from Huistec, protected from the wind by their tilted hats, the Pableños with their long red serapes. All the different dialects of Tzotzil could be overheard in the crowd's conversations.

The merchants unloaded their merchandise: string bags bursting with oranges, little heaps of salt, roughly woven fabrics, utensils made of wood and clay. Chicha and aguardiente sloshed in clay bowls and pitchers.

On all sides the hubbub of a market morning was heard. What a contrast between this little plaza, so much improved, and that of San Juan, silent and deserted for several Sundays past!

But the plaza of Tzajal-hemel was only a stopping place to rest a while. After relaxing and buying provisions, the pilgrims pressed on up the mountain until they reached the cave.

Since it was too small to contain all the visitors, many of them remained outside, waiting to go in. When Xaw's turn arrived, he was pushed by the crowd into a tiny enclosure, its air suffocatingly permeated with the smells of the flowers and burning candles that filled it.

On a makeshift altar stood the idols, unrecognizable now under the lengths and lengths of silk in which they had been enveloped. Some men burned incense or aromatic herbs; others started up songs the rest straggled to join in with and which then died down for no reason.

The incoherence of these actions made it clear that no one was authorized to direct them. They were spontaneous gestures, a crowd's spasmodic way of alleviating its impatience.

Finally what everyone was waiting for happened and was announced by a great silence: Catalina Díaz Puiljá came forward, making her way among the kneeling people. Without a glance, her companions brutally shoved aside all who sought to approach the ilol and participate (even if only through the fugitive impression of a touch) in the virtue that emanated from her body.

Catalina stopped before the altar and bowed down in a posture of reverence. Then she raised her voice, a voice hoarse with suffering. She did not intone syllables, she did not construct words. It was a simple moan, an animal or superhuman death rattle.

Xaw felt a shiver of horror run down his back. Was someone going to respond to this invocation? He wished desperately to be far from there, far from that place in which nameless and barbaric forces were about to be unleashed.

Now Catalina's voice was descending to a register so deep it was almost imperceptible, like the murmuring of a distant, subterranean spring.

The ilol's limbs appeared to have been overcome with lassitude. She stretched out on the ground and lay there motionless. Then a trembling, at first slight, then slowly becoming more and more violent, made her shake with wild convulsions. The spectators trembled as well, infected by the suggestive power of the scene which ended with a painful cry.

She is going to speak! She is going to speak! The rumor swept over the crowd.

As if the cry had freed her from her bonds, Catalina Díaz Puiljá stood up, transfigured. If someone had called her by her name she would not have understood. She was another woman now and did not recognize any kinship or link with anyone. Everything was erased from her eyes but this vision of the future, a future that had to become present. And now. Right now.

But Catalina was still incapable of expressing her visions. Stammering, she gesticulated, she beat her head with clenched fists. Or she repeated disjointed words, the sounds of an invented language that filled those who heard her with wonder and stupefaction.

But not Xaw. By a miracle the sacristan had managed to remain safely at the margin of the collective frenzy, and his attitude was still wary. This woman is lying, he repeated to himself. Her gestures are faked and her words are false. Her words. . . . What is she saying? That they must come to adore these images which are those of their protectors, the only living saints. Lies! The true saints live in the church of Chamula. The saints there really can ward off the injuries the brujos would do us; they can help the cornfield grow tall and the flocks multiply. But here. . . . Here they will devour us and by the time we realize it we will already be dead.

Xaw shifted, clearing his throat. In some way he wanted to demonstrate his disagreement, his protest. He was restrained by the severe gaze of those around him. No one would allow Catalina's ecstasy to be disturbed. If the sacristan had dared to shatter the atmosphere, if he had tried to distract the others with an irreverent word or gesture, they would have turned on him in rage to destroy him.

Xaw was afraid. He buried his face in his hands to protect himself from the ceremony he could not interrupt and stayed still. When he opened his eyes, Catalina and her companions had already left. A few minutes later the cave was empty.

Out of curiosity and a fear of being conspicuous, Xaw followed the crowd. All of them went along the path to the village, singing, wailing, shouting out prayers. When they got there they dispersed, seeking out the shade of the few trees to mix their posol with water and eat the tough tortillas they had brought with them on the journey. They did not speak. Or they spoke very little and of unimportant matters. In vain Xaw tried to discuss what he had witnessed. They avoided the subject as if it were necessary to be in a special state of grace in order to speak of it.

The hut Catalina went into was set apart from the others by the adornments hanging from its walls and doors and by the number of people trying to enter it.

The ilol did not have any fixed rules for receiving visitors. She acted on impulses no one succeeded in predicting. Yesterday she was ill-humored, withdrawn, unsociable, and refused to see anyone. But today she is wearing herself out listening to one person's complaints, another one's request for advice, the petition of yet another. To choose her next visitor she watches them from a distance and decides: that one. That one has just arrived and the others have been waiting for days on end, but no matter. That one is the one who goes in and the others submit to Catalina's arbitrary selection.

Not all of them can resign themselves to approaching her for a minute, listening to her for a short while. There are those who insist on remaining here, all of them women. They help with the tasks of the household, which is now without anyone in charge of it. For Marcela Gómez Oso is in a daze, she does not understand what is happening around her and cannot arrange or command. No one has ever relied on Lorenzo, "the innocent," and Domingo is still a little boy.

Pedro González Winiktón attends to the men. He takes them aside and discusses things with them. His face lights up when he sees Xaw's face among the crowd of strangers. But Xaw eludes him, mingles with the others, disappears.

Inside the hut, women busy themselves. They are grinding corn on the metate, throwing tortillas on the comal, checking the seasoning of the meats.

But those woman are . . . anyone. They take over for each other and no one notices the absence or the replacement. However, there are others, the privileged ones, who have access to the central room, to Catalina's intimacies. They help her with even her most trivial necessities. They do not allow the ilol to trouble herself with the slightest effort. They dress her and adorn her for her public appearances, they rid her of importunate or foolish people, they watch over her repose.

Outside, everything is commented on with envy and admiration. Xaw cannot go on listening and leaves abruptly. On his way back to Chamula, he thinks that his people, the people he taught, have gone mad.

"It is the devil," he mutters. "The pukuj has taken control of them."

He is afraid of what will happen next. Even if no one listens to his warnings, Xaw has the habit of feeling responsible for the tribe. Something must be done to bring them back to themselves, to make them come out of the bad dream.

Compassion gives away to anger in Xaw's soul. They have usurped his position. And who? A crowd of upstarts who know nothing about ritual or doctrine. Unscrupulous imposters.

But their crime would not go unpunished. Xaw would appeal to a higher authority. Padre Manuel would be informed of everything and he would put things back in their proper places. Those makeshift prophets would soon find out it was not so easy to dispense with Xaw Ramírez Paciencia.

CHAPTER XIX

PADRE MANUEL WAS BORED. The futility of his stay in San Juan had never been as evident to him as in the past weeks. Elbows leaning on the pine table he used as a writing desk, he listened to the monotonous and forever recurring fall of the rain.

His sister Benita entered the room.

"I brought you a cup of coffee, in hopes it would do you some good."

The priest smiled and made a sign of gratitude. Why would he vent his ill-humor, his discord, his powerlessness on this helpless woman? The spark of sympathy Benita surprised in her brother's eyes encouraged her to stay. She was so anxious for one minute of conversation, companionship!

"I don't know what's happening to everyone. . . ."

She spoke in haste, without choosing the words or the subject. She didn't know how long she would have and it was not a thing to waste.

"It's the bad weather," Padre Manuel interrupted. "We'll get used to it."

"Haven't you noticed Xaw? He used to stay quietly in the atrium of the church, sunning himself, picking off his lice. Now he wanders through the house all in a muddle, like a ghost, and he never calms down anywhere. Sometimes he's lost in the clouds and if someone comes up behind him he jumps as if he had seen visions."

Why do women place such importance on trivialities? It takes an exertion of Christian charity to endure them as they are.

"Maybe his conscience is troubling him about something? With these Indians you never know. . . . And it scares me. Why don't you talk to him? Not right now," Benita added, as if to excuse herself on seeing her brother's gesture of irritation. "Later, when the moment is right and it doesn't seem forced." Then, inconsistent as ever, she concluded, "Though maybe it would be better to do it quickly."

The cup was empty and Padre Manuel made no remark to

soothe his sister's apprehensions. Benita knew the audience was over.

Sighing, she went to the door. As she was closing it behind her, the priest's voice stopped her.

"Tell Xaw to come here. We'll talk for a while."

His recognition of the validity of his sister's fears was a way of compensating her for their conversation's brevity. Benita should be grateful to him. But how quickly, with what delight, she would have exchanged that compensation for a few moments of closeness to Manuel!

The sacristan appeared before his master, still not completely resolved to narrate the events he had witnessed in the cave. His memory retained them, with all their details vivid and exact, but they were becoming increasingly incomprehensible; he placed them at a level that was further and further beyond the reach of his words and his judgment. Though also, and contradictorily, those same events provoked a tumult within him (anger? rejection? offense?) that kept him from remaining silent.

Padre Manuel had Xaw sit down in front of him and offered him a cigarette. Xaw took a few, ceremonious puffs, without pleasure, and put it out on the floor.

"What does your heart say, sacristán?"

Xaw began a confused and vacillating response. His need to refer to other matters was easily glimpsed and Padre Manuel didn't fail to notice it.

"What does the heart of your people say, sacristán?"

The question was too direct for Xaw to sidestep. He stammered.

"They have left the straight path, padrecito. They no longer want to bring San Juan his candles or his incense. Before, when was a load of pine needles to scatter in the church ever lacking? When it was time to appoint the mayordomos and the other religious officials, we saw people quarreling."

"And now?"

"Now they do not want to, padrecito."

The priest felt wounded by his share of responsibility for this indifference. "What do they want, then? A meek little priest?" he inquired sharply.

Xaw remained suspended for several instants, turning his battered palm-leaf hat in his fingers.

"I will not offend your face by telling you what the people are doing and what they are saying. I tried to give them my advice: the fulfilment of the obligation is your repayment, I told them. But did they hear me? There is no more respect, ajwalil."

The priest went to the window. Beyond the glass planes stretched a misty landscape of sterile hills, scattered clusters of huts, stray animals.

Respect. Xaw felt a pang of jealousy when he pronounced the word. He had remembered how the multitude congregated in Tzajal-hemel bowed down as Catalina Díaz Puiljá went past.

Abruptly the sacristan stood up and turned his back on his superior.

"If San Juan tells them: it is fiesta time, come from your village carrying the harp or the three-string guitar so I can hear music, what do they answer? That it is time to go to the cornfield, that the corn will rot if they do not harvest it right away. And if San Juan tells them: I am walking in darkness and need candles; I want to smell pom and see garlands of flowers hanging in front of me, they claim: wait, tatic, this year we do not have the means and the harvest was poor and there is much sickness. If San Juan tells them: I want my mayordomos to take me to the river and wash my garments, they pay no attention. Tomorrow, patrón, or another time, or never. There is plenty of time. But when that woman talks to them. . . ."

Pedro Mandujano slowly turned around. In the tangle of complaints Xaw had thrown out he had caught nothing but the thread of the last two words.

"What woman?"

"She is evil, padrecito. She is marked. She has never had children."

"What woman?" the priest repeated.

Then Xaw spoke: of what he had seen in Tzajal-hemel, of what he knew about Catalina, of the catastrophes that were about to be unleashed. As his tale progressed, Padre Manuel's expression became more and more animated.

At first with misgiving (how could he trust the testimony of this man, befuddled by old age, stupidity and alcohol?) then with curiosity and finally with resolve, the priest of Chamula interrupted the sacristan: "There is no time to lose, Xaw. This is a very serious matter. You will guide me to this cave tomorrow."

Xaw was not expecting such immediate action. In an undefined way he was afraid of its consequences and wanted to delay it.

"Tomorrow? The rain is not going to clear up tomorrow, padrecito."

"That doesn't matter."

Manuel Mandujano was euphoric; all obstacles seemed insignificant.

"We'll take along our rubber ponchos. And what if we do get wet? We're not made of sugar paste, sacristán! Well, then: hurry up. You see to it that they catch my horse in the corral and saddle him up very early. I'll arrange for provisions to be prepared for the journey."

Once Padre Manuel was alone he could not stay still; excitement made him cross the room in all directions. When he stopped it was to move a piece of furniture from its place, leaf through a book impatiently and inattentively, drum his fingers on the windowpanes.

At last! The routine inertia, the compulsory immobility were over. The disobedience of these Indians, their hostility, their obduracy had finally shown its face. No more of these phantom shapes in the mist, these furtive sounds in the middle of the night, the threat that never solidified into a gesture, an act. Now the enemy had taken on a form, real dimensions, consistency. And how Manuel Mandujano's lust for battle flared when he got wind of the fight!

The priest and the sacristan left for Tzajal-hemel the following morning. Along the way they met small groups of Indians who hastily stood to one side to allow them to pass and looked at each other worriedly when they had gone by.

Padre Manuel fell on the congregation at the cave like a sparrow hawk on a henhouse. The crowd's fanaticism, exacerbated to the utmost by the ritual ceremonies, could have been violent and destructive. But taken by surprise as they were, they remained in a state of expectant bewilderment and allowed their adversary to win all the advantages.

The priest knew instinctively that he had to seize this moment. He made his way through the kneeling crowd, pushing aside the bodies with the threatening tip of a whip. He reached the mockery of an altar and with a violent shove moved Catalina aside. Xaw was trembling behind him, under the spell of his bravery, fearful that his audacity would break off in a moment of hesitation that would unleash the vengeful reaction of the multitude.

Knowing he would not be understood, Padre Manuel spoke. The volume of his impassioned, vibrant voice filled the cave's recesses. Those who were kneeling watched him in astonishment and began to feel that they were guilty of an unknown sin from which there was perhaps no redemption.

When Padre Manuel placed his hands on the idols a shudder of terror went down the spines of the believers. How would the dark powers respond to this sacrilege? Would the firmament collapse, would the waters recede, would the species be exterminated? The minutes throbbed by in every temple with an anguished gravity. The air seemed strangely empty, strangely available to receive a great event.

Padre Manuel did not stop talking as he tore down the lifeless stones, their adornments, their veils. The mirrors with celluloid frames were smashed to bits against the floor, the lengths and lengths of common fabrics in loud colors were heaped up formlessly. In the end, the idols appeared to all eyes, naked, in all the ugliness of their decomposed faces, their heavy hands, their impotent mineral mass.

The profanation engendered no more than a prolonged, incredulous ahhh! from the crowd. The mortar of the world remained solidly in place, nothing had been changed. Catalina Díaz Puiljá moaned, unable to ward off this dismay, this superhuman humiliation.

She turned her eyes towards her followers as if to ask for help but she found in them a more intense reproach than the one she could direct to the sacred images. She felt how, all at once, this intruder had torn her people's reverence and hope from her, how she appeared to them now in a garb of cheated illusions and inconsolable pain.

Suddenly the atmosphere became unbreathable. A sweat of agony impregnated everything; the lights began to dance, to merge with each other in capricious figures, in blossoming explosions. A wasp, a hundred wasps, a thousand wasps buzzed around her. The abyss opened its maw and vertigo threw her into it. The fall begins and goes on and on but it will never end. A woman, Catalina Díaz Puiljá, collapsed, unconscious. Those closest to her were aware of it but no one dared go to her aid. All of them had their eyes fixed on Padre Manuel who was still gesticulating, still haranguing with even greater intensity. Finally, he seized the hyssop, plunged it into holy water, and asperged the stone figures, the walls of the cave and the petrified crowd to chase away the demons that had taken possession of them.

Padre Mandujano left Tzajal-hemel with his conquered booty. No one opposed him when he dragged the idols out of the cave, across the ignominy of a plaza covered with rinds, residue, trash. There were even those who offered to carry them to Chamula, and later to Ciudad Real.

Padre Manuel presented himself before His Excellency with his evidence and with a witness to his triumph: Xaw Ramírez Paciencia.

Don Alfonso listened to the narration of the episode, distracted and indifferent. No, he could not share the alarm of the priest and the sacristan, who considered it an indicator of something whose nature, seriousness and extent they were unable to determine.

"The Indians' idolatry is not bad faith, it is ignorance," was the opinion he rendered. "And who is more responsible for that state of things than us? A great effort must be made to remedy it."

But Padre Manuel was not disposed to yield his prize so easily; he had achieved a magnificent pretext for leaving San Juan and he was not going to return there on an apostleship whose difficulties he was well acquainted with and whose absurdity no one could ever again refute.

"This matter is not our concern alone, Your Excellency. The civil authorities must also be made aware of the facts."

"What do they have to do with the Indians' nonsense?" was the Bishop's indifferent reply. "They may only blow it out of proportion in order to make themselves look important. Or they'll encourage it. The civil authorities are our enemies."

"If we don't inform them of what is happening in Tzajal-hemel they may accuse us of complicity later on. Don't you realize," said Padre Mandujano, pointing to the idols, "that this is the beginning of an uprising?"

Don Alfonso didn't want to put up any further opposition: old men, he reflected, lose their sense of proportion and no longer grant importance to anything but the subject of their own death.

The meeting, which was attended by Church dignitaries, civil servants and all the notables of Ciudad Real, took place in the Bishopric. Before an audience that was easily convinced and predisposed to condemn, Padre Manuel and Xaw Ramírez Paciencia repeated their story. They answered an infinity of questions, invented details they hadn't noticed in order to satisfy their questioners' curiosity. In the end, everyone agreed that the situation was perilous. What they differed on was the measures it would be appropriate to take. The municipal president and the members of the city council were inclined toward prudence, the slow but sure way of paperwork and bureaucracy. To write to the higher authorities in Tuxtla and even in Mexico, to inform them in minute detail, to await their instructions.

The men who held no political office proved to be more impetuous. While the letters came and went, who would protect their ranches, their businesses, from being attacked and ransacked? Who would defend their lives and those of their families? Because as soon as the Indians recovered from the confusion Padre Manuel's abrupt intervention had undoubtedly caused them, they would prepare to take revenge. They were numerous, far more numerous than the Ladinos scattered throughout the region and concentrated in Ciudad Real, and their savage spirit, inflamed by the offense they had endured, would lash out in uncontrollable destruction. It was imperative to take advantage of the Indians' moment of paralysis to render their chiefs and leaders powerless by imprisoning them.

The one who argued most vehemently that these decisions should be put to the vote was Leonardo Cifuentes. For some time, his political ambitions had been known and now he was presented with a set of circumstances in which to act, demonstrating not only the weakness and ineptitude of his rivals but also his own gift for leadership.

The bishop watched him, noting with a slightly disdainful cold-ness how the eagerness for power infused brio into a man's words, impetus into his resolutions. But he was unaware of one element that was having a considerable impact on Cifuentes' attitude. As he argued, Cifuentes was rubbing between his fingers a scrap of fabric—trampled, dirty, stained—that had been wrapped around the idols. What a strange way to recover the shawl by which he had once attested his love to La Alazana!

CHAPTER XX

CATALINA REMAINED ALONE. As in a dream she heard the last steps of the last person who abandoned her. She would have wanted to cry out, grab and hold back this unknown person who was taking away, irrevocably, her breath and her reason for living, but she knew it was useless. She remained still, in the same position she was in when the idols were hurled down and abducted: with her face humiliated against the ground, breathing a miasma, an unhealthy redolence of trampled pine needles and consumed wax.

She was there for a long time and she never knew if she was asleep or awake, dead or alive. Sudden sparks of pain were discharged into her consciousness and quickly muffled by a remote fog in which a minuscule insect buzzed in a spiral.

Pedro González Winiktón stood watch at the cave's threshold without resolving to cross it. The piece of refuse inside was his, but, just as he had been perturbed by the splendor that encircled the figure of his wife during the days of triumph, today he felt shame at her defeat and refused to share in it.

It was Domingo who rescued Catalina. In his own clay bowl he brought fresh water to splash on her wrists and temples. Without any fear, he touched the flesh that the crowd had worshiped as sacred and then repudiated as fraudulent. Catalina opened her eyes to the little boy's charity and her breast melted in a sob of gratitude. She could not get up, she could not speak. Only her pupils dilated in an anguished questioning: Why? Why?

Who could have answered her? With Lorenzo's help, Pedro put together a litter. Between the two of them, they transported Catalina back to her hut which was now silent, with no other presence than Marcela's aloofness.

They put Catalina down next to the fire. Her motionless eyes stared into the flame's mobility. And did not turn away even when the flame went out.

Catalina's convalescence was slow, troublesome, unassisted. The pulsetakers refused to attend to her, the brujos proffered weak pretexts for not fulfilling their duty. They were afraid to confront, in the person of the vanquished ilol, a reality they had not mastered, facts they had not succeeded in defining.

Only those closest to Catalina cared for her. Marcela placed infusions of beneficial herbs within her reach, simple dishes that the sick woman rejected for lack of appetite. Lorenzo always remained close by, looking on, watching over a faraway sleep, punctured by starts and sorrows, keeping between his own hands an inert hand he was unable to warm up.

For Domingo she had, at times, a trace of a smile, a blink of understanding. The ilol turned an anxious, expectant face toward the boy. Undoubtedly she wanted to speak, but her throat would not allow anything but incoherent sounds, aborted sobs, to pass through it. Domingo buried himself in her lap, blocking his ears so as not to hear the inhuman efforts Catalina was making to break her silence.

Strength returned little by little to the ilol's worn-out body and with it suffering. She could find no comfortable position and her desires were never understood. Catalina was suffocating in that hut thick with smoke; she wanted to go out to the field, yes, to the light. She no longer felt guilty, she felt betrayed. She needed to defy those who followed and then abandoned her. She was not afraid of being questioned; she was boiling inside with impassioned replies, harsh arguments. But she wore herself out in imaginary combats and the slightest real effort exhausted her. She lay in a corner of the hut, watching the others come and go, envying their freedom and their health.

One day Catalina perceived a palpitation, a sense of something imminent in the empty air around her. With panicky speed she stood up; she was going to ask for help but there was no one there. She was alone. With her eyes closed and a trickle of anguish on her forehead she dropped back onto the straw mattress.

Over the hill, horsemen were riding toward Tzajal-hemel. Without grace, without gallantry, stirred by sordid cruelty and invested with destructive power, the police had been sent by the authorities of Ciudad Real to seize all those responsible for the idolatrous cult, for secret associations and attempts at insurrection.

Xaw Ramírez Paciencia's reports gave the police precise names and exact locations. But who, advancing with the momentum of punishment, stops to verify such things? Who can tell the difference between a guilty Indian and an innocent Indian? Who listens to allegations made in a confused, rapid language that nobody has ever thought it worthwhile to understand?

The police fell on the village, avid as birds of prey. The men were absent, in the cornfields, on the mountain, and the women ran in disorderly flight, carrying small children in their arms, trying to save a suckling lamb, a newly fired clay utensil, a half-woven woolen cloth.

In her helplessness, Catalina heard the scurrying and shouting, the clatter of the horses' hooves, the shrill cackling, the agonized squealing of the pigs. Brutal guffaws mingled with the weak rasping breaths of the dying, and the weeping of children followed the clamor of smashed furniture, broken pots, ripped fabric.

Catalina saw the doors of her hut thrown wide open. She fell back against the wall as if to melt into it in a childish attempt to protect herself. Some men had entered the room, wearing threadbare, almost colorless uniforms, men whose coarse features were predominantly indigenous, but whose origins had been eclipsed by the abjection of a miserable life, degraded habits, petty vices.

The policemen lifted Catalina off the ground, holding onto her by her clothing. Since her feet could not support her, they dragged her out of the hut. She saw some soldiers robbing her belongings, then found herself outside in the harsh weather. A few minutes later the hut's straw was in flames.

The women and children had gathered in the center of the group of huts. They watched with inexpressive eyes as their town burned down.

Later, when the fire had gone out, the women (carrying their children on their shoulders or pulling them along by the hand if they could walk) were roped together and led to Ciudad Real. Catalina was thrown across a horse's croup.

The group's arrival in Ciudad Real caused an extraordinary commotion. People abandoned their daily tasks to lean out of windows and doorways, forming small circles on the sidewalks or joining the procession of policemen and prisoners, working themselves into a rage with jeering comments, threats and even quick, furious blows that the soldiers willingly tolerated.

The Indian women walked quickly, stumbling against each other, trying to protect their children. The hostile crowd grew larger as they approached the center of the city. By now their words had lost their initial timidity; they waved their fists with ever greater audacity and resolution against these exhausted women, gasping with fear, ready for any humiliation. Who would intercede on their behalf? Who would stand between their defenselessness and their enemies' fury? Their only hope of survival lay in reaching the Niñado jail before a collective scream of extermination burst from those throats.

Catalina came to her senses somewhat later. Her prison companions were jammed with her into a dark, narrow, reeking cell. She looked at them questioningly but could find no response in their faces, shuttered by panic and animosity.

That night the female guards brought each of them a cup of coffee and a few stale baked tortillas to divide up among all of them. The mothers gave their share to their children. Catalina rejected her portion and little by little fell back into a stupor.

The following day, the prisoners were taken from the Niñado to appear before their judges, accusers and witnesses.

The crowd was milling around the doors of the Palacio Municipal, eager for news and vengeance.

Catalina felt something stir inside her when she recognized the priest of San Juan Chamula and Xaw Ramírez Paciencia among those present in the courtroom.

They played the leading roles. Xaw accused Catalina of having founded and perpetuated an idolatrous cult in the cave at Tzajalhemel. With respect to the other women under arrest he could affirm only that they were her accomplices, that they had accompanied her during the ceremonies and had served her in her house "better than they would have served a patrona."

Xaw's declaration was made in Spanish. The Indian women did not understand the words that were condemning them and looked to the old sacristan's familiar, everyday figure as a refuge, a hope.

The lawyer who was prosecuting the arrested women was aware that freedom of religion was a right safeguarded by the Constitution, and though he in no way approved of the exercise of that right (he was a Catholic who regarded intransigence as a bulwark of the faith), he preferred to view the matter in another light that was just as effective in predisposing his listeners' minds against the accused women: a political light. These meetings, he said, which under the pretext of worshiping false gods took place in the cave at Tzajal-hemel, hid a much more dangerous intention, the intention the Chamulas had never given up: to rebel against the Ladinos of Ciudad Real.

The moment, the lawyer added, was favorable. Recently, the whole region had been agitated by the presidential decrees ordering that the property titles of the great haciendas be reviewed in order to reduce their boundaries to the limits set by the law and grant land to the ejidos by that means. This project, which while just (the lawyer did not wish to question the good intentions or the skill of the officials who held supreme power in the country), was also untimely and imprudent, should have had its implementation entrusted only to the most suitable hands. Unfortunately that was not the case in Ciudad Real; a person was appointed as executor of the agrarian policy, a person whose name the lawyer would not pronounce but it was in everyone's mind. A person who, far from reconciling warring interests, had systematically dedicated himself to making things worse by placing himself openly against the ranchers and stirring up the Indians by preaching equality and the recovery of their land to them.

The results of these errors were now making themselves felt. Here were a people who disregarded the advice and warnings of their parish priest, abandoned the practice of a religion of humbleness and obedience and began digging up images of a savage and bloody past, thus defying the wrath of their natural masters and endangering the established order. Where would all of this lead? To its logical end: the taking up of arms and the violent demand of rights which, even if they were granted by law, the Indians did not deserve. No one who knew their nature, their customs, their tendencies, could doubt that the Indians needed guardians. And who could exercise that guardianship better and more beneficially for all than the patróns?

The lawyer paused to leave time for the comments to burst out. All the Coletos present vehemently assented to his words, exaggerating the danger that confronted them and asking for rapid and effective measures to stave it off.

The lawyer went on. The harm, he said (which a clearer vision of reality on the part of those who drew up the agrarian law and a spirit more accessible to reason in those charged with implementing it could have avoided), was already done and there was no recourse but to try to remedy it. How? With a benevolence that would be taken for weakness by the very people who reaped its benefits? No: with a severity that would serve as an example. On these prisoners and especially upon the one whom they appeared to venerate as their leader, on Catalina Díaz Puiljá, all the weight of punishment should fall. That would have a pacifying effect on the restless spirits of all the Chamulas scattered across the mountains and the hills; that would put some good sense back into all the heads led astray by irresponsible advisors.

When his speech was finished, the lawyer returned to his place. From afar he answered the greetings, the gestures of approval, the mimicked applause by which his listeners sought to show their gratitude to him for having expounded so faithfully and so courageously the opinion they all shared.

The judge delayed the proceedings, pretending to review some papers, in order to allow these sympathies to be expressed. Then the priest, Padre Manuel Mandujano, was called upon to testify.

He began by stressing that his vows kept him from meddling in the historical events of the century. The concerns about properties and rights that had just been expressed were very foreign to him. The distinguished lawyer who had preceded him had given unto Caesar what belonged to Caesar, and generously. For him, as a priest, there remained only to consider the spiritual aspect of the question.

When His Excellency Don Alfonso Cañaveral honored him by naming him the parish priest of San Juan, he did not think he had been sent to a pagan land. Nevertheless, from the day of his arrival in the capital town of the municipality of San Juan Chamula he could see that he was in a world where the truths of Christianity had been corrupted by ignorance and had degenerated into crude rituals, barbaric superstitions.

The language made it difficult to penetrate his parishioners' souls; though he made an effort to learn it, it could never be very useful to him in an empty church, a closed confessional. He tried other approaches. But the Indian turned to the brujo, trusted the

pulsetaker, and yielded to the priest no more than a certain sum
of alms in which the soul was in no way committed.

That state of affairs was serious but not insoluble. The appearance of the idols at Tzajal-hemel complicated it further. Padre
Mandujano praised the zeal and acumen of his sacristan, Xaw Ramírez Paciencia, discoverer of the cult the Chamulas were paying
to those idols, as well as the loyalty he had faithfully shown to
the Holy Mother, whom he had served since his earliest youth.
As far as his own role in the events was concerned, the priest gave
himself no other merit than that of having proceeded rapidly to
confront a threat which did menace the security of the State, he
acknowledged, though that aspect of the matter was not his ulti-
mate concern, but also and above all which menaced the authority
of the Church. Before concluding, he did not fail to make a veiled
allusion to the secular powers' abusive intervention in problems
such as this which fell exclusively under the jurisdiction of the
Church.

Far from satisfying its audience, Padre Mandujano's declaration
disconcerted them. Why such mildness in pointing to the responsibility of the guilty parties? Why these distinctions between the
sacred and the profane, which were beside the point?

The prosecuting lawyer requested leave of the court to ask the
priest a few questions before he left the witness stand. The request
was granted, and the lawyer spoke as follows:

Padre Mandujano had lived among the Chamulas for some
time; did he think they were capable of the kind of wickedness it
would take to dig up idols and revive ancient ceremonies?

The priest of San Juan smiled condescendingly before answering that the idea did seem absurd to him, though, of course, he
did not see how else the events could have occurred.

The theory of the pernicious influence of a Ladino, a man of
reason, was unacceptable?

Padre Mandujano had to accept that that hypothesis seemed
more plausible. Because yes, in fact, the soul of the Indians is too
dull to invent a new form of idolatry, too stupid to remember the
customs of their ancestors.

The prosecuting lawyer persisted: did it not then remain only
to ask what influence the Chamulas have undergone recently? He

waited a few seconds for Padre Mandujano to speak Fernando Ulloa's name, but the priest's silence forced him to be more precise. Hadn't an agronomic engineer been travelling through the region for several months? The prosecuting lawyer was relying on the testimony of that engineer's former assistant, young Rubén Martínez, to prove that Ulloa did not confine himself to carrying out his assignment to survey the region, but also held public meetings at which he incited the Indians to commit acts of violence in order to reclaim their rights. "If the judge does not consider this evidence to be sufficient," the lawyer concluded, with a bow in His Honor's direction, "there are other proofs, definitive ones, that will demonstrate the engineer's complicity with the Chamulas of Tzajal-hemel."

Manuel Mandujano, who by his silence and reticence had managed, without compromising himself, to insure that the matter would continue in the direction that suited him, expressed his hope—standing up now—that the proofs which were being held in reserve by the accusing party were in fact as conclusive as the prosecutor had assured, because otherwise he was running the risk of committing the crimes of slander and defamation.

The final part of the proceedings consisted in bringing the witnesses face to face with the accused and questioning the latter. Catalina Díaz Puiljá was at the center of everyone's attention and everyone was amazed that a woman so insignificant and abject could have inspired an eager and credulous multitude to follow her. This also served to strengthen the idea of a secret mastermind, who had only used the Indian woman as his instrument.

The confrontations with witnesses and the examination of the defendants were carried out through an interpreter who was, in the first place, unaware of the exact meaning of the legal terms used by the prosecutor, and, furthermore, did not take into account the level of understanding of the accused women, their mental habits, their complete ignorance of justice as it was conceived of and practiced by the Coletos, their natural timidity, and the terror they felt at having been entrapped by a mechanism as complex as it was implacable.

The outcome of this series of misunderstandings was that all of them pointed hysterically to Catalina as the responsible party. To Catalina who had lost her power and prestige, to Catalina who was nobody to the people of Ciudad Real. From then on the prosecutor addressed Catalina alone.

It was not that Catalina refused to answer. It was that she could not grasp either the meaning or the intention of the questions. What relation could exist between her delirium, her desperate love for Pedro, her yearning for motherhood thwarted by Domingo, her return to childhood, her discovery at the cave, her enshrinement as a priestess, her people's fervor, and these words by which she was being designated? Catalina found no way out but denial. No, she had not received advice from anyone. No, she had not planned an uprising. No, she had no accomplices to give away. No, no, no.

Catalina answered in a very low voice, without raising her eyelids; she felt a lurching darkness growing within her, ravenous fissures yawning open, an endless cry echoing.

The defense lawyer remained negligently at the margin of the cross-examination. None of the professionals of Ciudad Real had wanted to put his orthodoxy in question or endanger himself or his future by taking on a case he knew in advance was lost. So the usual method was followed: the judge had to appeal to the public defender to take the case, and he did not miss an opportunity to show everyone how much it repelled him to carry out an assignment in which justice so obviously was not on his side.

The session concluded for the day, and resumed the following morning. Attendance was smaller the next day since curiosity had diminished from the moment the outcome was no longer in any doubt. The conviction was already a fact. The only thing that remained to be determined was the severity of the sentence.

Things had reached this point when a group of Chamulas led by Pedro González Winiktón came down from the mountain.

The people of Ciudad Real stopped to look at them with a tremor of dismay. The new arrivals were very numerous and perhaps for that reason they walked through the street looking not furtive but secure and, at certain moments, even defiant.

As everyone expected, they went to the house of Fernando Ulloa to ask him for advice and help.

CHAPTER XXI

WHILE HE WAITED for Virgilio Tovar to appear, Fernando Ulloa passed the time looking over the office he had been shown into.

If the room was a reflection of its owner's character, there were reasons for discouragement. The nakedness of the walls was hostile, the height of the ceiling disproportionate. The furniture was severe, uncomfortable. And the windows obstructed the light with heavy curtains.

Tovar's arrival was preceded by a quick sound of footsteps, an energetic clearing of the throat, the click of the latch. A man of medium stature, nervous and alert, came in. A man conscious of his own importance, though he did not appear to have abandoned himself to the delights of that sensation.

He was the most prestigious lawyer in Ciudad Real, praised more for his effectiveness than for the integrity of his methods. "He knows a lot more than your average shyster," they said. And that phrase summed up the general admiration for a talent on which passage through the halls of learning and the possession of an advanced degree had not exerted any inhibiting influence, for Tovar's inventiveness was still fresh and, on principle, he never rejected any opportunity which success could later anoint with respectability.

He greeted Fernando with the deference due to a representative of the federal government, but also with the reserve of someone who does not approve of his interlocutor's conduct or wish to express solidarity with his attitude. Both of them sat down in front of the large mahogany desk on whose naked surface stood an ivory cross.

"I hope," the lawyer said, pointing to it, "that such an open allusion to the beliefs I profess does not bother you. But what do you want? We Coletos are like that: frank. We don't know how to conceal our feelings."

That's exactly what they do best, Fernando thought to himself as he made his reply. "You must be badly informed about me, señor licenciado. I don't condemn anyone's beliefs. I don't even argue about them. That's why I demand that all beliefs be held in equal regard."

"You do not recognize any hierarchy?"

"No. And that brings us directly to the matter I have come to discuss: the women of Tzajal-hemel who were arrested for worshiping their idols."

Tovar opened his cigarette case.

"Would you like one, señor ingeniero?"

Fernando made a quick negative gesture after which the other man served himself, struck a match, and drew in the first avid mouthfuls of smoke.

These delaying tactics managed to imply several things: first, that it was impossible to catch Señor Tovar unprepared by mentioning a trial about which he was not already fully informed; second, that his interpretation of the matter usually differed from the generally accepted one since, in formulating his opinion, he had access to information that was not available to others; and, third, that any discrepancy between their opinions should be understood to result from a mistake on the part of his interlocutor and skilled judgment on his own part. Satisfied with this conclusion, the lawyer took the cigarette from his lips.

"It isn't a religious problem; it is political."

"Political?" Fernando repeated, as if the word had been used incorrectly.

"Precisely. What the women of Tzajal-hemel have been accused of, along with their accomplices—because there must still be quite a number of them at large and perhaps they are very influential as well—is sedition."

"And on what do you base such an absurd accusation?"

"You must know that better than I do."

"Why?"

Tovar crushed out the cigarette in the ash tray. He couldn't stand having anyone take him for naive.

"Because you've been singled out as the principal instigator of the rebellious movement among the Indians."

Fernando smiled with a touch of mockery.

"Yes, I heard about that. But I'd like to know your opinion señor licenciado."

"I'm going to do something for you that I don't generally do ingeniero. When all is said and done, we are colleagues, professional men, I mean. I won't charge you a fee, which is what I'm usually given for my opinions. Listen to me carefully because I speak to you as an impartial observer: you are in a difficult situation. I recommend that you place yourself in the hands of a capable defense lawyer."

"I had thought you would be that defense lawyer."

"Thank you for the compliment, but I cannot take on your case."

"It isn't my case, it's the case of the women who are in prison, their families, and all the towns in Chamula on which suspicion is now falling and reprisals will soon descend."

"I'll keep your secret and ask you for nothing in return for that, either. But I warn you, it isn't prudent for you to display your relations with those people, the interest you take in them or your concern to help them. I can understand the altruism of your motives. But others will see it as proof that you are inciting the Indians to an insurrection."

"But how could I have done that? I don't even speak Tzotzil."

"There are many ways. Your post, your mission, lend themselves to being taken advantage of."

"I've confined myself to the strict fulfillment of my duty."

"Have you?"

Tovar's reluctance to admit the truth of his words gave Ulloa his first glimpse of the extent to which his situation was adverse. Now he was sure the ranchers would stop at nothing to succeed in implicating him in the crime or, at least, in having him dismissed from his job.

"I need someone who is well versed in the law to defend me. I'm counting on you."

Tovar made an ambiguous gesture.

"I would be delighted to be of service, but. . . ."

Suddenly, the excuse the lawyer was going to proffer seemed unnecessary. There are men who deserve the truth, he thought, looking pityingly at Ulloa.

"Taking on the responsibility for your case would be a betrayal."

"Of whom?"

"Of my colleagues. We have a gentlemen's agreement not to intervene in this trial."

"And to allow that an injustice be carried out on innocent people. If I may say so, you and your colleagues have some very dubious professional ethics."

"They are not innocent, ingeniero. What was being plotted in that cave has happened before. Read our history: uprisings in 1712, in 1867, in 1917. Why not now? The difference is that they were discovered in time, before they could pose a threat to Ciudad Real."

"What are you talking about?"

"I'm talking about something we Coletos know far better than foreigners do: when the Indians gather together it is for no other reason than to do harm to the Ladinos. In their fiestas, in their drunken binges, the end result is always some Caxlán wounded or dead, some peddler's stall burned down. It takes very little to make them attack us. And on top of that you come and fan the flames with your sermonizing. They're afraid. That's natural, because every time they've tried to rebel they've always paid heavily for it. Believing their idols will protect them, they rush out to kill and destroy. They forget that our God is stronger and more powerful than theirs!"

Tovar had clamped his fist around the crucifix. His voice was trembling with indignation as he continued.

"Defend them! Would you defend the person who murdered your father, raped your sisters? Would you defend those who took all you had and left you in misery?"

"Is that what happened to you, licenciado?"

"It happened to me and to every other Coleto!"

"Things may have happened that way in the past, but that is no basis for declaring that they will happen the same way today. The Indians' guilt cannot be based on prophecies."

"No one is prophesying. We are remembering, that's all. You don't understand that."

"Even if I did understand it, I don't accept it!"

So childish a recalcitrance was in the end quite moving to Virgilio Tovar. He gave Ulloa a look of kindness.

"Don't put yourself between the horses' hooves, ingeniero.

Why? You're young, you have a career, a future. There is still time: ask to be transferred, resign, do whatever you want. But don't stay in Ciudad Real."

Fernando Ulloa wasn't deceived by the tone of the admonition. He said harshly, "Ciudad Real is no longer what all of you here believe it to be: the private domain of a few gentlemen and their crooked lawyers. Ciudad Real is Mexico, and in Mexico there are just laws and an honest President. I will not go. I do not betray my own either!"

Afterward, Fernando did not know how to explain the failure of his errand to the Tzotziles without damaging his prestige. And not out of vanity. The confidence the Indians placed in him was essential for the smooth flow of their relations. Finally he decided to take Pedro aside.

"We're not going to make anyone listen to us here," he said. "The Coletos are intent on making an example of the women who are in prison. But they won't stop there; they'll keep looking for 'the responsible parties.' They want to harm all of us."

"Are you going to complain to the president?"

For Pedro, in his ignorance, there was no man more trustworthy or closer at hand in circumstances like these. Fernando smiled without irony. No, he would not go so high up. But he would go to Tuxtla. There were authorities there with stronger hands than the shady lawyers of Ciudad Real.

He was accompanied on the trip by César Santiago who, with growing insistence, did not stop musing on—and exaggerating—the suspicions that had fallen on Fernando and the uselessness of trying to exonerate oneself in the eyes of Coletos.

"It would be better for us to teach them a lesson. If they think you're capable of stirring up the Chamulas. . . ."

"They're mistaken."

"Who knows. The Indians are very discontented and the hope of having land of their own has turned their world upside down. If the situation were used to threaten the ranchers. . . . Do you think they're actually going to allow their property to be divided up?"

"What else can they do?"

"Exactly what they're doing now: preparing a state of emergency that will paralyze the process of distributing ejidos. Meanwhile they gain time. They send negative reports to your superiors."

"Even if I were sent away from here. A substitute would come."

"Perhaps he would be more tractable."

Fernando remained pensive. The truck they were riding in was jolting along a road of mud and rocks. To the right was a steep cliff.

Power! Was it true that the will of a people was in his hands? Was it true that with a gesture Fernando Ulloa could establish the direction of events? For an instant the prospect fascinated him. Power, yes, and without remorse, because he wasn't going to go back on either his past or his ideals; because he wasn't going to satisfy any shady ambition or obtain any illicit advantage. Ah, the uses he would make of it! Against the doubletalk of the rich, against the bad faith of men who occupy positions from which they should defend those who have been trampled underfoot, those who are helpless, those who are destitute.

Fernando turned to look at Pedro's face as if seeking to confirm his hopes. But he found no more than the hardness that was always there, the secret closely guarded by the eyes, the words that were detained before reaching the fold of the lips. How could he draw closer to this race? It opened itself only in drunkenness, in danger, in cataclysm.

They had passed the highest point of the road and only a few scattered shreds of mist were left. The plain stretched out below, green and hot.

"When we get to Tuxtla. . . ."

"You have a lot of faith in the government."

César was younger, more ignorant. Why, then, did he speak with such assurance?

"The men who govern Chiapas are used to obeying. The patrón is the patrón on his finca and also in the Palacio. His footsteps ring out loudly there, just like everywhere else."

Evidently César had employed a figure of speech. Because in the Palacio de Gobierno in Tuxtla nothing could be heard but the clacking of the noisy and very antique typewriters, the murmurs in the waiting rooms, the docile steps of the employees and the governor's orders.

He didn't make Fernando Ulloa and his companions wait long. He supported the president's agrarian policy across the boards, he said. And his administration was always ready to listen to a complaint, to remedy an anomaly. Fernando Ulloa accepted this cordial reception and this promise almost with disappointment. Now he became aware of how much he had wanted the authorities to be indifferent or even frankly biased in favor of the ranchers, so he could justify using the power César Santiago had shown him he possessed.

"Now then, what is your problem?"

The Governor, a simple, benevolent man of the tropics, leaned back as if preparing to hear a lengthy narrative. However, Ulloa preferred to be brief. He summarized the essential facts and emphasized the slant the ranchers of Ciudad Real wanted to put on the forthcoming expropriation of the fincas.

"The question is very clear," Fernando concluded. "As Señor Tovar himself acknowledged when he refused to defend us, no man born in Ciudad Real or linked to it by financial interests can be a judge in this matter since all of them have something at stake in it. Therefore we've come to ask you to have the case thoroughly reviewed by skilled and unbiased individuals."

The governor agreed to this request.

"I know their crafty ways, and we're going to give them a taste of their own medicine. But," he inquired with a hint of doubt, "no danger of an uprising in fact exists?"

The question seemed to be addressed to Pedro in particular. All eyes turned toward him.

"We will not be satisfied, ajwalil, while other hands hold the land that belongs to us. Until we have been given a paper that says who is the owner."

The tone of the Indian's words was civil but not to the point of being conciliatory or, far less, servile. He was holding back a last resort, the last resort despair leaves to the weak: violence.

Fernando Ulloa wanted to erase that impression.

"As you see, señor Gobernador, it's easy to bring an end to this unrest. All we need to do is speed up the process that has already begun so that each ejido can receive its title of possession."

The governor stood up to bring the interview to a close and smiled elusively.

"Everything in its time."

The petitioners didn't want to insist. And their optimism about a favorable resolution of their problems was strengthened when the order for the immediate release of all those involved in the events at Tzajal-hemel reached Ciudad Real.

CHAPTER XXII

WHEN THE WOMEN of Tzajal-hemel returned to their village they were welcomed with jubilation. They had been unjustly touched by Ladino hands and that fact magnified them. Once again avid, furtive and expectant gazes were directed at Catalina, the gazes of those who wanted to plumb the depths of mystery. Anonymous donors came as far as the door of the ilol's recently reconstructed hut to leave handfuls of newly picked produce, fresh eggs, chickens with their legs tied together.

Marcela made use of these gifts, happy to stave off neediness even if only by halves and provisionally. But these tributes to her power, these recognitions of her prestige were like a thorn in Catalina's side. Ah, how painfully they were awakening her from the apathy into which she had fallen during the past weeks!

After the seizure of her gods, during the days of her captivity, Catalina's will and character were annihilated. She watched herself, as if from some very remote vantage point, coming and going along the pathways; she heard the orders of the guards who escorted the prisoners, the accusations of the witnesses, the judge's sentence, as if none of it had anything to do with her. She watched the hours pass, indifferent as to whether they brought her freedom or condemnation. And when the doors of the prison opened (she never knew who to thank for that, nor did she care) and Catalina was returned to her family and her home, she showed no surprise, gratitude, or joy. She retreated into herself so that the familiar stabbing would no longer pain her: the exhaustion of a responsibility, the weight of a destiny, the urgency of the hopes of others which rose up to demand their realization and their fulfilment from her, the ilol.

The signs were multiplying. One morning when she opened the door of her hut, she discovered, leaning against the wall, waiting, some pilgrims who had come from beyond the mountains to find her. They bowed respectfully before Catalina and then stayed there without saying a word, without addressing an entreaty or a petition to her. But there was in their silence a tenacious question, an irreducible when? when?

Catalina held out her hands in a gesture that sought to promise. But she herself had a dark future, an unresponding horizon before her. She pulled her hands back before her fingers touched the pilgrims' submissive foreheads.

When Catalina felt strong enough she went back to herding the flock. She went with the sheep to distant meadows where no human intrusion could disturb the moment when she peered down into the deepest depths of herself in desperate eagerness to find the echo of a voice, the reflection of a face, the memory of a name.

At times she caught herself directing her steps toward the cave. She stopped, as if on the brink of some danger, and abandoned the footpaths that her people's faith had made and that were now being overgrown little by little with brush.

Once she kept going all the way there. She hesitated an instant at the entrance, but the smell (a smell of burning wax, cut flowers, pine needles) drew her in irresistibly.

Where the altar had once been, some women were now kneeling. A low murmuring emanated from their mouths. And suddenly they burst out in a continuous, monotonous lament which then broke into words: the word *helpless,* the word *suffering,* the word *misery.* They were praying to absent gods, illuminating with dying candles that never quite finished going out the hollow the gods had left behind.

Catalina moved forward until she was part of the group; she wanted to mingle her plea with the others but as soon as she was recognized she was left alone. The women fell back with the mixture of reverence and fear that the sacred inspires. Catalina tried to go after them as they left, to confess to them that she had been dispossessed of her gifts, that she would never again be able to do anything for anyone, but the women were already scattering to their villages without listening to the voice they left behind them, hurrying to share with everyone the news that would set their souls on fire.

Catalina stayed in the cave. A sudden agitation replaced her former inertia. Why cross her arms? Why remain silent? Why not confront the inevitable? Suddenly all obstacles were insubstantial and everything was within her reach. But the excitement was vanishing without finding a way of expressing itself, an act into which it could flow, and Catalina spent hours and hours in the cave without managing to leave, without finding a reason to stay. A great stupor paralyzed her. And in the semidarkness she lost all notion of the passage of time. Pedro and Marcela had to come find her the following day.

Pedro reproached her bitterly for wandering off like that. But as Catalina listened, head hanging and lips motionless, her husband watched for the sign that would come to give shape to his suspicion that the gods had not died, that their veneration would be resumed and that the Chamula people had not been cheated once more.

It was impossible for Catalina to offer anything, not even to herself; she followed false trails within herself like a hungry beast of prey.

After that she went back to the cave once more, many times more. She would stay there, in the darkness, breathing the unhealthy air that peopled her senses with deliria. She stretched out face down on the ground, the same ground that the crowd had trampled in happier days, and she felt herself die. She made her hands go limp, releasing all the intentions she was clinging to; she chased all memories from her mind; she silenced her heart, erasing the wound of love, the bite of jealousy, the purulence of contempt. She left herself empty in order to make room for revelation.

And nothing happened. Not a glimpse, not a disclosure. The ilol returned to her opaque routine as impoverished and despairing as before.

Nevertheless, something was gestating. Neither her heart nor her head noticed it. It was her hands, blinder and more humble, but more obedient, that began to seek out, by touch, a material in which to palpate the form they had already foreseen.

How to make present once more the vanished image of the idols? Each hour, each day was spent fulfilling her task of striking out a trait of that face, altering an expression, blending in an attribute. Anxious to hold back this current, Catalina buried her hands in the clay where the tip of her finger was imprinting an image dictated by an imprecise, contradictory, unreliable memory.

The failure of her attempts made her furious with her work. Again and again she broke the grotesque figures she was modelling. Again and again she discarded almost formless chunks of clay. And she always breathed deeply in relief, as if she had moved aside an impediment and now the way was clearer, easier to proceed along.

The fever, the fever of the days of plenitude, came back to take possession of her. But it no longer beat against her like an enclosed wind; it bolstered her in her effort, illuminated her in her conception, sustained her in her dissatisfaction. And it was not repose that Catalina found when, at last, the work of her hands corresponded—however imperfectly—to the demands of her memory. It was not repose but a frenzy, the heaving of the female who is about to give birth.

She left the cave looking for someone to speak to along the footpaths; she found astonished shepherdesses who did not understand her halting and confused message; she found woodcutters who lightened the weight of her load; she found people who were returning from the market in Jobel and her news quickened the steps that took them back to their villages; it brought families together around the fire; it fueled conversations into the depths of the night.

When Catalina arrived at her hut, Pedro had already heard from other mouths that the gods were once again in their place. He was not as easily delighted by the news as others were. Why do they return? he said to himself. We do not know how to worship them, we cannot defend them. They come only to expose us to the anger of the Caxlán, they come to incite our enemies against us. Between man and god, Pedro thought, woman is no more than an unconscious instrument. That was why Catalina abandoned herself to the fascination of the miracle without seeing the abyss that was opening up below it.

Ay, if he could drop a word, one single word, into her ear as she slept. And if that word could be placed on the altar, so the idols would pick it up!

Pedro leaned over his wife's sleep and slowly pronounced the only prayer he knew: "Land, Catalina. Tell them to give the land back to us. If they ask us for blood, if they ask for our lives, we will give them. But let them give back the land."

A shiver ran through the ilol's body and she covered her ear with her hand. Pedro drew back, certain he had been heard.

But Catalina, still awake, had paid no attention to him. She was dreaming of what was to come. The great pilgrimages of supplicants filling the pathways with accordion music and the sounds of the harp; the heavy wax candles chasing darkness from the sacred precincts, day and night; the copal smoke slackening the priestess's senses until a channel was left clear for prophecy. And afterward the body, her own body, caving in like a squeezed fruit; the slow recuperation of her powers; the gaze that discovers, little by little, a circle of wondering faces, quick hands, docile ears. Once again, between her and her people there was no rupture. Catalina had taken their hand once again, as if it were a child's, to lead them.

CHAPTER XXIII

WHEN TERESA ENTZÍN LÓPEZ fled from Leonardo Cifuentes' house (the flight of an animal that has ceased to be useful and hides, seeking a place to die) she did not know where to go. Her first steps through the streets of the city that had ceased to belong to her now that she no longer had the backing of her masters were hesitant. She could not think about the possibility of looking for work with another Coleto family because, in her, servitude had taken the form of loyalty. Neither was she very certain of wanting to go back to the Indians. But for lack of a better alternative, she went to the market where, their day's transactions completed, the Chamula vendors were preparing to return to their villages.

Teresa joined a group of women. She inserted herself among them in silence, humbly, in order to dispel the attitude of distrust with which they greeted her. Since she was carrying nothing she was able to ingratiate herself by helping the other women carry their loads. That first night she slept next to the fire of some strangers, and when she was asked who she was and where she came from she told a story about years of confinement in the house of some rich people in Jobel; she spoke of bad treatment and threats. The others believed her. What was unusual about the events she recounted? And in exchange for her work in the hut and the cornfield, she came to form part of the family of the former martoma, Rosendo Gómez Oso, in the village of Majomut.

These abrupt changes of perspective (from high to low in Jobel and now, suddenly, on an equal footing) made Teresa observant. She listened, first with curiosity and then with irritation, to the endless disputes between the martoma and his wife, Felipa. The reason for the argument was always insignificant at first. But then it would grow like a vortex, pulling the most diverse details into its center and building to a final catastrophe, a drunken binge and a beating, in which the name of a girl Teresa had not met— Marcela—was frequently mentioned, along with the disadvantageous circumstances of her marriage.

With greater precaution, as if to keep Teresa from noticing, the figure of Catalina Díaz Puiljá was also sometimes evoked; to her, according to Felipa, were owed all the household's misfortunes. Rosendo tried to calm her by advising her to be prudent if she did not want those misfortunes to increase, now that Catalina had acquired such great power. But Felipa was not intimidated. All those tales of the appearance of some gods in a cave, she said, were no more than lies, the kind of cock-and-bull stories Catalina had always used to impose her will on others through terror. But what harm could Catalina do her now? She was not afraid of death, her own or that of those closest to her, she said, gazing malignantly at Rosendo. And he, who still wanted to live, who took pleasure in the drunkenness in which he felt important and respected, found no other way of silencing his wife's irreverences but with a blow. He was able to lower the volume of her voice, but Felipa continued fuming at this cowardly man who had given up his daughter Marcela for nothing.

When, the day's heavy labor done, Teresa lay down next to the half-extinguished fire, sleep took a long time to close her eyelids. The misery into which she had sunk made her remember the Cifuentes household with secret pride and a veiled feeling of superiority. The carpet in the sewing room, she said to herself, remembering the softness, the warmth in which her feet had so often delighted. Curled up into a ball to warm herself, Teresa murmured in Castilla the names of the things she felt nostalgic for: the flowerpots in the gallery, the knocker on the main entryway, the flagstones where she washed the clothes, the cot she slept on. She never murmured Idolina's name.

Because when one loses a child (ay, she would rather a thousand times have seen her dead than in the hands of an intruder, a thief like that Julia Acevedo) one cannot speak. On the beast's back fall the blows of a master who is feared, who is not understood. And the beast is bewildered and suffers and runs to escape, and it is chased and caught and can be punished once more. And the beast does not complain because it does not understand.

As the weeks passed Teresa began to discover within herself an emptiness that was not filled by pleasant memories of the past or the exhausting work of the present. Even if she were to say something—and what could she say to this Rosendo always unconscious from alcohol, this Felipa, bitter and whining—even the smallest and most insignificant word seemed like a waste. Because it was not heard by Idolina.

Idolina. Very early, when the first bell tolled for the first mass of the day, who would bring her coffee with bread? She liked the crunchy, ring-shaped rosquillas, the cazueleja fresh from its tin mold, the molde de yema, rich with egg yolks. And she, Idolina's nana, chose the tenderest and most golden morsels to give her. It was the only time Idolina ate. Because later, when all the inhabitants of the house were awake and the door of her bedroom was unbolted and her mother and stepfather could come in without warning, Idolina was no longer hungry. She picked here and there in order not to expose herself to the adults' reprimands. But she did not lift anything of any substance to her mouth, nothing that would make her blood red or strengthen her body. Only recently, when Julia arrived. . . .

Teresa wanted to chase away the image. But La Alazana intruded anyway, smiling, energetic, forcing Idolina to obey her in everything. Teresa finally fell asleep but in her sleep enemies would suddenly appear, faces twisted in hatred, their fists, strength and speed making her their victim.

She was not the only one who was suffering. Ever since the burning of the huts at Tzajal-hemel and the imprisonment of Catalina and the other women, everyone was trembling. When the Ladino remembers the Indian, it is to finish him off. Each one waited for his turn with a kind of somber fatalism which only in Felipa became a frantic rebellion, a passionate reproach against the guilty party who was responsible for the threats that were hovering over Chamula: Catalina.

One afternoon while she was carrying wood, Teresa left the pathway and sat down on her load to weep. She could not go ---- The work drained her to the point of annihilation. And w_, work? To have a roof under which to take shelter, a tortilla with salt to eat. Living was not worth the trouble. Because no one really needed her. The transitory invalid state of the former martoma Rosendo, always caused by overimbibing, was repulsive. And Felipa, despite her ailments and complaints, was a robust and capable woman. Teresa thought of them both with hostility. She could not have any pity for them. But her pity, which had had no object since it withdrew from Idolina, was always sloshing around inside her like water in a jug. And at times like today, the jug was so full it spilled over.

Why not go back to Ciudad Real? This thought crossed Teresa's mind like a flash of lightning. Enter the city at noon, when the doors of the houses are wide open. Go, with bare feet, silently, along the galleries. Reach Idolina's room. Would she be there? Now that she could walk she had acquired the habit of taking long strolls just outside the city with Julia. No, Teresa would not find Idolina. She would not even reach her room, or her house, because the Chamulas no longer dared go down to Jobel now that the fury of the Ladinos was unleashed.

Drying her tears with the back of her hand, Teresa stood up. The load of wood was lighter now that she had ascertained that her misfortune was irrevocable.

Arriving at the hut, Teresa found that the former martoma Rosendo Gómez Oso had donned his best serape and Felipa was making preparations to leave.

"Where are you going?" she asked, puzzled.

"To Tzajal-hemel," Rosendo answered with a triumphant air. "Our comadre, Catalina Díaz Puiljá, has returned."

"Comadre!" Felipa interrupted disdainfully. "How much money did you get for handing Marcela over to her?"

"She is an ilol. The Ladinos themselves cannot control her. She was in jail and suddenly none of the guards could keep the doors closed. Our comadre Catalina and the other women who were imprisoned there came flying out to their village. And you want to make an enemy of her? She is a very powerful ilol."

Felipa let out a defiant burst of laughter.

"Power! She couldn't even bear a child!"

"And what are the saints who were born to her in the cave?"

Felipa bowed her head, momentarily quelled. She had heard about those saints. That they were miraculous, that they protected the weak, that they healed the sick, that they gave advice to those who had gone astray. But she wanted to see them with her own eyes, touch them. No, it was not so easy to fool Felipa.

"They say," the former martoma continued, dizzied by his

sudden victory over his wife, "they say that when the saints were born the ilol was dirty with clay and not blood, like other females. And that the saints were born full grown."

"Ave María Purísima!"

This exclamation, so frequently used by the Ladina maids of Ciudad Real, came naturally to Teresa's lips. Rosendo and his wife looked at her with a flash of alarm. What had she said that they had not understood?

"You are going with us?" Felipa asked.

Teresa nodded. She was afraid of being left alone, afraid they would think she was different, afraid she would be accused of betrayal.

The group set off for Tzajal-hemel. When they reached the cave it was not easy to go in. As in the past, people were crowded together everywhere, excited and anxious. It was whispered that Catalina Díaz Puiljá was going to appear.

Jabbing with their elbows and shoving, the former martoma, Felipa and Teresa managed to make their way inside. At the back of the cave, surrounded by aromatic smoke and lighted candles, was the altar, covered with a sheet from Guatemala. Teresa was disappointed by the sight. She had hoped for a display of wealth and sumptuous offerings, but this was poorer than the poorest ranch chapel.

In contrast to the nakedness of the sanctuary, Catalina made her appearance weighed down with adornments, hieratic as a corpse, supported on both sides by the women of her retinue. She stood with her back to the altar, and made no genuflection before it. The idols being worshiped there, were they not her babies, her sons? No, she did not fear them. She had established herself as their equal. In their relationship, each side set the conditions that suited it and demanded the price that was just. Yes, they did look into the entrails of time and if they squeezed the world between their fingers they could lay it to waste. But without Catalina, through whom they had manifested themselves, without her to serve as their interpreter, what would they be reduced to? Invisibility and muteness once more.

Catalina faced the crowd without fear. A docile flock, but how quick to scatter at the least sign of danger! How quick to renounce their faith!

Teresa Entzín López observed the priestess's slow movements, heard her grave and unmodulated voice.

"The saints are not content. Like cattle, they want to lick their salt, so they can become stronger. And there is no salt. No one has money, no one wants to make the sacrifice, to bring candles and pom."

Somewhere, someone began to sob.

CHAPTER XXIV

TERESA QUICKLY GREW accustomed to the monotonous chanting of this woman whose face seemed made of stone. She stopped listening and began to look around. People sighed loudly to attract attention to themselves; their moans begged for forgiveness. Even Felipa, so hostile toward Catalina, had fallen beneath her spell and was now vying with the others in making a display of her repentance and remorse. Teresa looked at her in amazement, feeling herself to be on the bank of a fast-flowing river that, with increasing turbulence, was dragging everyone else in an unknown direction.

"What am I doing here?" Teresa wondered suddenly with a disgust fueled by the odor of closely packed bodies, rotting flowers, ignited wax.

If this woman who demands that we perform these duties were truly capable of doing anything, Teresa reasoned, I would not be here. I would be with Idolina.

When the former martoma and his wife left the cave they were deeply moved and drunk. At a certain distance, a distance she no longer wanted to close, Teresa followed them. The couple stopped every time the old man reeled and needed Felipa's support to keep walking. Teresa laughed at his clumsy efforts to keep his balance, to go forward. And she made no move to help, no considerate gesture. It seemed humiliating and contemptible to serve an Indian.

Teresa entered the hut only to collect her things: a rebozo, a small bundle of clothing. Immersed as she was in drunkenness, Felipa was unaware of her guest's actions.

Taking pains not to brush against anything, not even with the hem of her clothing, Teresa took her last steps through the hut. She placed the wide bowl she ate from, shining clean, on a shelf. And she left.

She walked along the road thinking about how the Cifuentes family would receive her. Had Idolina missed her? How grateful she would be for a longed-for smile of happiness. But she didn't

count on it too much. The one thing she could count on was
Isabel's reproach and perhaps the quick slap that concluded her
fits of temper.

And if they would not take her in? Teresa was paralyzed by
the possibility. Then she recovered and kept on walking, careful
of the stones she had to sidestep, the mud puddles, the thorns.
She was not thinking about anything any more.

In Ciudad Real, emotions were no longer running as high and
the sight of an Indian did not arouse the Caxlans' fury, only the
same disdainful indifference as before. An Indian had ceased to
be a sign of danger.

Teresa crossed the first streets without anyone's paying any
particular attention to her. Perhaps a lady she walked by (who
had known her in her patróns' house) gave the distracted half-
smile one gives to the piece of furniture that is always there.

Teresa stepped into the entryway of her masters' house, sticking close to the wall so as not to be noticed. But her arrival in the
kitchen caused such a stir among the servants that Isabel had to
find out about it.

Isabel appeared, furious. To have left her like that, without even
giving notice, a wretched, brazen Indian she had done so much
for! And like all those of her race, Teresa deliberately chose the
worst moment. Just when she was most needed because a parlormaid had left and the woman who washed the clothes couldn't
cope. At that precise moment it occurred to Teresa to go off half-
cocked. But, after all, said Isabel, it's just what I deserved for
having expected any gratitude from an Indian. Teresa wept with
contrition and promised never to do it again. She had been crazy,
someone had cast an evil spell on her, because otherwise she could
not explain what drove her to leave. And while she spoke, punc-
tuating her words with gasps that tried to seem like sobs, she
stimulated her tears by rubbing her eyes with the corner of her
rebozo.

Isabel let herself be softened. After all, what did it matter if she
were served by this one or another? At least she already knew
Teresa's ways. And she was dependable and diligent. After the
lesson she was going to be taught, she would have no inclination
ever to jump the traces again.

From that night on, Teresa was given a cold tortilla (because no one was going to waste good coal coddling flighty Indians) and a few swallows of coffee, also unheated, for dinner. Teresa chewed the hard mouthful, sad because she still hadn't seen Idolina, who was out visiting La Alazana.

Idolina came home late and cheerful. When she discovered that the person who was going to help her undress was Teresa she embraced her effusively, though it was an effusiveness born of other causes and directed toward other people.

Teresa felt the distance that persisted in this embrace, but she shut her eyes so as not to see this alien girl who moved about with ease—as if she had never been sick—and chatted endlessly about events and things of which Teresa knew nothing. When the time came to sleep, Teresa stayed awake for a long while, eyes wide open in the darkness, asking herself the same question she had asked in the cave: What do I have to do with this place?

The following days helped her to get back into a routine. She had no time for reflection and at night when it was time to lie down she fell exhausted onto the floor, because her old cot was now being used by a maid who had always jealously coveted it.

Teresa eagerly awaited the moments Idolina spent in the house but, in addition to being very brief, they were so taken up with plans and preparations for going out once more that it was impossible to exchange any words other than an order, an instruction or a sign of compliance. How different this rushing, restless Idolina, pink with excitement, was from the other one, the inert girl whose strength was used up by shifting positions in bed.

But the people that we are in succession are never entirely lost; they are not buried. They survive, they hide, and as soon as a favorable occasion arises, they come onstage once more and stand in the spotlight.

One rainy day Idolina woke up tired and didn't want to get out of bed. As in the old days, Teresa lit the brazier and knelt down in a corner of the room.

"Tell me a story, nana," the girl asked lazily.

Teresa, who was a fount of fantastical tales, didn't want to tell any story but the one the girl hadn't asked her about: the story of what she did during the months she abandoned the house.

Teresa began to speak. Idolina was distracted by the water drumming against the roof tiles and windowpanes and barely caught a few disconnected phrases of the narration. Teresa made a desperate effort to get the girl to listen; when she reached the point where she arrived at the cave of Tzajal-hemel with Rosendo and Felipa, she claimed that the ilol had spoken to her (as if, under Teresa's insignificant exterior, she had recognized a very powerful canán) to tell her that the promises of the ashes would be fulfilled. Her girl was already well again. Now it only remained for the stepfather and the mother to die, and she would be free.

Idolina sat up to gaze severely at her nana.

"Don't lie to me!"

Teresa made the sign of the cross over her mouth and Idolina fell back onto the pillows.

"When will it stop raining?" she asked, looking impatiently out the window.

"If you go, will you take me with you?" the nana wanted to know.

Idolina made a gesture of assent. But where would she go? What would she have to leave behind? Suddenly she was shaken by a shiver of fear. She needed to talk to Julia.

"Get me an umbrella. We're going out."

Idolina was already standing up, starting to dress.

Mistress and maid walked through the deserted streets, seeking a way to ford the torrent of mud, dirty water and trash at every corner. La Alazana had to change Idolina's soaking wet socks for some dry ones. The Indian woman went to warm up beside the stove.

While she let her friend help her, Idolina smiled, savoring in advance the succulent tidbit of news they were going to share. We'd see if Julia would dare mock her now, telling her she was a child, that she knew nothing of the world, that her conversation irritated her! She would marvel, yes, she would marvel to learn that Idolina knew the secrets of the very Indians the foreign woman always saw as remote and inaccessible.

But when Idolina conveyed Teresa's story to Julia, she didn't marvel over it. Her eyes grew large with surprise and fear.

"So they've gone back to their old ways."

Did Fernando know? Why hadn't he told her? Did he want to cover for the Chamulas? Or to betray her?

He hates me, Julia thought bitterly. He doesn't want to hold on to any of the things I have achieved.

She looked around her with the painful acuity of a farewell. The spaciousness, the solidity of this room, one among the many at her disposal in her house. The furnishings, in which wealth and taste were combined. The power of commanding an unconditional and submissive staff of servants. The security of having more than enough money to meet their needs. The prestige of being the wife of a civil servant and the mistress of a rancher. She had found in Ciudad Real the end point of a hazardous peregrination she did not want to recommence. And this stupid girl put her arms around her neck, urging her not to go away soon because she could not, really she could not, go on living with her family, not in this town, or . . . !

Julia passed her hand over Idolina's head to calm her down.

"You'll see, everything will come out all right."

But she was afraid. And when Leonardo came to see her that night, she told him about the cave at Tzajal-hemel.

CHAPTER XXV

LEONARDO ASKED QUESTIONS, wanted details. Julia invented them. The more care she took to deflect suspicion from Fernando, the more he thought about rash confidings, secrets poorly kept. He pretended to believe her in order to get her to say more, and he thanked her for the warning with the promise of some dangling gold earrings that had caught La Alazana's eye as she was strolling through the silversmiths' district.

When their conversation was over, Leonardo went straight to the Palacio Episcopal. He needed some advice before notifying the civil authorities of the facts. His Excellency begged heaven to grant him patience when he learned that the lesson administered by the imprisonment of the Indian women had been in vain. In addition to being stubborn, the Chamulas were now heartened by the impunity the government was publicly guaranteeing them.

"The Holy Scriptures said it well," Don Alfonso concluded. "There is a time for war and a time for peace."

"Precisely," Leonardo concurred. "And now is the time for war."

"What? That would make the government think we were the troublemakers, and they would mount a campaign of persecution against the Church as bad as the one in Tabasco. The government has been looking for a pretext, and if we give them one now. . . ."

"Su Ilustrísima," was Leonardo's smooth reproach, "You aren't talking like a Coleto."

"I'm not a Coleto."

The old man was digging up a distant origin, a different background, other customs, to evade his solidarity with a town he had assimilated to many years before.

"The shepherd must watch his sheep. But the flock of Chamula is untended. I've seen Padre Manuel Mandujano everywhere, except in his parish."

"He has the right to take a rest. And I'm wondering if it would be a good idea to send him back. Manuel has a very violent nature, and, like you, like everyone, he's gotten wind of some political booty in San Juan."

Leonardo made a gesture of alarm.

"And who will replace him? A weakling? A coward? Among the Indians you need a man who knows how to keep a tight hold on the reins, someone who has what it takes to face down Ulloa."

Don Alfonso Cañaveral yielded in the end. How was he going to manage things, he, a poor old dog, among so many barking mastiffs? But for one more moment he wanted to wield the weapon that had made him strong in his youth and middle age, and he imposed one condition.

"No one must ever know what we have said here, Leonardo. As if this were the confessional."

"Not even the ranchers, Monseñor? They must be put on their guard. They would be the first to suffer if an uprising breaks out."

"The uprising will break out if a panic breaks out. I said no one! You choose: if you're coming to me, it's because you want to keep the peace. If what you want is to carry out reprisals against Fernando Ulloa or the people of Tzajal-hemel then go to the municipal president's office, hold a meeting of the city council and have the town prepare for war. It's very easy to frighten them because all of them, some more, some less, have guilty consciences. And you know how to handle these people. One shout, one rumor is enough, and there they are, your blessed ranchers, racing for their rifles, hiding their women in the cisterns and the attics, burying their money behind the house."

Leonardo laughed at this description of the scene and made a gesture as if to erase it. Don Alfonso Cañaveral was leaning against the back of his chair, breathing laboriously.

"I'm ready to keep the secret, Monseñor. But I want to impose some conditions, too."

"What conditions?"

"One that is more important than any other: the priest who goes to San Juan must be Manuel Mandujano."

"Why?"

"He knows the territory."

The reasoning was indisputable and the Bishop had to accept it. With that acceptance, the conversation reached a more cordial conclusion than could have been foreseen at its beginning. Leonardo left the Palacio Episcopal in good spirits. This time, he reflected, he would keep his promise. It made no sense to start ringing the bells before the fruit had ripened. Step by step, the same story that had just taken place would repeat itself. And only one thing would be accomplished: the Indians would become even bolder and no one would be able to stop them when they demanded that the haciendas be dismembered for the benefit of their communities. On the other hand, if the situation were handled sensibly. . . .

When the order to leave for San Juan reached him, Manuel Mandujano had grown tired of parading his triumph through the sacristies and the gatherings of the devout. It was the right moment: he was beginning to fear that his laurels would wither in inaction, and he had noticed that interest in the momentary danger that had confronted the city was beginning to wane. Now people were talking with the same passion as before about lawsuits over inheritances, newborn children found in some gutter, the tale of the brother and sister who were living together in sin and went all the way to Rome to see if the Holy Father. . . .

Don Alfonso Cañaveral recommended tact and a conciliatory spirit to Padre Manuel. While the departing priest's horse was stamping with impatience to leave in the stable, Don Alfonso recalled the parable of the prodigal son, applying it to Tzajal-hemel.

Manuel said yes, yes to everything. He was determined that his absence from Ciudad Real would be brief and that his return would again be spectacular. For only a few days' stay in Chamula it wasn't necessary to trouble Benita. So he left her ensconced in a spacious house, with galleries that quickly filled up with flowerpots and birdcages so his sister would be distracted and wouldn't sigh too much after her absent brother.

". . . and do not condemn them because they are now idol-worshipers. It's their ignorance, their abandonment. Be a comfort to them, let them feel, through your ministry, that our Church gathers them in and protects them."

Mandujano nodded, no longer listening. His fingers were tormenting the whip he was going to lash his mount with. The whip that he would brandish in the cave at Tzajal-hemel, but that he could not bring hissing down because Catalina placed herself between him and the idols and seized it from him.

Padre Mandujano wanted to punish the ilol but some men restrained him from behind. Catalina broke the whip against her knee and it was like a signal. Some with sticks, others with machetes, the rest brandishing stones, all of them hurled themselves onto Padre Manuel. When they went away, there was nothing left but a sickening mass of bones and blood. The sacristan Xaw Ramírez Paciencia, who was with him, escaped only by a miracle.

CHAPTER XXVI

XAW RAMÍREZ PACIENCIA was afraid. Ever since he had returned to San Juan, alone (because Padre Manuel still had matters to take care of in Ciudad Real), he saw nothing around him but inexpressive faces, forced bows. And Xaw needed his people's respect, their sympathy. He was not used to being feared, much less hated. Every since Padre Manuel's ill-fated arrival in Chamula, something very similar to fear and hatred had been pushing Xaw farther and farther away from his tribe.

The sacristan had taken to drinking to chase away his sorrows. He drank with the saints' mayordomos during the sacred ceremonies which began again in the priest's absence. But he no longer found, even in alcohol, the words to make the others understand him.

And the mayordomos neglected their tasks. The strings of tecolúmate flowers withered on the altars and the pine needles had taken on the yellow color, the dry and brittle texture they have when they are about to die.

Xaw understood that something was happening. He did not want to ask what, since no one would have answered him. All he needed was to see the direction the pilgrimages were setting off in: the village of Tzajal-hemel.

Xaw continued drinking, now without companions. He rang the bells of the parish church at any random moment of the day when his anguish became intolerable and he needed to make a loud noise to break the brooding silence.

When Padre Manuel returned to San Juan, Xaw did not know whether to rejoice or to flee. He wanted to convince the priest to dismount from his horse and rest for a while in the sacristy. But Padre Manuel was in a hurry. He answered the sacristan's hesitant suggestions with a friendly tap of his whip. What did he have to fear? He was accompanied by several armed men, among them Rubén Martínez, who had been sent with him by Leonardo Cifuentes (without Don Alfonso Cañaveral's knowledge) in order to protect him.

Xaw would rather have stayed in San Juan, but the party needed a guide and he had to lead the way to Tzajal-hemel.

He did not go into the cave. He stayed outside, shrinking from people's gazes, intent on what was about to happen. When he heard the first cry and learned that the Caxláns had fallen, he ran without stopping all the way to Jobel, seeking the most secret, least frequented footpaths, hiding in the undergrowth when he heard human steps approaching.

He reached the Palacio Episcopal gasping with exhaustion, and the servants, who knew him from his previous journey, let him inside. They were frightened by the turmoil on his face, the panic in his gaze, and though he had not asked them to (he was still unable to speak), they led him into His Excellency's presence.

Don Alfonso understood nothing of the incoherent narrative, spoken half in Tzotzil and the rest in an uncertain Spanish. But little by little he was infected by the speaker's terrified shuddering, and shaking him violently by the shoulders, he was able to learn that Padre Manuel and his companions (what companions?) had been killed in Tzajal-hemel.

Doña Cristina, the housekeeper, and the other maids of lower rank who were listening behind the door scattered as soon as they heard the news. One of them ran to the stove to mix up water, brandy, sugar and nutmeg for the draques that would be necessary; another took cups and spoons from the cupboard. Others rushed out to the street, on any pretext, to reveal what they had just learned.

Don Alfonso paced the room with slow, unsteady steps. It didn't bother him to lose himself in his bewilderment with Xaw looking on because for him, as for all Coletos, an Indian was not a witness.

What trap had the ranchers sprung on him? From what Xaw said, it was easy to tell that Leonardo Cifuentes had not respected the commitment the two of them had made to each other. Cifuentes had alerted the others, given Padre Manuel an escort.

"They must have been the first to attack. They fired, made a show of force. How idiotically rash!"

But that doesn't free me from my responsibility, Don Alfonso repeated to himself. Knowing the character of Padre Mandujano, his aggressiveness, his pride, which had increased since his initial exploit in the cave, how could I have given in to Cifuentes' pressure and sent him to Chamula, when he was a powder keg? To calm his scruples, Don Alfonso had urged Padre Manuel to be sensible before his departure. What good was that? About as useful as recommending prudence to a lighted fuse. There could have been no other outcome but the one he was now contemplating.

"And I am the guilty party," he judged.

It was strange. The sentence sounded hollow and meaningless. He was so accustomed to absolving without even having a clear image of the sins he was hearing about (what is a calumny? what is a wicked thought? what is not loving God above all things?) that now, immediately after having formulated and assessed his own lapse, he felt calm, relaxed.

"Go to the kitchen. They'll give you a cordial," he told Xaw.

When he was alone, Don Alfonso went to sit down in an armchair. He did not notice when, but a steaming cup had appeared next to him. Thanking a shadow that vanished through the door, he began taking little sips, automatically.

What should his attitude be? Should he protest to Cifuentes? Don Alfonso gave a gesture of fatigue. Leonardo would deny the accusations and he couldn't prove the contrary. There wasn't a single survivor. In any case, Leonardo had the unconditional support of the ranchers, the sympathy of all Ciudad Real.

"What is all the hubbub about?" His Excellency asked the housekeeper who had just entered the room.

"The people. They are afraid."

Doña Cristina diligently removed the empty cup and pressed it against her breast.

"How have they found out . . . ?"

Don Alfonso stood up in a flash of anger. Doña Cristina stepped back, vaguely frightened. She had never seen him like that.

"I don't know. . . . Some peddlers, perhaps. They sell their wares throughout the region of Chamula."

"Peddlers!" Don Alfonso repeated bitterly. "Betrayals everywhere, intrigues. . . ."

"Monseñor!"

"No, I'm not talking about you. You don't know what lies at the bottom of all this."

The sounds in the street were building. People were milling around the doors and windows of the Palacio Episcopal murmuring excitedly. Already the events at Tzajal-hemel were unrecognizable on their lips. Each one had added something, invented something, remembered something. Xaw's version became a hodgepodge of verisimilitudes and exaggerations, predictions supported by distant memories. And with each new phrase, each new comment, the sense of danger increased in all of them and their anger justified itself anew. The crowd stayed where it was, in the expectation that from the place where the news of the murder of Padre Manuel and his companions had been divulged, some wisdom, some guidance would also come.

Someone came around the corner. It was a woman, her hair unkempt, and a black shawl floating around her shoulders, followed by other women making gestures so ambiguous it was impossible to know if they were holding her back or pushing her on. She wanted to make her way through the crowd. It was Benita Mandujano. She was shouting, in a hoarse, tired and curiously opaque voice. She was struggling, as if someone were keeping her from moving forward, though all of them had now stepped aside to allow her to walk freely to the door. She pounded on the wood with two clenched fists.

"They killed my brother, Monseñor! You sent him to his death!"

People were shaking their heads in commiseration. Those cl est to Benita made an effort to console her.

"The will of God. . . ."

"The will of God. . . ."

"The will of God. . . ."

The syllables followed one another mechanically, without inflection, without conviction.

"Damnation!" Benita replied in a fury. "It was not the will of God. It was the jealousy of these good-for-nothings"—she pointed to the Palacio Episcopal. "Not one of them had his talent."

Inside, the housekeeper choked back an exclamation of rage.

"Let her talk," Don Alfonso said with a gesture of agreement. "I think she's right."

"With people feeling the way they do," Doña Cristina replied, "that woman could stir them up. And they will rise up against us, Monseñor."

All her years of service to the clergy had made her feel like an integral part of it.

"Wouldn't this be the right time for you to speak to her, calm her down?"

An exorcism, anything, she finally stammered—she didn't know exactly what procedures the Church followed with those possessed by the devil. Don Alfonso had to smile.

"Let her in. But only her! I don't want the others getting my rug dirty!"

Benita did not kneel when she was in the bishop's presence. She did not even bend down to kiss his ring. She was no longer weeping and her gaze was firm and direct.

"Not even a burial, Monseñor," she began, in a neutral and glacial voice. "The vultures are going to eat him like a dead animal."

And suddenly the frenzy came over her again.

"It's your fault! You sent him to his death!"

Doña Cristina rushed forward to silence this irreverence with a slap. But it was no longer necessary. Benita had fallen onto the sofa, weeping.

"You killed him out of envy," she repeated, her voice muffled by the plush cushions.

"Monseñor!" Doña Cristina implored.

Don Alfonso watched with patient attention as the pulsation of rage slowly lost its intensity. In the end it would be extinguished, and all the more quickly the more it was bled by accusations.

"I can't bear it," the housekeeper moaned, her face hidden among the folds of her apron as she blindly searched her way out of the room.

It wasn't that someone was insulting Don Alfonso, who, in this case, if it seemed best to him, could swallow the insults. It was his dignity, his purple robes, the respect and submission that the faithful owe to their Holy Mother. No, Doña Cristina could not bear it.

When His Excellency was left alone with Benita, he moved toward her, little by little. The sobs had become a regular, rhythmic, evenly spaced breathing, the breathing of a person who is asleep.

Don Alfonso looked at the mouth, now half-open in sleep, which a few minutes before had uttered an accusation that was far too sordid and unnuanced, and based on a false motive (jealousy!), but was, in fact, just. Yes, he had sent Manuel Mandujano to his death. He tried once more to feel remorse, but the small wave, artificially generated, subsided in his heart.

The years had destroyed his belief in the sacred character of life. Of this life, anyway. If the young priest's life hadn't been cut short, what then? He would have become a respectable parish priest, or perhaps reached a higher rank. And perhaps, from the seat of his power, whatever it was, he would have sent one or another of his subordinates to his death.

Pain and guilt, Don Alfonso meditated, are the two banks of the river of adversity. He had crossed its rushing waters long before. And from his side he contemplated with a remote gaze the heartsick woman who was snoring, her body flung haphazardly across the sofa.

CHAPTER XXVII

THE CROWD, which was slowly growing larger with a succession of new arrivals, remained in front of the Palacio Episcopal for a long time. People cast frequent, furtive and rapid glances towards the windows and doors, waiting in some obscure way for the appearance of a leader who would guide their actions, who would decide for them, who would pronounce the words that would describe and justify their conduct.

Someone whispered the name of the municipal president. After all, he was the town's highest authority and they should turn to him in a moment of crisis like this.

The name echoed meaninglessly in many ears. Who was he? Oh, yes, that old man, fat and benevolent; it was murmured that he was the one who had allowed many women of easy virtue from the coast—"seagulls"—to set up shop in Ciudad Real.

His position was familiar to all of them. Who hadn't invoked it in order to curse it, on crossing a street mined with potholes the Ayuntamiento hadn't bothered to fill in? Who didn't blame him for every one of the small calamities that plagued the town: completely irrational sales taxes, the lack of security at night, unjustified arrests, extortionate property taxes levied without appeal, the proliferation of vice? Who hadn't secretly aspired at least once to occupy that dignified office, whose holders left it with an inevitable diminishment of prestige, but rich? A municipal president is an institution that is accepted, tolerated and required under normal circumstances. But in an emergency like this one, a municipal president has nothing to do.

And the commandante of the garrison? This suggestion wasn't even worth discussing. The commandante of the garrison was a foreigner in the pay of the government of the Republic. Those two factors alone were enough to disqualify him. It would have been madness to trust him.

No, what they needed was a caudillo. A caudillo who was a Coleto to the marrow of his bones and an energetic, audacious and ambitious man. Who incarnated these virtues? The crowd found out when Leonardo Cifuentes, followed by other ranchers, passed through it to knock at the door of the Palacio Episcopal.

He was received immediately. And from the moment Leonardo Cifuentes and his retinue disappeared inside the bishop's house, the crowd's wait acquired a meaning. Now they became agitated, they gesticulated, and the murmur swelled to a bellow. Now they were proposing plans of attack against the indigenous communities and measures for defending their own city. Now each one felt himself to be the hero of a coming adventure, responsible for the lives of his fellow citizens, guardian of the community's belongings.

When, after a lapse of time that seemed eternal to those who were waiting, Leonardo Cifuentes reappeared in the doorway, there was a sudden silence.

Leonardo stopped and behind him his companions did too. He knew then that he had to speak.

"His Excellency sends you his blessing," he said. "Events have left him so shattered that he cannot come to be near his flock."

An old woman sighed sympathetically. She felt strong, daring, protected. When had the Church ever abandoned them? During an uprising she had heard her grandparents talk about, the Virgen de la Caridad intervened between the Indians and the Caxláns, granting victory to the just. Now, who knew what miracles, what wondrous things would be seen!

"Each one must look out for himself and for everyone," Leonardo continued. "The men by taking up arms, the women by exercising prudence, the virtue that Coletas are famous for throughout the region."

Applause was heard. Chests expanded in pride at having been born in this valley encircled by high mountain crests, at descending from men who were famous for their daring exploits and the purity of their names, at speaking the language of the elect.

"Our elders will not be ashamed of us! By our deeds we will prove ourselves worthy of them!"

Leonardo's last words were greeted with a chorus of *Viva!* and hats thrown into the air. The women covered their blushes with the fringes of their shawls. A boy tossed up a firecracker, causing fright and anger at first, then laughter from those nearby.

After that everyone went their separate ways. Leonardo and

the ranchers went to the Ayuntamiento, where an urgent meeting of the "most prominent members" of the populace had been called. The rest went to their respective homes.

And suddenly everything had been transformed. The artisan no longer opened the door of the workshop where his labor ground him down without any compensation. Now he walked past the loom, past the leatherworking tools, past the anvil without giving them so much as a glance. He went to his back storage room and took out a rusty shotgun, an antique rifle, a pistol he had made with his own hands. He asked for some oil and a piece of chamois and sat down on the edge of a bed to rub the weapon's interstices patiently until the last vestige of the rust that had marred the metal was erased. His children did not dare approach this man, absorbed, for the first time in their memory, in an important task, and on the sly they imitated his movements with toy weapons. Their mother shooed them away noiselessly. Then she went to the kitchen to make a little coffee to cheer her husband up with.

At noon the church bells rang. It was the call to prayer, which each person usually said to himself. But today pedestrians knelt down in the middle of the street and joined hands to recite aloud the verses of the Annunciation.

The upheaval was more apparent in the center of town. The maids came and went, barefoot, catlike, quick, buying out the stock of stores and markets, accompanying the patrona to the hiding place used in situations like this, cleaning out the cistern in case anyone had to take refuge there.

There was something almost festive about these preparations. But it was a funereal festival. The great mourning cast over Ciudad Real by the death of Padre Mandujano and his escorts had erased the small particular mournings many families were dragging out, no longer remembering for whom.

Spinsters opened the doors that shut them in. Now, finally, they could move around, act, serve, without being paralyzed by mockery or disapproval. For the first time in years they saw the street, no longer through a windowpane or from behind a half-closed shutter, but in full daylight. They joined the groups natally, without giving rise to comments or sympathetic sighs. ho was going to notice them now? Who was going to to see their sterile bellies, their barren years? Who was going to count their wrinkles and white hairs? Who was going to negate their efforts to feel that there was still hope for them, that they still were not definitively excluded from the circle of other people's interests and work? They talked a lot, heatedly, and laughed noisily. They offered to help and used this unexpected respite as an outlet for their abnegation.

At an early hour, the married women left the bed of love and childbirth, the place where the man humiliated and exalted them, the throne of their idleness, their refuge against inclement weather, and vigorously grasped the reins of the household which they so frequently abandoned to the servants.

Since the routine had been interrupted, the maids no longer gave instructions. Now the tyrannical cook, the surly porter, the lascivious parlormaid champed under the inflexible orders of a mistress who was suddenly vigilant, bubbling over with great ideas she had just had, new projects that couldn't be delayed.

From the most ancient trunks emerged yellowed, heirloom sheets, venerable sets of china, smudged pictures. Long-overlooked shelves were dusted at last, properties and possessions were inventoried. From time to time, with aloof magnanimity, the patrona yielded up some useless shred of cloth to the greed of the maid who was helping her.

The young girls looked for an opportunity to join in. They quarreled over a piece of silk, a pitcher, a silver place setting for the dowry they would take to their hypothetical marriages. The mother mediated the disputes, promising that everyone would receive an equal share, but later, because now they were in a hurry to hide the objects that belonged to them as carefully as possible.

"Otherwise, after the looting, we'll be left without so much as a strand of thread."

"Who's going to loot, Mama?"

"The Indians, if they come into the city."

"And if they don't come?"

"Then the poor people will, the ones who live on the edges of town. They're always on the lookout for any kind of disorder that will give them the chance to steal. And the troops, too."

"Is it true that the soldiers carry girls off with them?"

The respectable lady gave a start.

"Make the sign of the cross over your lips and hush. Now, let's get on with this."

The respectable lady was displeased precisely because what she had been asked about was true. During the Revolution, how many times they had seen it happen! Poor Angélica Ortiz, so pretty and with a serious boyfriend, had to endure the officers' abuse, and in front of her family. Afterward she was like a madwoman, of course. And she could never marry.

The story had happened once and could repeat itself now. The victims would be these girls. The respectable lady observed her daughters with panic in her heart as they laughed in front of a mirror, trying on old-fashioned hats. Only one of them was still quiet, her eyes downcast and her cheeks reddening. She was the eldest.

"They would have to kill me first!" the respectable lady exclaimed violently. The girls turned to look at her in bewilderment. The eldest daughter smiled.

The gentlemen gathered in the parlor. They smoked one cigarette after another and had pots and pots of coffee brought in.

"The bishop is not with us."

Leonardo's gesture sought to lessen the impact of this exaggeration.

"He hasn't said that."

"He hasn't said he supports us either."

"And he should be the most enraged of all. After all, he raised Padre Manuel."

"For that very reason the news of his death has prostrated him. At his age, heavy blows can no longer be endured."

"He must have lost his mind! That's the only explanation for how he could have said what he said."

"All right," Leonardo proposed. "Let's leave Don Alfonso in peace since, for the moment, thank God, he is not indispensable. And let's think about the measures that have to be taken."

"The most important one has already been taken: our leader is you."

Leonardo made a quick bow.

"I've sent telegrams to Tuxtla, to Mexico. . . ."

"People in Tuxtla won't waste this opportunity to do us a bad turn. We're old rivals."

"What's more, I have it on good authority that Fernando Ulloa is there, talking to the governor."

"Don't worry, gentlemen. The governor will do only what those above him order him to do."

"And it's easier for us to reach those above him than a mere employee like Ulloa."

"I have a finca in the municipality of Chamula!"

"And I have some cultivated land at the edge of it."

"Those worthless Indians are going to demolish the stores."

"I already distributed weapons among the peons."

"And if they use them against you?"

"How could they desert me now? They're Ladinos, too."

"But poor Ladinos."

"They're not trustworthy."

"What else can you do? There's no other pole to hang yourself from."

"If the Indian uprising spreads, the first to die will be the peons on the ranches and the Ladinos who live on the outskirts of town."

"They'll have to be warned."

"They already know from experience, hermano. It's always happened the same way."

"If only we could get some information about what's happening in Chamula."

"Those Indians are so crafty! They're going to be on top of us when we're unprepared."

"The man who delivers wood to my house told me he's seen flickering lights in the hills for several nights now."

"They're already gathering together."

"There are no such lights. Those are fires. It's the season for burning off the fields."

"That's easier to believe than to verify."

"I have verified it," Cifuentes said.

The others looked at him in admiration. To a respectful silence, he continued, "I don't know if all of you remember a woman named Doña Mercedes Solórzano."

"How could we forget her! We knew her so well!"

"What times we had then!"

"Now don't you start bragging. You were always the one with cold feet."

Cifuentes let them have their fun for a while. In the end, he would be the only one left holding the reins.

"So what did you want to tell us about the old gal?"

"Oh the favors you owe her, compadre!"

"She serves the man who knows how to repay her."

"I've provided her with a small amount of capital so she can go into business for herself. She bought some mules and some salt and went to sell it where it's most needed right now: in Chamula."

"That broad has guts. Heading straight into the wolf's jaw like that. . . ."

"She's not in any danger," Leonardo assured them, to detract from her merits. "The Indians are used to seeing peddlers."

"What miserable work it must be! Going along those paths. . . ."

"Always in danger of an assault, an ambush."

"And there's not even anyone to talk to. There aren't any people of reason in those villages."

"The income makes up for it. After a few years the peddler, who'd never have been anything but a poor beggar if he'd stayed at home, can open a shop in the Calle Real de Guadalupe."

A few of those present cleared their throats, feeling that they were being alluded to.

"Any kind of work is honorable."

"Of course."

"So if Doña Mercedes hears about anything that might interest us, she'll pass it along to me immediately."

"And in the meantime?"

"In the meantime we drink our coffee and chat."

"But if we have to wait too long people are going to lose their morale."

"What can we do? We don't have any way of stirring up the hornets' nest."

"Even the authorities are against us."

"The government is a gang of crooks!"

"One thing is going to be very clear when all of this is over: the president will know that in Chiapas his laws aren't worth a pure and celestial heap of shit."

"Maybe they'll stop sending us these college boys who think they're so much sharper than anybody else."

"Fernando Ulloa doesn't even hold a degree. I have that on good authority," Leonardo added, to clinch the matter. The others smiled in complicity.

"To think that this is what it's come to! Señor Nobody shows up out of the blue and puts us—us!—in a bind like this."

"Because if the Indians didn't have him backing them up. . . ."

"If he hadn't inflamed them with his sermonizing . . ."

". . . they never would have dared get themselves fired up like this."

"Gentlemen," one of them who had a penchant for historical exactitude said, "let's not forget that this isn't the first uprising."

"The main thing is to make sure it's the last."

"From your lips to God's ears!"

"God will hear me, even if the bishop has gone deaf."

"Poor old man! He's getting weak in the head."

"They should make them retire, too, like every other employee. There are some priests who are smart men . . ."

". . . and who are figuring out how to fish in the turbulent river of circumstance."

"If the government persecutes them they have to defend themselves one way or another."

"Anyone can sound good from the pulpit. The day one of them lets out a yell, the entire town of Ciudad Real will rush out to destroy the Chamulas."

"Let's be careful they're not the ones who end up letting out the first yell."

"They're useful, but you can't give them too much leeway."

"We're the ones in control of this situation."

"And things aren't turning out badly. Reinforcements have arrived from Comitán and even from Guatemala."

"They smelled a fight."

"They know we're their buffer zone. If the Indians finish us off, they'll finish them off next."

"In any case, we should thank them."

The clock on the Cabildo rang eleven o'clock. The men stood up and prepared to go.

"So, what do we do, mi general?"

Leonardo smiled.

"We wait."

It was easy for them to wait, the rich men whose pantries were well stocked with provisions. But for those who were obliged to play a prominent role but did not have the means to do so, the matter was a bit more complicated.

Elderly serving-women left the giant, half-ruined houses very early, carrying some object under their rebozos to sell on the cheap. But those who could afford to purchase it didn't consider this to be the right moment, and after making a fruitless round of all the doorways and grocery stores, the servants returned to their points of departure, still carrying the objects, along with a few vegetables bought on credit in their shopping baskets.

The lady of the house sat despairing among the remnants of a former splendor that would see her die of hunger; the daughters swore to themselves that they would escape from these daily humiliations—which were worse now because of the virtual state of siege Ciudad Real was in—but they did not think of going to work, since they were unqualified for any job. They thought of making an advantageous marriage. If that weren't possible (and how many withered maidenhoods there were behind the wrought iron balconies) they would accept the flirtation, which was always available, of a sales agent, a bullfighter with a traveling fair, a roadway inspector.

The men, meanwhile, were out of the house all day, especially now that they had a very good pretext for not staying in to listen to the women's chronic laments. With their weapons on their shoulders they patrolled the streets, stopping to chat in doorways and cantinas, looking for the chance to strike up a conversation with the people they saw and to show themselves to be on their side. Between one such occasion and another, they had ample opportunity to make the usual joking displays of mutual cowardice.

Then there was the lowest class, so poor there was nothing to conceal their poverty and nothing to alleviate it, and they bore the brunt of the troubled situation.

In vain the Ladina attackers took up their posts, one early morning after the next, at the roads that entered Ciudad Real. No

Indian came down from the hills and they had to return to their miserable dwellings emptyhanded. Those who cultivated a strip of garden could cheat hunger a few days longer. But the others hurried out to beg in the city's main streets. It was useless. The shops were closed and the portals of the private homes as well. The beggar women pounded the iron knocker insistently, clamorously. One of the maids would open the giant door a crack and look out. Through the opening came the echo of laughter, fragments of conversation. The rich were gathering together, tightening their social connections, making danger a reason for recreation. And the needy woman was left outside with the door unceremoniously shut in her face.

The Congregation of the Daughters of María and the Ladies of the Sacred Heart were the first groups to take pity and organize a charitable committee. In the district of Mexicanos y Tlaxcaltecas, in Custatali and San Felipe, they distributed old clothes, small portions of coffee and brown sugar, a few bushels of corn.

The residents of those districts formed jubilant throngs to receive these charitable gifts, and the benefactresses returned to their homes, their consciences swollen with a feeling of satisfaction.

But they quickly discovered that what they were doing was not enough, that nothing was enough. Where to find more? The rich had used up their extra supplies and donated less each time. The Daughters and the Ladies began making their morning rounds with a trace of fear and a vexation they could no longer conceal. More ragged and famished families were constantly appearing, no one knew from where, and none of them maintained the initial stance of submission and gratitude any longer. The youngest ones screamed out their demands and the older ones did nothing to quiet them. Then the older ones began screaming themselves, importuning the devout ladies with their pleas, giving free rein to their bad manners and permitting themselves to make jokes and show a lack of respect.

The Daughters of María and the Ladies of the Sacred Heart complained, weeping, to their confessors. And the latter, led by Padre Balcázar, because the bishop was still ill, went (as if on a mission to a pagan land) to the miserable neighborhoods that surrounded the city and served as an almost imperceptible transition from the Ladinos' world to the Indians'.

The priests encountered the greatest resistance in the parish of San Diego, whose residents were by tradition practitioners of witchcraft. Without daring to overturn the profane altars, the priests energetically cast opprobrium upon the conduct of those who worshipped at them. They said High Masses in all the parishes and delivered sermons charged with fanaticism, and the tension appeared to move into other channels. But already the devout ladies refused to return to the poorer districts and the distribution of clothing and foodstuffs, which grew more scanty each day, had to be entrusted to the troops.

Ciudad Real was dirty, and no one was worried about sweeping it clean. Every night the families from the outskirts of town bundled up their household goods and slept all together in a heap under the arches of the Ayuntamiento. They left behind an accumulation of garbage and rinds and a smell of sour milk—there were so many babies!—stale sweat, and old wool that was replenished before it had time to fade.

The smell didn't bother the authorities because their deliberations were no longer held there. They had chosen the home of Leonardo Cifuentes as their general headquarters. After having been spurned for so long, its threshold was now crossed by the most prestigious merchants, the ranchers of the most ancient lineage, the most influential prelates. Among the ladies, La Alazana was never absent, wishing to demonstrate her solidarity with the decent people of Ciudad Real and to hush up the murmurs that were going around about Fernando Ulloa.

At every occasion—whether opportune or inopportune—Julia brought up Fernando's trip to Tuxtla, to explain it away with reasons no one accepted. Her listeners nodded disbelievingly, and she was left clinging to the shelter of Leonardo's passion and Idolina's submission.

How much longer would the waiting go on? What were they waiting for? Many of them had already forgotten. Others passed along the rumors, without conviction or enthusiasm. Telegrams had been sent, they said, to the president of the Republic and the state governor, requesting their protection in order to defend

Ciudad Real against the Indian threat. But the telegrams had ended up in the office of some subaltern and from there were sent on the slow, routine and labyrinthine path of bureaucracy. No one in Mexico could imagine how pressing the danger was, and in Tuxtla they were delighted by their neighbors' misfortune.

The auxiliary troops that were given such a warm welcome when they arrived from Comitán and Guatemala turned out to be counterproductive. Their presence weighed heavily on the impoverished, paralyzed town and they calmed their impatience for action by doing a little stealing. It was nothing of any significance, but nevertheless it offended and alarmed the Coletos.

And through it all, still no sign of Doña Mercedes Solórzano.

"Maybe the Chamulas killed her?"

"The bad seed never dies," Leonardo answered. "She'll be back soon. And with good news."

In the meantime, people's interest had to be sustained, their hatred had to be incited. Toward that end, a rancher had a group of Indians sent down from his ranch in the mountains. They brought no goods with them and on the express orders of their patrón all of them carried machetes and rifles.

Their faces, their presence, were enough to make the people of Ciudad Real rush into the streets. Screaming, they launched their attack. The soldiers couldn't rescue the Indians from the fray until more than one of them had been wounded.

The Indians slept in Ciudad Real's jail that night, and the next day they were taken by Leonardo Cifuentes, his partisans, and the guards, to the state capital.

Before the peevish and incredulous governor, the Indians were accused of trying to take Ciudad Real by assault and of conspiring together to plan a vast uprising. The interrogations, carried out through an interpreter, clarified nothing because the accused were unaware of the meaning of terms such as "take by assault" and "vast uprising." They answered every question yes or no, as it struck their fancy, without distinguishing between what incriminated them and what absolved them.

The Indians pleaded to be allowed to speak to their patrón because he was the only one who could put an end to the confusion. The patrón denied ever having seen them before and the

Indians were declared justifiably imprisoned and confined to the Tuxtla jail.

But the governor found excuses for refusing to accompany the gentlemen on their return trip to Ciudad Real, and for postponing the mobilization of the troops. He managed to appease them only by promising to put the screws on that rebel Fernando Ulloa.

CHAPTER XXVIII

WHAT NEITHER FRIENDLINESS nor persistence had accomplished was now being made possible by danger. Julia Acevedo planned out a complex series of maneuvers to make the ladies who gathered at Leonardo Cifuentes' house do so at the home of his mistress instead. The advantages were obvious and numerous: first and foremost, Julia was younger and more eager to please than Isabel, who only rarely appeared, and whose manner was always forced, irritable, bored or mocking when she did.

The first to desert was Idolina. Her advice, help and orders sped up the transformation of the Ulloa house's empty rooms into parlors for receiving guests.

Prices were not dickered over when the furnishings were acquired. The illustrious families who were ridding themselves of these relics of a glorious past, now fallen into decline, rubbed their hands together in satisfaction at a good deal. Hired hands from Cifuentes' ranches moved in whole dowries' worth of graceless, heavy furniture. Its merits resided in the lasting quality of the materials, the meticulousness of the craftsmanship. And in having belonged to famous, opulent ancestors whose portraits had also been put up for sale.

In decorating the parlors, the customary symmetry was scrupulously respected. Julia's tiniest alteration was corrected by Idolina as an intolerable sin against orthodoxy. La Alazana accepted the corrections obediently. Without a frame of conventionality to set her off, how would she be able to perform convincingly in her role as a Coleta lady?

On the day of the first reception, Julia was almost unable to enjoy her triumph. At one moment she was spying on the approving or critical reactions of her guests, at the next she was following the efficiency of the service with a vigilant gaze. Her worries didn't subside until the ritual had acquired the natural fluidity of an everyday occurrence. Only then did she notice that her guests were behaving in a way that, under other circumstances, she would have described as insulting.

Far from being grateful for Julia's hospitality, they reciprocated with small but not inoffensive acts of hostility.

The assiduity bordering on mania with which Julia kept her house clean was her first vulnerable point. The guests appeared not to have noticed the mats placed in the entryways, or to be unaware of the use for which they were intended, and they came into the house with shoes that were filthy with mud from the street.

Distracted by their state of distress, they kept a clumsy hold on the glasses of refreshments, the cups of coffee or chocolate with which Julia plied them, and the liquids splashed across the furniture, leaving obscene stains on the carpets.

A simple exclamation of annoyance, not apology, would bring an end to such an incident, which wouldn't even cause a break in conversations from which the lady of the house was excluded because no one had filled her in on the story or instructed her on the meaning of the local idioms or asked her whether or not she was interested.

When Julia sought to breach the circle of exclusion by venturing a question, she received a vague or impatient answer, as if her curiosity were neither appropriate nor justified.

As time passed, the abuses—which the visitors called informalities—grew more flagrant. Each guest began to make known her favorite foods. The maids hurriedly offered them pieces of cheese, pork sausage, little cakes. Some of them, once their own appetite was sated, did not blush to ask for a napkin to wrap more food up. It was "a little something to tide over" the sick child, the invalid grandfather, the man preoccupied by war. La Alazana heaped more on to what the visitor had already been given and made an exaggerated show of refusing to listen to her explanations.

Her extravagance earned her no gratitude, only suspicion. What was she going to want from those ladies in exchange for what she gave them? They kept themselves at the ready to respond to the first hint in the negative, but meanwhile they were able to save their own food supplies by eating hers.

Very soon the little morsels were no longer enough and the ladies stayed until it was time for lunch or dinner. They had to be invited to a properly laden table, from which they rose hurriedly to go as soon as they had finished eating.

Alone again, Julia weighed her efforts against the results. She was spending sums of money that Cifuentes found increasingly excessive and absurd. She neglected all her other duties and pleasures to ensure the success of her daily salons. And still she remained an outsider, from whom the other women didn't even bother to conceal their distrust. Was it worth making any further attempt to penetrate a world that was so closed, to ascend into a hierarchy that was so inaccessible?

I'm just having an attack of nerves, she decided abruptly. The current situation was not so much critical as incomprehensible. It couldn't go on like that much longer.

And as if to speed its denouement, she ordered the servants to clear away what was left and straighten up the parlors. Then, when things were in their places once more and order was producing the illusion of security, she locked herself in her room and drank a sedative in order to sleep.

She slept deeply, smiling at pleasurable dreams. The long rest strengthened her resolve to conquer, to dominate (and no longer only to be the equal of) these Coleta women who were now taking advantage of her.

La Alazana's imitation of their manners and behavior was becoming more and more spontaneous and fluent. She stopped asking questions and arranged her features in the self-sufficient expression of one who is in on the secret. Discreetly, expertly, she observed the reactions of others in order not to deviate from them. She was upset when it was appropriate, as it was appropriate, and to the appropriate degree. With enthusiasm, she celebrated anything that was amusing.

As she worked the pump of conversation, she became aware of how few subjects there were to fuel her guests' comments, secrets, memories, projects, hostilities and ambitions.

Men. The first one I knew was my father, they would say. The father, to whose will they were subject and from whom they inherited a family name, a place in life, a standard of conduct.

The father, that distant daily god whose flashes of lightning illuminated the home's monotonous sky and whose thunderbolts were hurled down, striking no one knew how, no one knew when, no one knew why.

The father, in whose presence children fell silent with terror and adults with respect. The father, who takes off his leather belt to punish, to tilt out the stream of golden coins onto the table.

The father, who pronounces a blessing at the table and at bedtime, who stretches out his hand so his kinsmen can kiss it in greeting and in taking their leave.

The father who once sat you down on his knees and caressed your long teen-aged braid. You were brave enough to look into his eyes and caught sight of a gleam of hunger or a veiled perturbation that made him close to you and fearful and desirable.

Men. The priest breathing heavily behind the bars of the confessional.

"I am guilty of having sinned against purity."

"In thought? In word? In deed? With yourself? With an accomplice? Have you done it again? How many times?"

When the temptation seizes you, commend yourself to the Most Holy Virgin, invoking her in any of her guises. Repent in your heart, carry out the penitence. Go in peace.

Men. When you and your cousin are hiding in the attic, you feel his hot breath on the back of your neck. His hands are searching for something and neither you nor he knows where it is nor how it is hidden, how it can be found. In the distance you can hear the sounds of the household, blotted out by the beating of your hearts.

Suddenly, doors are flung open as if to startle a guilty act and the governess is there clapping her hands energetically.

"Come out of there! Aren't you ashamed? You're not little Indian brats to be entertaining yourselves like that."

Men. The classmate who asks, while the teacher is intent on explaining a math problem, if you've seen your brothers naked when they're taking a bath. No, you haven't seen them, you don't want to see them. But after that you can't stay away from the keyholes, the chinks in the walls, and you don't find out anything but you feel dirty inside. And sad.

Men. The family friend makes a nervous joke about how your bodice is beginning to fill out. The maids rummage through the sheets, the underwear. Until one day the cry goes up. Blood. Wherever you go, a trickle follows you and gives you away: ailing female. No, you're not going to die. You're only going to stay in bed for a while, without drinking any thing acidic, making sudden movements or bathing. You don't know why. But the others do. And they smile.

Men. During the serenades they look at you insistently, deliberately. During the fairs they send you flowers and gifts. During the kermesses they shower you with confetti. During the dances they take you by the waist and spin you around until you're dizzy.

"Stand back, enemy! The heart of Jesus is with me!"

But how are you going to recognize the enemy's face in the dark corners, the lonely places? There they undermine your maidenhood, chipping away at the "no" that defended it.

You take off your clothes in front of the mirror and gaze at yourself with the fascination of someone leaning over an abyss, with the stubbornness of someone questioning a sphinx.

The body that for now you simply endure will be revealed to you by a man. You will grow up in the act of giving yourself to him, you will acquire your definitive form from his caresses.

The husband is the culmination of everything. To your longings, your pleasure, your empty spaces, he holds out fecundity. He will elevate you to the rank you are predestined for.

If the husband never arrives then you've been left behind, niña quedada: resign yourself. Button up your blouse, lower your eyelids, hush. Don't listen to the wood creaking in the rooms of those who sleep together; don't feel the belly of the woman who has conceived a child; run from the "ay" of the woman in labor. The restlessness that pounds in your temples will one day turn into a fistful of ashes. Seek the protection of your brother when your hair grows grey. That is the man you must twine the clinging vine of your life around.

Neither your lap nor your hands will remain empty or idle. Household chores, other women's babies, will besiege you until the day you die. And of all your coffins only the last one will be white.

Money. The dowry by which the father tries to cover up an excessive ugliness or a blemished virginity.

Money. The inheritance the relatives dispute around the dying man's bed.

Money. Interminable litigations in order to gain possession of a strip of land or a property title. From one generation to the next, the lawsuit, the greed and the hatred are passed on.

Money. Because this year you can't afford to spend a season in the lowlands. Because the girls want new dresses to show off at parties. Because the young men have had their first woman and are going out on sprees with their friends.

Money. Because the man of the house is making some risky business deals and the profits will come only in the long term. Money. Because he is making bets at the cockfighting arena, the casino's gaming table. Money. Because he supports his mistresses and his bastard children. Money, money, money is the litany of the lady of the house. Because things are costing more and more and appearances have to be kept up and she doesn't know what to do with so many trials and tribulations.

Money. The couple turn their backs on each other at night. People sit around a table in a threatening silence. Engagements are broken, friendships end, family ties cease to be acknowledged.

Money. The notary collects the last coins the doctor left you with. And you might hear the nails of your casket being pounded in. Because the heirs are impatient.

Reputation. You must make the sign of the cross over your mouth so your guardian angel will keep you from committing the crime—because it is a crime—of wounding the reputation of your fellow men, inventing slanders, propagating rumors.

But conversation would be so insipid without the grain of salt such whisperings add!

Gently, slowly, delicately the whited sepulchers are disturbed and the fetid odor of secrets that cannot be silenced because they cry out to heaven escapes. Of injustice, pain, misery.

They cannot be silenced. Because if the things that are hidden beneath the rooftops, beneath the sheets, were silenced they would rot until they polluted the entire world.

Talking is like lancing an abscess. The pus runs out; the swelling goes down; the fever and its delirium are calmed.

Julia witnessed this operation, mesmerized by disgust and curiosity. It was then that she confronted for the first time a true image of Ciudad Real.

All the prestige of those to whom she paid the tribute of her admiration, respect, and envy, was dissected in her presence. Under the ecclesiastical vestments, under the academic gowns of the professionals, writhed diseased entrails, twisted minds, inconsolable disgraces.

In the rear courtyard of a house whose front door ostentatiously displays aristocratic coats of arms and proofs of lineage is locked, thrashing around in his own excrement, the madman, who has attacks of fury on certain nights and breaks the bars of his cage and howls like a wounded animal.

In a windowless room lies a baby whose bones never hardened enough for it to stand up. Toothless, centuries old, an enormous, hollow head sways on a pile of large pillows.

There are families everyone shuns because the cry of a newborn child was heard unexpectedly, a wailing silenced without an echo, without an epitaph.

And how has he come up in the world so suddenly, the scavenger who lived on the outskirts of the city and now parades around the center insulting others with his insolent luxuries and dissipated ways? Did he dig up a treasure, as the stories say? Is it true that, night after a night, a lost soul appeared to him to show him the exact place where he should dig? The money was intended for masses and ceremonies that would rescue a dead man from the flames of purgatory. And it is being wasted without rhyme or reason on frivolities.

No, you shouldn't play tricks on the dead. It would have been better for him to have taken away a widow's ranch or all that an orphan had, as so many others have done. It would even have been better for him to have appropriated the goods of the clergy, betraying their trust by transforming himself from nominal depository to legitimate owner.

The women fall silent, having completed their task of fathoming other people's spirits. If they were overflowing with any satisfaction, it wasn't that of malevolence. It was the satisfaction of having turned the implacable attention of the judge and witness that every resident of Ciudad Real was toward lives that were not their own, the sins and suffering of others.

Having passed through these rites of initiation, Julia began to be treated as an accomplice. After making so many useless forays, she was finally inside the circle. And she felt safeguarded by a wall of shared secrets, memories held in common. Invulnerable under the title of Coleta lady.

Idolina leaned toward her to murmur in her ear, "Fernando and César have just arrived from Tuxtla."

Julia was barely able to hold back a startled gesture. She would not allow them to interrupt her salon. Idolina made a soothing motion. "They're saddling up their horses."

Amid the noise of voices, Julia strained for the other noise, so distant, so slight that she didn't notice when it faded away.

Her muscles relaxed and her whole face took on a look of repose, of certain mastery. In that atmosphere, the gathering was drawn out longer than on other nights.

After accompanying her guests to the door, Julia made, as always, a final round of inspection through the house. Everything was in order. Even Fernando's bedroom. No wardrobe had been opened, no object had changed its place. The only thing that caught her eye was a packet of letters tied with a ribbon lying on top of a desk.

Julia examined them. Ordinary envelopes, irregular handwriting, an uneducated person's poor spelling. The name Ulloa written many times.

Julia pulled out a page and began reading: "a person who holds you in esteem but believes it more prudent not to reveal her identity. . . ." And then Julia's own figure emerged. The letters twined together lasciviously, like two bodies in a bed, uniting her with Leonardo Cifuentes. Julia the adulteress. Julia the greedy woman. Julia the hypocrite.

Crude words and vulgar images denounced, condemned, and derided Julia. And behind every paragraph a hand could be discerned. The same hand she shook each day, which opened avidly to receive her largesse and closed forcefully on the booty. That hand had traced out these sordid marks with a schoolgirl's application.

How long had she been like that, carved up like a side of beef and exposed to Fernando's impassive gaze? She looked for a date to help her, without finding one. But some of the papers had begun to lose their color.

With clumsy fingers, Julia refolded the pages, replaced them in their envelopes, tied up the ribbon.

She gave a last glance at the empty bedroom, went out to the gallery and locked the door behind her.

A boundless night was spreading across the sky. Julia watched it, her eyes wide with fear.

CHAPTER XXIX

Night among the Indians. A smell of burnt resin, a rustling of brittle leaves, a distant howl. Fernando Ulloa shivered. Weren't there other kinds of night in the world? Brightly lit streets, clean interiors, conversations, laughter? For how long had all of that been nothing but a dream? Why was it coming back to him now with the sadness of something irrecuperable? Because it had belonged to his youth, because he foresaw that he was going to die?

A dog barked furiously at the new arrivals. Then it ran quickly and dolefully away, as if it had been kicked.

There was no light in the huts of San Juan Chamula. The doors of the Cabildo were shut from the outside with enormous padlocks. A large crossbar lay over the front portal of the church.

Fernando and César exchanged questioning glances.

"They're in hiding. They're afraid the troops might suddenly come down on them."

"There are spies in the hills. By now they must know we're here."

They dismounted and, with the help of a small lantern, went to the parish house stable. There, two old and tired beasts of burden were gravely munching their fodder.

"It looks like we're not the only ones here."

A tempting smell of food being cooked drew them to the kitchen.

"Ave María!" said an obese woman, getting to her feet. Her companion, a sinister-looking mule driver, clutched the hip from which his weapon was hanging. Fernando and César stopped in the doorway.

"Come in, come in. Arriving on time is better than being invited, as the saying goes. Look how fate makes things turn out! Who would ever have thought that a swank gentleman like Fernando Ulloa would be my guest!"

In order to wield the cooking utensils more easily she took off the shawl that was protecting her from the cold and Fernando recognized the features of Doña Mercedes Solórzano. He answered her cordiality with a smile.

"What are you doing here?"

"What a poor person does everywhere: struggling to make a living. It's good business to sell salt around here at Holy Week."

"But you're fixed up nicely down in Ciudad Real," César observed, not without malice.

"Damned if I am! Buried in debts! There was nothing left for me but to take to the mountains."

"The woman has guts," the mule driver put in.

"Shut your mouth, you, and help me serve these gentlemen who must be half-starved."

"We have food with us. It just needs to be heated up, that's all."

"Don't offend me, ingeniero. Are you going to turn me down because I can only offer you very little? A bowl of hot broth, a piece of chicken, a tortilla rolled up with salt. Don't take it for what it is, but for the good will it's offered with. I would have wanted to have given you a feast!"

Fernando and César made themselves comfortable next to the fire. The heat was pleasant and the company picturesque. They began eating with a hearty appetite.

César paused between two mouthfuls to ask, "Where did you just come from?"

"From where the Negro Cimarrón runs."

Doña Mercedes splashed coffee into two large pewter cups. Then she sat down, laughing silently. She didn't want to say anything more.

"I won't ask you where you're going. Who is a poor peddler woman to make herself the equal of a pair of patróns? But I will tell you to be careful, because these aren't the times for rushing into anything."

The mule driver had finished his dinner and was rinsing out his mouth with a sonorous swig he then spat onto the brick floor.

"When the Indians see me arriving at a little hamlet with my team of mules, they run and hide as if the devil himself had appeared among them. Only when they're sure I'm coming in peace, then they start showing their faces again. They buy salt, which is the only thing I carry. But they'd like me to sell them other things."

Doña Mercedes and the mule driver glanced at each other. He felt authorized to say, "They have a powerful need for gunpowder."

Doña Mercedes shrugged her shoulders as if to subtract any importance from this observation.

"These must be the months when it's open season. There's a lot of deer around here."

The mule driver brushed the crumbs off his pants. He was standing up now, grouchy and drowsy.

"I'd swell up with cash if I could sell those Indians what they're asking for!"

The mule driver interrupted his boss's digression. "We have to get up early tomorrow, Doña."

"So? Who's holding you back? But before you go off to sleep, take a look in on the mules. Make sure the bogeyman doesn't scare them."

The mule driver left the kitchen, yawning. Doña Mercedes cleared off the dishes and washed them none too carefully.

"However I can serve you gentlemen, you know it's my great pleasure."

"Are you going straight back to Ciudad Real?"

"That depends. If I can unload all my merchandise. . . ."

"Who's going to buy it from you in San Juan? There's no one here."

"There's no one right now, niño. But I know the color of my cattle. They're not going to let Holy Week go by without a fiesta. And besides the salt, I can sell them candles and incense for their saints."

They were impressed by her certainty. How could the Indians assemble at a time like this? Unless they had weapons and had already resolved to put up a fight. Or they were unaware of the danger.

CHAPTER XXX

THE DAWN OF Holy Thursday broke with a clamor of bells and firecrackers. From the plaza came the sound of a growing, milling throng.

Fernando and César awoke with a start and hurried to get dressed. As they left the wide corridors of the parish house they heard Doña Mercedes' voice urging the mule driver to move a load to the stand where it would be sold. She interrupted herself to greet the engineer and his assistant.

"God got up on the right side of bed this morning! People have come, even from the farthest villages. They need things, and where there's a need there's got to be money. Business is going to be good because they all have to come to me. Nobody else wanted to take a chance on coming out here to the boondocks."

Responding with no more than a smile and a wave, Fernando and César continued on their way toward the plaza.

Despite the early hour (the mist had not yet lifted entirely) the number of people congregated there was already great and was increasing at every moment with the addition of families that emerged from the various footpaths, dressed in their best clothes and carrying their household goods and their children with them.

"Look," César said, pointing to the church's bell tower.

There, several martomas were trying to hang a Judas, a grotesque effigy filled with straw whose mask depicted a Ladino face with a threatening expression. Fernando watched their maneuvering attentively. Suddenly he thought he recognized one of the participants.

"Isn't that the sacristan?"

He mistrusted his memory and his eyesight. What was more, he hadn't learned to tell one Indian from another.

César strained to pick him out in the distance amid the constant movement of the figures.

"Xaw Ramírez Paciencia. What the hell is he doing here?"

"He'd gone to hide out in Ciudad Real. He was afraid. If he came back, things must be getting better. Everything seems calm."

Fernando registered this with a mixture of relief and disappointment. So deeply had the idea of intervening in the conflict, resolving it through his mediation, taken root in him. •

"Don't be naive, ingeniero! Just having the Indians beg their pardon isn't going to be enough for the Coletos. They want to punish those responsible for the death of Padre Mandujano, teach them a good lesson. Otherwise, what assurance do they have that the crime won't happen again?"

"It depends largely on them. Padre Mandujano was a firebrand."

"Who cares about Padre Mandujano? The point is not to give free rein to the Indians, and to make them feel the bit on their tongues. So they'll acknowledge their place and their status and won't even think about asking for the land to be redistributed."

And what if the Indians had renounced their rights and the patróns had been appeased by the promise that everything would stay as it was?

"We must speak to Pedro González Winiktón. He can set us straight."

Neither César nor Ulloa knew where to find him. They started walking aimlessly. The Chamula men, wearing hats sumptuously decorated with ribbons, heavy black wool serapes and high leather sandals, stood respectfully to one side to make way for them. Many of them hid a bottle of liquor among their clothing; others suspended their work weaving palm leaves together. They gave no impression of feeling alarm or animosity because a pair of Caxláns was circulating among them. They probably knew who Ulloa and Santiago were, though none of them made any sign of recognition.

The women conceded them no more than a sidelong glance. They remained absorbed in their work of caring for the belongings they had brought to trade, the objects that would be used in the ceremonies. Many of the children were dressed as angels, with white robes and paper crowns on their heads. They were the ones who most aroused the outsiders' curiosity, and they were also the ones who watched the outsiders with the most astonishment and went along behind them, snickering into their hands, imitating the foreigners' words and gestures.

Though the mockery made them uncomfortable, Fernando and

César didn't let their irritation show. Mainly to rid themselves of their followers, they moved toward the church, whose doors were thrown wide open.

They paused for an instant on the threshold, so forcefully were they assaulted by the smell of flowers, burnt resin, burning wax, a compact and sweating multitude.

They could hardly move forward between the bodies seated or stretched out on the ground. The women were enraptured in an uninterrupted psalmody; the men had fallen to the ground in fatigue or drunkenness. The children were entertaining themselves by braiding the pine needles that served as a carpet.

In the center of the church, enclosed by a wooden railing and covered with wild orchids, lay an image of Christ with his hands crossed on his breast and the pale, sharp profile of a dying man.

Protecting him, at his head and feet, were two crossed rifles and four men wearing their bandanas across their chests like cartridge belts.

Fernando wanted to communicate his unease to César. What did those weapons mean? Was this a custom that was simply being repeated this year? Or were the Chamulas exhibiting them today to demonstrate their warlike mood? Fernando was brutally pushed away by the guards of the Holy Sepulcher when he tried to approach them.

Near the central altar, eight women were seated. Against the dark wool of their serapes, colored yarns stood out in geometrical figures. On their heads they wore yaguales, the padded rings used for balancing heavy loads, which were also made of colored yarns; from the yaguales, heavy, brilliant mantles hung down to the soles of their feet. Each woman had a basket filled with sweet-smelling nichimes in front of her and held a rosary from which ribbons hung. Those who approached the women were given the rosaries to kiss.

These were the women who illuminate the sacrament.

César bent down, simulating a bow, in the hope of finding Catalina Díaz Puiljá among them. He had to move away, disappointed.

The two Ladinos left the church and returned to the plaza. How greedily they breathed the cold, pure air! The spot where Doña Mercedes had set up her stand was visible in the distance.

She could hardly cope with the clientele. The mule driver was lending an awkward and unwilling hand.

"Come on over here, patróns. Didn't I tell you that today I had made the sign of the cross with my right hand? With all I earn this Easter season, I'll certainly be able to hold my head high in Ciudad Real again, God willing."

Fernando and César took shelter under the awning that protected the two vendors from the strong, sharp light of the morning sun.

"Make a little place for them, mi alma, they're refined people and have to be treated as they deserve. Pile the diabolos and dancing puppets up over here; after all, there's no point in damaging them. Take away those parcels of brown sugar. Run quickly and hurry back with a little leather stool, so they can sit down, even if they have to take turns."

"We don't want to trouble you, Doña."

"What trouble? A big lug like him isn't going to be able to shoot to the parish house like an arrow. Look at him, here he comes already, one gasp after another. Catch your breath, little one; God will reward you."

The mule driver placed the stool in a small empty space.

"Go ahead, ingeniero, make yourself comfortable."

Out of courtesy, Ulloa tried to yield the seat to his assistant, but Doña Mercedes strenuously objected.

"That's all we need! You're the man of respect here. César's just a boy; he won't embarrass himself by perching on a stool like we do. He's young, he's used to discomfort."

During the conversation, Doña Mercedes did not interrupt her mercantile transactions. She weighed candy on a Roman balance and measured out ribbon, coarse cotton cloth and dried herbs with her thick, stubby-fingered hands. More customers were constantly arriving, and she came and went with ease and precision m the place where she kept the copper pots, the hand mills, : cacao.

The hours passed slowly. The shadow on the sundial in the center of the plaza barely moved one, two millimeters. Fernando stared at it as if each minute had the power to make what he most desired a reality: the arrival of Pedro González Winiktón.

César had picked up some hazelnuts and was playing with them distractedly. He smiled.

"Do you know what I'm thinking? What would happen if federal troops showed up right now?"

Fernando had also considered that possibility.

"It would be a bloodbath. Very few of them have weapons. Almost all of them are drunk by now."

"And on top of that they don't have a leader."

"If Pedro spoke to them he might be able to get them to disperse."

Among the Indians who came to Doña Mercedes' stand were some whose faces were familiar to Ulloa. But he didn't dare address them for fear of being mistaken.

"Do you speak Tzotzil, César?"

César's first reaction to this question was defensive. Then two reflections came to calm him: he was with a man whose criteria were the opposite of those of the ranchers. And even the ranchers, despite their disdain for everything that had to do with the Indians, generally mastered the language of their serfs, who weren't allowed to speak Spanish.

"I understand it a little."

Fernando made an impatient motion.

"That's not enough."

César kept playing with the hazelnuts. The sundial looked exactly the same.

"Isn't that Winiktón, that man over there?"

Fernando had stood up and was pointing to a distant spot. They couldn't see the faces clearly.

"Let's go over there before we lose him."

César deposited the hazelnuts in a basket and dusted himself off. Doña Mercedes watched his effort to get up off the ground with suspicion.

"Is anything wrong, patróns? Why do you want to go?"

"We're just going to stretch our legs a little, shopkeeper."

They set out, threading their way among the little groups. The Indians' attitude was neither cordial nor indifferent as it had been at first. They seemed menacing. They were beginning to be drunk. The men swayed, leaning against each other and watching the outsiders with a stupid fixity. The women, seated on the ground, did not raise their eyelids. They moved their heads as they suckled their children. Other women gave their children small sips of liquor from a flask or squeezed a rag soaked with posh between their lips. The children grimaced with disgust but then stopped resisting.

"Pedro, we've been looking for you."

Ulloa accompanied the words with a friendly pat on the shoulder. The Indian quickly turned his head. Catalina stood up, pulling little Domingo to her. Lorenzo and Marcela gave no more than a brief, incurious glance at the newcomers.

"What's going on, Pedro? Why have the people come together? Don't they know the troops can attack Chamula at any moment?"

Pedro wanted to clear himself of his responsibility while excusing the others at the same time.

"It is the fiesta of Holy Week, ajwalil. If we do not celebrate it, there is no water for planting the fields."

Catalina dropped her eyelids so they would not notice the flash of hatred that jolted through her. San Juan's church full of decorations and offerings, and the cave at Tzajal-hemel empty and abandoned!

"Didn't you warn them about the danger, Winiktón?"

Yes, Pedro had grown weary of offering them his advice when they paid no attention. The people had endured more anguish and fear than they could bear. The wait had been too long and had ended up losing its meaning. Little by little the Indians were forgetting their precautions and returning to the routine of daily life. They came out from their hiding places, took up their ordinary tasks again, dared to occupy their houses once more. They were hungry and sought sustenance.

"In Ciudad Real, feelings are running very high, Winiktón."

Pedro nodded and Catalina looked at him pityingly. She had listened to his discussions with the principal men. They were obstinate and feared that if the ritual of Holy Week were not followed exactly the powers that had protected them until then would turn against them. Catalina herself was mistaken in believing her influence could persuade them to revoke those decisions. When she said, in one of the trances she frequently fell into, that the idols of Tzajal-hemel demanded to be worshiped in exclusivity, those who heard her were left dumbfounded with fear and astonishment. But after long deliberations, the leaders reached an agreement: they would offer extraordinary gifts to the idols as proof of their submission. But they would celebrate Holy Week in San Juan's church because he, too, was powerful and capable of doing harm.

Catalina saw how her followers deserted her as Easter approached. She exaggerated her threats and predictions of adversity, only to learn that they were useless. Then she chose to be silent and, in the end, consented to attend the ceremonies as well. Contact with the multitude had become her vice, and she had not lost hope of playing the leading role in front of the crowd once again.

"If you explained it to them, ajwalil, perhaps they would pay attention to you. You are a man of reason."

"Assemble them as quickly as you can, and let me know when it's done."

Catalina walked away, holding little Domingo's hand. They were going toward the church.

"Ask the municipal secretary to open the Cabildo. The meeting will be in the Cuarto del Juramento."

Pedro made a motion of obedience and moved away.

When Ulloa and Santiago returned to Doña Mercedes' stand it was almost dismantled.

"What happened, shopkeeper?"

Doña Mercedes interrupted her work, but not before ordering the mule driver to hurry up putting away the lengths of fabric that had protected them from the sun. She put her hands on her hips and gave César her answer.

"Good business! We've run out of merchandise. Ay, if all my clients were like these Chamulitas, a different cock would crow for me."

One of the trunks was still wide open. It was overflowing with objects. César's gaze met Doña Mercedes's above it. Without changing her expression, she clarified, "Some things aren't in demand. But the salt. . . . I don't have a grain left. I'll have to go back to Ciudad Real for a few more loads."

Doña Mercedes closed the trunk.

"Can I take any messages for you? I'll be back here tomorrow, at the latest. I'll make time to pay a visit to little Julia," she added, looking meekly at Ulloa.

"Don't bother. We'll be on our way back to Ciudad Real very soon, too."

"Good, then. Well, he who says many goodbyes doesn't really want to go. Remember, so you won't have to trouble yourselves, there's food in the kitchen. It only needs warming up."

The mule driver brought the mules. Doña Mercedes mounted one of them and urged it forward with an energetic lash of the whip. Fernando and César watched her leave without finding words to express their unease.

CHAPTER XXXI

THE MEETING could not be arranged until nightfall. The principal men unwillingly abandoned the ceremonies in which they were playing an active part or the unceremonious huddles in which they were getting drunk. The false security of alcohol, the strength they felt in the number of those who had congregated, the time that had passed (empty of the events they had feared) reduced their worry and alarm to a remote and meaningless reality. What was Jobel but something these men could smash with their fists? And they clenched those fists with rage and obstinacy and unsheathed their machetes which flashed for an instant like bolts of lightning, and for an instant the air vibrated with danger.

The whole valley of Chamula was resounding with music. The accordion, panting and uneven like a drunken man's breathing; the harps, with their delicate strings that were invisible in the distance and the darkness. The rhythm of feet, shod in sandals of thick, crudely tanned leather. Everywhere at once—beginning, continuing, reaching its end—was the Bolonchón, the dance of the tiger and the snake, the metamorphoses of the god who is suddenly recognizable in an animal the eyes are accustomed to seeing. The animal that presides over births, accompanies and sustains life, strips death of its horror. The Bolonchón, continuous, ever the same, endless.

What can the will of men do against the things the gods have ordained? Why does Pedro González Winiktón come at so untimely a moment to urge prudence? And those foreigners, Fernando Ulloa and César Santiago, whose intentions are unintelligible, whose language is untranslatable. Let them all be silent! The people of Chamula are establishing their alliance with the dark powers, paying their tribute to the true masters, ransoming their right to live another year.

But some men, the community's leaders, have been momentarily removed from this communion. They left the freedom of the night, the echoes, the bonfires; guided by an ancestral instinct to obey, they have come to the Cuarto del Juramento. They squeeze together in order to fit in. Their features are difficult to see in the light of a gasoline lamp. They laugh and spit. They are nervous. Winiktón has announced that Ulloa, the engineer, is going to speak to them.

"I come from Tuxtla. I was with the governor."

Winiktón translated. A few of the men let out belches of self-importance. They were not unaware of what that was, Tuxtla. As for the governor, they had heard him speak once or twice, when he was touring the state. The Indians did not remember the speech, to which a representative of their community gave a response in their own language. They remembered the jolting of the truck in which they had been transported, their long immobility in front of a kiosk or a balcony, the coin that repaid them for their time. What did the authorities assembled here (each one of the principal men represented a village, down to the smallest one in the Tzotzil region) have to do with the other ones Ulloa was invoking? Why did they always have to fear, always have to submit? They were sick of patróns. The president of the Republic, who was something more than the governor, promised them they would be free.

"The matter of the land redistribution is going very well."

Fernando was lying. The process could be delayed for years. But he was counting on their intervention to make it go more quickly.

César listened to him skeptically. Led by this phlegmatic, dispassionate man who believed in the law, the Indians' unrest wouldn't go anywhere. But César placed his faith in circumstances rather than individual decisions. The present ones could be favorable. The people of Ciudad Real were terrified and the governor was authorizing measures that only increased their alarm, rather than offering them any security. And the Indians . . . the Indians were an unknown quantity. They were probably frightened as well. It's easy to transmute fear into violence. When a man is already afraid he can't tell the difference between self-defense and defiance. He throws himself into action like a bull charging the red cape that ripples in front of its eyes.

Knowing how to manage the deception is all that is required. César didn't think very highly of the engineer's skill. He didn't think Ulloa had even formulated a concrete plan of action. The engineer was more inclined to calm the Indians than to inflame them.

"The ranchers are looking for a pretext so as not to carry out the orders. Let's not give them one! Let's not put the noose around our own necks!"

Winiktón stammered, trying to get the words out. He didn't really understand what they meant, and it would damage his prestige in the eyes of the others if he showed his ignorance. He said that now was the time to make use of force.

One of the principal men raised his hand to protest. Here, far from Tzajal-hemel, within another religious sphere, Pedro and his wife, the ilol, were not persons to be feared. Why should their council be followed?

Other leaders broke in. They spoke energetically. Ulloa suspected that his message had been misinterpreted. Trying not to let anyone else hear him, he said to Pedro, "The army is coming. They're after you and your wife, for the death of Padre Mandujano. But they'll take everyone. Right now there is still time for all of you to escape."

Pedro finally succeeded in silencing the murmurs and comments. Suddenly he was pained, not for himself and Catalina, but for all those who would be punished for a crime that by now no one knew who had committed.

"We must go back to the mountain. We must hide."

"And leave San Juan's church empty?" one of the men asked in disbelief. The others were silent, stupefied.

"During Holy Week!"

What foolishness! As if San Juan and the Virgen de los Dolores and Santiago and the dead Christ would allow their fiestas to be interrupted.

"There are soldiers, many of them. They have rifles, bullets."

Fernando was gesticulating. His useless efforts to be understood made Santiago give a quick smile.

"You'll be responsible for the slaughter if you don't make them disperse!"

He had seized Winiktón's shoulders and was shaking him hard. Pedro was shaking his head in anguish. He had never wanted that: the death of his people. He wanted justice. But in his imagination the image of justice always went together with the image of blood.

Winiktón extricated himself from Ulloa's clutches and went to mingle with the others. He tried to make himself heard, but in vain. They were excited and unafraid. What did this Ladinified Indian want from them? He had always baffled them and on many occasions he had succeeded in making his will prevail. But he was not going to make anyone run to take refuge in the mountains today. They were fine as they were, all gathered together. Alone they would lose their courage, they would go to their enemies and surrender, they would betray those who had fled. No one wanted to be alone.

"The troops are coming."

"How? Along the roads, every stone is transformed into a guardian, every boulder into an obstacle, every grove of trees into an army. Such is the power of San Juan, whose double is in the sky and watches over us when the image in Chamula rests."

The principal men of Chamula folded their arms. Where did strength lie? In arms, in guns? No: in this body that has drunk from the waters of the sacred spring. In this head where the emanations of pom penetrate. In these hands that hold up the saints' platforms, that sprinkle water over the pine needles for the festivities, that string together the garlands of flowers. What can the blaspheming Caxlán, careless of his religious duties, do against these invulnerable men? What can his lead bullets do against this flesh to which divinity has communicated its attributes. Nevertheless, one of the old men wanted to know: "Have the Ladinos of Jobel brought out the Virgen de la Caridad in a procession?"

Pedro was going to say yes, that the Virgen de la Caridad had appeared on the Mount of Tzontehuitz, wearing the insignia of a general. But César Santiago spoke first.

"No. The Virgen de la Caridad is in her niche inside the church."

A collective laugh of relief went up among the Indians. Their immemorial enemy, who can be found in several places at once during a battle, encouraging the fainthearted, restoring the dying to life, setting out fatal traps for the Chamulas, had taken no part in this conflict. Therefore it could be won. They embraced one another, uncorked the bottles of liquor, laughed until tears flowed from their eyes.

Fernando went over to César.

"What did you tell them?"

"The truth."

Indifferent, he gave Fernando the details he wanted.

"And you didn't realize it would make them bolder?"

Naturally. And he had done it for that reason. César had intervened once before, as well. When he first learned of the discovery of the idols in the cave of Tzajal-hemel. Not that he believed in their miraculous origin. Stones like that could be found anywhere; he had seen some very similar ones on his father's ranch near Ocosingo. But the real and startling fact was the people's devotion, the great hope that awoke within them at the mere sight of the images, the ferocity with which they were prepared to defend their worship. César thought it would enhance Ulloa's reputation with the Tzotziles if he were to demonstrate his support for those beliefs. He hinted this to Ulloa quite directly. But Fernando never agreed to sanction with his presence or his words a rite he considered nothing but a crude superstition.

The Indians didn't understand such insensitivity from one who showed them so much sympathy in other respects. They didn't dare ask. But something inside them closed up when this man, Ulloa, asked for their trust or spoke to them of justice and deliverance.

César realized where the failing lay and, convinced that Fernando would never condescend to make amends, he did what he thought was best: he stole Julia's shawl and gave it to Catalina so she could wrap her idols in it. To Pedro González Winiktón, who functioned as the interpreter, he gave lengthy explanations of the garment's meaning and of who the woman was that it had belonged to. La Alazana, too, had the supernatural power to make cripples walk again. She respected the Chamula ilol and was sending her a present. Why hadn't her husband brought it? César made a vague gesture with his hand. It's a secret. You must never mention the shawl in front of him.

The Indians had nodded in acquiescence. And when they thought of La Alazana, they felt in some vague way that Fernando Ulloa was not an outsider and that the silence with which he observed the ceremonies in the cave was one of complicity and consent. From then on they were less disinclined to entrust him with their things. Those who had kept their papers—titles, maps

—hidden until then, dug them up and gave them to him. They pulled up the undergrowth that concealed the markers which indicated the boundary between one property and another; they pointed out the former beds of the rivers. The engineer did his work quickly and precisely. And when he congratulated himself on his good luck and speculated on the reasons for the Indians' obedience, César couldn't help smiling. And he smiled to himself, too, when the echo of Julia's voice bemoaning the disappearance of the shawl, making accusations, reached his room in Ciudad Real.

"Tell them right now that you take back what you said about the Virgen de la Caridad, that you were mistaken!"

"The engineer is such a scrupulous man, yet he wants to help himself with a lie. Worse yet, a useless lie. Look at your Indians, your poor little lambs. They're running wild, and when they decide to launch an attack on the Ladinos no one can stop them."

"And you're happy about that?"

"At least I'm not going to make myself an obstacle so they can trample me underfoot."

They were facing each other. César was dominating the situation, and in a slightly condescending tone he said, "There's nothing for me to do but follow wherever the current takes them. But you, who feel sorry for them, who think they're victims of exploitation and injustice, why don't you take command?"

"Because I don't believe in violence."

"You won't believe in it even when all these people are put to the knife before your eyes?"

"I came to try to avoid that."

"And you're asking them to disband. As if that would be of any use! The ranchers have convinced the governor to teach them a lesson. And they will be taught a lesson. They'll look for the last Indian, in the last corner, to kill him. At least here, together, they can defend themselves better."

"With what weapons?"

"They'll find something. A machete, a hoe, a rock. Anything will do. Haven't you ever been told how the Chamulas covered the mouths of the guns with their palm-leaf hats during the Revolution?"

"And?"

"And they were blown to bits, as you would expect. But another one came, with another hat. There are a lot of them. An endless number."

From out in the night, the echo of a drum reached them along with broken sounds of weeping and song.

"He who wants to dance must pay the piper, ingeniero. You talked to them about land. But the ranchers aren't going to give land to the Indians just for their pretty faces. You have to be prepared to lose something."

César had passed imperceptibly from condescension to arrogance. His provincial maliciousness made him feel superior in age and experience to this engineer from the capital.

"You have to be practical, ingeniero."

"Yes. I'm not opposed to what you're suggesting or to what these people want to do on moral grounds. I know you don't keep your hands clean or your conscience easy in politics. But what justifies that are results. And what would we achieve if we were to become the leaders of this uprising?"

"We'd scare the Coletos."

"That's not enough. Tell me that we'll win and I'll accept it. But fear brings reprisals, not concessions."

"And if we win?"

"I don't have faith in miracles. I know the history. All the Chamulas' rebellions have always been like this, hatched in drunkenness and superstition. A tribe of desperate men hurls itself against its oppressors. All the disadvantages are on their side, even justice. And again, they fail. But not from cowardice, understand. Not from stupidity either. It's just that in order to gain a victory you need something more than a fit of rage and a stroke of luck: you need an idea to implement, an order to put in place."

"That's precisely what you can give them, ingeniero."

The principal men asked for permission to withdraw. They were going to deliberate.

Winiktón went out behind them, pensive. The hallway of the Cabildo was in darkness. From time to time, bursts of sound and light reached it from the assembly in the valley.

They sat down in a circle. They coughed solemnly. The bottle of liquor circulated continually.

"The Virgen has not come out in a procession. But the Caxláns can bring her out."

"Perhaps they are bringing her out now."

"Who will we raise up to look into her face?"

"Our patrón is San Juan."

"San Juan herds flocks. He has no sword."

"Santiago is a horseman."

"He cures horses when they step on harmful plants. He does not want to fight."

"And the Dolorosa?"

There was no response to this suggestion. The Dolorosa wandered through the nights' darkness lamenting her lost children. A sad, deranged mother; how could she defend them?

Pedro did not take part in this discussion. He forgot that the ones the Ladinos of Jobel wanted were Catalina and his family. He forgot that if he surrendered to them, Ulloa had promised there was a possibility of saving his people. He only wanted, in that moment, to help. He said to the Indians, "And what if we went to Tzajal-hemel?"

They looked at him suspiciously. Go to Tzajal-hemel now? What a sacrilege! What was more, the cave's idols had still given no signs of their power. They had not measured themselves even against the saints of Chamula, much less against the god of the Caxláns.

"They nailed him to a cross and killed him and drank his blood. Ever since then, no one can beat them."

They were still for a moment. They thought of their abandoned villages, the hiding places in the mountain.

"The police know how to track us down. They sniff out a trail and follow it."

"My wife is with child. In the last months."

"And my children are only just learning to walk."

"It is a difficult life."

"It is."

This fatalism made Winiktón rebellious.

"It could be otherwise."

No one listened. They felt no curiosity. It didn't interest them to contradict him. That encouraged him to continue.

"Do you remember the ancient stories?"

"Old men's tales. No one knows now what happened."

"When the first Caxláns came, centuries ago, there were many who preferred to die than to give in to them."

An old man nodded. Yes, he had heard his grandparents say something. Something about a group of warriors who had thrown themselves from a crag to the bottom of a river.

"From that time on the Sumidero canyon has been sacred."

The sacrifice of so many souls sanctified every stone, every branch, every slope of the chasm. And Chamula was going to remain helpless? In this immense territory, the spirit of San Juan, the spirit of the builder and the master of the flocks would no longer reign? This land, where so many springs welled up, where the mist came down to rest so frequently, would be defiled? How unworthy of living on it they would have been if they were incapable of disputing its possession with the Ladinos now!

The wild, chaotic force of galloping horses would come, razing everything to the ground, leaving ashes, ruin and slavery behind. Traditions would be abolished, the positions of the principal men would be usurped, the sanctuary would be profaned. What would become of the sky if the Chamulas surrendered their land?

A group of the principal men, headed by Pedro González Winiktón, stood up to go and speak to Ulloa.

"Ajwalil, tomorrow is the fiesta of Good Friday. We want you and your assistant to attend because it will be a great and solemn ceremony."

CHAPTER XXXII

THIS CATALINA DÍAZ PUILJÁ knew: that Lent is the belly of the
year. In its hours—long, transparent and motionless—ferment the
seasons that will hold sway over the tribe's destiny. The parched
earth is waiting: the emaciated animals are waiting. The soothsayer
invokes the signs of rainfall and conjures away the ragged ghost
of drought.

Lent is the time for propitiation. The saints leave the shade of
their niches, the shelter of their altars, and go out on the shoulders
of their mayordomos to the center of the plaza. There, food,
health and life are prayed for. And sacrifices are offered in return.

But during Holy Week, the last week, the decisive week, no
one, neither saints nor mayordomos nor the faithful, can bear bad
weather. All of them take refuge inside the church, because a bolt
of lightning will fall and no one knows whom it will strike down.

Catalina leads Domingo by the hand. She grasps him firmly so
the crowd will not separate them.

The ilol's appearance in San Juan's church does not mean she
is betraying her gods, her children in Tzajal-hemel. Sustained by
their memory she moves forward, more defiant than reverent, to
the place where the wise ones direct the order of the ceremonies,
the order that is necessary to keep the world from straying off its
path. And to keep men's customs from breaking down.

Catalina, who does not release her hold on Domingo, who uses
him as a shield, approaches the prone, bloodless image of Christ.
She does not lower her eyelids before it; for some time now she
has no longer feared to look into the face of mystery. And this
body, crushed by suffering, demolished by death, does not move
her. She despises its flaccid muscles which were unable to triumph,
its white skin whose delicacy did not protect its owner from lacerations and in which each laceration has festered and become a
gaping wound.

Around Catalina the women are wailing. What are they asking
this deaf, defenseless, lifeless man for? That he protect them from
the very ones who crucified him? That he help them bear their

burden of suffering and misery when he could not even bear his own cross? Why don't they leave him to the tomb that is crying out for him and return with Catalina to Tzajal-hemel? Catalina does not understand. And the women remain there, stubborn. Some of them, the neediest ones, perhaps, lick the blood on the feet, the hands, the side. Then they stand erect as if they had fortified themselves with a sacrament.

Moving with the throng of the faithful, Catalina and Domingo reach the place where Xaw Ramírez Paciencia is officiating, with a basin of water thick with rose petals. He holds the basin in his left hand and with his right hand he sprinkles the faces of the congregation.

Catalina received the benediction without looking at Xaw. She feared that her former rival would recognize her in his moment of triumph and reject her. She enveloped as much of herself as she could in her woolen headcloths. Xaw distractedly traced out the gesture. For him there existed no more than a single head, bowed, successive and anonymous: that of his people, over whom he had recovered his power.

It was Domingo's turn. As the sacristan was preparing to sprinkle his face, the basin (precariously balanced in Xaw's clumsy, rheumatic fingers) tilted until it spilled completely over the boy, covering him with water and petals. The sacristan let out a kind of moan of fatigue, pain and impatience. Domingo did not dare wipe away the liquid that was flattening his hair and running down his temples. The witnesses were paralyzed by alarm at the singularity of the situation. Catalina abruptly took off her woolen headcloth—leaving her face uncovered—and tried to wipe Domingo's face with it. Many arms stopped her. Xaw, who had not recognized her, who had not even looked at her (because all of his attention, questioning, humble, was turned toward the boy), let the empty basin fall to the ground and knelt before him. With an almost inaudible syllable, he implored the boy to permit him to continue carrying out his duty.

"Sacristán, apostle!" Catalina exclaimed in a loud voice. Only then did Xaw and the others recognize her and it became clear to them that Domingo was the one born at the eclipse. And their consternation increased.

When Catalina had finished cleaning the petals and water from her nephew, she moved off with him. Arrogant and masterful, she made her way through the people who were kneeling or lying flat on the ground as if she were hoisting a conquered trophy.

She was gripped by an abrupt certainty that the idols of Tzajalhemel had just won a battle against the saints of Chamula. It struck her like a sudden rush of blood, like a gulp of aguardiente, and dizzied her for an instant, then gave her senses an unbearable acuteness so that she could perceive even the slightest of the vibrations that were electrifying the church's atmosphere.

All activity was now concentrated around the Great Cross of Good Friday. Certain religious officials were moving it away from the wall against which it was leaning.

The Cross swayed in the air, threatening to crash down on many of those around it. But the religious officials managed to support it and slowly, in an open space left by the crowd, the Cross was lowered until it lay on the ground.

The dexterity of the officials was extolled. Those closest to them (and everyone was trying to get close to them) offered them flasks of liquor and small funnels so that they could drink their fill. From afar, Catalina watched them: the gestures with which they expressed thanks for the invitation, the speed with which they accepted. They needed to recover their strength before continuing with their duties.

Those duties now consisted in unwrapping the fabric that swathed the Cross. They pulled at the cloth, trying not to rip it. But when, despite their precautions, a tear occurred, the religious officials kept even the tiniest of the unruly threads in a special case.

Finally the Cross was stripped of its coverings and the old, solid, unpolished wood was exposed to the eyes of those who were witnessing the ritual. The madrinas quickly flocked around it to clean it with cotton cloths. After that the wood was covered over again, this time with fresh and fragrant forest leaves.

Then came the incense burners. Seven incense burners, Pom was slowly consumed on the hot coals and wafted through the air, evoking in those who breathed it the great pine forests, the height and solitude of the mountain range.

Catalina closed her eyes. An unease she recognized was stealing over her. At what moment would the seizure overcome her? How much longer until she fell into the dark well of unconsciousness? Because it was impossible for this agony to go on any longer. A cold sweat of sickness, anguish, broke from her pores and permeated her clothing.

She let go of Domingo without caring whether the crowd's movements swept him away from her. She groped blindly for a space to fall down in. She did not find it, and could only fall to her knees.

At that level, the air was so foul it was almost unbreathable. Catalina was panting rapidly, which forced the rhythm of her pulse (already so tormented) to accelerate, and made her heart lurch. And still unconsciousness did not fully take her.

Catalina opened her eyes again. No one had paid the least attention to her pallor, her pained movements. But she was not alone. These people who were repudiating her today, who were ignoring her, were the same ones who once put on the shoes of pilgrimage to take the paths to the idols' cave. They were the same ones who exalted the priestess into a trance with their chanting, who pleaded, day after day, for the favor of an audience. Because they needed to discharge their guilt or their punishment onto someone else. Or they wanted their hope to be revived. Or to share in the ilol's power by touching the hem of her skirt, brushing the tips of her fingers.

The same ones. Yes, Catalina knew their names and their faces, remembered their sorrows. The taste of the promises she had uttered was still in her mouth. Why had they gone away? Had Catalina ever put her fatigue before the needs of her petitioners, even once? Had she ever refused, even once, to throw herself into the vortex in which revelation whirls? Had she ever tried, even once, not to share her discoveries? Catalina scrutinized her own conduct, prepared to be contrite, and found nothing to reproach herself with.

Catalina, the barren woman who knew more of motherhood than many mothers, had given of herself, as in childbirth, in every act of adoration, admonition, council. Her body (was it still her body?) had become a receptacle, meekly lodging the supernatural, transparent so the miracle could manifest itself. When Catalina felt herself to be overflowing with gifts she did not dare protect herself. Defenseless, she placed herself within everyone's reach.

Let those who are thirsty come and drink of the cool, clear water! Let those who are hungry devour the sustenance that will comfort them! And she burned to illuminate the darkness where those who are ignorant become lost. And she hardened herself so that those who vacillate would have something to hang on to. And she stood still, like a signpost, for those who cannot find their way.

These were the arduous sciences Catalina had practiced. One by one she untied the knots that bound her. First the knots of her own complacency. Then the attachments to others. She did not aspire to freedom, but to absolute slavery. To obey what came from far away and what went far away. To give. To give herself.

Each unknotting (the appetites that demand their satisfaction, the kinsmen that complain of her coldness, or nothing more than the fatigue of incessant effort) was a sickness, a wrenching. So lengthy an agony, and without any resolution!

But the ilol accepted her fate, agreed to it, obedient. Hers was the destiny of water that fructifies the place it passes through. Until suddenly it plunges headlong into the void.

It is impossible to go back. Hopelessly she searched in Pedro's presence for the love, the storminess, the anguish of former days. And in Domingo for the consolation of past times. One of them rejected her because he was shut up inside himself, the other thwarted her because he was happy. And neither the sight of Lorenzo nor her interaction with Marcela was capable now of reviving pity or disdain within her.

Catalina became sullen. Sullen even with the idols, which she would have wanted to damage, to break, as if the matter that sheathed them were the source of their muteness. The silence was not in the mouths of others but in Catalina's own stopped-up ears and worn-out eardrums.

Inside her only one question reverberated: why did they abandon me? Her family, her people. No, they had not abandoned her because they were surfeited. Many times the ilol saw them leave unsatisfied, doubtful, unrelieved, despite her longing to give herself to them. And though she called to them and they returned, they stood there looking at her uselessly.

Had the wealth of her mines been exhausted or was Catalina an inept prospector? She felt it was her right to demand a respite. But the people, ever fickle, and now betraying her again, were already far away. And the cave of Tzajal-hemel was empty. And the idols were without sacrifices. And the ilol was abandoned.

Abandoned. As a sick person keeps returning to, touching, probing the point from which his pain radiates, Catalina returned to the feeling of her isolation, her uselessness. She wanted to arouse a hostility inside herself, but she experienced only a hazy dismay, without any fixed handhold. The evil was not sinking its roots into the others. It was sinking them into her.

Ah, how well she knew herself, how long she had endured herself. A childless woman. The nut that does not break open to make way for the growth and fullness of the seed. The rock, ugly and immobile, against which the passer-by stumbles. The fist that imprisons the bird and strangles its death rattle.

What had her mistaken tenacity done for her? Nothing belonged to her. Pedro was always someone else and not the man Catalina loved, the man Catalina needed. She could not hold him inside herself, not even as a child is held. A child. That was the name of her solitude, her destitution, her failure.

Catalina wants to expiate the guilt. She humbles herself before her husband, then raises herself up, maddened with wounded pride; she serves Lorenzo but disdains him for his feebleness. She tolerates her sister-in-law, but only when jealousy does not rise into her mouth like a bitter foam.

Only with Domingo did she sometimes take sustenance and learn to find some rest. Domingo, who was warmed against her body when he was a newborn, who received food from her hands, and care and the little favors that make life possible.

Who but Catalina had surprised the first flash of intelligence in the little boy's eyes? To whom did he stretch out his arms for the first time, to be picked up and held? What name did he learn to babble before any other?

In those years, Catalina wore her love for Domingo like a resplendent jewel upon her breast. After that she passed through a vast and hostile desert until the absolute appeared and made her its shelter and its dominion.

But the absolute is jealous. One by one it was casting away the memories that the notches in the surface of everyday life preserve; it was weakening the habits that ease the day's work; it was erasing all faithfulness to others, to herself.

Catalina evaded even Pedro's gaze; she allowed Lorenzo to become covered in lice and Marcela to be careless in her tasks. Even Domingo became a stranger to her, and she saw his face from very far away, as if through a mist, as if from another world.

Now Catalina is like an animal marked by a glowing brand: the brand of the gods. Before her lies the great stupefaction of the unknown. Behind her, the mass of her people. The people who pray, who implore, who may threaten. Words, murmurings, confessions. And suddenly everything disintegrates, sinks into silence.

Silence is the ravenous mouth of the abyss. It must be placated by flinging the only thing that will satiate its hunger into its depths: a victim.

Catalina is a tree that has been shaken, a coffer that has been ransacked. She no longer has anything to give. And the silence persists. Nothing to give. Because she defends the last thing that she possesses, and her nakedness is not perfect like the Cross's.

The Cross cries out for its crucifixion. One by one, to all of them. But who has taken upon himself the duties of the tribe? Who has laid claim to the office of intermediary? No one but Catalina. And therefore the echo of the Cross's clamoring is magnified in her, and into her flank digs the spur that demands action.

Drunken, terrible, innocent, Catalina lets out a scream. The silence, at last, is broken. She and that which raises up her head and supports her advance together amid the trampled pine needles and scattered debris and expectant people, to the Cross.

The religious functionaries stand back; the madrinas flee; the sacristan trembles. What will happen is what must happen. The moment when what is possible and what is necessary flow together and mingle and culminate is a moment that cannot be endured.

Catalina contemplates the Cross with the same compassion with which she contemplates herself. It is wood cut down by blows of an ax; it is contradiction and knot and paralysis; it is total privation. And she, the ilol, has in her hands what the cross is missing in order to be not an inert symbol but the instrument of salvation for all. One gesture, the simplest gesture, is enough to solidify hope into reality. And Catalina makes the gesture.

CHAPTER XXXIII

How small the world is if a child can become its center.

His birth was marked by omens: he is "the one born at the eclipse." But his destiny was concealed by the humbleness of his position and the routine of daily tasks. Today that destiny is revealed to the tribe. An ilol, a woman who has given birth to gods, holds him in her arms and speaks the words that anoint those who are chosen.

Domingo was not afraid of crowds. At Tzajal-Hemel he mingled with the crowd and took part in its adoration and propitiation of the idols. The crowd had thronged around his house like an animal, hungry but tame; it would scatter at the least sign of danger. The crowd that now encircles him does not dare go beyond a certain limit, though no one knows who marked that limit.

Domingo must be alone with the Cross. Catalina herself withdraws to stand among the men who have fallen silent, the women who are holding back their breath, the Tzotzil people who wait.

The period of atonement has now ended. The signs of proof have been fulfilled. The dark powers are reconciled with their slaves and have given them the gift that will make them equal in strength and power to the Caxláns. When the blood of an innocent is spilled, those who drink it will rise up with new might. Christ was what the Ladino had over them. Now they would have Christ.

The mayordomos recognize the victim who will ransom them and approach him to place the offerings of gratitude at his feet.

It does not frighten Domingo when they kneel before him. Grown-ups tend seedlings and light the fire on their knees; they kneel down to speak to small children.

Domingo is still a child. Though his days are not filled with games but are a succession of duties and tasks, though his teeth have often chewed the bone of hunger, though his skin has already been toughened by the elements and his intelligence sharpened by scarcity and danger, "the one who was born at the eclipse" is no more than a child.

A greedy child. When the mayordomos bring bottles, he does not seek out Catalina's eyes to see if he may accept the treat. He drinks. His throat burns. He coughs. But afterward a pleasant warmth spreads through his body and he feels free and wishes he were in an open field, running wild like a puppy or a suckling lamb.

Catalina watches him fixedly, sternly. Who is this strange creature she has handed over as a natural counterpart to the Cross? The bastard of a Caxlán from Jobel; the dishonor of a girl of her own race; Lorenzo's hidden shame; her husband's reproach; her own open wound. The open wound that never stops bleeding, that never scars over, because Domingo is always there. At midnight, when everyone else is resting, Catalina listens to the boy's breathing. If it is calm she relaxes, but if it comes in quick pants she runs to conjure away the threat of fever, harm, illness. Before the weeping can begin, sweet words are already flowing from her.

Catalina does not sleep. She watches in the darkness. She dotes in the light. And now, at last, she is face to face with the thief who has stolen her nights, the thorn that punctures her repose. She wants to cry out in bitterness: she was the mother of no one so that no one could tear her apart like that.

Domingo drinks from the mayordomos' bottles. Why should he refuse a gift when all he does is take? He has never even asked. In Pedro González Winiktón's house, food is not divided into equal portions. If there is too little, the boy never knows. Catalina pretends not to be hungry, or to feel ill, and gives him her share. During the times of abundance she chooses the sweetest ears of corn, the tenderest pieces of meat, the lushest vegetables. Today, these renunciations demand their compensation. Catalina wants to weep, like a women who has been cheated, because nothing can give her back the child she herself has placed beyond her own reach.

Uselessly she stretches her hands toward him. The hands that helped him from Marcela's belly and wiped away his original filth, hands that shaped him, day by day, with more patience than when they shaped the idols, and that can no longer add even the lightest touch, now that perfection has been achieved.

Because Domingo's body is sacred, and only the sacramental

madrinas have access to it. Troubled, awkward, they remove his wool jacket, his shirt, his coarse cotton breeches, his leather sandals. His best clothes, but they are not fine enough for the ceremony that is about to be consummated.

His cheeks inflamed by the liquor, Domingo gives himself over to the women's ministrations. He is not cold; he is not afraid. Gently they stroke his back, arms and thighs with pieces of cotton soaked in oil.

A low chant (from where? all mouths are closed) summons him to unconsciousness. Domingo lets his eyelids droop and is dazzled by a landscape of hills guarded by trees, clearings licked by mist, puddles that mirror the stag's bewilderment.

Passively carried along by the movement of the throng, Marcela and Lorenzo have arrived at its center, which is the Cross. What disproportion there is between the two sizes! Yet, on the scales of justice, the soul weighs more than wood. A blade of grass is enough to make the emptiness of the universe overflow.

These mysteries no longer shock Catalina, who has been spinning them out from the time of her earliest youth. How often the skein unravelled into countless threads! How often she found the strands, tied the knots, and wove a sturdy fabric whose design was simple and clear!

But she did not understand how a sacrifice could be consummated without pain. Her own flesh, emaciated by its familiarity with the divine, rebelled against the idea.

Domingo appeared to be sleeping. What did the mayordomos add to the posh that had tranquilized the will, enfeebled the limbs and crushed the resistance of "the one who was born at the eclipse."

No. Such a death, like a vegetable or a stone, would be worthless in the eyes of the dark powers. And they would demand another hostage. Catalina seized the basin from Xaw Ramírez Paciencia. Before the terrified faces, she poured the water that was left in it onto the victim's temples to revive him.

Domingo came to himself with a shiver of alarm. The image that filled his horizon calmed him. He knew well the anguished tension, the alarm that had always appeared on Catalina's face at the least threat to his health or happiness. Now, as always, she was bending over him to protect him. But why, instead of the warm softness of her lap, was he given the geometric rigidity of the Cross?

Domingo wanted to move, to change position, and realized that he could not. His arms had been fully extended and around his wrists a tightly knotted cord held them in place. He struggled to free himself but only succeeded in deepening the furrow the cord was making in his flesh.

Domingo stayed still, as an animal caught in a trap does, so as not to hasten its end. Only his eyes, more than astonished, stunned, stared insistently at Catalina's as if to implore her not for help but for an explanation.

Spellbound, Catalina followed these movements, this prudent and useless paralysis. Now death would take possession of this body as the gods always took possession of her, making a show of their power over an enemy subjugated in an unequal battle, an enemy brought down by force, whose every nerve—and there are so many!—has been shredded.

The mayordomos, interpreters of the divine will, are wise. They thrust where the pain is deepest, where the scream is crouched. But they do not allow the scream to echo through the church. They drown it out with their weeping, their lamentations. Their own voices, in a furious pack, pursue the cracked voice of agony. In every corner they find it and annihilate it.

The first rush of blood (from the side, as in all crucifixions) blinds Catalina. Yet she tries to brush away the mist that clouds her vision and to wipe the face of agony, as with the shroud of Veronica, to leave it clean and clear.

With the first rush of blood, the impetus that was making Domingo pitch upward, that was keeping him at the sharp peak of pain, rushes away and he breathes a moment of respite. With blood, it becomes possible to escape far from this sweat, this ceaseless nausea, the intolerable expectation of the blow about which nothing is known except that it must come.

Far, far. The nightmare will vanish, the horror will disappear. With a smile of tranquility, Domingo loses consciousness.

Catalina watches him, pained. Has he given in so quickly, with so little resistance? His martyrdom will not satiate the hunger of the gods. His death will not suffice to redeem the tribe!

What are the mayordomos doing? Are they distracted from their ritual duties by endless mutual bows? And the madrinas? Are they trying to veil the spectacle with smoke from the censers? Only one person remains attentive to the order that must be maintained: the sacristan, who squeezes a bitter liquid onto Domingo's mouth.

Domingo feels the pain of the wound, multiplied. He resists instinctively, but does not ask himself how or why what is happening began to happen. He is a child, but his childhood has not been sheltered from the sight of the unequal fight between beings. From the moment of his birth he has been marked by the indelible cipher of the only law that governs the world: the law of force. Shaking, he has watched the coyotes' nocturnal assaults on the henhouses, he has seen the sparrow hawk fall on its prey, rapid and sure as an arrow; he has defended himself from the attackers on the outskirts of Jobel; and during the celebration of the holy days, he has witnessed the fistfights of rivals. He has seen without horror how the heavy-soled sandal of the winner kicks the face of the beaten man again and again until it is disfigured.

But nothing was equal to the misfortune that had been unleashed on him. Nothing. Not even the moment when the whole tribe raised stakes, machetes and luks to finish off a mad dog. Or a brujo.

Domingo understood suddenly that somehow he had become the thing he had always feared most: a mad dog. He wanted to help the others in the task of extermination: he twisted, trying to break the cords, and yelled to excite his executioners. The wound began to bleed again but this time the loss of blood brought no relief or weakness.

This time Domingo does not faint. He will be the victim, but also the witness of his own execution.

The nails that are going to pierce his hands and feet are large and rusty because they have been stored away for a long time. As they penetrate the flesh, they pulverize the bones, burst open the arteries, scrape the tendons.

Domingo moans, he no longer knows why. If someone were to ask him if he was suffering he would be unable to answer. Suffering is a word that has a certain dimension and a predetermined weight, all it takes is a voice to speak it. Domingo has gone beyond all voices, all dimensions.

He is dying. But it is not him or his body that will disintegrate. It is the world. He opens his eyes and a kind of vertigo rushes over him. Figures draw close, blur, merge. Proportions change. It isn't only that his perceptions are wobbling. The Cross to which Domingo has been nailed is moving. The religious officials carry it to the center of the altar and there it is planted and raised. Every vibration of the wood is painfully prolonged into Domingo's flesh and tears the last howls from his throat, cuts the last ties.

The blood is still flowing, but not in a gush or a torrent. It drips. Every drop is caught below by the sacramental madrinas' fine handkerchiefs, which are stained red. The blood that runs down the wood is licked by the mayordomos, the sacristan, Catalina.

Those who are farthest from the Cross can see all of it. The distance hides the details that make the crucified boy ugly. He hangs inert now; his end lacks the beauty or serenity of statues. Against all other wills and even against his own, Domingo's body refuses to die. His rebellion takes the form of grotesque contractions of the muscles, a movement of cowardice, confusion, repulsion.

After the consummation a leaden silence drops over the crowd. Even the crying of a newborn is quickly stifled by the mother's breast; even the drunkard's incoherent mutter trails off. In this silence, prophecy is gestating. Because what has happened means nothing if words do not give it form.

But who will speak? Xaw stammers and does not succeed in understanding the deep meaning of things. The functionaries, the mayordomos and the madrinas, are good only for servile tasks, spiritual beasts of burden who do not know what they carry. The ilol alone remains, and hopeful, yearning eyes turn toward her.

Catalina knows that gaze, responds to it. For the first time she does not stray onto false paths. She knows what must be said and finds the right words. Neither babbling nor enigmas. And the revelation does not announce itself as it has before, as it always has, from within a delirium. Catalina keeps her senses; she is in control of herself; she is free. The stone of the sepulcher has been pushed aside.

"We have all reached the end of the story with the Ladino. We have suffered injustice and persecution and adversity. Perhaps some of our ancestors sinned and that is why this tribute was exacted from us. We gave what we had and paid the debt. But the Ladino wanted more, always more. He has dried up the marrow of our bones with work; he has robbed us of our possessions; he has made us guess at the orders and punishments he gives in a foreign language. And we endured the suffering without protest because no sign told us that it was enough.

"But suddenly the gods showed themselves, the dark powers spoke. And it is their will that we become equal to the Ladino who grew haughty in the possession of his Christ.

"Now we, too, have a Christ. He was not born in vain and has not suffered and died in vain. His birth, his suffering and his death have placed the Tzotzil, the Chamula, the Indian on the same level as the Ladino. If the Ladino threatens us we must not flee but confront him. If he pursues us we must turn to face him.

"What can we fear? On our heads the blood of baptism has fallen. It is said that those who are baptized with blood instead of water will not die.

"Let us go out to meet the Ladino. Let us defy him, and we will see how he runs and hides. But if he resists we will join together in the fight. We are equals now that our Christ offsets his Christ.

"You women must not tremble for your husbands and your sons. They are going to the place where men are measured. And they will return dragging victory by the hair. Whole, even if they have many wounds. Resurrected, after the necessary end. Because it is said that none of us will die."

CHAPTER XXXIV

THE CRY WITH WHICH Domingo Díaz Puiljá died on the Cross resonated into every corner of the Tzotzil region. It echoed in the air, desolate as a hunting horn, awakening the men's rapacious and oppressive instincts.

The farmers pulled their luks from half-cut furrows and raised them like weapons; the stealthy woodsmen pulled the ax from the tree's trunk before they had finished cutting it down and busied themselves filing away the notches that blunted its edge. Those who forded streams, who frequented watering holes, wrung out the cloths they had just beaten against the riverbank stones and placed them to dry in the sun; the merchants who went to and from Jobel left off their traffic to go to their villages, their huts, and instruct their families in the duties of orphanhood, widowhood, absence.

The old people, the women and the children remained where they were.

Neither the pregnant ewe about to give birth nor the young sheep nor the randy billy-goat could be exposed to the hazards of adventure or flight. They, at least, could run away—but the other things? The earthenware utensils whose surfaces were shaped and known by long habit; the wooden coffer, enclosing small, hidden treasures; the loom which gives rank and dignity to the weaver; the three tenamastates that the cooking pots rest on, warm from the embers. Who could carry the foodstuffs that would sustain them? The dried beef, hanging from a rough hook; the various kinds of beans and corn; the comfort of dried chiles and roasted coffee.

What roots them to the land are the things that have roots: the defenseless vegetable garden, the helpless fruit tree.

Each thing, as at the time of creation or during a time of peace, remains with its guardian.

Meanwhile the tribe moves like a great, clumsy animal, disjointed and headless, changing direction whenever it finds an obstacle in its path. The hills are blackened and the valleys echo with the sound of its movement.

Each one knows the place of hostility, the place where vengeance will be fulfilled; each one wants to present himself there and be satiated. The tribe disperses. A few men band together around Winiktón's will and Ulloa's orders. Their goal is Ciudad Real.

The others fall on the hamlets where the Ladinos have taken refuge, on the cattle ranches and coffee farms, on the towns. They kill when they are afraid or when they are shaken by rage. The people surrender and the Indians take possession of the land. There is no fight and their triumph has no heroic dimension. They abandon what they have conquered and continue on. It does not matter where. They must go farther.

The long-memoried among them recall: the ranch of El Vergel, where they loudly demanded surrender. There was no answer. Crouching behind the fences, they waited for the cover of night to advance. With the butts of their guns they broke through an iron grating that protected nothing but a dilapidated courtyard. As they checked the corridors and broke open the potted plants searching for who knew what, they were followed by a skinny, mangy dog that howled piteously. There was no need to force open any lock. In the bedrooms they found the disorder of a sudden departure. Smashed, empty vials on the floor, broken furniture, closets in disarray. The Indians carried away several bundles of clothing but left them one by one along the road because they were very cumbersome. They also took a double-barreled shotgun.

Everyone had fled from Arbenza except a woman who could not walk because she was paralyzed. She greeted them with insults, stiff in her wooden chair. When one of them tried to stop her mouth she bit his hand. They hit her on the head until she lost consciousness, then left her there, unconscious, as they went through the house and its surroundings. They were tired, hungry. Enraged at having found nothing, they went back to the crippled woman's room. She moaned weakly, and tried to grasp something with hands knotted by rheumatism. On one finger a gold ring gleamed. An Indian wanted to take it off, but the knuckles were too swollen. Another took a quick whack with his machete. Blood spattered the faces of those who were closest. They wiped it away with their sleeves and finished off the woman on the spot.

In Laguna Petej they overtook a group of children, their stomachs swollen and full of worms, dressed in rags through which their ribs could be counted. The children tried to escape, but as if it were a game. Their pursuers were numerous, and more agile than they. They harassed them with questions that the children, weeping in terror and fatigue, were incapable of answering. One Indian, an old man, told them he would take them to his village because he needed some help in the cornfield. Another wanted them too, and all the others quickly became embroiled in their dispute. Finally, one of them who was half drunk wanted to settle the problem: with quick thrusts of a spear he killed the children. Afterward, all of them headed off somewhere else, like sleepwalkers. It was noon and they were tormented by thirst.

In a meadow in Baalchen they found a she-goat grazing. Her udders were full and there seemed to be no young nearby to relieve them. They approached her cautiously so as not to frighten her—an unnecessary precaution because the she-goat was tame and allowed them to grab her and stand her in the best position for milking. When not a drop of milk was left, they killed her.

They had started a large bonfire, and they roasted strips of meat on it. They took a long time eating, unsatisfied because none of them had a large enough portion nor anything to wash the meal down with. One of them took out a small violin he had hidden among his clothes and began to play a sound. The sound of a jaguar fighting a snake; the sound of the defeat of the men who were transformed into monkeys; the sound of the wise men who studied the sky and knew how many stars it held. The music made the thought of death less bitter.

In Cruz Obispo, an old man confronted them. Stories of his wealth and avarice were told throughout the region. The Indians knew him very well as an unscrupulous indenturer of workers and a severe master. With him, an arm in a sling was not a reason to work a little less; the story of a sick child would not increase the amount of a loan.

"We're going to pull together, Chamulita," he would say. He was up before sunrise to oversee the work. He rode to the farthest edges of his ranch on a fat she-mule, slow and solemn. Wherever he found anything the least bit out of order he immediately stopped and corrected it. He never let go of the whip that was the warning sign and the executor of his punishments.

There was no woman in his house and there were no friends he went to see outside it; he only went to Ciudad Real when he was obliged to by some litigation.

When this old man learned of the uprising, he gave strict orders to his laborers to double their workload. That would keep them from losing their heads, he thought. And when the rebelling Indians arrived at the big house, he was alone.

He seemed neither surprised nor afraid. He was used to seeing them in groups and speaking to several of them at once. The old man did not rise from his chair or lift his eyes from the accounts he was going over. The Indians were troubled by his serenity.

Finally, one of them, who had once been in the old man's employ and had overheard rumors about treasures he had stored away, stepped forward and demanded that he hand those treasures over.

The old man raised his eyes and gave him a look of scandalized fixity. Was he crazy? In hard times like these, could anyone prosper or grow rich? At that moment especially, when he had just looked over his papers, he could tell them that if things continued on in the same way he would soon have to declare himself bankrupt. But that was his problem. As for the Indians, he advised them to leave off their foolishness and go back to their cornfields because it was the season for sowing.

What were they after? It was a shame to see them like that, ragged, filthy, wandering around like madmen.

One of the Indians answered that Ladinos were no longer allowed to speak to them that way, because now they were equals. At the old man's mocking laugh, he added the irrefutable argument: the Chamulas had their own Christ, and they had heard the promise that they would not die.

"Shall we put it to the test?" the old man asked. "I have no weapons. But if one of you will give me a gun and let me take a shot, he won't be telling the tale afterward."

An Indian held out a rifle and asked the old man to aim at him. The old man gave a questioning glance at those who seemed to be most respected and saw signals of approval. He raised the rifle to his face and aimed it at the Indian's heart. The explosion and the cloud of powder made the Chamulas step back as their companion slumped to the ground. The old man reloaded the rifle.

"Anyone else want to give it a try?"

No one did. Many of them were upset by the fact that their companion had fallen and appeared to be lifeless. Others thought they should wait. Their opinion prevailed and the Indians sat around the corpse until nightfall. The old man occupied the place of honor and watched the incidents of the vigil with mild amusement. He had refused to light the gasoline lamp and only a single pine torch illuminated the house. The rifle rested on his knees.

By early dawn most of them had left. The ranch's own laborers were all that remained for the burial.

Far from Cruz Obispo, the insurrectionaries rejoined each other. They did not want to discuss what had happened because they were incapable of understanding or interpreting it. But all of them experienced the event as an impulse to faster and more ambitious actions.

Even the most dull-witted of them realized it was no longer possible to go back, it was necessary to move ahead, even though they could not count on invulnerability. Their despair drove them to turn on populous and well-fortified towns, against which they had no advantage other than the initiative of their attack, surprise, and their numbers.

The nearest place was San Pedro Chenhalhó. They fell on it without warning, without allowing time for any resistance. The townsmen (craftsmen and campesinos, not warriors) took up positions they thought were favorable because they were concealed from their enemies' eyes. But this also prevented them from firing with a sure aim.

The Indians paid no attention to the fallen bodies, of which, moreover, there were few. They advanced through the narrow street, up to their ankles in mud, stumbling against rocks. The most impatient, the most curious, the most exhausted among them jumped over the walls of the houses, went into the stables and henhouses, tore the locks off doors to penetrate the family's quarters, to find a table still bearing the remains of the last breakfast, beds that still retained the warmth of bodies, the storage room in which a variety of impractical objects were scattered, unused.

Other Indians kept walking, seeking the heart of the battle. There was no barracks in San Pedro Chenhalhó and the Palacio Municipal was deserted. From inside the church came a murmur of people, hiding, huddled together. The Indians attacked.

They broke down the ancient wooden doors, eaten away by insects, with the butts of their rifles. Each blow was met with hysterical shrieks that were quickly stifled. When the way was clear, the Indians went in.

Inside the church there was nothing except women surrounded by their sons and their grandfathers. They were kneeling, their backs to the enemy, their eyes fixed on the altar. The commotion of the splintering doors and the invaders' cries did not make them turn around. Their sole horizon was an image bent under the weight of its own miracles.

The Indians consulted with each other, unable to decide. The lack of an adversary paralyzed them. But then one of them discovered a piece of bread in the hands of a small boy and tried to grab it away. The boy cried in protest and his mother intervened, castigating the man's behavior.

"Such a winikón! Why don't you pick on someone your own size? Let go of that, you miserable Indian!"

And she gave him a slap in the face. The Indian flung himself against the woman and shook her violently. Those who were nearby made a movement to interfere. An old man justified his inaction: "If my ailments didn't nail me to the spot, I'd be standing up to you Indian wretches!"

"Don't think you're going to get out of this mousetrap alive! Our men will give you what's coming to you."

The threats turned into blows. The women brandished the scissors they had been hiding in their bodices. Others had armed themselves with saddler's needles, with fistfuls of pepper they blew in their attackers' faces.

"Bitch! You blinded me!"

"That and more is what you deserve, rebel Indian! I want to see you crawling to beg my forgiveness!"

The machetes came out, glittering. They hummed through the air, falling onto empty space or onto a body that split in half as a puddle of blood formed below.

In silence the encounter continued. The besieged townspeople retreated to the walls. Which were smooth and straight. Without a place to hide in, without a handhold to climb by. The children became entangled in the adults' legs; they lost their balance; they could not get up from the ground; they were trampled on. They were the first to begin to cry.

Suddenly a howl went up and the Chamulas hurled themselves on their victims. They put their hands on the women, ripped off their clothes, laughed uproariously at their nakedness. They played at tossing the children into the air and running them through with the points of their spears. The old men implored their pity in vain. They died trembling ignobly.

One of the Indians applied himself to cutting apart a corpse, carefully, painstakingly. He wanted to find something that was different from an animal's carcass or an Indian's remains. The thing that allowed the Ladinos to command. Not finding it, he moved his head, dissatisfied, uncertain. He abandoned that useless corpse to look for another.

Those who had come down from the highest mountains were hungry for women. Who was there to stop them? They raped the nubile young girls, the pregnant wives, the old women. They concluded their work with a blow to the skull, a gunshot at point-blank range, or by lopping off a limb.

Others opened up a path to the altar, it didn't matter how, in order to satisfy their craving to profane the objects of worship. They broke the chalices, shattered the monstrances, ripped the wigs off the saints and tore out their glass eyes. The uprooted mannikins and broken cases tumbled to the ground. False eyelashes were scattered across the floor.

After some time, the episode ended. The Indians were tired and the air inside the church was unbreathable. They came out bloodstained, with bits of brain encrusted in the soles of their sandals. Their booty was scant. But many of them made do with it and returned to their villages.

Others, however, as soon as they learned what had happened, began gathering together provisions in order to leave. Without order, without regularity, senselessly, the raids, the looting, the torching continued. The settlements became heaps of ashes, the planted fields were razed, the flocks were sent stampeding.

Up the mountain go those who are fleeing and those who pursue. Each side is afraid to confront the other. They run into each other because there is only one spring to drink from, one cave to hide in, one trail going up or down.

Inchinton, Ya'alcuc, Corralchen, Bechiltic. Where haven't the Indians gone? With hunger, despair, rage.

The one who stays behind is forgotten. No one asks about his fate. Did that one come back? Did they bury him? Because only one thing sustains them in their endless peregrination, one beacon: Catalina's promise. Those who died will come back to life bearing a weight that others have not yet experienced: that of not having died. And if they do not come back to life. . . .

Do not think any more, Chamulita, just walk. Loneliness is not a good counselor. Join up with a companion, and another, and yet another. Do not ask any questions. Because the foundation you built yourself on could crack and you could collapse.

CHAPTER XXXV

JULIA STRETCHED HER HAND out over the always damp (and therefore clammy) surface of the sheet. She touched a solid shoulder and said timidly, "Are you asleep?"

Leonardo's silences, which grew longer each day, frightened her. She wanted to attribute them to a natural cause. But the tension, the alarm that emanated from the body that had once been so tractable to her spell, did not let her deceive herself. A detached voice answered, "No."

And then, more for himself than for her, "I'm thinking."

Julia was well acquainted with the distances that worrying and preoccupation with matters other than love could visit upon the most intimate proximity. And she hated them. At another time, when she was the one holding the reins in this love affair, she would have protested vehemently. Now, she limited herself to getting up, trying not to make any noise, trying not to bother him.

What Leonardo was thinking (in a difficult, painful way that was impossible for him to put into words) was that it wasn't worth the trouble of having made such an effort to become an integral, vital part of Ciudad Real. Then he raised his head.

"Do you know what happened to the men on the night watch yesterday?"

La Alazana had lit a small lamp in front of the dressing table mirror and was gathering up her hair to fasten it with a ribbon. Unable to keep a note of irritation from her voice, she answered.

"The Indians killed them. The burial processions passed in front of my house. They were singing hymns and swearing vengeance."

Leonardo was looking at the roof with his hands clasped behind his head.

"But the Indians didn't kill them. We made that up."

Julia turned, puzzled.

"What then?"

"They killed each other. Out of fear."

Leonardo spoke the last word with rage. He knew himself and therefore thought he knew his men. He was not a coward. He did not tremble when the supreme moment came, standing in front of Isidoro, when the two of them settled their differences once and for all. Thanks to that feat he had considered himself the equal of the town's leading men, and he had shared many adventures with them in which bravery was the essential element: hunting parties that enabled him to show off his sure eye and steady nerves; brutalities committed to punish and give a lesson to peons; abductions of women. And from time to time, as well, an ambush to rid himself of a rival.

Consequently, Leonardo was now scandalized by the conduct of the others. As their leader—which he was in the present emergency—he had assigned them very specific duties, all of which were to their direct benefit. Nevertheless, they evaded those duties on the most implausible pretexts. They left the town, the district, the danger, so as not to have to take part in the patrols. And their own homes were left at the mercy not only of the invaders but of any passing thief because they had forsaken them to go and take refuge in some hiding place.

The news that one of their ranches had been burnt down by Indians didn't inflame them or fill them with rage; it made them afraid. They spoke of fleeing. At first in whispers, in secret. But now their discretion was gone. And some of them had fled.

Leonardo raised his head to see Julia already dressed for her afternoon salon. But who would be there? The women who weren't sealed in by stones and mud or hiding out in warehouses or inside empty cisterns were wandering through the streets as if mad, yelling out confessions of all their sins, kneeling down in front of any passer-by to beg for his forgiveness. Because Ciudad Real had to be cleansed of its sins and their penitence would achieve that. The obdurate sinners would have to be cast out, stoned. The obdurate sinners like Leonardo, who took advantage of the situation's abnormality to consummate his abominations. He visited La Alazana without taking the slightest precaution, as if he were issuing a challenge. And thus the wrath that the Coletos had built up against their enemies, which they dared not unleash, was turned against the man who had made it his duty to defend them. Who was this parvenu? Isidoro's murderer, Julia's lover, the traitor who would reach an agreement with foreigners on the onditions under which Ciudad Real would be surrendered to em.

Every morning, without fail, Leonardo received anonymous letters in which the charges against him were enumerated, insults were repeated, and his plots were guessed at. In the letter's unsigned folds, a hatred was battling to find its way out, a hatred accumulated over inert years; like a snail shell inhabited by the wind, it was now alive, moving, resonating.

Julia rubbed her hands together impatiently. She came and went through the room, she moved objects around on the dressing table.

"Calm down; you're going to make me nervous. When do your visitors arrive?"

"Since I no longer have anything to offer them, my visitors always give one reason or another for not coming."

"That's natural."

"And is it also natural that the servants have invaded the house with droves of their relatives, all loaded down with their belongings, who eat everything they find in their paths?"

"Throw them out."

Yes, it was so easy to solve other people's problems. Throw out the servants! And who would do the household chores? Julia was incapable of sweeping the enormous courtyards or of cooking anything on the coal stove. Or of being alone.

She waited for Leonardo's reaction. It wasn't impatient, or concerned, or even curious. Almost smiling, he started to get dressed.

"You're afraid, too, aren't you? Now you can really call yourself a Coleta."

Julia took his face between her hands, anxious.

"Is it true that the Indians have us under siege? And that we haven't done anything to defend ourselves?"

Leonardo pulled away roughly.

"You believe what the papers say, too."

Julia hadn't wanted to read them again after they published the fact that the idols that Xaw Ramírez Paciencia brought to Ciudad Real were wrapped in a shawl from Guatemala that many witnesses could identify as belonging to her. From that to accusing her of being an accomplice or an instigator was a step many people took. The editorials clamored for a thorough investigation of the matter.

"Let whoever falls fall," they said. And Julia refused to read them, though she couldn't disobey Leonardo's order to buy them. He spent a large part of their meetings on those papers, which were now lying scattered and crumpled around the bed.

"Before, there was only one, remember? Now every day new ones spring up, like mushrooms after a cloudburst. We were used to *¡Plus Ultra!* Not that it had anything important to say. On the contrary. Social notes, weather forecasts, tips for curing distemper. A measured but firm denunciation of the Ayuntamiento for allowing the streets to flood or to be used as garbage cans. Now you can't turn a page any more without reading some prophet who's tearing his hair and lamenting the calamities that are going to befall us. And that's only when you aren't faced, instead, with the generous bearer of the most efficient and rapid solutions to our problems."

"Are they exaggerating when they talk about the problems?"

Leonardo, gun tucked into his belt, did not look very reassuring.

"They aren't seeing them clearly. The danger doesn't lie with the Indians. There are a lot of them, I won't deny that. But they have no arms, no leaders."

He looked at Julia with a touch of mockery in his eyes.

"I didn't mean to offend you. For a second I forgot that one of the men who's commanding them is your husband."

Julia turned her back on him to declare, "He's not my husband."

The confession humiliated her, and did not even succeed in surprising or gratifying Leonardo. To him, it was no more than a triviality, a detail that didn't change the situation in the least.

"We don't have any means of defending ourselves either. A toy cannon and some chocolate soldiers. And we're not going to get any help. Mexico is very far away. And as far as Tuxtla is concerned. . . ."

Leonardo opened the curtains to let in a chilly darkness.

"There are old grudges that haven't been forgotten. And they have their own interpretation of the events. According to them, the Indian uprising is nothing but a story we've come up with.

When we ask for their help it's only because we want to distract their troops, then fall on a defenseless city, declare that its authority has disappeared, and return that authority to its place of origin: Ciudad Real."

The misunderstanding seemed absurd to Julia, and very simple to clear up.

"Can't they come here and see for themselves that the information is true?"

"Their dignity keeps them from doing so. They haven't forgotten that we accepted the assistance of a foreign country, Guatemala."

And what assistance it was. A few poor mercenaries who hadn't even been issued uniforms and didn't know how to stand at attention in front of their commanding officers. They played out the charade for a few days but then abandoned the barracks in groups. They took up with women from the outskirts of town and sold their work at much lower prices than the artisans of Ciudad Real. Since they were skilled, as well, they stole all the customers. Those whose luck wasn't as good sponged in the houses of the rich. Julia could testify to that from experience. And if anyone tried to draw the line on their abuses, they gave vent to an endless litany on the Coletos' lack of gratitude, which left the Coletos mute.

"What are you going to do?"

"What can I do? It's not easy to transform a harness maker into a captain. There's something civilians don't have and can only get from lengthy training: discipline. Of course I could try to teach it to them, drill it into them—by my example and also by certain measures that must absolutely be established. . . . But I'm boring you. This is no kind of conversation for a woman. I should ask you what you are going to do."

There was no real interest. Only a forced and distant courtesy. Julia felt wounded.

"That depends on what happens. And what happens depends on you."

It was such an abrupt conclusion that she had to add: "You're the Chief of Operations in the highlands. Isn't that the title they gave you at the last meeting?"

"They gave me that title because they were scared. And because there wasn't anyone else who was inclined to face what's coming."

"Don't belittle yourself," La Alazana responded heatedly. "This is a promising situation, and it's only the beginning for you. You were born to go very high. Ciudad Real isn't much. Chiapas either."

"Please, that's enough."

Leonardo protested without conviction. And Julia, for whom, until then, flattery had been closely related to mockery, discovered in astonishment that she now believed her own words and longed for them to become a reality. Disturbed, she added glibly, "I'm foretelling your future. I've got a little bit of witch in me, did you know? If you don't believe me, ask Idolina."

"Right now it isn't easy to talk to her. She spends all day locked in her room."

"Is she sick again?"

"I don't know and don't care."

"She stopped coming to see me. Like that: all of a sudden. Without any explanation. Without any reason."

"Maybe she found out about us and was offended."

"Did Isabel tell her?"

"Isabel doesn't need to tell her, the stones in the streets can. It's one secret that's shouted from the housetops."

Leonardo came closer to examine Julia's face. Its sharp angles had disappeared, dissolved into smooth curves that gave it a tranquil, meek expression like a domestic animal. So: he had captured the hawk, swift, high-strung and rapacious; he had fattened it up patiently, and now it was heavy, it moved with difficulty, it had acquired sedentary habits. Would his triumph over Ulloa amount to no more than this conquest? Would the two of them never confront one another on any other terrain?

Uncomfortable, Julia ducked away from her lover's stare, which was both fixed and distracted.

"Your prophecies aren't going to come true, Alazana. Because those prominent citizens who are now under my command don't trust me. No, they don't have any doubts about my bravery. Only about my loyalty. Because of you."

It was only an instant, the instant of the somnambulist who walks to the edge of the void and suddenly awakens. Across Julia's face flashed a fleeting appeal for help. But then it subsided back into reserve. Just in time she remembered that she could appeal to this man's sensuality, to his anger, to his disdain, but not to his compassion. She left his side and went to sit with her back to him in a rocking chair.

"You were telling me about discipline."

Leonardo began pacing the room, glad that the conversation had turned toward his natural element: action. When he was in the throes of an important project, all other ideas, all other events, paled and disappeared.

"Discipline is a very simple thing: a few rules that can be taught and learned. But since we have neither the time nor the place to do that directly, we'll have to rely on a kind of . . . of. . . ."

"Manual."

"No, that's not what it's called. It has its own name. Let me remember. . . . Directives. . . . That's it. Military directives."

"Are you going to issue them?"

"I already have the essentials, I've been turning them over in my head from the beginning. But I need someone whose mind is more polished than mine to write it all out clearly for me."

"A letter-writer?"

"No, por Dios. Someone of a higher class."

"A lawyer."

"Fortunately there's no lack of them in Ciudad Real."

"What do you want him to say?"

"What he knows as well as I do: that this problem of the Indians and their uprisings is not going to be resolved as long as we go on making excuses for evading it. We have to cut it out at the root."

"How?"

"Like the song says, the best Indian is a dead Indian."

"And you think a piece of paper will be enough to make the Coletos dedicate themselves to killing the Indians."

"It will be a good push in the right direction. Until now they've had scruples: they don't want an Indian to die any more than they want their herds of cattle to be diminished. They feel that the Indians are something that belongs to them and they don't fully understand that the Government has taken them away. And that's why, as I've said many times, the Indians must be finished off."

The simplicity of this conclusion stunned Julia, who could do nothing but burst out laughing.

"The ladies of Ciudad Real complain that they can never have done with the plague of red ants. And you want their husbands to finish off all the Indians!"

"There are many ways of doing it and we must make use of all of them. For the rebels, the most conspicuous ones who have placed us between the sword and the wall, death is little enough. Yes, their death, their families' death, the destruction of their villages and towns. Then we'll have to throw salt on their fields so that not a single seed ever sprouts there again."

"That would take care of a few of them, the leaders. And the rest?"

Carried away by his own oratory, Leonardo had forgotten that the vast majority of the Indians were neither rebellious nor conspicuous, but indifferent, with a submissiveness they inherited from their parents and grandparents. He rapidly improvised a response.

"Let the government send them somewhere else. The map of the state is full of areas of federal land. Let them colonize that land."

"And if the Indians don't want to go?"

"They'll be killed!"

Before turning around, Julia asked one more question, "Have you discussed this with the other ranchers?"

"Of course. We talk about it every day, all the time."

"What do they think?"

"At first they thought it was a trap, that I was trying to leave them without anyone to work their ranches for them, to ruin them so I could get my hands on their property and pay them a pittance for it."

"Did they tell you that?"

"When does a Coleto tell you what he's thinking? But I'm as sly a fox as they are and I know their cunning ways. I played the offended party and threatened to let them find out on their own whatever lesson it was that God wanted to teach them."

"If you issue the directives, who's going to carry them out?"

"The soldiers."

"You yourself just said they have no guts."

"Because they haven't smelled blood or gunpowder yet. They're holed up here behind their mothers' skirts, waiting for the Indians to come down on them and finish them off. I'm going to force those worthless beggars to take some initiative and stop being so gun-shy."

"I'm going to leave."

"Where will you go? Are you crazy? What are you talking about?"

"It's still possible to leave, isn't it? A lot of families have moved away from the city."

Leonardo did not see in Julia's features any sign that she was upset or confused. Her calmness annoyed him. I'm not going to be the one to beg, he told himself. And then, aloud, "You'll have to leave everything in the house behind you. People won't want to buy anything at a time like this."

"I'm going to give my things to Doña Mercedes Solórzano if she helps me prepare for the trip."

"Have you already agreed on this with her?"

"I wanted to have your consent first. Now I can go ahead and send for her."

"Don't worry about it. I'll give her the message."

"Thank you very much."

That last phrase sounded like a dismissal. Before going their separate ways, the pair of them looked at one another, each offended by the other's blindness and lack of love. And they each promised themselves that the final goodbye would at least leave their pride intact.

CHAPTER XXXVI

CATALINA DÍAZ PUILJÁ was shivering. In vain she had covered her body with the rags that her finest and her everyday clothes had been worn to over the course of this demented, delirious march that had begun with Domingo's death.

Domingo's death. Now, at a distance, Catalina could contemplate it with a lucidity that made it totally incomprehensible. The lone boy, placed in the center of an inviolate circle; his spilled blood, drunk by ravenous dogs as well as by those who witnessed the sacrifice and those who consummated it. Catalina beat at her temples to make herself remember what spot she was standing in while Domingo was dying. Distracted, absorbed, frenetic, yes, but where? If only she could know that she would know all the rest, too.

But it was not possible. The sepulchral slab that did not quite cover the corpse of the boy, her boy, had been covering her ever since. Under it, immobile, lay the ilol whose powers had been lost. The woman who made the marvelous discovery in the cave had forgotten it; the woman who, with her own hands, gave shape to some distant and perhaps already nonexistent idols; the woman who, in her barrenness, rejoiced in the proximity of a childhood. And that was the part of Catalina that was most dead, most buried, most rotted away.

The woman who survived Good Friday was someone else, with a perpetual shudder that made her jaws lock and erased every trace of color from her face. Her only solace lay in not having to decide anything ever again.

She set out walking at a sign from those who led the tribe and in the direction her shepherds indicated. She stopped when the others did: when the difficulties of the path impeded the march; when some enemy waylaid them; when night fell.

Sometimes, in a moment of repose, Catalina saw—in the shape of a crag, in the mirroring surface of a body of water, in a fugitive cloud—the image of a crucified boy. She saw it and the words that would have given this mirage the name that would conjure it away did not rise to her lips.

What was more, whether she herself or anyone else spoke words, she did not hear them, deafened as she was by the pandemonium of fury that burst her eardrums after Domingo's death.

She watched other people's gestures without understanding them either. One man would hoist a machete or a hoe; another would be brandishing some rocks. In front of him went Pedro González Winiktón, his eyes fixed on no one knew what. At his sides the Ladinos: Ulloa and Santiago.

In the confusion and disorder of the exodus no one saw to anyone but himself. What happened to Lorenzo Díaz Puiljá, Catalina's brother, the innocent? Those who were questioned could not say. He was with them at the beginning, they were sure; Marcela helped him with his needs. But he gradually began to lag behind; he was always slower than the others and gave in more easily to fatigue. Or he died in some combat. Or he simply decided to go back to his hut.

The others went on, up and down hills, protecting themselves from the rain under the trees' foliage or in a sheepfold. They descended on the settlements, starving, blind with rage, seeking, almost groping for an end to their exhaustion. Then they would go, leaving behind them a smoking ruin, a field laid to waste, some animal or human remains.

They would walk away, looking at each other suspiciously, trying to hide what they had managed to steal.

Catalina, to whom no one paid any particular deference, plundered the granaries and nosed around the hooks where meat is hung out of reach to be smoked and dried. She wanted to eat, always, at all times. She finished off the stew abandoned in the kitchen by those who had taken flight; she went to the storerooms and ripped open bags of grain that she chewed long and painfully and then was unable to swallow. She threw stones to knock down clusters of fruit, and she sucked on her fingers which were impregnated with a juice long since consumed, an absent aroma.

Catalina's agility as she scurried from place to place, driven by obscure instincts, by dire needs, was astonishing to Marcela who had once known her wearied by her priestess's robes, marked by

a hieratic reserve as if she feared her every movement could unleash a catastrophe. But Marcela had stopped trying to understand
Catalina from the very beginning. For many years, she had sub-
mitted to her like an ox allowing itself to be yoked to the instrument of labor. But now something had cracked, and the figure of
the ilol, once respected, feared, venerated, was collapsing at her
feet. Marcela turned her face away so as not to see it. Without
anger, without amazement, without disillusionment, without happiness. At last she was free.

And Catalina was, too. She joined with the other women to
carry out the lowliest tasks. She merged with them. No sign of
exemption set her apart, not even the mark, arbitrary and terrible,
which all of them glimpsed, though she hid it as if it were leprosy.

Catalina forgot herself and her former tasks. She grazed meekly
in anonymity. But at times, when hope abandoned the pilgrims,
when victory turned its back on them and the uncertainty was
too piercing, the others turned their eyes toward Catalina with a
gaze at once imperious and reverent, pleading for and demanding
an unconditional surrender: the gaze of the devout.

At those moments, Catalina felt as if she were being hunted
down. Her breathing quickened and her pulse pounded roughly
in her temples like an animal captured in a trap.

She tried to run away; she was no longer capable of resurrecting
any of her bygone gestures. And the others made way, not for
her current and obvious fear, but for the memory of a majesty
that would never abate or end.

Catalina went to find sanctuary among the only ones who
never tortured her with such gazes: the Ladinos. Ulloa and
Santiago, protected from the cold nocturnal winds by the Indians' coarse woolen shirts, allowed her to draw near their half-
extinguished campfire as if she were a harmless dog without a
master.

Disconnected fragments of conversation reached her, not spoken in her language or for her ears or for her understanding.

At first Fernando Ulloa had obstinately, tenaciously refused to
wear the clothing Pedro and the other principal men offered him.
Eventually he had to give in; his own clothing was falling apart
on the long trek and becoming useless as the severity of the

weather increased. He had to give up the cleanliness he was accustomed to as well, and his scraggly beard gave his face a sickly,
sullen expression.

César Santiago seemed to be in greater harmony with the element he found himself moving in; he had taken on an air of irritation, of acceptance of certain facts that were not, in his
opinion, modifiable, but that he would try to the best of his abilities to adapt to his own purposes.

"Ingeniero, why all the arguments with Winiktón?"

Fernando and the Indian became entangled in disputes on any
subject whatsoever. They never agreed.

Ulloa clasped his hands together nervously.

"He must understand that the only thing we are achieving with
this senseless coming and going is to weaken our forces and give
the people of Ciudad Real time to organize and strike against us."

"Winiktón is an Indian, ingeniero. And all those who follow
him are Indians. Neither he nor the others understand. Even if
you give them the most satisfactory reasons and explain everything in the most minute detail. You're just wasting your time."

"So I'm supposed to let them pick us up and carry us from
one end of the highlands to the other?"

"They have picked us up and carried us; they'll keep on picking
us up and carrying us as long as they can. As long as the Coletos
haven't killed us."

Santiago's statement was so obvious that the other man had no
reply.

"There's no point in cursing fate, but it was a mistake not to
have taken control from the beginning. With orders. But you
wanted to treat them as equals."

How many times had Ulloa reproached himself for this? At
first he defended himself on the basis of his belief that no man is
superior to another. But now, with the results of his stance before
his eyes, he couldn't help but recognize that César was right, and
he had been mistaken. Moreover, he knew it was no longer the
moment, it was no longer even possible to make any attempt to
exercise the authority he had so mindlessly and so hastily discarded.

"At this point, ingeniero, I would advise you to be prudent.
Winiktón is no longer eating out of your hand, and that's natural,

since at every opportunity that has arisen you have opposed the
desires he shares with those who follow him."

"But what are those desires?"

"There aren't many: robbery, murder. It's a release for them;
afterward they can sleep peacefully."

"But that wasn't the point. . . ."

"No one remembers what the point was any more."

"I do: to strike out against Ciudad Real and beat the ranchers.
When we left the church of San Juan, the night of Good Friday,
there were a lot of us and we had courage and impetus. We would
have triumphed."

"You really believed the Chamulas were capable of defying
their patróns?"

"I thought they were capable of anything when they crucified
the boy."

It repelled him to allude to that. He hadn't dared prevent it—
more out of fascination than out of fear. And he stayed until the
end of the ceremony, mute and paralyzed. He let himself be carried away by the same impulse that flung the others against their
oppressors. But later, when he became fully conscious that this
impulse was the blood of a victim, he was filled with horror. He
shared his misgivings with Santiago, and then did not conceal
them from Pedro and the other caudillos. He remembered the
murmurs of surprise, shock and indignation that his words provoked. And the silence that grew up around him. A silence sometimes broken by Winiktón who argued with him over any
triviality. Neither Domingo nor his death were ever mentioned
again. Until now, when Fernando was invoking them as winning
cards. The incongruence of his conduct made him pause for an
instant; he wanted to feel ashamed but couldn't. None of the recent events could be understood rationally or assessed morally.
He was revolving in an orbit that was alien to his most intimate
convictions, his most deeply rooted habits. He did not recognize
himself. He was part of the mechanism of an unintelligible world.

"The Chamulas rose up to come to us from the most distant
villages. Was it so absurd to imagine that an upheaval like that
would lead to something more than a kind of ambulatory delirium?"

"That the movement had a goal, you mean? And that the goal

was Ciudad Real? If you were paying any attention to the map, ingeniero, we've never gone in that direction. On the contrary. We chose the paths that would take us away from it, protect us from it. In reality, we started fleeing from the very moment of the crucifixion."

"But why? Who are we fleeing from? They hadn't defeated us even once."

"The Virgen de la Caridad appeared to the Ladinos and stands guard over the town. The Indians don't dare fight her."

"They believe that? That is what's stopping them? Winiktón has never said anything to me about it."

"He doesn't trust you any more."

The answer was simple, irrefutable. Ulloa's first reaction was not bitterness but alarm. But he didn't want to let it show. He didn't trust the others any more, either. None of them. Not even Santiago.

César shook Catalina awake with the tip of his foot and said a few phrases to her in Tzotzil. The woman made an effort to understand and obey the order she was given. She stood up and began a clumsy search of the ground around her. She gave the impression of not knowing very well what she was looking for. She picked up pebbles, looked at them stupidly for long seconds, then let them fall. César, who was following her movements with a mocking gaze, said a word, repeating it many times until Catalina could distinguish, among the enormous, the inexhaustible mass of objects that surrounded her, the only one she was being asked for. And she began to gather up branches and bits of dry wood to revive the fire.

The new fuel crackled tranquilly; hissing flames leaped up. Catalina faded into the darkness.

"And the Coletos? What are they waiting for to put an end to all of us?"

Santiago made a gesture of ignorance, indifference.

"Does it really matter to you whether we're killed by the Coletos or by the Indians?"

"Us? Killed by the Indians?"

"Yes. You and I. They can decide one day that we're a couple of traitors, a couple of Caxláns, after all, and do away with us."

Fernando did not want to believe that this conjecture was viable. But Pedro's gaze, the other men's gazes—evasive, when not openly hostile—destroyed his sense of security.

"And if the other side takes us alive, you can imagine what the consequences will be. They're not going to demote us from the position of leaders of the uprising. And before they can make a more detailed investigation, we'll be shot."

There was a kind of spiteful satisfaction in the way Santiago exhibited the evidence, the hard facts. As if demonstrating Ulloa's own naiveté to him were filling his mouth with a pleasant substance. As if he were unaware that following another man's naiveté was an even more serious mistake, and, ultimately, an even more ridiculous one.

Fernando didn't answer. By a series of chance circumstances—many of them involuntary and none of them, he now understood, valid—he had been caught in a trap. Bemoaning his lot wouldn't solve anything. The urgent thing was to find some way out. Because there must be a way out. It wasn't logical for things to end like that.

Must be . . . logical. . . . I'm incorrigible, in spite of it all, Fernando said to himself. And burst out laughing.

CHAPTER XXXVII

THE PALACIO EPISCOPAL was seething with covert agitation. The servants were making an unsuccessful effort to obey two contradictory orders: not to break the silence and repose of the house in which a sick man lay suffering, and to prepare that house to receive distinguished guests. Brief, minor catastrophes erupted (a broken vase, a stumble, a loud ripping) and were quickly brought to an end by the energetic scolding of Doña Cristina or her right hand, Benita.

The cleanliness of all the rooms (even those the guests would not see) was painstaking. And the consultations on the most appropriate dishes to serve for dinner were prolonged. But fruitful. When the day and the hour arrived, everything flowed with perfect ease.

Padre Balcázar (who would do the honors of the master of the house, since His Excellency's age and illness made him unable to play the role of host) and other lesser members of the clergy went out to meet the commission. At its head came the governor of the state and Leonardo Cifuentes. Surrounding them and striving to seem close and intimate were the ranchers from the oldest families, the merchants whose capital was most unencumbered, the professionals whose prestige was greatest. And after them, the civil servants of Ciudad Real and Tuxtla, the train on power's robe.

The salutations—which began at the doorway and concluded in the parlor—were less ceremonious than those the Coletos were used to and more ceremonious than the governor could bear.

They took their seats, not without disputing, with simulated courtesy, the privileged spots. When all of them had made themselves comfortable, a kind of timidity overcame them. Convulsive coughs and clearings of the throat were heard. But not a word. Until Leonardo spoke.

"Why are the decorations still in storage? It's all over now."

He indicated the bare walls whose discolorations marked absent crucifixes, mirrors and paintings.

"His Excellency is aware of that. But in old age we repent of the errors of our conduct and sprinkle ashes on our heads; we become austere."

Padre Balcázar employed the fictive plural which the great reserve for themselves.

"But what happened to the things?"

"They were put away. Though Don Alfonso believes they were sold. He thinks they could be sold, that they were his own property and not the Palacio's. He believes that the money from the sale is being used to attend to the needy."

"And why is he being deceived?"

It was the direct, brutal voice of the governor. Padre Balcázar smiled smoothly.

"You will understand, Excelencia, when you see Don Alfonso."

The Coletos exchanged knowing glances and made signs of approval.

"But before that we want to take advantage of this occasion, which may not arise again, to thank you for having honored us at last with your visit. At last, after we had entreated you to come so many times and with such urgency."

Padre Balcázar had placed such an obvious dose of reproach in his welcome that the governor felt the dignity of his position to be wounded and it was impossible for him to feign an apology.

"I don't know what you needed me for. Everything is as it should be."

"Now it is, Excelencia, now it is. But we have been sorely tried. We have been on the verge of. . . ."

"Of what?"

It was one of the civil servants from Tuxtla. With his boss's bad manners, but without his rank.

"Of perishing at the hands of the Indians."

"In the tour I have been making of the state, on which your town is neither the only nor the principal stop, I am particularly concerned with finding out what state of mind the Indians are in, whether they are calm or agitated. With my own eyes, therefore, I have been witness that the Chamulas are obeying the laws and are not resorting to violence to stand up to those who are riding roughshod over their belongings and their persons."

Another civil servant, who must not have been as insignificant if he allowed himself to make such a comment, said, "Everywhere we hear the same complaint: the Ladinos of Ciudad Real are stealing from them and killing them."

"There are towns, even towns of some prominence, abandoned as if a plague had struck them."

"They were decimated by epidemics, señor Gobernador. But we're not the ones who should be accused of that—it's the filth they wallow in."

"Yes, it's true; they are dirty. We saw dried blood in the empty huts."

"How revolting!"

"And the bones of women, children, even men were scattered across the countryside, picked clean by animals."

"That shows you, señor Gobernador, the seriousness of the situation we found ourselves endangered by. Vigorous measures had to be taken. First to defend ourselves, then to teach our enemies a lesson."

"We were without defenses, Excelencia. Our garrison is manned for times of peace."

"And the volunteers from Guatemala and Comitán?"

"We will never be able to thank our neighbors enough for their good intentions, for their demonstration of friendship. But the men they sent were few in number and were not fighting men."

"If they had been, we wouldn't have begged you so desperately, Excelencia. Each time we sent a letter, a telegram, or one of us went to Tuxtla to ask for the favor of a meeting, we never failed to consider the immense burden of work that you bear and the importance of the affairs you deal with. Beside that, what could we mean to you?"

"But our situation did not allow for any delay. . . ."

"We were between the sword and the wall."

"And when I do come here, I find that you have the sword in your hand and the wall has disappeared."

"We would have wanted to owe our salvation to you, Excelencia, to the government over which you so worthily preside."

"But even though it hasn't turned out that way, because circumstances did not allow it to, nevertheless we feel the same gratitude for your will to listen to us, your desire to examine the facts yourself, at first hand."

"And since we are speaking of gratitude, it is fitting that we should inform the governor of the name of the man to whom we owe the order he has found re-established."

"I've heard praises for Leonardo Cifuentes on everyone's lips."

Leonardo did not want and did not know how to feign modesty. Moreover, the subject interested him passionately.

"Times like those we have just passed through in Ciudad Real make a man discover his true capacities. I wanted to defend myself—who doesn't?—and to defend my interests. I thought of each one of the gentlemen here as if he were myself. For that reason I accepted the title they chose to honor me with."

"Chief of Operations."

"Only temporarily, señor Gobernador. While the state of emergency lasted. Or as long as the authorities under whose jurisdiction it fell did not take charge of the matter. At this point, I no longer bear that title or any other."

"That won't last long, Cifuentes. Your fellow townsmen have decided, and have informed me of their decision, to launch your candidacy for the Federal Congress."

Leonardo reddened with satisfaction. He hoped the others would interpret the flush as a sign of surprise.

"I don't know if I'll be able to serve them if they uproot me from the only place I know well and take me away from the people to whom I am bound by so many ties."

"You'll make the sacrifice, Leonardo; you'll make the sacrifice."

The women entered with trays of refreshments and platters of sweets. There was a pause while the guests helped themselves.

"Leonardo has the support not only of the respectable people of Ciudad Real but also of the common people. Wherever he goes, he is greeted affectionately, applauded."

"But that alone is not enough to meet the criteria of the Party's leaders."

"What party do you belong to, Leonardo?"

"Your question offends me, señor Gobernador. What party could I belong to? The official party."

"The requirements are minimal. They'll ask about your background, they'll request certain information. They'll want to know everything related to the Chamula uprising led by Winiktón."

"Winiktón wasn't responsible. He's only an Indian."

"Who, then?"

"Fernando Ulloa. He was the one who goaded the Chamulas on with his ranting, then acted as their caudillo."

"Do you have any proof of this?"

"We wouldn't be talking if we couldn't prove it. It's a serious accusation."

"Ulloa was with the Indians until he saw he was lost and wanted to negotiate with us."

"Actually, he wanted to put a price on his surrender."

"An unacceptable price: complete amnesty."

"He thought he was very smart. But when we saw him arriving at the appointed place on his own, we knew that either Ulloa had betrayed the Indians, and in that case his promises were no longer worth anything, or the Indians had dispersed and were no longer a threat. So we took him prisoner."

"We interrogated him and he described the Indians' weapons, positions, and plans in detail."

"Was a written record made of this?"

"Yes."

"Signed by Ulloa?"

"Yes."

"Thanks to that we became aware of the extent of the danger we were in. And of the measures that would best enable us to ward it off."

"Those measures were the directives issued by Leonardo Cifuentes?"

"Among other things."

"They are very harsh. If they had been carried out to the letter not a single Chamula would be left alive."

"Señor Gobernador, these things are like bargaining in the market. You ask for twice as much so the other will offer you a quarter of that and in the end you settle for half."

"You were counting on a lack of zeal among those who carried out the mandate, then."

"And on their lesser numbers and the disadvantage of operating on enemy territory."

"You must be pleased with the results."

"There is order. There is peace. You yourself said so."

"If peace and order are being maintained, what is there to complain about?"

"There will certainly be no more disturbances. The cause has disappeared, hasn't it?—Ulloa."

"Another man may come to take his place."

"He'll take care to be more prudent. He'll be told about his predecessor's fate."

"It was unfortunate, wasn't it? When we were considering his case, we decided that since he had been a federal employee before launching the uprising the matter did not fall under our jurisdiction."

"He had to be sent to Mexico."

"Where there is no death penalty, as there is in Chiapas."

"The utmost precautions had to be taken for the journey. On the chance that Ulloa would try to escape. . . ."

"If he had tried to escape there wouldn't have been anything to do but shoot him in the back. . . ."

". . . but also to protect him from the common people, señor Gobernador."

"The common people were outraged. They surrounded the jail day and night, they took turns standing watch."

"When they realized Ulloa was being taken to Mexico, they revolted and took justice into their own hands."

"No one defended him?"

"Who was going to defend him? Ulloa's guards were Coletos, too."

And that justified everything. At least in the minds of the gentlemen who were present. The governor had nothing to say in reply and all of them fell silent. The tinkling of spoons against glasses and glasses against plates, the measured swallowing of liquids could be heard. . . .

"Will the bishop see me?"

Padre Balcázar gazed at the governor with a benevolence that was not without compassion. What carelessness in selecting the proper turn of phrase!

"We have been taking advantage of your time, Excelencia. I will go and announce you right now."

While the priest was leaving the room, the governor turned to Leonardo Cifuentes and patted his thigh with rough familiarity.

"So, this is the fighting cock."

A chorus of exclamations drowned out Cifuentes' faint protest.

"Tireless. . . ."

"Right on target. . . ."

"Bold. . . ."

"Decisive. . . ."

"Smart. . . ."

"A true hero."

Padre Balcázar opened the door that led to His Excellency's rooms.

"Don Alfonso awaits you, Excelencia."

The governor stood up and a few others followed him; he signalled them to stop.

"I want to speak to him alone."

As he left the room, Padre Balcázar went back to his seat.

"It is a comfort," he said, "to see how the oppositions between the earthly powers and the spiritual authority amount to nothing and how all is reconciled when common goals are pursued: justice, order and peace."

CHAPTER XXXVIII

THE GOVERNOR MOVED cautiously. From daylight, he had passed into an almost total darkness and from a soft rug onto cold, uneven and echoing tiles.

An old man's voice, halting and oddly creaky as if from lack of use, said, "Doña Cristina, someone I need to see has come."

A shadow, a woman's shape, crossed the room and stopped in front of the window. Slowly the curtains were pulled back to let in some light.

The image that appeared before the governor's eyes startled him. On a crude wooden platform lay Don Alfonso Cañaveral. Wearing a homespun habit, he was rigid, with his hands crossed over his chest like a corpse. And he kept his eyes closed.

"Kneel."

Doña Cristina's order—whispered but clearly not subject to appeal—was obeyed.

"Kiss his hand."

The governor looked for the finger where the ring ought to be. But the hands were bare of gems. He turned a questioning face towards the housekeeper.

Doña Cristina shrugged. What importance could a piece of jewelry have? Even without it, Don Alfonso was still the bishop of Chiapas.

"Like this."

Once the gesture of submission had taken place, Doña Cristina pointed to an uncomfortable, vertical chair, made of planks.

"You can sit down now."

The distance between the interlocutors would facilitate their dialogue. Doña Cristina gazed appreciatively at the setting and appeared to approve of it.

"Can I not bring you anything, Monseñor?"

Don Alfonso shook his head; he did not open his lips until the sound of the closing door told him they were alone.

"You will forgive me for not receiving you as you deserve."

"On the contrary. My presence here is a great imposition on you."

"It's an imposition that benefits the shepherds of the flock."

"How?"

"Those who saw you (and everyone saw you) going toward the Palacio Episcopal and coming to my room will be astounded. Aren't we living in the time of a new Nero? Weren't you expected to make me appear before you, by force if necessary?"

"Why would I behave so disrespectfully? I have some consideration for your white hair."

"And you've always been tolerant, too. More than we deserved. But those details escape the people. They see nothing but your walk to the Bishopric and your visit and they say the years of the fat cows have returned for the Church. And those who were kept at the threshold by respect for human affairs go in at last, and those who were lukewarm become fervent, and religious devotion spreads and increases. And all of them pay tithes and offerings."

The governor was dumbfounded, while Don Alfonso smiled with a sad twist of his lips.

"How unfitting it is for a high dignitary such as myself to refer to such sordid, such basely material matters as money. No, I haven't forgotten what Our Lord Jesus Christ preached: 'Man does not live by bread alone.' But I say unto you: he lives by bread, too. And lately there have been times when we were lacking it."

"Why?"

"Haven't those hypocrites out there told you that we were in a state of siege for months, many months? Naturally, food became scarce."

"When they were going hungry they must have cursed me for not sending help."

"Perhaps."

"Do you think they were right to do so?"

"My perspective on events is different. In any case, God could have chosen to make you an instrument of his punishment."

"I am not a Catholic, señor."

"Monseñor."

"I am not a Catholic, Monseñor. Yet I still have some regard for priests. And what I would not confide to any other man. . . ."

"You have come to confess to me."

"I want your opinion. I'm fed up with the barbed remarks and indirect allusions of your townsmen."

"I am not a Coleto, Excelencia."

"Señor Gobernador."

"I am not a Coleto, señor Gobernador. What do they accuse you of?"

"Of having proceeded with negligence and bad faith during the Chamula rebellion."

"Do you acknowledge that to be true?"

"It's true that I didn't send troops as quickly as they wanted and in the numbers they asked for. But I had reasons which I considered valid at the time."

"What reasons."

"Every day, several times a day, I received letters postmarked in Ciudad Real. Do you want to see them? I brought them with me?"

Don Alfonso covered his eyes with his hands as if to reinforce his blindness.

"No."

"In those letters, I was assured that the situation was not serious, that the ranchers had armed their own peons to simulate a nonexistent danger."

"For what purpose?"

"For the purpose of concretely demonstrating to my government and the federal government that the laws on the redistribution of land could not be put into practice in Chiapas without the risk of bloodshed."

"And what did you do?"

"I conducted my own investigation. I sent people in whose good judgment and prudence I believed. And they came back to tell me that in Ciudad Real the atmosphere was more festive than fearful. That under the pretext of the Indian uprising, daily gatherings were being held and morals were becoming lax."

"Did that seem unlikely to you?"

"No. I'm from a town where people are bored, too."

"And the Indians. They didn't pose any threat?"

"There wasn't a trace of them in the area surrounding the town. The villages were and still are abandoned."

"So?"

"How could I justify to my superiors a decision to provide the ranchers with the means to make a mockery of the application of the law? They would say I had been bribed."

"Are you very protective of your reputation?"

"I have a future, Monseñor."

"Under the circumstances, señor Gobernador, you proceeded with good judgment."

That sentence appeared to be the end of the consultation. Don Alfonso could no longer conceal his exhaustion or his lack of interest in the subject. But the governor was not yet satisfied.

"My informers also determined something that didn't bother me before, but that worries me now: the names of the people who signed the letters were false. And the addresses, as well."

"Why does that surprise you? Aren't you from a town where anonymous letters are written, too?"

"Yes, but. . . ."

"But you don't like having been deceived. And yet how very easily you excuse yourself for having made a mistake, having taken affliction for festivity, anxiety for happiness. A mistake that has cost so much suffering, so many losses, so many lives."

"What happened can no longer be remedied, Monseñor. And I'm glad my hands are clean of the crimes that have been committed here."

"You could have prevented them."

"The ranchers wanted to use the army as an executioner, not as a defender."

"If you're so sure of that, I don't understand why you come to speak to me."

"Since my arrival in Ciudad Real, I've been receiving letters again."

"Writing! The mania of lonely women."

"This time they make reference to a very serious matter which I must confirm. Because it has to do with the man who, sooner or later, will be my successor."

"Leonardo Cifuentes?"

"They say that from the beginning he has been playing a dirty game. They say he was in league with Fernando Ulloa through a woman known as La Alazana."

"That woman no longer lives in Ciudad Real."

"Could you swear to that, Monseñor? The letters say she never left the city. That Leonardo faked her journey and arranged for a hiding place where he is keeping her shut away. That he ordered Ulloa killed so he could be with her."

There was a pause. A long pause. Charged with unspoken words.

"Before you go, señor Gobernador, I must beg you to close the curtains. I cannot bear the light."

"I'm not leaving without an answer, Monseñor."

"Why do you suppose I can give you an answer? What do you want me to answer? That it isn't true? I don't know. That it isn't possible? Everything is possible."

"How did the person who made the accusation know about it?"

"When someone is alone, fundamentally alone, and for a very long time, they can guess other people's intentions even before those intentions have taken shape in actions; they can feel other people's deliria and give a name and a form to the creatures others dream of unknowingly."

Don Alfonso's hands were hanging limply from the edges of the platform. He was pale and his breathing was labored.

"That girl has always been alone."

The governor bent toward the bishop, anxious not to miss even the slightest inflection of his voice.

"What girl?"

"The one who writes."

"Do you know who it is?"

"It's someone who has as much trust in priests as you do. And I'm not going to let her down. Because it is enough already with Manuel Mandujano . . . and so many others."

The governor rose to his feet and began closing the curtains.

"Go in peace, hijo mío. Let the dead bury their dead."

The governor groped his way out. At his back, he heard the deep sigh of someone who is at rest.

"Ah, at last! Darkness again!"

CHAPTER XXXIX

JOBEL RISES UP once more, walled by injustice, a city that can only be entered through the portal designated for the herds.

The valley of Chamula—once a place of mists and brooks—is now dense with smoke. What once was village, sown field, town is now smoke. Smoke: scorched earth, tainted air, ruin and annihilation.

The tribe of the Tzotzils wanders, scattered and persecuted. The punishment of the Caxláns reaches them even in the most remote spots, the most hidden corners. And even further than the Caxlán can reach come hunger, fear, cold, madness.

The rebels perished at the hands of their enemies and the meek were taken captive by the victors, who raped the women and put the mark of slavery on the rumps of newborn babies.

The survivors climbed to the highest slopes where the air they breath is sharp-edged, where the Caxlán's heart, though it is so hard, bursts.

The survivors do not know how many of them there are. They never gather together, neither around a fire nor around food nor around the old people who give counsel nor around the long-memoried ones who recount. They hide from each other so as not to have to share the prey that will sustain them, the refuge that will shelter them.

Alone, these men forget their lineage, the dignity they once displayed, their past. They learn the sciences of furtiveness from fearful animals. They slip across the dry leaves without causing the least sound, they sidestep the trap, they play dead at the menace of danger.

Naked, barely covered with rags or loincloths of half-tanned leather, they have abolished the time that once separated them from bygone ages. Neither before nor today exists. It is always. Always defeat and persecution. Always the master who is not appeased by the most abject obedience or the most servile humility. Always the whip falling onto the submissive back. Always the knife lopping off the gesture of rebellion.

In this eternity, the tribe's destiny is fulfilled. Because it is the will of the gods that the Tzotzils remain. In caves and in the open air, at night and under the blazing sun, females and males join together to perpetuate themselves. The fecundated woman walks slowly and hides near running water when the time comes to give birth.

The farmer, who kept the seed within his closed fist, lets it fall in the propitious place. He does not wait for the harvest. Someone else must come after him who will gather it in.

The weaver woman spins the tuft of wool. The work, whose design was taught to her parents by her grandparents, progresses.

Between skilled fingers, clay takes on the shape of a utensil and wood is smoothed down.

The shepherd, the midwife, the potter, repeat their trades as the earth repeats the cycle of the seasons, as the stars revisit the points of their orbit. Out of submission to the law, out of fidelity.

The soothsayer is also working. He recognizes his equals with a single glance, from far away. He exchanges the secret signal with them. And together they set out to give the gods what they clamor for: prayer, which their servants only succeed in stammering, and ceremony, which they guess at, invent, remember.

The search for darkness leads them to the caves. They chase away the predatory animals; they adorn the caves with forest branches; they fill their enclosures with the beneficial emanations of pom. And there they congregate, on certain nights when the coyote howls in desperation and the moon rises pale and bloodless.

In the center of the cave, in the center of the circle formed by those congregated there, lies the ark. They have defended it from the greed of marauders and more than one man has died before he would allow it to be seized. They shield it from inclement weather as if it were a sickly infant; they protect it from carelessness; they surround it with devotion and reverence. Because in the ark, the divine word reposes. There the testament of those who were and the prophecy of those who are to come is kept. There is the record of what the dark powers dictated to their slaves. There radiates the promise that brings comfort in days of uncertainty and adversity. There is the substance the soul eats in order to live. The pact.

On solemn occasions (dates which the profane would never succeed in determining), the ark is opened and what it contains is manifested before the elect.

They kneel, faces hidden in their hands, wailing, praying, while the leader among them officiates.

The torches of ocote pine splutter as they illuminate the instant when the lock yields and the lid of the ark opens. A bundle appears. Each one, in order of rank, takes a turn untying a knot, unwrapping the cloths. Meanwhile the flask of liquor sates the thirst of expectation. It is emptied, filled, emptied again.

At last the book appears. There are only a few pages. A few pages, but nevertheless the bridge between humanity and the divine.

The book is exposed to their adoration. The leader raises it between his hands with exquisite care. He brings it close to the faces of those who are present so they may testify to its existence and make it known to those who do not have access to the ceremony.

They are the witnesses that the book exists. That it has not been lost in the vicissitudes of flight or in disaster's ransacking. It exists, so that hope will not grow faint. It exists.

Now the eyes that brim with tears can close forever. What they have seen is their salvation.

And there remains exposed, like a communion wafer, the page that an unknown hero rescued from the catastrophe. The first page, on which a title flames:

Military Directives.

CHAPTER XL

STRETCHED OUT ON her bed, her face turned toward the wall, Idolina lies awake.

It's the same night or day. At all hours the churchbells echo, along with the confused murmur in the street, the sounds of the house.

The sound of voices chattering in the parlor, arguing, remembering. The sound of laughter that bursts out in the galleries, whispers of complicity. The sound of orders the servants hurry to carry out.

The sound of footsteps. Slow, when the person walking by is important and is being awaited and is received with jubilation. The diligent steps of the person who wants to curry favor and doesn't want to lose his turn. The light steps of young girls.

Idolina wants to recognize among the voices, among the footsteps, her mother's. Not to call out to her (from her remote confinement no one would hear her) but to feel betrayed.

Does Isabel attend the gatherings Leonardo holds? Does she do the honors as lady of the house? Does she share in the triumph? Is she proud of the homages he is paid?

Sometimes Idolina thinks she can make out her voice among those of strangers. But then she doubts, at an inflection she doesn't recognize, a new tone. The person speaking is a secure and satisfied woman. A happy woman.

Idolina drowns out the echoes by burying her head in the pillows. She shuts her eyes to make the world disappear once and for all.

And suddenly the sound is gone. The house is left unvisited, without guests, without a master. Idolina refuses to find out what has happened. Whether Leonardo and Isabel left. Whether they are going somewhere together, and where. Whether they will come back.

The sound is gone. Idolina hears nothing any more but her own delirium. What an uproar of battle! Cannon and rifles fire, the slingshot responds, the taut bow whistles. The one who hurls himself on his enemy screams; the one who collapses moans. The one who is dying moans. And the one who dies dies without a lament.

The sound is gone. There's nothing left but the insomniac throbbing of the crickets. Crickets in the garden, the courtyard, the back courtyard. Close, domestic, identifiable. And those out in the country. Between all of them they raise, little by little, a wall that will keep out the thing that lies waiting for the tiniest crack of silence to steal through. The thing that is feared by those who are sleepless, those who walk through the night, those who are lonely, children. That thing. The voice of the dead.

Suddenly the wall caves in. And the mouths suffocated with earth speak.

Catalina repeats a senseless litany. Fernando says the word law and deaf ears reject it and return it to him transformed into a sneer. "The one born at the eclipse" cries out as the Cross is crucifying him. Winiktón harangues an army of shadows. Xaw Ramírez Paciencia stammers out the false testimony that will condemn his people. Julia laughs. Doña Mercedes Solórzano mumbles a secret. Marcela and Lorenzo, the martoma and his wife, Felipa. And others who had no name or face. And others who fell along the roadways. And others who were abandoned. And others who dragged themselves along until they met their end.

Idolina listens for an instant, seized with terror. And she cries out as if she, too, were being crucified, and Teresa Entzín López, her nana, runs to her side, solicitous, and takes her in her lap and strokes her hair and tells her a story to soothe her and put her to sleep.

"In other times—you weren't born yet, child, and maybe I wasn't born yet either—there was in my village, the old people say, an ilol of great power.

"With one glance at a horizon she knew if it brought prosperity or scarcity; she recognized destiny in the appearance of men and expelled disease from the bodies of those who suffered from it.

"To everyone's great fright, this ilol had a son made of stone. He spoke as people of reason speak; he gave counsel to the pilgrims who came to witness this prodigy; he made cripples walk and abundant harvests pour out from the cornfields.

"The fame of the ilol and her son spread in all directions throughout the highlands. Her name was repeated in Huistán and in Tenejapa, in Mitontic and in Oxchuc, in Zinacantan and in Pantelhó.

"The stories came to be told even in Ciudad Real itself. The lords who dwell there were moved to amazement, but they did not consider it prudent to show their approval as long as they were not certain of the truth.

"So they sent as their emissary a servant of God. He went along the roads asking where the ilol's stone son had his lodging.

"He found them both at last in a cave. They were richly dressed and bejeweled and he asked them, in the name of the lords of Ciudad Real, to consent to accompany him and be known and examined.

"This was agreed upon and the ilol and her son arrived in Ciudad Real and were received with honors by its principal men. And after the festivities and the banquets, the testing commenced.

"The judges asked the ilol what the source of her powers was and she said she had received them not from the Holy Spirit, but from San Jerónimo, he of the tiger in his belly, the secret patrón of brujos. And at each answer that came from her mouth a blazing light as if from a bonfire could be seen.

"After that, the caretakers made her pass through many mansions. She came out intact from the mansion of wild beasts, and she was not harmed by cold nor burned by fire, nor was she troubled by darkness. And finally she broke the chains that bound her and the walls that held her in and returned to her village.

"Along with her went her son and the two of them occupied the place of command before the face of the tribe. They received offerings that Indians and Caxláns set at their feet and in their fists they grasped the reins of the days.

"But as their authority grew their pride grew also. It was no longer enough to offer them the choicest lambs, the first fruits of the harvests or the most beautiful flowers. The ilol had grown taciturn. She and her son were hungry and they needed to eat every family's first-born son.

"The tribe, which feared their sorcery, handed over a victim who was devoured. But then they demanded another and another and still another. They were insatiable. The Tzotzils walked about in disarray and did not know what to do. Until the elders went to complain to the lords of Ciudad Real.

" 'What are we to do with these devourers of human flesh?' they asked. And the lords did not wish to rush into violence, but called for harmony. So a messenger went off, who never returned because the ilol and her stone son sacrificed him. And they sacrificed the next one, too, and the last one.

"Then the lords of Ciudad Real and the elders said: there is nothing left for us but force.

"They armed themselves as best they could and marched together, followed by the bulk of the Indians, in pursuit of the ilol and her stone son.

"How they made fun of their enemies, those two! They appeared in two places at the same time and set up effigies of themselves so their opponents would exhaust their energy and their rage on them. And the ilol and her son laughed at these tricks and exposed themselves to bullets without fear. Because the bullets rebounded off of them to bring death to those who had fired the guns.

"What must we do to free ourselves of these demons? everyone wondered in anguish. And an old sacristan advised them, 'Let us tell this woman that her stone son is cold and he must be wrapped up so he can be warm. And then we will give her a shawl woven by the brujos of Guatemala so that it will fetter his might.'

"As soon as he was wrapped in the shawl, the stone son could no longer move or live. In despair the ilol broke her head open against the slowly disintegrating matter.

"Their corpses strewed pestilence and harm to all the winds. Animals died, fields dried up, men fell as if struck by lightning.

"Out of ten families, one was saved; out of ten villages, none was completely preserved.

"The lords of Ciudad Real observed nine days of mourning and ordered the tribe's survivors to cleanse themselves of their guilt by acts of penitence. Those same lords furnished the guilty with the instruments for inflicting the punishment.

"The name of that ilol, which was once spoken by all with

hope and reverence, has been outlawed. The man who feels himself stung by the temptation to speak it spits and the saliva helps to erase her image, to erase her memory."

The nana was silent. Gently she set the sleeping girl's head on the pillow.

Silently she went back to her place.

It was still a long time before dawn.

AFTERWORD

"Writing has been, more than anything, explaining to myself the things I don't understand."
—Rosario Castellanos

"Love is not consolation. Love is light."
—Simone Weil

THE TERM THAT HAS come into the English language as "magic realism" (in Spanish, *lo real maravilloso*), was coined by the great Cuban writer Alejo Carpentier, who argued in a 1949 essay that European ideas of the fantastic had faded to an exhausted reworking of a few familiar themes and twists, while the reality of America held out wonders still far beyond anything dreamed of by Europe. The essay's final question—"What is the history of America but a chronicle of this marvelous reality?" rang out as a challenge to all Latin American writers.

By the time Carpentier's essay appeared, the technique of magic realism had already been pioneered by, among others, the Guatemalan novelist Miguel Angel Asturias, winner of the 1967 Nobel Prize. In 1925, at the beginning of his literary career, Asturias translated the sacred Maya text known as the Popol Vuh, or Book of the Council, into Spanish. Maya myth became one of the wellsprings of Asturias's vision, yielding a fantastical dimension of existence where the laws of the material world no longer hold sway, yet which is portrayed in realist detail, interwoven with depictions of ordinary life and human beings.

Asturias was Rosario Castellanos's friend ("What tiny little Mayan hands you have!" Elena Poniatowska once overheard him exclaim to her). She was very much aware of the technique he had devised to incorporate the world view of a pre-Columbian culture into a modern European literary genre. After all, she faced the same challenge in writing about the Maya of Chiapas, which shares more than just a border with Guatemala. She had to be aware, as well, of the ascendency of magic realism in Latin American literature, which would reach its apex with the 1967 publication of Gabriel García Márquez's dazzling *One Hundred Years of Solitude*.

Though Asturias's influence is detectable in the detached, hyperreal, and almost balletic depiction of violence in Castellanos's 1962 novel *The Book of Lamentations*, (the machetes that whir through the air as if of their own accord), her book can be read as a virtual manifesto against magic realism. The only magic in the unrelieved starkness of its landscape is the all too familiar spell of one human being's power over another. In his great poem, *El Desdichado*, the French poet Gerard de Nerval speaks of "the black sun of melancholy." *The Book of Lamentations* was written by the cold light of that sun, and emphatically not out of Carpentier's vision of the marvels of American reality, though the historical events it is based on are as staggering as any of the wonders Carpentier enumerates.

Its insistence on the minute specifics of a single area places *The Book of Lamentations*, instead, in the tradition of intensive regionalism that characterizes the nineteenth-century Latin American novel. This was the very literary tradition the Latin American writers of the generation that came to be known as the "Boom" had vehemently rejected. Castellanos, in turn, repudiated the trappings of magic realism (the blood that flows from the dead body through the village to stop at the murderer's door, the human beings who transform themselves into animals at will) and of modernist narrative experimentation—the novel with chapters in a seemingly random arrangement, or that is a single endless paragraph—that were the predominant features of the Latin American novel of her time. Instead, she wrote what struck many as a curiously antiquated document—an anachronism.

The rejection of magic realist forms of "wonder" does not mean that myth itself is absent in *The Book of Lamentations*. The narrative develops out of a Tzotzil myth of the origin of the church of San Juan Chamula, a collective, inherited myth engraved in the portals of the church, and ends in a mythical retelling of the events of the novel itself (with echoes of the Popol Vuh), invented by the Chamula nursemaid Teresa Entzín López to soothe Idolina, her insomniac charge, and put her to sleep. This brief, final myth places the novel's events in an enigmatic light: in Teresa's tale, Indians and Ladinos are not pitted against each other, but join forces against a nameless ilol and her stone son (though in the end, it is the Indians who are punished—who punish themselves—for the ilol's excesses). The first and most immediate function of this final myth is to mold catastrophic events into a recognizable, intelligible form: a story with a clearly demarcated beginning and end, connected by a simple sequence of actions, bearing a resemblance to a very familiar and much older story. Recast in this way, the events become bearable, even soothing, and thus forgettable. The final sentence of Teresa's myth speaks of the Indians' desire to eradicate the ilol from their collective memory.

As an antidote to this sedative, corrosive power it fears in myth, the novel offers its own rigorous, pitiless lucidity. Its plot is loosely based on a singularly resonant historic episode—the crucifixion of one of their own by a group of Tzotzil rebels in Chiapas in 1867, who are thought to have believed that by creating their own Christ they would achieve the same power as their Christian oppressors. Though the historic accuracy of the story has in recent years been disputed by U.S. anthropologist Jan Rus, it is widely believed in Mexico and has taken on a life of its own. In addition to Castellanos's book, the story has inspired at least two other novels: Flavio Paniagua's *Florinda* (San Cristóbal, 1889) and Carter Wilson's *A Green Tree and a Dry Tree* (New York, 1972). And who knows if some echo of it didn't find its way into Jorge Luis Borges' searing paradox, "El Evangelio según Marcos" (The Gospel According to Mark) (Buenos Aires, 1970). In any case, the clarity Castellanos sought is something entirely different from factual accuracy. The events of 1867 are transposed in time to the 1930s and altered in many other ways as well. Castellanos began by researching the history, but then, she told an interviewer in 1965, "As I progressed, I realized that historical logic is absolutely different from literary logic. However much I wanted to, I could not be faithful to history. Little by little, I abandoned the real event."

Instead, her method was to reimagine each element of the story on its own terms and within the echo chamber of everything she brought to the writing of the novel. She then juxtaposed the various strands in all their radical incompatibility. "When they are written out, incidents adjoin one another so closely that their proximity looks like coherence," the reader of *The Book of Lamentations* is cautioned. Without calling attention to its resistance by using experimental narrative techniques ("The story is, in and of itself, complex and confused enough not to add further architectonic and stylistic difficulties," Castellanos said), *The Book of Lamentations* tacitly combats this illusion of coherence, representing an infinitely-faceted event in such a way as to include the silent abysses that gape between each participant's understanding of it.

Like the nineteenth-century Latin American novels of the tradition that it recuperates and transforms, this book is concerned, above all, with synthesis. Unlike those novels, *Lamentations* aims not to reassure its readers of the peaceful fusion of all the disparate elements of their nation but to depict the shattering absence of any such fusion. As it rejects a narrative synthesis that would gather different viewpoints into a seamless whole, it also rejects the overarching myth of racial and cultural synthesis (of mestizaje and syncretism) that is the foundation of Mexico's national self-image.

The story begins with the rape of Marcela, a Tzotzil girl, by Leonardo Cifuentes, a Caxlán or Spanish-descended landowner (and here it's worth mentioning that when I first visited San Cristóbal in 1990 there were huge graffiti everywhere that said "Stop the rape of indigenous women," which apparently continues to be a favorite local pastime). Likewise, Mexican history begins with the conquest and ravishment of indigenous peoples by European invaders, a violation that gives birth to la raza, the people of modern Mexico. But the mestizaje of Castellanos's novel is a forced and unwilling proximity, without community, without understanding, without fusion. Despised by whites for being an Indian, Domingo, the child born of rape, is rejected by his mother because of the European blood that his curly hair betrays. Later, when the people of Chamula put him to death, the question arises: Does the fact of his Caxlán blood make it easier and more tempting for them to crucify him?

Syncretism, the merging of pre-Columbian religious beliefs with Catholic rituals—another of the pillars of Mexican cultural identity—is viewed with similar suspicion, though in this respect, at least, *The Book of Lamentations* is willing to acknowledge some kind of amalgamation. The Tzotzil religious universe includes the brujos, ilols, and pulsetakers of Maya tradition alongside a panoply of Catholic saints presided over by San Juan. But just as a word that moves from one language into another can take on an entirely different or opposite meaning, the Catholicism practiced by the Tzotziles is something else altogether. Their belief is intense, but very far removed from what their catechizers set out to imbue in them.

Syncretism exists: that much *Lamentations* will grant. But it does not exist as the simple persistence of a few old traditions within a slightly modified Catholicism. It is the new monster that has slouched towards Bethlehem and that has been born. The crucifixion which is the central event of the novel achieves its unendurable power because it takes place in the narrow space where the spheres of Mayan and Catholic belief overlap: human sacrifice. Domingo's death echoes both Christ's solemn, singular sacrifice and the exuberant, kaleidoscopic human sacrifices of the Popol Vuh. In both traditions, sacrifice holds out the promise of overthrowing the constraints of the material world, cheating death, and achieving eternal life.

The hero twins of the Popol Vuh, Hunahpu and Xbalanque, defeat their enemies, the Lords of Xibalba, by voluntarily sacrificing themselves. The Lords of Xibalba have prepared a wide stone oven, and the twins throw themselves into it, headlong. Afterwards, by a plan prearranged between the boys and two seers, their bones are ground up and spilled into the river where they sink to the bottom and the boys become whole again. When the hero twins reappear, they have defeated death. They can kill themselves and come back to life at will, and they cavort about, gleefully killing and resurrecting animal and human sacrificial victims. When the Lords of Xibalba witness this prowess they beg the twins, "Do it to us! Sacrifice us!" and voluntarily submit to what Dennis Tedlock's brilliant translation of the Popol Vuh calls "the heart sacrifice"—the extraction of their living hearts.

Having tricked the Lords of Xibalba into willing their own

death, the hero twins do not, of course, bring them back to life, and so the Xibalbans are vanquished and the twins pass judgment on them by speaking a variant of the lines that Castellanos chose as the epigraph to *The Book of Lamentations*. This episode of the Popol Vuh resonates throughout her book ("I wrote the Popol Vuh," Poniatowska remembers Castellanos joking), but never more strongly than in the passage where the rebelling Indians tell a cunning old Ladino that they have defeated death. At the old man's prompting, one of them volunteers to be shot in the chest to prove it. The old Ladino fires the shot; the Indian dies. The Tzotziles fall for the hero twins' own stratagem, tricked by their own myth. Death cannot be cheated. The laws of the material world are supreme and unalterable.

Its incorporation of the Popol Vuh is, however, the point where the novel's obsession with synthesis can come to seem more affirmative. For even as it resists and argues against the dominant Mexican myths of cultural and racial fusion, *The Book of Lamentations* proposes a syncretism all its own. In 1959, three years before *Lamentations* was published, the woman who joked about having written the Popol Vuh wrote (with, it must be said, mixed results) two lyric dramas, *Salomé* and *Judith*, which recast Old Testament stories in terms of the conflict between Chamula and Ladino in Chiapas. *The Book of Lamentations* is clearly a project along similar lines, except that the story it retells is the Gospel itself.

This gospel according to Chiapas is not some pristine and incorruptible Word of God, but a human, hybrid revelation, shot through with traces, echoes and reflections of other texts and outside forces. There are, first and foremost, the Bible and the Popol Vuh; there is the historical record of the 1867 Chamula uprising and the land redistribution project attempted by Lázaro Cardenas in the 1930s. There is also Emily Bronte's *Wuthering Heights*, echoed in the story of Leonardo Cifuentes' early years and in the novel's clinical dissection of romantic passion. There is the fictionalized autobiography of Castellanos's own earlier novel *Balún-Canán*, which resurfaces in the relationship between the neurotic invalid Idolina and her Tzotzil nana. There is the work of the French philosopher Simone Weil, whose ideas had influenced Castellanos to return to Chiapas to work with Mexico's National Indigenist Institute in the years before she wrote this

novel. And finally, there was the birth, in 1960, of the only sur-
viving child of this woman writer who had quipped to her dis-
sertation defense committee ten years earlier that "Women writers
are writers because they don't have children." (For this book is,
among other things, the story of a woman who quite literally
sacrifices her child to her own ambition.)

This hybridity is soaked into the very fabric of the text, which
is interlaced with Tzotzil words, used casually and without explanation, as a natural part of the bilingual world the novel in-
habits. This bilingualism can be detected even in the cadences of
Castellanos's prose, the preference for three words where one
would do that is typical of Tzotzil phrase-making. In this way,
Castellanos's novel embraces the one thing neither Indian nor Ladino can bear to acknowledge: the fact that the two groups are
inextricably part of each other, mutually interwoven and inter-
dependent, indivisible.

Castellanos's ambition to portray all sides of the cultural divide
between Indian and Ladino has recently met with some criticism
in the United States. Since she was not an Indian herself, the logic
goes (and from a strictly genetic perspective, this is already a dubious proposition where any Mexican is concerned, and particularly one with tiny Mayan hands and a Mayan profile), she had
no right to speak for Indians or represent them and by doing so
was collaborating in the oppression and exploitation of indigenous
peoples. That logic—that no one has the right to speak except as
a representative of their individual gender, class, sexual persuasion,
ethnic background, religion, etc.—presupposes a vision of the
world far blacker than the one depicted here. The one possibility
of redemption this profane gospel holds out can be found in its
own imaginative leap, its will to see reality in its entirety, to overcome the limitations of any individual viewpoint. That such an
achievement can always only be partial does not mean it should
ever be rejected. The complex act of understanding that this book
embodies is the one hope it offers of a real understanding, somewhere, somehow, outside its pages.

For the most part, however, the gospel according to *The Book
of Lamentations* holds out little hope of salvation. Its only god is
force, its only ideology the universal struggle for power. These
are unusual qualities in a work involving a political struggle in

Latin America published only three years after Fidel Castro's triumphant revolution. Its complete rejection of Cold War ideologies is another of the ways in which this novel goes against the grain of its time.

Fernando Ulloa, the reformer sent by the Mexican government to redistribute land, is accused of being a Communist, but his accusers have little idea what the term means: their charge is motivated by Ulloa's assertion that all men are equal. And the categories of subversion and order are hopelessly jumbled: Ulloa is not a guerilla, but a civil servant charged with upholding the law and returning private property to the rightful owners from whom it had been confiscated. From the perspective of the late 1990s, this dismissal of the Cold War mindset seems highly prescient; the battle that rages in this novel is exactly the kind of ethnic conflict that has become all too familiar over the last decade.

The Book of Lamentations turns its back on the ideological hysteria of its time at least partly as a result of the extraordinary impact on Castellanos of the work of Simone Weil, whose 1939 essay, "The Iliad, Poem of Might," is fundamental to an understanding of *The Book of Lamentations*. (To such a degree that certain passages of Castellanos's novel—"the smooth orbit without resistance or objection" in which Leonardo Cifuentes moves, for example—seem to be cited directly from Weil's essay: "He who possesses strength moves in an atmosphere which offers him no resistance.") After serving as a volunteer in the Spanish Civil War, Weil found in the *Iliad* a way of explaining to herself what she saw there: "That might which is wielded by men rules over them," she wrote. "The human soul never ceases to be modified by its encounter with might." And the effect of might on the soul is brutally simple: "Might is that which makes a thing of anybody who comes under its sway. When exercised to the full, it makes a thing of man in the most literal sense, for it makes him a corpse."

In the *Iliad*, according to Weil, "The cold brutality of the facts of war is in no way disguised, because neither victors nor vanquished are either admired, despised or hated." Over the later course of European history, Weil said, the purity of this knowledge was lost or distorted; it became difficult not to believe "first, that degradation is the innate vocation of the unfortunate; second, that a soul may suffer affliction without being marked by it, without changing all consciousness. . . ." Like Castellanos after her, Weil was an acute observer of the ways in which oppression transforms human beings, grinding them down, diminishing them, attenuating their humanity; her argument, in this respect, resonates with Hegel's dialectic of the master and the slave. "On no occasion has the slave a right to express anything if not that which may please the master. This is why, if in so barren a life a capacity to love should be born, this love could only be for the master." This is the love Teresa Entzín López has for Idolina, the only convincing example of love in Castellanos' entire novel.

The miracle of the *Iliad*—a miracle, Weil believed, that barely endured beyond the limits of ancient Greek civilization—was this: "The bitterness of it is spent upon the only true cause of bitterness: the subordination of the human soul to might, which is, be it finally said, to matter."

No political or economic system, however just and equitable, is likely to free us from the dominion of matter. But the fact that Weil's philosophy does not easily lend itself to political application does not render it any less illuminating. And in Castellanos's reading of them, Weil's ideas do not lead to mere fatalism, but are a moral challenge—the only possible moral challenge. Each character in Castellanos's novel, from the most powerful to the most abject, is simultaneously oppressed and oppressing, victim and perpetrator. It is very clear that some groups disproportionately bear the crushing weight of oppression, and it is their tragedy that moves Castellanos to write here. But she refuses to complete the work of oppression by reducing them to no more than the passive victims of might's blind force. Each character wields power and cannot choose not to. Ulloa, who tries to evade the exercise of power out of an idea of democracy, finds that it cannot be evaded, and that in trying to do so he has simply abdicated his responsibility to stave off disaster. Even Cifuentes, whose sway seems virtually uncontested, reaches a point where almost everyone has turned against him and only the arbitrary and unforeseeable course of events saves him. Each character's drama lies essentially in the nature of his or her relationship with the power all of them battle to wield. And the novel's most ambitious, powerful, and devastating character is simultaneously one of its most oppressed, Catalina Díaz Puiljá, an Indian woman.

Catalina Díaz Puiljá takes on the dimensions of a great, tragic character because she makes a gesture—a gesture she was absolutely free not to make. She offers Domingo, the child she has raised since birth, as a sacrificial victim. And the choice destroys her. In the end, crushed under the weight of her own power, her own ambition, she is reduced to little more than an object, alien even to language. "That might which is weilded by men rules over them." Castellanos leaves little doubt that this goes for women, too; she challenges our need to divide the world into easy categories of victim and victimizer. No matter who you are, *Lamentations* works at making you suspicious of the self-congratulatory note that sounds in your voice as you denounce those who oppress others, even as it compels you to denounce them.

The Book of Lamentations can be read purely as a roadmap to the political situation in Chiapas. Those who reread it in the aftermath of the 1994 Zapatista uprising will testify that it provides an excellent guide, down to the uncanny parallels between Subcomandante Marcos, the eloquent Ladino outsider who refuses to be called the Zapatista's leader, and Fernando Ulloa. But the lucidity of its vision transcends its regionalism; it can tell us about the place that used to be Yugoslavia, about certain regions of Africa, about any conflict between groups that are bound together yet set against one another. Castellanos has provided us with a vision of the incalculable consequences of force, the terrible, inexorable momentum that builds once it has been unleashed. If we know how to read it, this novel can help us stop looking for innocence and start trying instead to understand the ways that force destroys the soul.

Teresa Entzín López, the nana, the almost invisible woman who passes unnoticed between the Caxlán's world and the Indian's, is given the final word. As she weaves her myth, Teresa is Castellanos's own counterpart, making a leap of understanding from the other side of the cultural divide. And what Teresa sees, what the myth she so artfully devises tells us, is that the lines of battle are not ultimately between ethnic groups, races or genders, but between the force that ceaselessly works to render the world inanimate and the animate humanity that struggles to persist.

—Esther Allen

A BRIEF GLOSSARY OF
TZOTZIL AND SPANISH TERMS

THE FOLLOWING GLOSSARY does not include a number of words taken from Spanish and Nahuatl—finca, jícara, capataz, brujo, cabildo, querida, vaquero, nixtamal, petate, campesino, caudillo, ejido, latifundio, etc.—which appear in *Webster's Third New International Dictionary*.

The glossary was prepared with the extremely kind and expert assistance of Jan Rus, who cautions that three of the terms— canán, tatic, and winikón—are not Tzotzil words but are taken from a contiguous Maya language, Tzeltal (spoken in the area around Comitán, the Chiapas town where Rosario Castellanos grew up).

Without going deeply into the complexities of Tzotzil pronunciation, readers may find it helpful to know that the Tzotzil "x" is pronounced "sh," and the Tzotzil "j" is the equivalent of a strong "h." —EA

ajwalil (Tz) Master, lord. A term of reference and address for a powerful, highly respected man, usually a Ladino.

alcalde (Tz/Sp) A high-ranking official with both political and religious duties. (In Spanish, mayor.)

alférez (Tz/Sp) Religious official of a higher rank than the mayordomo, also assigned to care for a particular saint. (In Spanish, second lieutenant.)

Castilla (Sp) Chiapas slang for Castellano (the Spanish language).

Caxlán (Tz) Any Spanish-speaking person; derived from the Spanish word Castellano (Castilian).

canán (Tz) Star.

chulel (Tz) Innate soul.

Ciudad Real (Sp) The colonial name of San Cristóbal de Las Casas which was restored during the 1920s and 1930s when the Mexican government attempted to ban saints' names as part of its persecution of the Catholic Church. Ciudad Real is the name of the Spanish city to the south of Toledo in Castilla-La Mancha that was the home of the conquistador of the Chiapas highlands.

Coleto,-a (Sp) Resident of the town of Ciudad Real. The name is derived from the little pig tail worn by colonial Spaniards, which is much like the ones worn today by bullfighters.

copal (Nahuatl) Resin used as incense.

enganchador (Sp) Labor contractor who persuades Indians to become migrant workers on distant plantations.

enganchado (Sp) Indentured laborer, induced into running up a debt to his "employer" for more than he will ever be able to pay off. "The enganchados are guarded most carefully, for there is the ever present danger of their running away on the slightest opportunity," from a 1909 news article quoted by John Kenneth Turner in *Barbarous Mexico* (1910).

gobernador (Tz/Sp) A village official with a variety of duties, just above the alcalde in rank. (In Spanish, governor.)

ilol (Tz) A shaman or seer who can be male or female.

Jobel (Tz) Ciudad Real. Lit. "Grass" (the valley of San Cristóbal was once a meadow).

Ladino,-a (Sp) A person of mixed or pure Spanish descent who does not belong to an Indian community.

luk (Tz) "Long pole with a question mark of sharpened metal used for weeding."—Carter Wilson, *A Green Tree and a Dry Tree* (1972).

madrina (Sp) Used by Castellanos to refer to the wife of a mayordomo (see below) who also has ceremonial duties. (In Spanish, godmother.)

mayordomo (Tz/Sp) A religious official appointed to maintain and serve a specific saint for one year. (In Spanish, steward.)

martoma (Tz) Tzotzil form of mayordomo, also used as a term of address.

nana (Sp) Grandmother; nanny; nurse; mother.

nahual (Tz) The animal that is the double or alter ego of a human soul.

pasión (Tz) Tzotzil religious official with specific duties involving the celebration of Carnival.

patrón,-a (Sp) Boss; master, mistress.

pichulej (Tz) Strips of woven palm used for making hats and other things.

pom (Tz) Incense made from the resin of the Copal tree.

posh (Tz) Rustic sugar cane liquor drunk—and often made—by Tzotzils.

posol (Na) Finely ground corn kneaded into a ball for storage and transportation, then mixed with water and drunk.

pukuj (Tz) Demon. "Because things (all things: those we see and also those we use) don't belong to us. They have another owner. And the owner punishes when someone takes possession of a place, a tree, even a name. The owner—no one would know how to invoke him if the brujos had not shared their revelations—the pukuj, is a spirit. Invisible, he comes and goes, listening to the desires in mens' hearts."—"The Truce" in Rosario Castellanos' *Ciudad Real* (1961).

pus (Tz) Sweathouse.

regidor (Tz/Sp) Mid-ranking village official. (In Spanish, alderman.)

síndico (Tz) Village civil official. (In Spanish, trustee.)

tatic (Tz) Affectionate term of respect for older male relatives or elders of the tribe.

tenemastes (Nahuatl) Three stones on which cooking pots rest over a fire.

tzec (Tz) Traditional skirt of Tzotzil women.

Tzotzil (Tz) A Maya language spoken by about half a million people, most of whom live in the central highlands of Chiapas around San Cristóbal. Also, a person who speaks Tzotzil.

winikón (Tz) Lit., "I am a man." Some Ladinos who affect familiarity with Indian words use it simply to mean "man."

FOR THE BEST IN PAPERBACKS, LOOK FOR THE

In every corner of the world, on every subject under the sun, Penguin represents quality and variety—the very best in publishing today.

For complete information about books available from Penguin—including Penguin Classics, Penguin Compass, and Puffins—and how to order them, write to us at the appropriate address below. Please note that for copyright reasons the selection of books varies from country to country.

In the United States: Please write to *Penguin Group (USA), P.O. Box 12289 Dept. B, Newark, New Jersey 07101-5289* or call 1-800-788-6262.

In the United Kingdom: Please write to *Dept. EP, Penguin Books Ltd, Bath Road, Harmondsworth, West Drayton, Middlesex UB7 0DA.*

In Canada: Please write to *Penguin Books Canada Ltd, 90 Eglinton Avenue East, Suite 700, Toronto, Ontario M4P 2Y3.*

In Australia: Please write to *Penguin Books Australia Ltd, P.O. Box 257, Ringwood, Victoria 3134.*

In New Zealand: Please write to *Penguin Books (NZ) Ltd, Private Bag 102902, North Shore Mail Centre, Auckland 10.*

In India: Please write to *Penguin Books India Pvt Ltd, 11 Panchsheel Shopping Centre, Panchsheel Park, New Delhi 110 017.*

In the Netherlands: Please write to *Penguin Books Netherlands bv, Postbus 3507, NL-1001 AH Amsterdam.*

In Germany: Please write to *Penguin Books Deutschland GmbH, Metzlerstrasse 26, 60594 Frankfurt am Main.*

In Spain: Please write to *Penguin Books S. A., Bravo Murillo 19, 1° B, 28015 Madrid.*

In Italy: Please write to *Penguin Italia s.r.l., Via Benedetto Croce 2, 20094 Corsico, Milano.*

In France: Please write to *Penguin France, Le Carré Wilson, 62 rue Benjamin Baillaud, 31500 Toulouse.*

In Japan: Please write to *Penguin Books Japan Ltd, Kaneko Building, 2-3-25 Koraku, Bunkyo-Ku, Tokyo 112.*

In South Africa: Please write to *Penguin Books South Africa (Pty) Ltd, Private Bag X14, Parkview, 2122 Johannesburg.*

Printed in the United States
by Baker & Taylor Publisher Services